NEW YORK REVIEW BOOKS
CLASSICS

VARIETIES OF EXILE

MAVIS GALLANT was born in Montreal and worked as a journalist at *The Standard* before moving to Europe to devote herself to writing fiction. After traveling extensively she settled in Paris, where she still resides. Her stories first appeared in *The New Yorker* in 1951. *Paris Stories*, selected and introduced by Michael Ondaatje, was published by New York Review Books Classics in 2002. *Varieties of Exile* is her fourteenth book to appear in this country.

RUSSELL BANKS is a novelist and short story writer. His most recent works are *Cloudsplitter*, a novel, and *The Angel on the Roof: New and Selected Stories*. He is president of the International Parliament of Writers and a member of the American Academy of Arts and Letters. He lives in upstate New York.

VARIETIES OF EXILE

STORIES

MAVIS GALLANT

Selected and with an introduction by
RUSSELL BANKS

NEW YORK REVIEW BOOKS

New York

This is a New York Review Book
Published by The New York Review of Books
1755 Broadway, New York, NY 10019

Library of Congress Cataloging-in-Publication Data
Gallant, Mavis.
  Varieties of exile / Mavis Gallant ; selected and with an introduction
by Russell Banks.
    p. cm. — (New York Review Books classics)
  ISBN 1-59017-060-1 (pbk. : alk. paper)
  1. Exiles—Fiction. I. Banks, Russell, 1940– II. Title. III. Series.
  PR9199.3.G26A6 2003
  813'.54—dc22

                        2003020764

ISBN 1-59017-060-1

Book design by Lizzie Scott
Printed in the United States of America on acid-free paper.
10 9 8 7 6 5 4 3 2 1

December 2003
www.nyrb.com

CONTENTS

INTRODUCTION

IN A CHARACTERISTIC mingling of modesty and fierce pride, Mavis Gallant has said that "one of the hardest things in the world is to describe what happened next." It's hard because of the value- and emotion-laden nature, not just of memory, but of human consciousness itself. Though nothing truly escapes us, memory and mind from the moment of our birth are notoriously, almost hopelessly, selective, elliptical, and inventive. And memory and mind, for expression, perhaps for their very existence, depend upon language—than which, of course, there is no more evasive and deceptive a medium. Now in her eighties, Gallant has spent a long lifetime doing that hardest thing, describing what happened next, in stories that are not only moving and powerful but true to memory and mind. Born and raised bilingual in French-speaking Quebec and residing most of her adult life in France, Gallant chose to write in English, and in it fewer than a handful of living story writers are her equal: William Trevor, and her countrywoman Alice Munro, perhaps, and—since the death of Eudora Welty—no American that I can think of.

The tension—and sometimes outright conflict—between remembered and felt experience on the one hand and, on the other, the known truth of what happened lies at the heart of all great short stories. It's the argument that generates plot and structure, which, finally, gives a story meaning. Since Gogol and Chekhov, the flexible and still rapidly evolving form of the short story has unfolded that argument, and in doing so it has universalized and dignified the experience, the pain and sorrow and desire and fear, of the ordinary, solitary man, woman, and child. It has extricated the isolato from the masses and made Everyman. Frank O'Connor called the modern short story "the lonely voice," and more than any other literary form it speaks to and for every human being who thinks of him- or herself as alone, cut off from God, and counted as unimportant and unworthy of attention except when considered *en masse*. It is, in a sense, the most democratic literary form. And it is in this tradition that Mavis Gallant has made herself a master.

Her stories follow no formula and obey no laws other than Robert Musil's "one law of life, and that is the law of narrative order." Which is to say, they are digressive, regressive, and circular; they leap forward in time one minute and linger in pockets of loss the next; they ruminate and fulminate and explicate. There are asides, self-reflexive inquiries, and rapid shifts in point of view—none of which stop or hinder the forward motion of the story. Quite the opposite; they keep the story flowing, like a meandering stream crossing a broad plain to the sea, like consciousness. But Gallant's intent is always to dramatize consciousness, not merely to portray it. Consequently, her stories are as difficult to describe or to reduce to a synopsis as any truly lived experience is—not because of their variety or obscurity (her stories are never obscure) or some esoteric quality (her characters, settings, situations, and language are always instantly familiar, intimate, and homegrown, whether planted in Montreal, an Eastern Township village, Paris, Moscow, Florida, or the French Mediterranean), but because of their economy and precision and the sublime integration and inseparability of their elements—form, structure, content, and style.

In terms of locale, her stories, perhaps as a reflection of her somewhat bifurcated life, can be divided roughly between those that take place in Europe, usually Paris, and those set in Canada, usually Montreal and its nearby environs. I have for personal reasons (I am half Canadian with three Canadian grandparents and grew up and live today just south of the border) an abiding affection if not an outright preference for the North American stories, if only because Gallant has attended there to lives that are familiar and matter greatly to me and rarely make it into literature: an adolescent girl, nearly crushed by the claustrophobic religious culture of her family, refusing to exchange her spirit for her soul ("The Chosen Husband"); a boy, abandoned by his feckless dad, but obliged to care for the old man when, years later, he turns up dying in France ("The End of the World"); a grown daughter, returning to the city of her childhood, tracking the secret sources of her gauzy memories of her father and mother and their torn marriage ("Voices Lost in Snow"). None of these characters has money or property or much education; none of them is secure in society. Characters and situations like these seem peculiarly American, *North* American. It's not easy to imagine them in the hands of a British or European or Latin American writer. I fear they would be treated far less kindly.

In Gallant's stories, the conflicts, obsessions, and concerns —the near-impossibility of gaining personal freedom without inflicting harm on those whom you love and who love you; the difficulty of forgiving a cruel and selfish parent without sentimentalizing him; or the pain of failed renewal—are limned with an affectionate irony and generated by a sincere belief in their ultimate significance, significance not just for the characters who embody them, but for the author and, presumably, the reader as well. Such themes and perspectives as these have characterized the work of the best American story writers of the last half-century, from John Cheever to Raymond Carver to Lorrie Moore, and the best Canadians, from Alice Munro to Margaret Atwood to Clark Blaise. We respond to them on both sides of the long, porous border between our two nations with the same sad shock of self-recognition that we feel contemplating the imagery and atmosphere of a painting by Edward Hopper or a Duke Ellington orchestral suite. There is stringently expressed nostalgia, and then a bite, a redemptive edginess, that by undercutting the nostalgia gives it dignity and makes it worthy of our attention and admiration. As Samuel Beckett noted, "There is no escape from yesterday because yesterday has deformed us, or been deformed by us." The memory doesn't simply linger on; it instructs the present and prepares for the future that will sabotage it.

Here is Gallant:

> The end of the afternoon had a particular shade of color then, which is not tinted by distance or enhancement but has to do with how streets were lighted. Lamps were still gas, and their soft gradual blooming at dusk made the sky turn a peacock blue that slowly deepened to marine, then indigo. This uneven light falling in blurred pools gave the snow it touched a quality of phosphorescence, beyond which were night shadows in which no one lurked. There were few cars, little sound. A fresh snowfall would lie in the streets in a way that seemed natural. Sidewalks were dangerous, casually sanded; even on busy streets you found traces of the icy slides children's feet had made. The reddish brown of the stone houses, the curve and slope of the streets, the constantly changing sky were satisfactory in a way I now realize must have been aesthetically comfortable. This is what I saw when I read "city" in a book; I had no means of knowing that "city" one day would also mean drab, filthy, flat, or that city blocks could turn into dull squares without mystery.
>
> ("Voices Lost in Snow")

Time is the great subject of all Gallant's work, but in this collection we also see how much she is a writer of the American North, of the region and culture that overlap the US/Canada border from Maine and the Maritimes all the way west to Seattle and Vancouver. In these stories, darkness comes early and stays late; summer is not a condition, it's an all-too-brief holiday. Cities are gray, skies are mauve or milky, and there are always wet boots slumped in entryways.

Many of the stories take place in Montreal, the city of Gallant's childhood, and its suburbs. Born there in 1922 to English-speaking, Protestant, middle-class parents, she was an only child who, at the age of four, was sent for several years to a French Catholic boarding school; whose father died early, and whose mother quickly remarried. She was, as she says, "set afloat." Consequently, from the beginning she has been situated simultaneously inside and outside her given worlds, a person forced to navigate her way on her own along the straits that lie between children and adults, men and women, and family and strangers; between the French language and English, provincial Catholic culture and urbane humanism; between Canada and the United States, and North America and Europe. Gallant's life has placed her at the Borderlands, the ideal site for a writer of short stories.

It's apparent from Mavis Gallant's fiction that, like Henry James, nothing is ever lost on her; for she seems to have remembered everything that occurred in Montreal in the 1930s and 1940s and everyone whom she even so much as glanced at. It should not surprise us that she has been, especially for her time and place, an unusually independent woman. For six years she worked as a reporter for the *Montreal Standard*. She married young, soon divorced, and in the late 1940s started publishing her first stories in Canadian literary magazines. In 1950, at the age of twenty-eight, she made the bold decision to run off to France and live as a fiction writer, saying of that move simply, "I have arranged matters so that I would be free

to write. It's what I like doing." Which, while guarding her
privacy and solitude with care, is what she has done ever
since.

With gratifying regularity her stories have appeared in the
pages of *The New Yorker* for nearly five decades now (which
fact alone justifies the existence of that magazine); she has
won numerous prizes and awards, yet here in the United
States, despite having long been ensconced at Parnassian
heights, she has mostly been viewed as a "writers' writer."
Surely this is due more to her residency abroad, her absence
from book-chat circles, and her well-known aversion to in-
trusions on her privacy than to any particular difficulty or
preciousness or exoticism in her work. For what is a writers'
writer, anyhow? Merely one who honors in every sentence
she writes the deepest, most time-honored principles of composition: honesty, clarity, and concision. So, yes, in that sense
she is a writers' writer. But only in that sense.

The fifteen stories gathered together here are the ones I
love best from Gallant's so-called "Canadian stories." They
are "Canadian," not by virtue of where they are set, but
only because their protagonists happen to hail from that
country, regardless of where they turn up in the world of
the story. Gallant is fond of revisiting some of her characters
in subsequent stories, viewing them at different times and
places and from different points of view, producing sequences
of three or four or more stories about the same individual
and his or her family members and giving an almost novel-
istic take on their individual and familial histories, all the
while remaining faithful to the short story form. I've included
selections from these series here, the Montreal stories about
Linnet Muir, the set about the Carette sisters, Berthe and
Marie, as well as a new sequence of three extraordinary stories, "Let It Pass," "In a War," and "The Concert Party," nar-
rated by a man, *un homme d'un certain âge,* whose life's
story and sad fate ought forever to disabuse any critic of sug-

gesting that Ms. Gallant is hard on her male characters. Ironic, perhaps, but always sweetly forgiving. The Linnet Muir and Carette sisters stories are justly famous and often anthologized, but this is the first time that this new group has ever appeared in a book.

In an afterword that appears in her collection *Paris Stories*, Gallant says, "Stories are not chapters of novels. They should not be read one after another, as if they were meant to follow along. Read one. Shut the book. Read something else. Come back later. Stories can wait." Yes, but believe me, these can't.

—RUSSELL BANKS

VARIETIES OF EXILE

THE FENTON CHILD

1

IN A LONG room filled with cots and undesired infants, Nora Abbott had her first sight of Neil, who belonged to Mr. and Mrs. Boyd Fenton. The child was three months old but weedy for his age, with the face of an old man who has lost touch with his surroundings. The coarse, worn, over-sized gown and socks the nuns had got him up in looked none too fresh. Four large safety pins held in place a chafing and voluminous diaper. His bedding—the whole nursery, in fact—smelled of ammonia and carbolic soap and in some way of distress.

Nora was seventeen and still did not know whether she liked children or saw them as part of a Catholic woman's fate. If they had to come along, then let them be clear-eyed and talcum-scented, affectionate and quick to learn. The eyes of the Fenton baby were opaquely gray, so rigidly focused that she said to herself, He is blind. They never warned me. But as she bent close, wondering if his gaze might alter, the combs at her temples slipped loose and she saw him take notice of the waves of dark hair that fell and enclosed him. So, he perceived things. For the rest, he remained as before, as still as a doll, with both hands folded tight.

Like a doll, yes, but not an attractive one: No little girl would have been glad to find him under a Christmas tree. The thought of a rebuffed and neglected toy touched Nora deeply. She lifted him from his cot, expecting—though not precisely—the limpness of a plush or woolly animal: a lamb, say. But he was braced and resistant, a wooden soldier, every inch of him tense. She placed him against her shoulder, her cheek to his head, saying, "There you go. You're just grand. You're a grand little boy." Except for a fringe of down around his forehead, he was perfectly bald. He must have spent his entire life, all three months of it, flat on his back with his hair rubbing off on the pillow.

In a narrow aisle between rows of beds, Mr. Fenton and a French-Canadian doctor stood at ease. Actually, Dr. Alex Marchand was a pal from Mr. Fenton's Montreal regiment. What they had in common was the recent war and the Italian campaign. Mr. Fenton appeared satisfied with the state and condition of his son. (With her free hand Nora pulled back her hair so he could see the baby entirely.) The men seemed to take no notice of the rest of the room: the sixty-odd puny infants, the heavily pregnant girl of about fourteen, waxing the floor on her hands and knees, or the nun standing by, watching hard to be sure they did not make off with the wrong child. The pregnant girl's hair had been cropped to the skull. She was dressed in a dun-colored uniform with long sleeves and prickly-looking black stockings. She never once looked up.

Although this was a hot and humid morning in late summer, real Montreal weather, the air a heavy vapor, the men wore three-piece dark suits, vest and all, and looked thoroughly formal and buttoned up. The doctor carried a panama hat. Mr. Fenton had stuck a carnation in his lapel, broken off from a bunch he had presented to the Mother Superior downstairs, a few minutes before. His slightly rash approach to new people seemed to appeal. Greeting him, the nuns had been all smiles, accepting without shadow his alien presence, his confident ignorance of French, his male sins lightly borne. The liquor on his breath was enough to knock the Mother Superior off her feet (he was steady on his) but she may have taken it to be part of the natural aura of men.

"Well, Nora!" said Mr. Fenton, a lot louder than he needed to be. "You've got your baby."

What did he mean? A trained nanny was supposed to be on her way over from England. Nora was filling in, as a favor; that was all. He behaved as if they had known each other for years, had even suggested she call him "Boyd." (She had pretended not to hear.) His buoyant nature seemed to require a sort of fake complicity or comradeship from women, on short notice. It was his need, not Nora's, and in her mind she became all-denying. She was helping out because her father, who knew Mr. Fenton, had asked if she would, but nothing more. Mr. Fenton was in his late twenties, a married man, a father, some sort of Protestant—another race.

Luckily, neither the girl in uniform nor the attendant nun seemed to know English. They might otherwise have supposed Nora to be Neil's mother. She could not have been the mother of anyone. She had never let a man anywhere near. If ever she did, if ever she felt ready, he would be nothing like Mr. Fenton—typical Anglo-Montreal gladhander, the kind who said "Great to see you!" and a minute later forgot you were alive. She still had no image of an acceptable lover (which meant husband) but rather of the kind she meant to avoid. For the moment, it took in just about every type and class. What her mother called "having relations" was a source of dirty stories for men and disgrace for girls. It brought bad luck down even on married couples unless, like the Fentons, they happened to be well-off and knew how to avoid accidents and had no religious barrier that kept them from using their knowledge. When a mistake did occur—namely, Neil—they weren't strapped for cash or extra space. Yet they were helpless in some other way, could not tend to an infant without outside assistance, and for that reason had left Neil to founder among castaways for his first twelve weeks.

So Nora reasoned, gently stroking the baby's back. She

wondered if he had managed to capture her thoughts. Apparently infants came into the world with a gift for mind reading, an instinct that faded once they began to grasp the meaning of words. She had been assured it was true by her late Aunt Rosalie, a mother of four. The time had come to take him out of this sour place, see him fed, washed, put into new clothes and a clean bed. But the two men seemed like guests at a disastrous party, unable to get away, rooted in place by a purely social wish to seem agreeable.

How sappy they both look, ran Nora's thoughts. As sappy as a couple of tenors. ("Sappy-looking as a tenor" was an expression of her father's.) I'll never get married. Who wants to look at some sappy face the whole day.

As though he had heard every silent word and wished to prove he could be lively and attentive, the doctor looked all around the room, for the first time, and remarked, "Some of these children, it would be better for everybody if they died at birth." His English was exact and almost without accent, but had the singsong cadence of French Montreal. It came out, "Most of these child*ren*, it would be bet*ter* for eve*ry*body . . ." Nora held a low opinion of that particular lilt. She had been raised in two languages. To get Nora to answer in French, particularly after she had started attending an English high school, her mother would pretend not to understand English. I may not be one of your intellectuals, Nora decided (an assurance her father gave freely), but I sound English in English and French in French. She knew it was wrong of her to criticize an educated man such as Dr. Marchand, but he had said a terrible thing. It would have sounded bad spoken heedfully by the King himself. (The King, that August morning, was still George the Sixth.)

The stiff drinks Mr. Fenton had taken earlier in the day must have been wearing off. He seemed far away in his mind and somewhat put-upon. The doctor's remark brought him to. He said something about shoving off, turned easily to the nun, gave her a great smile. In answer, she placed a folded document in his hands, said a cool "Au revoir" to the doctor and did not look at Nora at all. In the hall outside Mr. Fenton stopped dead. He appealed to the doctor and Nora: "Look at this thing."

Nora shifted the baby to her right arm but otherwise kept her distance. "It's a certificate," she said.

"Baptismal," said the doctor. "He's been baptized."

"I can see that. Only, it's made out for 'Armand Albert Antoine.' She gave me the wrong thing. You'd better tell them," for of course he could not have made the complaint in French.

"Those are just foundling names," said the doctor. "They give two or three Christian names when there's no known family. I've seen even *four*. 'Albert' or 'Antoine' could be used as a surname. You see?"

"There damn well is a known family," said Mr. Fenton. "Mine. The name is Neil Boyd Fenton. When I make up my mind, it's made up for good. I never look back." But instead of returning the certificate he stuffed it, crumpled, into a pocket. "Nobody asked to have him christened here. I call that overstepping."

"They have to do it," said the doctor. "It is a rule." In the tone of someone trying to mend a quarrel, he went on, "Neil's a fine name." Nora knew for a fact he had suggested it. Mr. Fenton had never got round to finding a name, though he'd had three months to think it over. "There's another name I like. 'Earl.' Remember Earl Laine?"

"Yeah, I remember Earl." They started down a broad staircase, three in a row. Mr. Fenton was red in the face, either from his outburst or just the heat and weight of his dark clothes. Nora might have sympathized, but she had already decided not to do that: What can't be helped must be borne. Her mother had got her to wear a long-sleeved cotton jacket, over her white piqué dress, and a girdle and stockings, because of the nuns. The dress was short and allowed her knees to be seen. Nora had refused to let the hem down for just that one visit. Her small gold watch was a graduation present from her uncle and cousins. The blue bangle bracelets on her other wrist had belonged to her elder sister.

The mention of Earl Laine had started the men on a last-war story. She had already noticed their war stories made them laugh. They were not stories, properly speaking, but incidents they remembered by heart and told back and forth. Apparently, this Earl person had entered an Italian farmhouse ("shack" was the word Mr. Fenton actually used) and dragged a mattress off a bed. He wanted it for his tank, to make the tank more comfortable. A woman all in black had followed him out the door, clawing at the mattress, screaming something. When she saw there was no help for it, that Earl was bigger and stronger and laughing the whole time, she lay down in the road and thumped the ground with her fists.

"That Earl!" said the doctor, as one might speak of a bad but charming boy. "He'd do anything. Anything he felt like doing. Another time . . ."

"He was killed in '44," Mr. Fenton said. "Right? So how old would that make him now?"

It sounded very silly to Nora, like a conundrum in arithmetic, but the doctor replied, "He'd be around twenty-three." Dr. Marchand was older than Mr. Fenton but much younger than her father. He walked in a stately, deliberate way, like a mourner at a funeral. There was a wife-and-children air to him. Unlike Mr. Fenton he wore a wedding ring. Nora wondered if Mrs. Fenton and Mme. Marchand had ever met.

"Earl's people lived up in Montreal North," said Mr. Fenton. "I went to see them after I got back. They were Italians. Did you know that? He never said."

"I knew it the first time he opened his mouth," said the doctor. "His English wasn't right. It turned out his first language was some Sicilian dialect from Montreal North.

Nobody in Italy could make it out, so he stayed with English. But it sounded funny."

"Not to me," said Mr. Fenton. "It was straight, plain Canadian."

The doctor had just been revealed as a man of deep learning. He understood different languages and dialects and knew every inch of Montreal far better than Nora or Mr. Fenton. He could construe a man's background from the sound of his words. No, no, he was not to be dismissed, whatever he had said or might still come out with. So Nora decided.

Downstairs, they followed a dark, waxed corridor to the front door, passing on the way a chapel recently vacated. The double doors, flung wide, revealed a sunstruck altar. Mr. Fenton's antipapal carnations (Nora gave them this attribute with no hard feelings) stood in a vase of cut glass, which shed rainbows. A strong scent of incense accompanied the visitors to the foyer, where it mingled with furniture polish.

"Is today something special?" said Mr. Fenton.

A blank occurred in the doctor's long list of reliable information. He stared at the wall, at a clock with Roman numerals. Only the hour mattered, he seemed to be telling himself. Nora happened to know that today, the twenty-third of August, was the feast of Saint Rosa de Lima, but she could not recall how Saint Rosa had lived or died. Nora's Aunt Rosalie, deceased, leaving behind three sons and a daughter and sad Uncle Victor, had in her lifetime taken over any saint on the calendar with a Rose to her name: not just Saint Rosalie, whose feast day on September fourth was hers by right, but Saint Rosaline (January) and Saint Rosine (March) and Rosa de Lima (today). It did not explain the special Mass this morning; in any case, Nora would have thought it wrong to supply an answer the doctor could not provide.

Although someone was on permanent duty at the door, making sure no stranger to the place wandered in, another and much older nun had been sent to see them off. She was standing directly under the clock, both hands resting on a cane, her back as straight as a yardstick. Her eyes retained some of the bluish-green light that often goes with red hair. The poor woman most likely had not much hair to speak of, and whatever strands remained were bound to be dull and gray. The hair of nuns died early, for want of light and air. Nora's sister, Geraldine, had the same blue-green eyes but not yet the white circle around the iris. She was in the process now of suppressing and concealing her hair, and there was no one to say it was a shame, that her hair was her most stunning feature. So it would continue, unless Gerry changed her mind and came home to stay and let Nora give her a shampoo with pure white almond-oil soap, followed by a vinegar rinse. She would need to sit at the kitchen window and let the morning sun brighten and strengthen her hair to the roots.

The old nun addressed Mr. Fenton: "Your beautiful flowers are gracing our little chapel." At least, that was how Dr. Marchand decided to translate her words. Nora would have made it, "Your flowers are in the chapel," but that might have sounded abrupt, and "gracing" was undoubtedly more pleasing to Mr. Fenton.

"That's good to hear," he said. A current of laughter set off by the story of Earl and the mattress still ran in his voice. Nora was afraid he might pat the nun on the cheek, or in some other way embarrass them horribly, but all he did was glance up at the clock, then at his watch, and make a stagy sort of bow—not mockingly, just trying to show he was not in his customary habitat and could get away with a gesture done for effect. The clock struck the half hour: twelve-thirty. They should have been sitting down to lunch at Mr. Fenton's house, along with his wife and Mrs. Clopstock, who was his wife's mother. Nora had never before been invited to a meal at a strange table. This overwhelming act of hospitality was her reason for wearing white earrings, white high-heeled shoes, and her sister's relinquished bracelets.

The hard midday light of the street stunned them quiet at first, then the baby set up a thin wail—his first message to Nora. I know, she told him. You're hungry, you're too hot. You need a good wash. You don't like being moved around. (For a second, she saw the hairline divide between being rescued and taken captive. The idea was too complex, it had no end or beginning, and she let it go.) You've dirtied yourself, too. In fact, you reek to high heaven. Never mind. We're going to put everything right. Trying to quiet him, she gave him one of her fingers to suck. Better to let him swallow a few germs and microbes than cry himself sick. Mr. Fenton had parked in shade, around the corner. It wasn't much of a walk.

"Nora can't remember the war," he said to the doctor, but really to her, trying the buddy business again. "She must have been in her cradle."

"I know it's over," she said, thinking to close the subject.

"Oh, it's that, all right." He sounded sorry, about as sorry as he could feel about anything.

The doctor had replaced his panama hat, after three times at achieving the angle he wanted. He made a reassuring sort of presence in the front seat—solid, reliable. Nothing would knock him over. Nora's father was thin and light as a blown leaf. The doctor said, "There's another name I like. 'Desmond.' "

"Des?" said Mr. Fenton. He struggled out of his jacket and vest and threw them on the backseat, next to Nora. His white carnation fell on the floor. The doctor remained fully dressed, every button fastened. "Des Butler?"

"He married an English girl," said the doctor. "Remember?"

"*Remember*? I was best man. She cried the whole time. She was called Beryl—no, Brenda."

"Well, she was in the family way," said the doctor.

"She hightailed it right back to England," said Mr. Fenton. "The Canadian taxpayers had to pay to bring her over.

11

Nobody ever figured out where she got the money to go back. Even Des didn't know."

"Des never knew anything. He never knew what he should have known. All he noticed was she had gotten fat since the last time he saw her."

"She arrived with a bun in the oven," said Mr. Fenton. "Four, five months. Des had already been back in Canada for six. So . . ." He turned his attention to Nora. "Your dad get overseas, Nora?"

"He tried."

"And?"

"He was already thirty-nine and he had the two children. They told him he was more useful sticking to his job."

"We needed civilians, too," said Mr. Fenton, showing generosity. "Two, did you say? Ray's got two kids?"

"There's my sister, Gerry—Geraldine. She's a novice now, up in the Laurentians."

"Where?" He twisted the rearview mirror, so he could see her.

"Near St. Jerome. She's on the way to being a nun."

That shut him up, for the time being. The doctor reached up and turned the mirror the other way. While they were speaking, the baby had started to gush up some awful curdled stuff, which she had to wipe on the skirt of his gown. He had no luggage—not even a spare diaper. The men had rolled down the front windows, but the crossbreeze was sluggish and smelled of warm metal, and did nothing to lighten the presence of Neil.

"Want to open up back there?" said Mr. Fenton.

No, she did not. One of her boy cousins had come down with an infected ear, the result of building a model airplane while sitting in a draft.

"At that stage, they're only a digestive tube," said the doctor, fanning himself with his hat.

"How about the brain?" said Mr. Fenton. "When does the

brain start to work?" He drove without haste, as he did everything else. His elbow rested easily in the window frame. Ashes from his cigarette drifted into Nora's domain.

"The brain is still primitive," the doctor said, sounding sure. "It is still in the darkness of early time." Nora wondered what "the darkness of time" was supposed to mean. Mr. Fenton must have been wondering too. He started to say something, but the doctor went on in his slow singsong way, "Only the soul is fully developed from birth. The brain . . ."

"Newborn, they've got these huge peckers," said Mr. Fenton. "I mean, really developed."

"The brain tries to catch up with the soul. For most people, it's a lifelong struggle."

"If you say so, Alex," Mr. Fenton said.

The baby wasn't primitive, surely. She examined his face. There wasn't a hair on him except the blond fluff around his forehead. Primitive man, shaggy all over, dragged his steps through the recollection of a movie she had seen. Speak for yourself, she wanted to tell the doctor. Neil is not *primitive*. He just wants to understand where he's going. Her duty was to hand over to its mother this bit of a child, an only son without a stitch to his name. Socks, gown, and diaper were fit to be burned, not worth a washtub of water. So her sister had gone through an open door and the door had swung to behind her. She had left to Nora everything she owned. So Marie Antoinette, younger than Nora, had been stripped to the skin when she reached the border of France, on the way to marry a future king. Total strangers had been granted the right to see her nude. The clothes she had been wearing were left on the ground and she was arrayed in garments so heavy with silver and embroidery she could hardly walk. Her own ladies-in-waiting, who spoke her native language, were turned back. (Nora could not remember where Marie Antoinette had started out.) "For we brought nothing . . . ," Nora's Methodist Abbott grandmother liked to point out, convinced that

Catholics never cracked a Bible and had to be kept informed. "Naked we came..." was along the same line. Nora knew how to dress and undress under a bathrobe, quick as a mouse. No earthquake, no burglar, no stranger suddenly pushing a door open would find Nora without at least one thing on, even if it was only a bra.

"...from Mac McIvor," the doctor was telling Mr. Fenton. "He's out in Vancouver now. It's a big change from Montreal."

"He'll crawl back here one day, probably sooner than he thinks," said Mr. Fenton. Something had made him cranky, perhaps the talk about souls. "I consider it a privilege to live in Montreal. I was born on Crescent and that's where I intend to die. Unless there's another war. Then it's a toss-up."

"Crescent's a fine street," said the doctor. "Nice houses, nice stores." He paused and let the compliment sink in, a way of making peace. "He's buying a place. Property's cheap out there."

"It's a long way off," said Mr. Fenton. "They can't get people to go and live there. That's why everything's so cheap."

"Not being married, he doesn't need a lot of room," the doctor said. "It's just a bungalow, two rooms and a kitchen. He can eat in the kitchen. It's a nice area. A lot of gardens."

"Sure, there are stores on Crescent now, but they're high-quality," said Mr. Fenton. "I could sell the house for a hell of a lot more than my father ever paid. Louise wants me to. She can't get used to having a dress shop next door. She wants a lawn and a yard and a lot of space between the houses."

"Mac's got a fair-size garden. That won't break his neck. Out there, there's no winter. You stick something in the ground, it grows."

"My father hung on to the house all through the Depression," said Mr. Fenton. "It'll take a lot more than a couple of store windows to chase me away." So saying, he made a sudden rough swerve into his street, having almost missed the corner.

It jolted the baby, who had just fallen asleep. Before he could start to cry or do anything else that could make him unpopular, she lifted him to the window. "See the houses?" she said. "One of them's yours." A few had fancy dress shops on the first floor. Others were turned into offices, with uncurtained front windows and neon lights, blazing away in broad daylight. The double row of houses ran straight down to St. Catherine Street without a break, except for some ashy lanes. Short of one of these, Mr. Fenton pulled up. He retrieved his vest and jacket, got out, and slammed the door. It was the doctor who turned back to help Nora struggle out of the car, held her arm firmly, even adjusted the strap of her white shoulder bag. He wasn't trying anything, so she let him. Anyone could tell he was a family man.

Neil seemed more awkward to hold than before, perhaps because she was tired. Shielding his eyes from sunlight, she turned his face to a narrow house of pale gray stone. On her street, it would indicate three two-bedroom flats, not counting the area. She was about to ask, "Is the whole thing yours?" but it might make her sound as if she had never been anywhere, and the last thing she wanted was Mr. Fenton's entire attention. In the shadow of steps leading up to the front door, at a window in the area, a hand lifted a net curtain and let it fall. So, someone knew that Neil was here. For his sake, she took precedence and climbed straight to the door. The men barely noticed. Mr. Fenton, in shirtsleeves, vest and jacket slung over a shoulder, spoke of heat and thirst. Halfway up, the doctor paused and said, "Boyd, isn't that the alley where the girl was supposed to have been raped?"

"They never caught him," said Mr. Fenton at once. "It was dark. She didn't see his face. Some kids had shot out the alley light with an air gun. Her father tried to sue the city, because of the light. It didn't get him anywhere. Ray Abbott knows the story. Light or no light, it wasn't a city case."

"What was she doing by herself in a dark lane?" said the doctor. "Did she work around here?"

"She lived over on Bishop," said Mr. Fenton. "She was visiting some friend and took a shortcut home. Her father was a principal." He named the school. Nora had never heard of it.

"English," said Dr. Marchand, placing the story in context.

"They moved away. Some crazy stories went around, that she knew the guy, they had a date."

"I knew a case," said the doctor. "An old maid. She set the police on a married man. He never did anything worse than say hello."

"It was hard on Louise, something like that going on just outside. Nobody heard a thing until she ran down to the area and started banging on the door and screaming."

"Louise did that?"

"This girl. Missy let her in and gave her a big shot of brandy. Missy's a good head. She said, 'If you don't quit yelling I'll call the police.' "

"Her English must be pretty good now," said the doctor.

"Missy's smart. When my mother-in-law hired her, all she could say was, 'I cook, I clean.' Now she could argue a case in court. She told Louise, 'Some guy grabs *me* in a lane, I twist him like a wet mop.' Louise couldn't get over it." He became lighthearted suddenly, which suited him better. "We shouldn't be scaring Nora with all this." Nora found that rich, considering the things that had been said in the car. She was at the door, waiting. He had to look up.

He took the last steps slowly. Of course, he was closer to thirty than twenty and not in great shape. All that booze and his lazy way of moving were bound to tell. On the landing he had to catch his breath. He said, "Don't worry, Nora. This end of Crescent is still good. It isn't as residential as when I was a kid but it's safe. Anyway, it's safe for girls who don't do dumb things."

"I'm not one for worrying," she said. "I don't wander around on my own after dark and I don't answer strangers. Anyways, I won't ever be spending the night here. My father doesn't like me to sleep away."

A word she knew but had never thought of using— "morose"—came to mind at the slow change in his face. Sulky or deeply pensive (it was hard to tell), he began searching the pockets of his vest and jacket, probably looking for his latchkey. The doctor reached across and pressed the doorbell. They heard it jangle inside the house. Without Dr. Marchand they might have remained stranded, waiting for the earth to turn and the slant of the sun to alter and allow them shade. Just as she was thinking this, wondering how Mr. Fenton managed to get through his day-by-day life without having the doctor there every minute, Dr. Marchand addressed her directly: *"On ne dit pas* 'anyways.' *C'est commun. Il faut toujours dire* 'anyway.'"

The heat of the day and the strain of events had pushed him off his rocker. There was no other explanation. Or maybe he believed he was some kind of bilingual marvel, a real work of art, standing there in his undertaker suit, wearing that dopey hat. Nora's father knew more about anything than he did, any day. He had information about local politics and the private dealings of men who were honored and admired, had their pictures in the *Gazette* and the *Star*. He could shake hands with anybody you cared to mention; could tell, just by looking at another man, what that man was worth. When he went to Blue Bonnets, the racetrack, a fantastic private intuition told him where to put his money. He often came home singing, his hat on the back of his head. He had an office to himself at City Hall, no duties anybody could figure, but unlimited use of a phone. He never picked a quarrel and never took offense. "Never let anyone get under your skin," he had told Gerry and Nora. "Consider the source."

She considered the source: Dr. Marchand had spent a horrible morning, probably, trying to sidestep Mr. Fenton's temporary moods and opinions. Still, the two of them were friends, like pals in a movie about the Great War, where actors pledged true loyalty in a trench before going over the top. Wars ran together, like the history of English kings, kept alive in tedious stories repeated by men. As a boring person he was easy to forgive. As a man he had a cold streak. His reproof stung. He had made her seem ignorant. Mr. Fenton didn't know a word of French, but he must have caught the drift.

Just as Nora's mother could predict a change in the weather from certain pains in her wrists, so the baby sensed a change in Nora. His face puckered. He let out some more of that clotted slobber, followed by a weak cough and a piercing, choking complaint. "Oh, stop," she said, hearing a rush of footsteps. She gave him a gentle shake. "Where's my little man? Where's my soldier?" Her piqué dress, which had been fresh as an ironed handkerchief just a few hours before, was stained, soiled, crumpled, wetted, damaged by Neil. She kissed his head. All she could find to say, in a hurry, was "Be good." The door swung open. Without being bidden Nora entered the house. The doctor removed his hat, this time with a bit of a flourish. Mr. Fenton, she noticed, was still looking for a key.

In rooms glimpsed from the entrance hall the shades were drawn against the burning street. A darker and clammier heat, like the air of an August night, condensed on her cheeks and forehead. She smiled at two women, dimly perceived. The younger had the figure of a stout child, wore her hair cut straight across her eyebrows, and had on what Nora took to be a white skirt. In the seconds it took for her pupils to widen, her eyes to focus anew, she saw that the white skirt was a white apron. In the meantime, she had approached the young woman, said, "Here's your sweet baby, Mrs. Fenton," and given him up.

"Well, Missy, you heard what Nora said," said Mr. Fenton. He could enjoy that kind of joke, laugh noisily at a mistake, but Missy looked as if a tide had receded, leaving her stranded and unable to recognize anything along the shore. All she could say was "There's a bottle ready," in a heavy accent.

"Give it to him right away," said the older woman, who could not be anyone but Mrs. Clopstock, the mother-in-law from Toronto. "That sounds to me like a hunger cry." Having made the observation, she took no further notice of Neil, but spoke to the two men: "Louise is really knocked out by the heat. She doesn't want any lunch. She said to say hello to you, Alex."

The doctor said, "Once she sees him, she'll take an interest. I had another case, just like that. I can tell you all about it."

"Yes, tell us, Alex," said Mrs. Clopstock. "Do tell us. You can tell us about it at lunch. We have to talk about something."

It pleased Nora that Dr. Marchand, for the first time, had made a "th" mistake in English, saying "dat" for "that." He wasn't so smart, after all. Just the same, she had spoiled Neil's entrance into his new life; as if she had crossed the wrong line. The two errors could not be matched. The doctor could always start over and get it right. For Nora and Neil, it had been once and for all.

2

Nora's uncle, Victor Cochefert, was the only member of her family, on either side, with much of consequence to leave in a will. He had the place he lived in—four bedrooms and double garage and a weeping willow on the lawn—and some flats he rented to the poor and improvident, in the east end of the city. He was forever having tenants evicted, and had had beer bottles thrown at his car. The flats had come to him through his marriage to Rosalie, daughter of a notary. Her father had drawn up a tight, grim marriage contract, putting Rosalie in charge of her assets, but she had suffered an early stroke, dragged one foot, and left everything up to Victor. The other relatives were lifelong renters, like most of Montreal. None were in want but only Victor and Rosalie had been to Florida.

Her own father's financial arrangements were seen by the Cocheferts as eccentric and somewhat obscure. He never opened his mouth about money but was suspected of being better off than he cared to let on; yet the Abbotts continued to live in a third-floor walk-up flat, with an outside staircase and linoleum-covered floors on which scatter rugs slipped and slid underfoot. His wife's relations admired him for qualities they knew to exist behind his great wall of good humor; they had watched him saunter from the dark bureau where he had stood on the far side of a counter, wearing an eyeshade (against what light?), registering births and delivering certificates, to a private office in City Hall. He had moved along nonchalantly, whistling, hands in his pockets—sometimes in other people's, Victor had hinted. At the same time, he held Ray in high regard, knowing that if you showed confidence, made him an accomplice, he could be trusted. He had even confided to Ray a copy of his will.

Victor's will was locked up in a safe in Ray's small office, where nothing was written on the door. "Nothing in the safe except my lunch," Ray often remarked, but Nora once had seen it wide open and had been impressed by the great number of files and dossiers inside. When she asked what these were, her father had laughed and said, "Multiple-risk insurance policies," and called her pie-face and sniffy-nose. She thought he must be proud to act as custodian to any part of Victor's private affairs. Victor was associate in a firm of engineers, established since 1900 on St. James Street West.

The name of the company was Macfarlane, Macfarlane & Macklehurst. It was understood that when Macfarlane Senior died or retired, "Cochefert" would figure on the letterhead—a bit lower and to the right, in smaller print. Three other people with French surnames were on staff: a switchboard operator, a file clerk, and a bilingual typist. During working hours they were expected to speak English, even to one another. The elder Macfarlane harbored the fear that anything said in an unknown language could be about him.

Nora's father knew the exact reason why Uncle Victor had been hired: It had to do with Quebec provincial government contracts. Politicians liked to deal in French and in a manner they found pertinent and to the point. Victor used English when he had to, no more and no less, as he waited. He was waiting to see his name figure on the firm's stationery, and he pondered the retreat and obscuration of the English. "The English" had names such as O'Keefe, Murphy, Llewellyn, Morgan-Jones, Ferguson, MacNab, Hoefer, Oberkirch, Aarmgaard, Van Roos, or Stavinsky. Language was the clue to native origin. He placed the Oberkirches and MacNabs by speech and according to the street where they chose to live. Nora's father had escaped his close judgment, was the English exception, even though no one knew what Ray thought or felt about anything. The well-known Anglo reluctance to show deep emotion might be a shield for something or for nothing. Victor had told his wife this, and she had repeated it to Nora's mother.

He had taken the last war to be an English contrivance and had said he would shoot his three sons rather than see them in uniform. The threat had caused Aunt Rosalie to burst into sobs, followed by the three sons, in turn, as though they were performing a round of weeping. The incident took place at a dinner given to celebrate the Cochefert grandparents' golden wedding anniversary—close relatives only, twenty-six place settings, small children perched on cushions or volumes of the Littré dictionary. The time was six days after the German invasion of Poland and three after Ray had tried to enlist. Victor was in such a state of pacifist conviction that he trembled all over. His horn-rimmed glasses fell in his plate. He said to Nora's father, "I don't mean this for you."

Ray said, "Well, in my family, if Canada goes to war, we go too," and left it at that. He spoke a sort of French he had picked up casually, which not everyone understood. Across the table he winked at Nora and Geraldine, as if to say, "It's all a lot of hot air." His favorite tune was "Don't Let It Bother You." He could whistle it even if he lost money at Blue Bonnets.

Just before Victor's terrible outburst, the whole table had applauded the arrival of the superb five-tier, pink-and-white anniversary cake, trimmed with little gold bells. Now, it sat at the center of the table and no one had the heart to cut it. The chance that one's children could be shot seemed not contrary to reason but prophetic. It was an unlucky age. The only one of Victor's progeny old enough to get into uniform and be gunned down by her father was his daughter, Ninon— Aunt Rosalie's Ninette. For years Victor and Rosalie had been alone with Ninette; then they had started having the boys. She was eighteen that September, just out of her convent school, could read and speak English, understand every word of Latin in the Mass, play anything you felt like hearing on the piano; in short, was ready to become a superior kind of wife. Her historical essay, "Marie-Antoinette, Christian Queen and Royal Martyr," had won a graduation medal. Aunt Rosalie had brought the medal to the dinner, where it was passed around and examined on both sides. As for "Marie-Antoinette," Victor had had it printed on cream-colored paper and bound in royal blue, with three white fleurs-de-lys embossed on the cover, and had presented a copy to every person he was related to or wished to honor.

Nora was nine and had no idea what or where Poland

might be. The shooting of her cousins by Uncle Victor lingered as a possibility but the wailing children were starting to seem a bit of a nuisance. Ninette stood up—not really a commanding presence, for she was small and slight—and said something about joining the armed forces and tramping around in boots. Since none of them could imagine a woman in uniform, it made them all more worried than ever; then they saw she had meant them to smile. Having restored the party to good humor, more or less, she moved around the table and made her little brothers stop making that noise, and cleaned their weepy, snotty faces. The three-year-old had crawled under the table, but Ninette pulled him out and sat him hard on his chair and tied his napkin around his neck, good and tight. She liked the boys to eat like grown-ups and remember every instructive thing she said: The Reverend Mother had told Victor she was a born teacher. If he would not allow her to take further training (he would not) he ought to let Ninette give private lessons, in French or music. Nothing was more conducive to moral disaster than a good female mind left to fester and rot. Keeping busy with lessons would prevent Ninette from dwelling on imponderables, such as where one's duty to parents ends and what was liable to happen on her wedding night. The Reverend Mother did not care how she talked to men. She was more circumspect with women, having high regard for only a few. Uncle Victor thought that was the best stand for the director of an exceptional convent school.

Having thoroughly daunted her little brothers, Ninette gave each of her troubled parents a kiss. She picked up a big silver cake knife—an 1889 wedding present, like the dictionary—and sliced the whole five-tier edifice from top to bottom. She must have been taught how to do it as part of her studies, for the cake did not fall apart or collapse. "There!" she said, as if life held nothing more to be settled. Before she began to serve the guests, in order, by age, she undid the black velvet ribbon holding her hair at the nape of her neck and gave it to Geraldine. Nora watched Ninette closely during the cake operation. Her face in profile was self-contained, like a cat's. Ray had remarked once that all the Cochefert women, his own wife being the single exception, grew a mustache by the age of eighteen. Ninette showed no trace of any, but Nora did perceive she had on mascara. Uncle Victor seemed not to have noticed. He wiped his glasses on his napkin and looked around humbly, as though all these people were too good for him, the way he always emerged from tantrums and tempers. He said nothing else about the war or the English, but as soon as he started to feel more like himself, remarked that it was no use educating women: It confused their outlook. He hoped Ray had no foolish and extravagant plans for Nora and Geraldine. Ray went on eating quietly and steadily, and was first to finish his cake.

Nora's father was a convert, but he fitted in. He had found the change no more difficult than digging up irises to put in tulips. If something annoying occurred—say, some new saint he thought shouldn't even have been in the running—he would say, "I didn't sign on for that." Nora's mother had had a hard time with him over Assumption. He came from Prince Edward Island. Nora and Geraldine had been taken down there, just once, so Ray's mother could see her grandchildren. All her friends and neighbors seemed to be called Peters or White. Nora was glad to be an Abbott, because there weren't so many. They traveled by train, sitting up all night in their clothes, and were down to their last hard-boiled egg at the end of the journey. Their Abbott grandmother said, "Three days of sandwiches." Of course it had not been anything like three days, but Nora and Gerry were trained not to contradict. (Their mother had made up her mind not to understand a word of English.)

Grandmother Abbott had curly hair, a striking shade of white, and a pink face. She wore quite nice shoes but had been forced to cut slits in them to accommodate her sore toes. Her apron strings could barely be tied, her waist was that thick around. She said to Gerry, "You take after your grandpa's side," because of the red-gold hair. The girls did not yet read English, and so she deduced they could not read at all. She told them how John Wesley and his brothers and sisters had each learned the alphabet on the day they turned five. It was achieved by dint of being shut up in a room with Mrs. Wesley, and receiving nothing to eat or drink until the recitation ran smoothly from A to Z.

"That's a Methodist birthday for you," said Ray. It may have stirred up memories, for he became snappy and critical, as he never was at home. He stood up for Quebec, saying there was a lot of good in a place where a man could have a beer whenever he felt like it, and no questions asked. In Quebec, you could buy beer in grocery stores. The rest of Canada was pretty dry, yet in those parched cities, on a Saturday night, even the telephone poles were reeling-drunk. Nora was proud of him for having all that to say. On their last evening a few things went wrong, and Ray said, "Tough corn and sour apple pie. That's no meal for a man." He was right. Her mother would never have served it. No wonder he had stayed in Montreal.

On a warm spring afternoon the war came to an end. Nora was fifteen and going to an English high school. She knew who George Washington was and the names of the Stuart kings but not much about Canada. A bunch of fatheads— Ray's assessment—swarmed downtown and broke some store windows and overturned a streetcar, to show how glad they felt about peace. No one knew what to expect or what was supposed to happen without a war. Even Ray wasn't sure if his place on the city payroll was safe, with all the younger men coming back and shoving for priority. Uncle Victor decided to evict all his tenants, give the flats a coat of paint, and rent them to veterans at a higher price. Ninette and Aunt Rosalie went to Eaton's and stood in one of the first lines for nylon stockings. Nora's mother welcomed the end of rationing on principle, although no one had gone without. Geraldine had been moping for years: She had yearned to be the youngest novice in universal history and now it was too late. Ray had kept saying, "Nothing doing. There's a war on." He wanted the family to stick together in case Canada was invaded, forgetting how eager he had been to leave at the very beginning, though it was true that in 1939 the entire war was expected to last about six months.

Now Gerry sat around weeping because she could leave home. When Ray said she had to wait another year, she suddenly stopped crying and began to sort the clothes and possessions she was giving up. The first thing she turned over to Nora was the black velvet ribbon Ninette had unfastened all those years ago. It was as good as new; Gerry never wore anything out. To Nora it seemed the relic of a distant age. The fashion now was curved combs and barrettes and hair clips studded with colored stones. Gerry went on separating her clothes into piles until the last minute and went away dry-eyed, leaving an empty bed in the room she had shared with Nora all Nora's life.

The next person to leave was Ninette. She came down with tuberculosis and had to be sent to a place in the Laurentians—not far from Gerry's convent. She never wrote, for fear of passing germs along by mail. If Nora wanted to send a letter, she had to give it, unsealed, to Aunt Rosalie. The excuse was that Ninette had to be shielded from bad news. Nora had no idea what the bad news might be. Ninette had never married. Her education had gone to waste, Nora often heard. She had inherited her father's habit of waiting, and now life had played her a mean trick. She had slapped her little brothers around for their own good and given private French lessons. Her favorite book was still her own "Marie-Antoinette." Perhaps she secretly had hoped to be martyred and admired. Ray had thought so: "The trouble with Ninette was all that goddamn queen stuff."

"Was," he had said. She had fallen into their past. After a short time Nora began to forget about her cousin. It was impossible to go on writing to someone who never replied. The family seemed to see less of Aunt Rosalie and Uncle Victor. Tuberculosis was a disgraceful disease, a curse of the poor, said to run through generations. Some distant, driven ancestor, a victim of winter and long stretches of émigré hunger, had bequeathed the germ, across three centuries, perhaps. The least rumor concerning Ninette could blight the life of brothers and cousins. The summer after she vanished, Aunt Rosalie had a second stroke and two weeks later died.

One person who came well out of the war was Ray. He was in the same office, an adornment to the same payroll, and still had friends all over. He had devised a means of easing the sorrow of childless couples by bringing them together with newborn babies no one wanted to bring up. He had the satisfaction of performing a kindness, a Christian act, and the pleasure of experiencing favors returned. "Ray doesn't quite stand there with his hand out," Uncle Victor had been heard to say. "But a lot of the time he finds something in it." Ray had his own letter paper now, with "Cadaster/*Cadastre*" printed across the top. "Cadaster" had no connection to his job, as far as anyone could tell. He had found sheaves of the paper in a cardboard box, about to be carted away. The paper was yellowed and brittle around the edges. He enjoyed typing letters and signing his name in a long scrawl. He had once said he wanted his children to have names he could pronounce, and to be able to speak English at his own table if he felt like it. Both wishes had been granted. He was more cheerful than any man Nora had ever heard of and much happier than poor Uncle Victor.

Nora had to herself the room she had shared with her sister. She placed Gerry's framed high school graduation portrait on the dresser and kissed the glass, and spread her belongings in all the dresser drawers. Before long, her mother moved in and took over the empty bed. She was having her change of life and had to get up in the night to put on a fresh nightgown and replace the pillowcases soaked with sweat. After about a week of it, Ray came to the door and turned on the overhead light. He said, "How long is it going on for?"

"I don't know. Go back to bed. You need your sleep."

He walked away, leaving the light on. Nora went barefoot to switch it off. She said, "What does it feel like, exactly?"

Her mother's voice in the dark sounded girlish, like Gerry's. "As if somebody dipped a towel in boiling-hot water and threw it over your head."

"I'm never getting married," Nora said.

"Being married has nothing to do with it."

"Will it happen to Gerry?"

"Nuns get all the women's things," said her mother.

The August heat wave and her mother's restlessness kept Nora awake. She thought about the secretarial school where she was to begin a new, great phase of her life on the Tuesday after Labor Day—twelve days from tomorrow. Her imagination traveled along unknown corridors and into classrooms where there were rows of typewriters, just delivered from the factory; the pencils, the erasers, the spiral notebooks had never been touched. All the girls were attractive-looking and serious-minded. At a front-row desk (should they be seated in alphabetical order) was Miss Nora Abbott, with her natural bilingual skills and extensive wardrobe—half of it Gerry's.

As children, she and Gerry had taken parental magic on trust, had believed their mother heard their unspoken thoughts and listened from a distance to their most secret conversations. Now her mother said, "Can't you get to sleep, Nora? You're all impressed about taking that course. Are you wanting to leave home with your first paycheck? Papa wouldn't want that."

"Gerry was eighteen when she went away."

"We knew where she was going."

"I'll be over nineteen by the time I start to work."

"And starting off at fifteen dollars a week, if you're lucky."

Nora said, "I've been wondering how Dad's going to manage to pay for the course. It's two hundred dollars, not counting the shorthand book."

"It's not for you to worry about," said her mother. "He's paid the hundred deposit. The rest isn't due until December."

"Uncle Victor had to chip in."

"Uncle Victor didn't *have* to do anything. When he helps out, it's because he wants to. Your father doesn't beg."

"Why couldn't he pay the whole hundred dollars on his own? Did he lose some of it at Blue Bonnets?"

Her mother sat up all of a sudden and became a looming presence in the dark. "Did you ever have to go to bed on an empty stomach?" she said. "You and Gerry always had a new coat every winter."

"Gerry did. I got the hand-me-down. Grandma Abbott sent Gerry presents because she had red hair."

"Gerry's old coats looked as if they came straight from the store. She never got a spot or a stain on any of her clothes. Grandmother Abbott sent her a chocolate Easter egg once. It broke up in the mail and your father told her not to bother with any more parcels."

"Why would Uncle Victor have to lend Dad fifty dollars? What does he do with his money?"

"Did you ever have to go without shoes?" said her mother. "Did you ever miss a hot meal? Who gave you the gold chain and the twenty-four-karat crucifix for your First Communion?"

"Uncle Victor."

"Well, and who was he trying to be nice to? Your father. He's been the best father in the world and the best husband. If I go before he does, I want you to look after him."

I'll be married by then, Nora thought. "It's girls that look after their old dads," Ray had said when Victor had once commiserated with him for not having a son. Ninette was now back from the place in the Laurentians—cured, it was said— and had taken Aunt Rosalie's place, seeing to it that the boys did their homework and Uncle Victor got his meals on time. She wore her hair short (apparently the long hair had been taking all the strength) and had put on weight. Her manner had changed more than her appearance. She was twenty-six, unlikely to find a husband. A nagging, joyless religiosity had come over her. Nora had seen her only once since her return: Ninette had instructed Nora to pray for her, as though she were gradually growing used to giving spiritual orders. Nora had said to herself, She's like a sergeant-major. The whole family had been praying for Ninette for well over a year, without being pushed. Perhaps she had chosen this new, bossy way of behaving over another possibility, which was to sit with her head in her hands, thinking, Unfair! Either way, she was not good company.

Nora said to her mother, "You mean you want me to look after Dad the way Ninette takes care of Uncle Victor?"

"Poor Ninette," her mother said at once. "What else can she do now." Who would marry Ninette, she was trying to say. Ninette kept herself to herself; it may have been that one kept away from her—not unkindly, not dismissing the devaluation of her life, but for fear of ill luck and its terrible way of spreading by contact.

In the next room, Ray thumped on the wall and said, "Either we all get up and waltz or we pipe down and get some sleep."

Her last waking thoughts were about Gerry. When the time came to take over Ray's old age—for she had assumed her mother's wild requirement to be a prophecy—Gerry might decide to leave her convent and keep house for him. She could easily by then have had enough: Ray believed her vocation to be seriously undermined by a craving for peanut clusters and homemade fudge. In a letter she had run on about her mother's celebrated Queen of Sheba chocolate cake, artfully hollowed and filled with chocolate mousse and whipped cream. Nora tried to see Gerry and Ray old and middle-aged, with Gerry trying to get him to drink some hot soup; her imagination went slack. Old persons were said to be demanding and difficult, but Gerry would show endless patience. Would she? Was she, any more than most people, enduring and calm? Nora could not remember. Only a year or so had gone by, but the span of separation had turned out to be longer and more effacing than ordinary time.

The next morning, and in spite of the heat, Ray requested pancakes and sausages for breakfast. No two of the Abbotts ever ate the same thing; Nora's mother stood on her feet until the family was satisfied. Then she cleared away plates, bowls, and coffee cups and made herself a pot of strong tea. Ray picked his teeth, and suddenly asked Nora if she wanted to do a favor for a couple he knew: It involved fetching this couple's baby and keeping an eye on it just a few hours a day, until the end of the week. The infant's mother had suffered a nervous breakdown at his birth, and the child had been placed in a home and cared for by nuns.

"Why can't they hire a nurse?" Nora said.

"She's on her way over from England. They're just asking you to be around till she comes. It's more than just a good turn," her father said. "It's a Christian act."

"A Christian act is one where you don't get paid," Nora said.

"Well, you've got nothing better to do for the moment," he said. "You wouldn't want to take money for this. If you take the money, you're a nursemaid and have to eat in the kitchen."

"I eat in the kitchen at home." She could not shake off the picture of Ray as old and being waited on by Gerry. "Do you know them?" she said to her mother, who was still standing, eating toast.

"Your mother doesn't know them," said Ray.

"I just saw the husband once," said his wife. "It was around the time when Ninette had to stop giving lessons. Mrs. Fenton used to come once a week. She must have started being depressed before the baby came along, because she couldn't concentrate or remember anything. Taking lessons was supposed to pull her mind together. He brought a book belonging to Ninette and I think he paid for some lessons his wife still owed. Ninette wasn't around. Aunt Rosalie introduced us. That was all."

"You never told me about that," said Ray.

"What was he like?" said Nora.

Her mother answered, in English, "Like an English."

Nora and her father took the streetcar down to the stone building where Ray had worked before moving into his office at City Hall. He put on his old green eyeshade and got behind an oak counter. He was having a good time, playing the role of a much younger Ray Abbott, knowing all the while he had the office and the safe and connections worth a gold mine. Mr. Fenton and his doctor friend were already waiting, smoking under a dilapidated NO SMOKING sign. Nora felt not so much shy as careful. She took in their light hot-weather clothes—the doctor's pale beige jacket, with wide lapels, and Mr. Fenton's American-looking seersucker. The huge room was dark and smelled of old books and papers. It was not the smell of dirt, though the place could have done with a good cleanout.

Nora and the men stood side by side, across from her father. Another person, whom she took to be a regular employee, was sitting at a desk, reading the *Gazette* and eating a Danish. Her father had in front of him a ledger of printed forms. He filled in the blank spaces by hand, using a pen, which he dipped with care in black ink. Mr. Fenton dictated the facts. Before giving the child's name or its date of birth, he identified his wife and, of course, himself: They were Louise Marjorie Clopstock and Boyd Markham Forrest Fenton. He was one of those Anglos with no Christian name, just a string of surnames. Ray lifted the pen over the most important entry. He peered up, merry-looking as a squirrel. It was clear that Mr. Fenton either could not remember or make up his mind. "Scott?" he said, as if Ray ought to know.

The doctor said, "Neil Boyd Fenton," pausing heavily between syllables.

"Not Neil Scott?"

"You said you wanted 'Neil Boyd.' "

Nora thought, You'd think Dr. Marchand was the mother. Ray wrote the name carefully and slowly, and the date of birth. Reading upside down, she saw that the Fenton child was three months old, which surely was past the legal limit of registration. Her father turned the ledger around so Mr. Fenton could sign, and said "Hey, Vince" to the man eating Danish. He came over and signed too, and then it was the doctor's turn.

Mr. Fenton said, "Shouldn't Nora be a witness?" and her father said, "I think we could use an endorsement from the little lady," as if he had never seen her before. To the best of Nora's knowledge, all the information recorded was true, and so she signed her name to it, along with the rest.

Her father sat down where Vince had been, brushed away some crumbs, and ran a cream-colored document into a big clackety typewriter, older than Nora, most likely. When he had finished repeating the names and dates in the ledger, he fastened a red seal to the certificate and brought it back to the counter to be signed. The same witnesses wrote their names, but only Nora, it seemed, saw her father's mistakes: He had typed "Nell" for "Neil" and "Frenton" for "Fenton" and had got the date of birth wrong by a year, giving "Nell Frenton" the age of fifteen months. The men signed the certificate without reading it. If she and her father had been alone, she could have pointed out the mistakes, but of course she could not show him up in front of strangers.

The doctor put his fountain pen away and remarked, "I like Neil for a name." He spoke to Mr. Fenton in English and to Ray and Nora not at all. At the same time he and Nora's father seemed to know each other. There was an easiness of acquaintance between them; a bit cagey perhaps. Mr. Fenton seemed more like the sort of man her father might go with to the races. She could imagine them easily going on about bets and horses. Most of the babies Ray was kind enough to find for unhappy couples were made known by doctors. Perhaps he was one of them.

It was decided between Ray and Mr. Fenton that Nora would be called for, the next morning, by Mr. Fenton and the doctor. They would all three collect the child and take him home. Nora was invited to lunch. Saying good-bye, Mr. Fenton touched her bare arm, perhaps by accident, and asked her to call him "Boyd." Nothing in her manner or expression showed she had heard.

That evening, Ray and his wife played cards in the kitchen. Nora was ironing the starched piqué dress she would wear the next day. She said, "They gave up their own baby for adoption, or what?"

"Maybe they weren't expecting a child. It was too much for them," her mother said.

"Give us a break," said Ray. "Mrs. Fenton wasn't in any shape to look after him. She had *her* mother down from Toronto because she couldn't even run the house. They've got this D. P. maid always threatening to quit."

"Does he mind having his mother-in-law around the whole time?" said Nora.

"He sure doesn't." Nora thought he would add some utterly English thing like "She's got the money," but Ray went on, "She's on his side. She wants them together. The baby's the best thing that could happen."

"Maybe there was a mistake at the hospital," said Nora's mother, trying again. "The Fentons got some orphan by mistake and their own baby went to the home."

"And then the truth came out," said Nora. It made sense.

"Now when you're over there, don't you hang out with that maid," Ray said. "She can't even speak English. If somebody says to you to eat in the kitchen, I want you to come straight home."

"I'm not leaving home," said Nora. "I'm not sure if I want to go back to their place after tomorrow."

"Come on," said Ray. "I promised."

"You promised. I didn't."

"Leave your dress on the ironing board," said her mother. "I'll do the pleats."

Nora switched off the iron and went to stand behind her father. She put her hands on his shoulders. "Don't worry," she said. "I'm not going to let you down. You might as well throw your hand in. I saw Maman's."

3

Obliged to take the baby from Nora, Missy now held him at arm's length, upright between her hands, so that no part of him could touch her white apron. Nora thought, He'll die from his own screaming. Missy's face said she was not enjoying the joke. Perhaps she thought Mr. Fenton had put Nora up to it. His laughter had said something different: Whatever blunders he might have committed until now, choosing Missy to be the mother of a Fenton was not among them.

"You'd better clean him up right away," said Mrs. Clopstock.

Missy, whose silences were astonishingly powerful, managed to suggest that cleaning Neil up was not in her working agreement. She did repeat that a bottle was ready for some reason, staring hard at the doctor.

"The child is badly dehydrated," he said, as if replying to Missy. "He should be given liquid right away. He is undernourished and seriously below his normal weight. As you can tell, he has a bad case of diarrhea. I'll take his temperature after lunch."

"Is he really sick?" said Nora.

"He may have to be hospitalized for a few days." He was increasingly solemn and slower than ever.

"Hospitalized?" said Mr. Fenton. "We've only just got him here."

"The first thing is to get him washed and changed," said Mrs. Clopstock.

"I'll do it," said Nora. "He knows me."

"Missy won't mind."

Sensing a private exchange between Mrs. Clopstock and Missy, Nora held still. She felt a child's powerful desire to go home, away from these strangers. Mrs. Clopstock said, "Let us all please go and sit down. We're standing here as if we were in a hotel lobby."

"I can do it," Nora said. She said again, "He knows me."

"Missy knows where everything is," said Mrs. Clopstock. "Come along, Alex, Boyd. Nora, don't you want to wash your hands?"

"I'm feeling dehydrated too," said Mr. Fenton. "I hope Missy put something on ice."

Nora watched Missy turn and climb the stairs and disappear around the bend in the staircase. There'll be a holy row about this, she thought. I'll be gone.

"It was very nice meeting you," she said. "I have to leave now."

"Come on, Nora," said Mr. Fenton. "Anybody could have made the same mistake. You came in out of bright sunlight. The hall was dark."

"Could we please, please go and sit down?" said his mother-in-law.

"All right," he said, still to Nora. "It's O.K. You've had enough. Let's have a bite to eat and I'll drive you home."

"You may have to take Neil to the hospital."

Mrs. Clopstock took the doctor's arm. She was a little woman in green linen, wearing pearls and pearl earrings. Aunt Rosalie would have seen right away if they were real. The two moved from the shaded hall to a shaded room.

Mr. Fenton watched them go. "Nora," he said, "just let me have a drink and I'll drive you home."

"I don't need to be driven home. I can take the Sherbrooke bus and walk the rest of the way."

"Can you tell me what's wrong? It can't be my mother-in-law. She's a nice woman. Missy's a little rough, but she's nice too."

"Where's Mrs. Fenton?" said Nora. "Why didn't she at least come to the door? It's her child."

"You're not dumb," he said. "You're not Ray's girl for nothing. It's hers and it isn't."

"We all signed," Nora said. "I didn't sign to cover up some story. I came here to do a Christian act. I wasn't paid anything."

"What do you mean by 'anything'? You mean not enough?"

"Who's Neil?" she said. "I mean, who *is* he?"

"He's a Fenton. You saw the register."

"I mean, *who* is he?"

"He's my son. You signed the register. You should know."

"I believe you," she said. "He has English eyes." Her

voice dropped. He had to ask her to repeat something. "I said, was it Ninette?"

It took him a second or so to see what she was after. He gave the same kind of noisy laugh as when she had tried to place the child in Missy's arms. "Little Miss Cochefert? Until this minute I thought you were the only sane person in Montreal."

"It fits," said Nora. "I'm sorry."

"Well, I'll tell you," he said. "I don't know. There are two people that know. Your father, Ray Abbott, and Alex Marchand."

"Did you pay my dad?"

"*Pay* him? I paid him for *you*. We wouldn't have asked anyone to look after Neil for nothing."

"About Ninette," she said. "I just meant that it fits."

"A hundred women in Montreal would fit, when it comes to that. The truth is, we don't know, except that she was in good health."

"Who was the girl in the lane? The one you were talking about."

"Just a girl in the wrong place. Her father was a school principal."

"You said that. Did you know her?"

"I never saw her. Missy and Louise did. Louise is my wife."

"I know. How much did you give my dad? Not for Neil. For me."

"Thirty bucks. Some men don't make that in a week. If you have to ask, it means you never got it."

"I've never had thirty dollars in one piece in my life," she said. "In my family we don't fight over money. What my dad says, goes. I've never had to go without. Gerry and I had new coats every winter."

"Is that the end of the interrogatory? You'd have made a great cop. I agree, you can't stay. But would you just do one last Christian act? Wash your hands and comb your hair and sit down and have lunch. After that, I'll put you in a taxi and pay the driver. If you don't want me to, my mother-in-law will."

"I could help you take him to the hospital."

"Forget the Fenton family," he said. "Lunch is the cutoff."

Late in the afternoon Ray came home and they had tea and sandwiches at the kitchen table. Nora was wearing Gerry's old white terry-cloth robe. Her washed hair was in rollers.

"There was nothing to it, no problem," she said again. "He needed a hospital checkup. He was run-down. I don't know which hospital."

"I could find out," said Ray.

"I think they don't want anybody around."

"What did you eat for lunch?" said her mother.

"Some kind of cold soup. Some kind of cold meat. A fruit salad. Iced tea. The men drank beer. There was no bread on the table."

"Pass Nora the peanut butter," said Ray.

"Did you meet Mr. Fenton because of Ninette," said Nora, "or did you know him first? Did you know Dr. Marchand first, or Mr. Fenton?"

"It's a small world," said her father. "Anyways, I've got some money for you."

"How much?" said Nora. "No, never mind. I'll ask if I ever need it."

"You'll never need anything," he said. "Not as long as your old dad's around."

"You know that Mrs. Clopstock?" said Nora. "She's the first person I've ever met from Toronto. I didn't stare at her, but I took a good look. Maman, how can you tell real pearls?"

"They wouldn't be real," said Ray. "The real ones would be on deposit. Rosalie had a string of pearls."

"They had to sell them on account of Ninette," said her mother.

"Maybe you could find out the name of the hospital," Nora said. "He might like to see me. He knows me."

"He's already forgotten you," her mother said.

"I wouldn't swear to that," said Ray. "I can remember somebody bending over my baby buggy. I don't know who it was, though."

He will remember that I picked him up, Nora decided. He will remember the smell of the incense. He will remember the front door and moving into the dark hall. I'll try to remember him. It's the best I can do.

She said to Ray, "What's the exact truth? Just what's on paper?"

"Nora," said her mother. "Look at me. Look me right in the face. Forget that child. He isn't yours. If you want children, get married. All right?"

"All right," her father answered for her. "Why don't you put on some clothes and I'll take you both to a movie." He began to whistle, not "Don't Let It Bother You," but some other thing just as easy.

THE END OF THE WORLD

I NEVER LIKE to leave Canada, because I'm disappointed every time. I've felt disappointed about places I haven't even seen. My wife went to Florida with her mother once. When they arrived there, they met some neighbors from home who told them about a sign saying NO CANADIANS. They never saw this sign anywhere, but they kept hearing about others who did, or whose friends had seen it, always in different places, and it spoiled their trip for them. Many people, like them, have never come across it but have heard about it, so it must be there somewhere. Another time I had to go and look after my brother Kenny in Buffalo. He had stolen a credit card and was being deported on that account. I went down to vouch for him and pay up for him and bring him home. Neither of us cared for Buffalo.

"What have they got here that's so marvelous?" I said.

"Proust," said Kenny.

"What?"

"Memorabilia," he said. He was reading it off a piece of paper.

"Why does a guy with your education do a dumb thing like swiping a credit card?" I said.

"Does Mother know?" said Kenny.

"Mum knows, and Lou knows, and I know, and Beryl knows. It was in the papers. 'Kenneth Apostolesco, of this city...'"

"I'd better stay away," my brother said.

"No, you'd better not, for Mum's sake. We've only got one mother."

"Thank God," he said. "Only one of each. One mother and one father. If I had more than one of each, I think I'd still be running."

It was our father who ran, actually. He deserted us during the last war. He joined the Queen's Own Rifles, which wasn't a Montreal regiment—he couldn't do anything like other people, couldn't even join up like anyone else—and after the war he just chose to go his own way. I saw him downtown in Montreal one time after the war. I was around twelve, delivering prescriptions for a drugstore. I knew him before he knew me. He looked the way he had always managed to look, as if he had all the time in the world. His mouth was drawn in, like an old woman's, but he still had his coal-black hair. I wish we had his looks. I leaned my bike with one foot on the curb and he came down and stood by me, rocking on his feet, like a dancer, and looking off over my head. He said he was night watchman at a bank and that he was waiting for the Army to fix him up with some teeth. He'd had all his teeth out, though there wasn't anything wrong with them. He was eligible for new ones provided he put in a claim that year, so he thought he might as well. He was a bartender by profession, but he wasn't applying for anything till he'd got his new teeth. "I've told them to hurry it up," he said. "I can't go round to good places all gummy." He didn't ask how anyone was at home.

I had to leave Canada to be with my father when he died. I was the person they sent for, though I was the youngest. My name was on the back page of his passport: "In case of accident or death notify WILLIAM APOSTOLESCO. Relationship: Son." I was the one he picked. He'd been barman on a ship for years by then, earning good money, but he had nothing put by. I guess he never expected his life would be finished. He collapsed with a lung hemorrhage, as far as I could make out, and they put him off at a port in France. I went there. That was where I saw him. This town had been shelled twenty years ago and a lot of it looked bare and new. I wouldn't say I hated it exactly, but I would never have come here of my own accord. It was worse than Buffalo in some ways. I didn't like the food or the coffee, and they never gave you anything you needed in the hotels—I had to go out and buy some decent towels. It didn't matter, because I had to buy everything for my father anyway—soap and towels and Kleenex. The hospital didn't provide a thing except the bed-sheets, and when a pair of those was put on the bed it seemed to be put there once and for all. I was there twenty-three days and I think I saw the sheets changed once. Our grandfathers had been glad to get out of Europe. It took my father to go back. The hospital he was in was an old convent or monastery. The beds were so close together you could hardly get a chair between them. Women patients were always wandering around the men's wards, and although I wouldn't swear to it, I think some of them had their beds there, at the far end. The patients were given crocks of tepid water to wash in, not by their beds but on a long table in the middle of the ward. Anyone too sick to get up was just out of luck unless, like my father, he had someone to look after him. I saw beetles and cockroaches, and I said to myself, This is what a person gets for leaving home.

My father accepted my presence as if it were his right—as if he hadn't lost his claim to any consideration years ago. So as not to scare him, I pretended my wife's father had sent me here on business, but he hardly listened, so I didn't insist.

"Didn't you drive a cab one time or other?" he said. "What else have you done?"

I wanted to answer, "You know what I've been doing? I've been supporting your wife and educating your other children, practically single-handed, since I was twelve."

I had expected to get here in time for his last words, which ought to have been "I'm sorry." I thought he would tell me where he wanted to be buried, how much money he owed, how many bastards he was leaving behind, and who was looking out for them. I imagined them in ports like this, with no-good mothers. *Somebody* should have been told—telling me didn't mean telling the whole world. One of the advantages of having an Old Country in the family is you can always say the relations that give you trouble have gone there. You just say, "He went back to the Old Country," and nobody asks any questions. So he could have told me the truth, and I'd have known and still not let the family down. But my father never confided anything. The trouble was he didn't know he was dying—he'd been told, in fact, he was getting better—so he didn't act like a dying man. He used what breath he had to say things like "I always liked old Lou," and you would have thought she was someone else's daughter, a girl he had hardly known. Another time he said, "Did Kenny do well for himself? I heard he went to college."

"Don't talk," I said.

"No, I mean it. I'd like to know how Kenny made out."

He couldn't speak above a whisper some days, and he was careful how he pronounced words. It wasn't a snobbish or an English accent—nothing that would make you grit your teeth. He just sounded like a stranger. When I was sent for, my mother said, "He's dying a pauper, after all his ideas. I hope he's satisfied." I didn't answer, but I said to myself, This isn't a question of satisfaction. I wanted to ask her, "Since you didn't get along with him and he didn't get along with you, what did you go and have three children for?" But those are the questions you keep to yourself.

"What's your wife like?" my father croaked. His eyes were interested. I hadn't been prepared for this, for how long the mind stayed alive and how frivolous it went on being. I thought he should be more serious. *"Wife,"* my father insisted. "What about her?"

"Obedient" came into my head, I don't know why; it isn't important. "Older than me," I said, quite easily, at last. "Better educated. She was a kindergarten teacher. She knows a lot about art." Now, why that, of all the side issues? She doesn't like a bare wall, that's all. "She prefers the Old Masters," I said. I was thinking about the Scotch landscape we've got over the mantelpiece.

"Good, good. Name?"

"You know—*Beryl*. We sent you an announcement, to that place in Mexico where you were then."

"That's right, Beryl." "Burrull" was what he actually said.

I felt reassured, because my father until now had sounded like a strange person. To have "Beryl" pronounced as I was used to hearing it made up for being alone here and the smell of the ward and the coffee made of iodine. I remembered what the Old Master had cost—one hundred and eighty dollars in 1962. It must be worth more now. Beryl said it would be an investment. Her family paid for half. She said once, about my father, "One day he'll be sick; we'll have to look after him." "We can sell the painting," I said. "I guess I can take care of my own father."

It happened—I was here, taking care of him; but he spoiled it now by saying, "You look like you've done pretty well. That's not a bad suit you've got on."

"Actually," I said, "I had to borrow from Beryl's father so as to get here."

I thought he would say, "Oh, I'm sorry," and I had my next answer ready, about not begrudging a cent of it. But my father closed his eyes, smiling, saving up more breath to talk about nothing.

"I liked old Lou," he said distinctly. I was afraid he would ask, "Why doesn't she write to me?" and I would have to say, "Because she never forgave you," and he was perfectly capable of saying then, "Never forgave me for what?" But instead of that he laughed, which was the worst of the choking and wheezing noises he made now, and when he had recovered he said, "Took her to Eaton's to choose a toy village. Had this shipment in, last one in before the war. Summer '39. The old man saw the ad, wanted to get one for the kid. Old man came—each of us had her by the hand. Lou looked round, but every village had something the matter, as far as Her Royal Highness was concerned. The old man said, 'Come on, Princess, hurry it up,' but no, she'd of seen a scratch, or a bad paint job, or a chimney too big for a cottage. The old man said, 'Can't this kid make up her mind about anything? She's going to do a lot more crying than laughing,' he said, 'and that goes for you, too.' He was wrong about me. Don't know about Lou. But she was smart that time—not to want something that wasn't perfect."

He shut his eyes again and breathed desperately through his mouth. The old man in the story was his father, my grandfather.

"Nothing is perfect," I said. I felt like standing up so everyone could hear. It wasn't sourness but just the way I felt like reacting to my father's optimism.

Some days he seemed to be getting better. After two weeks I was starting to wonder if they hadn't brought me all this way for nothing. I couldn't go home and come back later, it had to be now; but I couldn't stay on and on. I had already moved to a cheaper hotel room. I dreamed I asked him, "How much longer?" but luckily the dream was in a foreign language—so foreign I don't think it was French, even. It was a language no one on earth had ever heard of. I wouldn't have wanted him to understand it, even in a dream. The nurses couldn't say anything. Sometimes I wondered if they knew who he was—if they could tell one patient from another. It was a big place, and poor. These nurses didn't seem to have much equipment. When they needed sterile water for anything, they had to boil it in an old saucepan. I got to the doctor one day, but he didn't like it. He had told my father he was fine, and that I could go back to Canada anytime—the old boy must have been starting to wonder why I was staying so long. The doctor just said to me, "Family business is of no interest to me. You look after your duty and I'll look after mine." I was afraid that my dream showed on my face and that was what made them all so indifferent. I didn't know how much time there was. I wanted to ask my father why he thought everything had to be perfect, and if he still stood by it as a way of living. Whenever he was reproached about something—by my mother, for instance—he just said, "Don't make my life dark for me." What could you do? He certainly made her life dark for her. One year when we had a summer cottage, he took a girl from the village, the village tramp, out to an island in the middle of the lake. They got caught in a storm coming back, and around fifty people stood on shore waiting to see the canoe capsize and the sinners drown. My mother had told us to stay in the house, but when Kenny said, to scare me, "I guess the way things are, Mum's gone down there to drown herself," I ran after her. She didn't say anything to me, but took her raincoat off and draped it over my head. It would have been fine if my father had died then— if lightning had struck him, or the canoe gone down like a stone. But no, he waded ashore—the slut, too, and someone even gave her a blanket. It was my mother that was blamed, in a funny way. "Can't you keep your husband home?" this girl's father said. I remember that same summer some other woman saying to her, "You'd better keep your husband away from my daughter. I'm telling you for your own good, because my husband's got a gun in the house." Someone did say, "Oh, poor Mrs. Apostolesco!" but my mother only answered, "If you think that, then I'm poor for life." That was only one of the things he did to her. I'm not sure if it was even the worst.

———

It was hard to say how long he had been looking at me. His lips were trying to form a word. I bent close and heard, "Sponge."

"Did you say 'sponge'? Is 'sponge' what you said?"

"Sponge," he agreed. He made an effort: "Bad night last night. Awful. Wiped everything with my sponge—blood, spit. Need new sponge."

There wasn't a bed table, just a plastic bag that hung on the bedrail with his personal things in it. I got out the sponge. It needed to be thrown away, all right. I said, "What color?"

"Eh?"

"This," I said, and held it up in front of him. "The new one. Any special color?"

"Blue." His voice broke out of a whisper all at once. His eyes were mocking me, like a kid seeing how far he can go. I thought he would thank me now, but then I said to myself, You can't expect anything; he's a sick man, and he was always like this.

"Most people think it was pretty good of me to have come here," I wanted to explain—not to boast or anything, but just for the sake of conversation. I was lonely there, and I had so much trouble understanding what anybody was saying.

"Bad night," my father whispered. "Need sedation."

"I know. I tried to tell the doctor. I guess he doesn't understand my French."

He moved his head. "Tip the nurses."

"You don't mean it!"

"Don't make me talk." He seemed to be using a reserve of breath. "At least twenty dollars. The ward girls less."

I said, "Jesus God!" because this was new to me and I felt out of my depth. "They don't bother much with you," I said, talking myself into doing it. "Maybe you're right. If I gave them a present, they'd look after you more. Wash you.

Maybe they'd put a screen around you—you'd be more private then."

"No, thanks," my father said. "No screen. Thanks all the same."

We had one more conversation after that. I've already said there were always women slopping around in the ward, in felt slippers, and bathrobes stained with medicine and tea. I came in and found one—quite young, this one was—combing my father's hair. He could hardly lift his head from the pillow, and still she thought he was interesting. I thought, Kenny should see this.

"She's been telling me," my father gasped when the woman had left. "About herself. Three children by different men. Met a North African. He adopts the children, all three. Gives them his name. She has two more by him, boys. But he won't put up with a sick woman. One day he just doesn't come. She's been a month in another place; now they've brought her here. Man's gone. Left the children. They've been put in all different homes, she doesn't know where. Five kids. Imagine."

I thought, You left *us*. He had forgotten; he had just simply forgotten that he'd left his own.

"Well, we can't do anything about her, can we?" I said. "She'll collect them when she gets out of here."

"If she gets out."

"That's no way to talk," I said. "Look at the way she was talking and walking around . . ." I could not bring myself to say "and combing your hair." "Look at how *you* are," I said. "You've just told me this long story."

"She'll seem better, but she'll get worse," my father said. "She's like me, getting worse. Do you think I don't know what kind of ward I'm in? Every time they put the screen around a patient, it's because he's dying. If I had TB, like they tried to make me believe, I'd be in a TB hospital."

"That just isn't true," I said.

"Can you swear I've got TB? You can't."

I said without hesitating, "You've got a violent kind of TB. They had no place else to put you except here. The ward might be crummy, but the medicine . . . the medical care . . ." He closed his eyes. "I'm looking you straight in the face," I said, "and I swear you have this unusual kind of TB, and you're almost cured." I watched, without minding it now, a new kind of bug crawling along the base of the wall.

"Thanks, Billy," said my father.

I really was scared. I had been waiting for something without knowing what it would mean. I can tell you how it was: It was like the end of the world.

"I didn't realize you were worried," I said. "You should of asked me right away."

"I knew you wouldn't lie to me," my father said. "That's why I wanted you, not the others."

That was all. Not long after that, he couldn't talk. He had deserted his whole family once, but I was the one he abandoned twice. When he died, a nurse said to me, "I am sorry." It had no meaning, from her, yet only a few days before, it was all I thought I wanted to hear.

NEW YEAR'S EVE

ON NEW YEAR'S Eve the Plummers took Amabel to the opera.

"Whatever happens tonight happens every day for a year," said Amabel, feeling secure because she had a Plummer on either side.

Colonel Plummer's car had broken down that afternoon; he had got his wife and their guest punctually to the Bolshoi Theater, through a storm, in a bootleg taxi. Now he discovered from his program that the opera announced was neither of those they had been promised.

His wife leaned across Amabel and said, "Well, which is it?" She could not read any Russian and would not try.

She must have known it would take him minutes to answer, for she sat back, settled a width of gauzy old shawl on her neck, and began telling Amabel the relative sizes of the Bolshoi and some concert hall in Vancouver the girl had never heard of. Then, because it was the Colonel's turn to speak, she shut her eyes and waited for the overture.

The Colonel was gazing at the program and putting off the moment when he would have to say that it was *Ivan Susanin*, a third choice no one had so much as hinted at. He wanted to convey that he was sorry and that the change was not his fault. He took bearings: He was surrounded by women. To his left sat the guest, who mewed like a kitten, who had been a friend of his daughter's, and whose name he could not remember. On the right, near the aisle, two quiet unknown girls were eating fruit and chocolates. These two smelled of oranges; of clothes worn a long time in winter; of light recent sweat; of women's hair. Their arms were large and bare. When the girl closest to him moved slightly, he saw a man's foreign wristwatch. He wondered who she was, and how the watch had come to her, but he had been here two years now—long enough to know he would never be answered. He also wondered if the girls were as shabby as his guest found everyone in Moscow. His way of seeing women was not concerned with that sort of evidence: Shoes were shoes, a frock was a frock.

The girls took no notice of the Colonel. He was invisible to them, wiped out of being by a curtain pulled over the inner eye.

He felt his guest's silence, then his wife's. The visitor's profile was a kitten's, to match her voice. She was twenty-two, which his Catherine would never be. Her gold dress, packed for improbable gala evenings, seemed the size of a bathing suit. She was divorcing someone, or someone in Canada had left her—he remembered that, but not her name.

He moved an inch or two to the left and muttered, "It's *Ivan*."

"What?" cried his wife. "What did you say?"

In the old days, before their Catherine had died, when the Colonel's wife was still talking to him, he had tried to hush her in public places sometimes, and so the habit of loudness had taken hold.

"It isn't *Boris*. It isn't *Igor*. It's *Ivan*. They must both have had sore throats."

"Oh, well, bugger it," said his wife.

Amabel supposed that the Colonel's wife had grown peculiar through having lived so many years in foreign parts. Having no one to speak to, she conversed alone. Half of Mrs. Plummer's character was quite coarse, though a finer Mrs. Plummer somehow kept order. Low-minded Mrs. Plummer chatted amiably and aloud with her high-minded twin—far more pleasantly than the whole of Mrs. Plummer ever talked to anybody.

"Serves you right," she said.

Amabel gave a little jump. She wondered if Mrs. Plummer's remark had anything to do with the opera. She turned her head cautiously. Mrs. Plummer had again closed her eyes.

The persistence of memory determines what each day of the year will be like, the Colonel's wife decided. Not what happens on New Year's Eve. This morning I was in Moscow; between the curtains snow was falling. The day had no color. It might have been late afternoon. Then the smell of toast came into my room and I was back in my mother's dining room in Victoria, with the gros-point chairs and the framed embroidered grace on the wall. A little girl I had been ordered to play with kicked the baseboard, waiting for us to finish our breakfast. A devilish little boy, Hume something, was on my mind. I was already attracted to devils; I believed in their powers. My mother's incompetence about choosing friends for me shaped my life, because that child, who kicked the baseboard and left marks on the paint . . .

When she and her husband had still been speaking, this was how Frances Plummer had talked. She had offered him hours of reminiscence, and the long personal thoughts that lead to quarrels. In those days red wine had made her aggressive, whiskey made him vague.

Not only vague, she corrected; stubborn too. *Speak*? said one half of Mrs. Plummer to the other. Did we speak? We yelled!

The quiet twin demanded a fairer portrait of the past, for she had no memory.

Oh, he was a shuffler, back and forth between wife and mistress, said the virago, who had forgotten nothing. He'd desert one and then leave the other—flag to flag, false convert, double agent, reason why a number of women had long, hilly conversations, like the view from a train—monotonous, finally. That was the view a minute ago, you'd say. Yes, but look now.

The virago declared him incompetent; said he had shuffled from embassy to embassy as well, pushed along by a staunch ability to retain languages, an untiring recollection of military history and wars nobody cared about. What did he take with him? His wife, for one thing. At least she was here, tonight, at the opera. Each time they changed countries he supervised the packing of a portrait of his mother, wearing white, painted when she was seventeen. He had nothing of Catherine's: When Catherine died, Mrs. Plummer gave away her clothes and her books, and had her little dog put to sleep.

How did it happen? In what order? said calm Mrs. Plummer. Try and think it in order. He shuffled away one Easter; came shuffling back; and Catherine died. It is useless to say "Serves you right," for whatever served him served you.

The overture told Amabel nothing, and by the end of the first act she still did not know the name of the opera or understand what it was about. Earlier in the day the Colonel had said, "There is some uncertainty—sore throats here and there. The car, now—you can see what has happened. It doesn't start. If our taxi should fail us, and isn't really a taxi, we might arrive at the Bolshoi too late for me to do anything much in the way of explaining. But you can easily figure it out for yourself." His mind cleared; his face lightened. "If you happen to see Tartar dances, then you will know it is *Igor*. Otherwise it is *Boris*."

The instant the lights rose, Amabel thrust her program at him and said, "What does that mean?"

"Why, *Ivan*. It's *Ivan*."

"There are two words, aren't there?"

"Yes. What's-His-Name had a sore throat, d'you see? We

knew it might all be changed at any moment. It was clever of them to get these printed in time."

Mrs. Plummer, who looked like the Red Queen sometimes, said, "A life for the tsar," meanwhile staring straight ahead of her.

"Used to be, used to be," said the Colonel, and he smiled at Amabel, as if to say to her, "Now you know."

The Plummers did not go out between acts. They never smoked, were seldom thirsty or hungry, and they hated crowds. Amabel stood and stretched so that the Russians could appreciate her hair, her waist, her thin arms, and, for those lucky enough to glimpse them, her thighs. After a moment or two Mrs. Plummer thought the Russians had appreciated Amabel enough, and she said very loudly, "You might be more comfortable sitting down."

"*Lakmé* is coming," said the Colonel, for it was his turn to speak. "It's far and away my favorite opera. It makes an awful fool of the officer caste." This was said with ambiguous satisfaction. He was not really disowning himself.

"How does it do that?" said Amabel, who was not more comfortable sitting down.

"Why, an officer runs off with the daughter of a temple priest. No one would ever have got away with that. Though the military are awful fools most of the time."

"You're that class—caste, I mean—aren't you?"

The Colonel supposed that like most people he belonged to the same caste as his father and mother. His father had worn a wig and been photographed wearing it just before he died. His mother, still living, rising eighty, was given to choked melancholy laughter over nothing, a habit carried over from a girlhood of Anglican giggling. It was his mother the Colonel had wanted in Moscow this Christmas—not Amabel. He had wanted to bring her even if it killed her; even if she choked to death on her own laughter as she shook tea out of a cup because her hand trembled, or if she laughed and said, "My dear boy, nobody forced you to marry Frances." The Colonel saw himself serene, immune to reminders; observed a new Colonel Plummer crowned with a wig, staring out of a photograph, in the uniform his father had worn at Vimy Ridge; sure of himself and still, faded to a plain soft neutral color; unhearing, at peace—dead, in short. He had dreamed of sending the plane ticket, of meeting his mother at the airport with a fur coat over his arm in case she had come dressed for the wrong winter; had imagined giving her tea and watching her drink it out of a glass set in a metal base decorated all over with Soviet cosmonauts; had sat beside her here, at the Bolshoi, at a performance of *Eugene Onegin*, which she once had loved. It seemed fitting that he now do some tactful, unneeded, appreciated thing for her, at last— she who had never done anything for him.

One evening his wife had looked up from the paperback spy novel she was reading at dinner and—having waited for him to notice she was neither eating nor turning pages—remarked that Amabel Bacon, who had been Amabel Fisher, that pretty child Catherine roomed with in school, had asked if she might come to them for ten days at Christmas.

"Nothing for children here," he said. "And not much space."

"She must be twenty-two," said his wife, "and can stay in a hotel."

They stared at each other, as if they were strangers in a crush somewhere and her earring had caught on his coat. Their looks disentangled. That night Mrs. Plummer wrote to Amabel saying that they did not know any young people; that Mrs. Plummer played bridge from three to six every afternoon; that the Colonel was busy at the embassy; that it was difficult to find seats at the ballet; that it was too cold for sight-seeing; Lenin's tomb was temporarily closed; there was nothing in the way of shopping; the Plummers, not being great mixers, avoided parties; they planned to spend a quiet Christmas and New Year's; and Amabel was welcome.

Amabel seemed to have forgotten her question about the officer caste. ". . . hissing and whispering behind us the whole time" was what she was saying now. "I could hardly hear the music." She had a smile ready, so that if the Colonel did look at her he would realize she was pleased to be at the Bolshoi and not really complaining. "I suppose you know every note by heart, so you aren't bothered by extra noise." She paused, wondering if the Colonel was hard of hearing. "I hate whispering. It's more bothersome than something loud. It's like that hissing you get on stereo sometimes, like water running."

"Water running?" said the Colonel, not deafly but patiently.

"I mean the people behind us."

"A mother explaining to a child," he said, without looking.

Amabel turned, pretending she was only lifting her long, soft hair away from her neck. She saw a little girl, wearing a white hair ribbon the size of a melon, leaning against, and somehow folded into, a seal-shaped mother. The two shared a pear, bite for bite. Everyone around them was feeding, in fact. It's a zoo, Amabel thought. On the far side of the Colonel, two girls munched on chocolates. They unwrapped each slowly, and dropped the paper back in the box. Amabel sighed and said, "Are they happy? Cheap entertainment isn't everything. Once you've seen *Swan Lake* a hundred times, what is there to do here?"

Mrs. Plummer slapped at her bangles and said, "We were told when we were in Morocco that children with filthy eye diseases and begging their food were perfectly happy."

"Well, at least they have the sun in those places," said Amabel. She had asked the unanswerable only because she herself was so unhappy. It was true that she had left her husband—it was not the other way around—but he had done nothing to keep her. She had imagined pouring all this out to

57

dead Catherine's mother, who had always been so kind on school holidays because Amabel's parents were divorced; who had invited her to Italy once, and another time to Morocco. Why else had Amabel come all this way at Christmastime, if not to be adopted? She had fancied herself curled at the foot of Mrs. Plummer's bed, Mrs. Plummer with a gray braid down on one shoulder, her reading spectacles held between finger and thumb, her book—one of the thick accounts of somebody's life at Cambridge, the reading of the elderly— slipping off the counterpane as she became more and more engrossed in Amabel's story. She had seen Mrs. Plummer handing her a deep blue leather case stamped with dead Catherine's initials. The lid, held back by Mrs. Plummer, was lined with sky-blue moire; the case contained Catherine's first coral bracelet, her gold sleeper rings, her first locket, her chains and charm bracelets, a string of pearls, her childless godmother's engagement ring.... "I have no one to leave these to, and Catherine was so fond of you," said a fantastic Mrs. Plummer.

None of it could happen, of course: From a chance phrase Amabel learned that the Plummers had given everything be- longing to Catherine to the gardener's children of that house in Italy where Catherine caught spinal meningitis and died. Moreover, Amabel never saw so much as the wallpaper of Mrs. Plummer's bedroom. When she hinted at her troubles, said something about a wasted life, Mrs. Plummer cut her off with, "Most lives are wasted. All are shortchanged. A few are tragic."

The Plummers lived in a dark, drab, high-ceilinged flat. They had somehow escaped the foreigners' compound, but their isolation was deeper, as though they were embedded in a large block of ice. Amabel had been put in a new hotel, to which the Colonel conducted her each night astonishingly early. They ate their dinner at a nursery hour, and as soon as Amabel had drunk the last of the decaffeinated coffee the

Plummers served, the Colonel guided her over the pavement to where his Rover was waiting and freezing, then drove her along streets nearly empty of traffic, but where lights signaled and were obeyed, so that it was like driving in a dream. The sidewalks were dark with crowds. She wiped the mist away from the window with her glove, and saw people dragging Christmas trees along—not for Christmas, for the New Year, Colonel Plummer told her. When he left her in the hotel lobby it was barely half past eight. She felt as if her visit were a film seen in fragments, with someone's head moving back and forth in front of her face; or as if someone had been describing a story while a blind flapped and a window banged. In the end she would recall nothing except shabby strangers dragging fir trees through the dark.

"Are you enjoying it?" said Mrs. Plummer, snatching away from the Colonel a last-ditch possibility. He had certainly intended to ask this question next time his turn came round.

"Yes, though I'd appreciate it more if I understood," said Amabel. "Probably."

"Don't you care for music?"

"I love music. Understood Russian, I meant."

Mrs. Plummer did not understand Russian, did not need it, and did not miss it. She had not heard a thing said to her in French, or in Spanish, let alone any of the Hamitic tongues, when she and the Colonel were in Morocco; and she had not cared to learn any Italian in Italy. She went to bed early every night and read detective novels. She was in bed before nine unless an official reason kept her from going. She would not buy new clothes now; would not trouble about her hair, except for cutting it. She played bridge every afternoon for money. When she had enough, she intended to leave him. Dollars, pounds, francs, crowns, lire, deutsche marks, and guldens were rolled up in nylon stockings and held fast with elastic bands.

But of course she would never be able to leave him: She

would never have enough money, though she had been saving, and rehearsing her farewell, for years. She had memorized every word and seen each stroke of punctuation, so that when the moment arrived she would not be at a loss. The parting speech would spring from her like a separate Frances. Sentences streamed across a swept sky. They were pure, white, unblemished by love or compassion. She felt a complicity with her victim. She leaned past their guest and spoke to him and drew his attention to something by touching his hand. He immediately placed his right hand, the hand holding the program, over hers, so that the clasp, the loving conspiracy, was kept hidden.

So it appeared to Amabel—a loving conspiracy. She was embarrassed, because they were too old for this; then she was envious, then jealous. She hated them for flaunting their long understanding, making her seem discarded, left out of a universal game. No one would love her the way the Colonel loved his wife. Mrs. Plummer finished whatever trivial remark she had considered urgent and sat back, very straight, and shook down her Moroccan bangles, and touched each of her long earrings to see if it was still in place—as if the exchange of words with the Colonel had in fact been a passionate embrace.

Amabel pretended to read the program, but it was all in Russian; there wasn't a word of translation. She wished she had never come.

The kinder half of Mrs. Plummer said aloud to her darker twin, "Oh, well, she is less trouble than that damned military-cultural mission last summer."

Tears stood in Amabel's eyes and she had to hold her head as stiffly as Mrs. Plummer did; otherwise the tears might have spilled on her program and thousands of people would have heard them fall. Later, the Plummers would drop her at her hotel, which could have been in Toronto, in Caracas, or in Amsterdam; where there was no one to talk to, and where she was not loved. In her room was a tapped cream-colored telephone with framed instructions in a secret alphabet, and an oil painting of peonies concealing a microphone to which a Russian had his ear glued around the clock. There were three thousand rooms in the hotel, which meant three thousand microphones and an army of three thousand listeners. Amabel kept her coat, snow boots, and traveler's checks on a chair drawn up to the bedside, and she slept in her bra and panties in case they came to arrest her during the night.

"My bath runs sand," she said. Mrs. Plummer merely looked with one eye, like a canary.

"In my hotel," said Amabel. "Sand comes out of the tap. It's in the bathwater."

"Speak to the manager," said Mrs. Plummer, who would not put up with complaints from newcomers. She paused, conceding that what she had just advised was surrealistic. "I've found the local water clean. I drink quarts of it."

"But to bathe in . . . and when I wash my stockings . . ."

"One thing you will never hear of is typhoid here," said the Colonel, kindly, to prevent his wife from saying, "Don't wash your damned stockings." He took the girl's program and looked at it, as if it were in some way unlike his own. He turned to the season's events on the back page and said, "Oh, it isn't *Lakmé* after all," meanwhile wondering if that was what had upset her.

Amabel saw that she would never attract a man again; she would never be loved, for she had not held even the Colonel's attention. First he sat humming the music they had just heard, then he was hypnotized by the program, then he looked straight up at the ceiling and brought his gaze down to the girls sitting next to the aisle. What was so special about them? Amabel leaned forward, as if looking for a dropped glove. She saw two heads, bare round arms, a pink slip strap dropped on the curve of a shoulder. One of the girls divided an orange, holding it out so the juice would not drip on her knees.

They all look like servants, thought the unhappy guest. I can't help it. That's what they look like. They dress like maids. I'm having a rotten time. She glanced at the Colonel and thought, They're his type. But he must have been good-looking once.

The Colonel was able to learn the structure of any language, given a few pages of colloquial prose and a dictionary. His wife was deaf to strangers, and she barely noticed the people she could not understand. As a result, the Colonel had grown accustomed to being alone among hordes of ghosts. With Amabel still mewing beside him, he heard in the ghost language only he could capture, "Yes, but are you happy?"

His look went across the ceiling and came down to the girls. The one who had whispered the question was rapt; she held a section of orange suspended a few inches from her lips as she waited. But the lights dimmed. "Cht," her friend cautioned. She gathered up the peelings on her lap in a paper bag.

Mrs. Plummer suddenly said clearly to herself or to Amabel, "My mother used to make her children sing. If you sing, you must be happy. That was another idea of happiness."

Amabel thought, Every day of the year will be like tonight.

He doesn't look at women now, said Mrs. Plummer silently. Doesn't dare. Every girl is a wife screaming for justice and revenge; a mistress deserted, her life shrunk down to a postage stamp; a daughter dead.

He walked away in Italy, after a violent drinking quarrel, with Catherine there in the house. Instead of calling after him, Mrs. Plummer sat still for an hour, then remembered she had forgotten to leave some money for the postman for Easter. It was early morning; she was dressed; neither of them had been to bed. She found an envelope, the kind she used for messages to servants and the local tradesmen, and crammed a thousand-lire note inside. She was sober and cursing. She scribbled the postman's name. Catherine, in the garden, on her knees, tore out the pansy plants she had put in the little crevices between paving stones the day before. She looked up at her mother.

"Have you had your breakfast?" her mother said.

"It's no use chasing *them*," Catherine answered. "They've gone."

That was how he had done it—the old shuffler: chosen the Easter holiday, when his daughter was home from school, down in Italy, to creep away. And Catherine understood, for she said "them," though she had never known that the other person existed. Well, of course he came shuffling back, because of Catherine. All was safe: Wife was there, home safe, daughter safe, books in place, wine cellar intact, career unchipped. He came out of it scot-free, except that Catherine died. Was it accurate to say, "Serves you right"? Was it fair?

Yes! Yes! "Serves you right!"

Amabel heard, and supposed it could only have to do with the plot of the opera. She said to herself, It will soon be over.

The thing he was most afraid of now was losing his memory. Sometimes he came to breakfast wearing two kinds of shoes. He could go five times to a window to see if snow was falling and forget each time why he was standing there. He had thrown three hundred dollars in a wastepaper basket and carefully kept an elastic band. It was of extreme importance that he remember his guest's name. The name was royal, or imperial, he seemed to recall. Straight down an imperial tree he climbed, counting off leaves: Julia, Octavia, Livia, Cleopatra—not likely—Messalina, Claudia, Domitia. Antonia? It was a name with two *a*'s but with an *m* and not an *n*.

"Marcia," he said in the dark, half turning to her.

"It's Amabel, actually," she said. "I don't even know a Marcia." Like a child picking up a piece of glass and innocently throwing it, she said, "I don't think Catherine knew any Marcias either."

The woman behind them hissed for silence. Amabel

swung round, abruptly this time, and saw that the little girl had fallen asleep. Her ribbon was askew, like a frayed birthday wrapping.

The Colonel slept for a minute and dreamed that his mother was a reed, or a flower. "If only you had always been like that!" he cried, in the dream.

Amabel thought that the scene of the jewel case still might take place: A tap at the hotel-room door tomorrow morning, and there would be Mrs. Plummer, tall and stormy, in her rusty-orange ancient mink, with her square fur bonnet, first visitor of the year, starting the new cycle with a noble gesture. She undid a hastily wrapped parcel, saying, "Nothing really valuable—Catherine was too young." But no, for everything of Catherine's belonged to the gardener's children in Italy now. Amabel rearranged tomorrow morning: Mrs. Plummer brought *her own case* and said, "I have no one to leave anything to except a dog hospital," and there was Amabel, sitting up in bed, hugging her knees, loved at last, looking at emeralds.

Without speaking, Colonel Plummer and his wife each understood what the other had thought of the opera, the staging, and the musical quality of the evening; they also knew where Mrs. Plummer would wait with Amabel while he struggled to the cloakroom to fetch their wraps.

He had taken great care to stay close behind the two girls. For one thing, he had not yet had the answer to "Are you happy?" He heard now, "I am twenty-one years old and I have not succeeded . . ." and then he was wrenched out of the queue. Pushing back, pretending to be armored against unknown forces, like his wife, he heard someone insult him and smiled uncomprehendingly. No one knew how much he understood—except for his wife. It was as though he listened to stones, or snow, or trees speaking. ". . . even though we went to a restaurant and I paid for his dinner," said the same girl, who had not even looked round, and for whom the Colonel had no existence. "The next night he came to the door very late. My parents were in bed. He had come from some stuffy place—his coat stank. But he looked clean and important. He always does. We went into the kitchen. He said he had come up because he cared and could not spend an evening without seeing me, and then he said he had no money, or had lost his money somewhere. I did not want my mother to hear. I said, 'Now I know why you came to see me.' I gave him money—how could I refuse? He knows we keep it in the same drawer as the knives and forks. He could have helped himself, but instead he was careful not to look at the drawer at all. When he wants to show tenderness, he presses his face to my cheek, his lips as quiet as his forehead—it is like being embraced by a dead animal. I was ashamed to think he knew I would always be there waiting. He thinks he can come in whenever he sees a light from the street. I have no advantage from my loyalty, only disadvantages."

Her friend seemed to be meditating deeply. "If you are not happy, it might be your fault," she said.

The cloakroom attendant flung first the girls' coats and woollen caps on the counter, and then their boots, which had been stored in numbered cubbyholes underneath, and it was the Colonel's turn to give up plastic tokens in exchange for his wife's old fur-lined cloak, Amabel's inadequate jacket, his own overcoat—but of course the girls were lost, and he would never see them again. What nagged at him was that disgraceful man. Oh, he could imagine him well enough: an elegant black marketeer, speaking five languages, wearing a sable hat, following tourists in the snow, offering icons in exchange for hard currency. It would explain the watch and perhaps even the chocolates and oranges. "His coat stank" and "he looked clean and important" were typically feminine contradictions, of unequal value. He thought he saw the girls a moment later, but they may have been two like them, leaning on a wall, holding each other's coats as they tugged their boots on;

then he saw them laughing, collapsed in each other's arms. This is unusual, he told himself, for when do people laugh in public anywhere in the north—not only in this sullen city? He thought, as though suddenly superior to the person he had been only a minute ago, what an iron thing it would be never to regret one's losses.

His wife and Amabel looked too alert, as if they had been discussing him and would now pretend to talk about something else.

"That didn't take long," remarked Mrs. Plummer, meaning to say that it had. With overwhelming directness she said, "The year still has an hour to run, so Amabel tells me, and so we had better take her home with us for a drink."

"Only an hour left to change the year ahead," said Amabel without tact.

The Colonel knew that the city was swept by a Siberian blizzard and that their taxi would be nowhere in sight. But outside he saw only the dust of snow sifting past streetlights. The wind had fallen; and their driver was waiting exactly where he had promised. Colonel Plummer helped Amabel down the icy steps of the opera house, then went back for his wife. Cutting off a possible question, she said, "I can make a bed for her somewhere."

Wait, he said silently, looking at all the strangers disappearing in the last hour of the year. Come back, he said to the girls. Who are you? Who was the man?

Amabel's little nose was white with cold. Though this was not her turn to speak, Mrs. Plummer glanced down at her guest, who could not yet hear, saying, " 'He is not glad that he is going home, nor sorry that he has not had time to see the city....' "

"It's 'the *sights* of the city,' I think," said the Colonel. "I'll look it up." He realized he was not losing his memory after all. His breath came and went as if he were still very young. He took Amabel's arm and felt her shiver, though she did not complain about the weather and had her usual hopeful smile ready in case he chose to look. Hilarity is happiness, he thought, sadly, remembering those two others. Is it?

Mrs. Plummer took her turn by remarking, "Used to read the same books," to no one in particular.

Without another word, the Plummers climbed into the taxi and drove with Amabel back to the heart of their isolation, where there was no room for a third person; but the third person knew nothing about this, and so for Amabel the year was saved.

THE DOCTOR

Who CAN REMEMBER now a picture called *The Doctor*? From 1891, when the original was painted, to the middle of the Depression, when it finally went out of style, reproductions of this work flowed into every crevice and corner of North America and the British Empire, swamping continents. Not even *The Angelus* supplied as rich a mixture of art and lesson. The two people in *The Angelus* are there to tell us clearly that the meek inherit nothing but seem not to mind; in *The Doctor* a cast of four enacts a more complex statement of Christian submission or Christian pessimism, depending on the beholder: God's Will is manifest in a dying child, Helpless Materialism in a baffled physician, and Afflicted Humanity in the stricken parents. The parable is set in a spotless cottage; the child's bed, composed of three chairs, is out of a doll's house. In much of the world—the world as it was, so much smaller than now—two full generations were raised with the monochrome promise that existence is insoluble, tragedy static, poverty endearing, and heavenly justice a total mystery.

It must have come as a shock to overseas visitors when they discovered *The Doctor* incarnated as an oil painting in the Tate Gallery in London, in the company of other Victorian miseries entitled *Hopeless Dawn* and *The Last Day in the Old Home*. *The Doctor* had not been divinely inspired and distributed to chasten us after all, but was the work of someone called Sir Luke Fildes—nineteenth-century rationalist and atheist, for all anyone knew. Perhaps it was simply a scene from a three-decker novel, even a joke. In museum surroundings—classified, ticketed—*The Doctor* conveyed a new instruction: Death is sentimental, art is pretense.

Some people had always hated *The Doctor*. My father, for one. He said, "You surely don't want *that* thing in your room."

The argument (it became one) took place in Montreal, in a house that died long ago without leaving even a ghost. He was in his twenties, to match the century. I had been around about the length of your average major war. I had my way but do not remember how; neither tears nor temper ever worked. What probably won out was his wish to be agreeable to Dr. Chauchard, the pediatrician who had given me the engraving. My father seemed to like Chauchard, as he did most people— just well enough—while my mother, who carried an uncritical allegiance from person to person, belief to belief, had recently declared Chauchard to be mentally, morally, and spiritually without fault.

Dr. Chauchard must have been in his thirties then, but he seemed to me timeless, like God the Father. When he took the engraving down from the wall of his office, I understood him to be offering me a portrait of himself. My mother at first refused it, thinking I had asked; he assured her I had not, that he had merely been struck by my expression when I looked at the ailing child. "*C'est une sensible*," he said—an appraisal my mother dismissed by saying I was as tough as a boot, which I truly believe to have been her opinion.

What I was sensitive to is nearly too plain to be signaled: The dying child, a girl, is the heart of the composition. The parents are in the shadow, where they belong. Their function is to be sorry. The doctor has only one patient; light from a tipped lampshade falls on her and her alone.

The street where Dr. Chauchard lived began to decline around the same time as the popularity of *The Doctor* and is now a slum. No citizens' committee can restore the natural elegance of those gray stone houses, the swept steps, the glittering windows, because, short of a miracle, it cannot resurrect the kind of upper-bourgeois French Canadians who used to live there. They have not migrated or moved westward in the city—they have ceased to exist. The handful of dust they sprang from, with its powerful components of religion and history, is part of another clay. They were families who did not resent what were inaccurately called "The English" in Montreal; they had never acknowledged them. The men read a newspaper sometimes, the women never. The women had a dark version of faith for private drama, a family tree to memorize for intellectual exercise, intense family affection for the needs of the heart. Their houses, like Dr. Chauchard's, smelled of cleanness as if cleanness were a commodity, a brand of floor wax. Convents used to have that smell; the girls raised in them brought to married life an ideal of housekeeping that was a memory of the polished convent corridor, with strict squares of sunlight falling where and as they should. Two sons and five daughters was the average for children; Simone, Pauline, Jeanne, Yvonne, and Louise the feminine names of the decade. The girls when young wore religious medals like golden flower petals on thin chains, had positive torrents of curls down to their shoulder blades, and came to children's parties dressed in rose velvet and white stockings, too shy to speak. Chauchard, a bachelor, came out of this world, which I can describe best only through its girls and women.

His front door, painted the gloomy shade my father called Montreal green, is seen from below, at an angle—a bell too high for me during the first visits, a letter box through which I called, "Open the door; *c'est moi*," believing still that "*moi*" would take me anywhere. But no one could hear in any language, because two vestibules, one behind the other, stood in the way. In the first one overshoes dripped on a mat, then

71

came a warmer place for coats. Each vestibule had its door, varnished to imitate the rings of a tree trunk, enhanced by a nature scene made of frosted glass; you unbuckled galoshes under herons and palm trees and shed layers of damp wool under swans floating in a landscape closer to home.

Just over the letter box of the green door a large, beautifully polished brass plate carried, in sloped writing:

> Docteur Raoul Chauchard
> Spécialiste en Médecine Infantile
> Ancien Externe et Interne
> des Hôpitaux de Paris
> Sur Rendez-vous

On the bottom half of the plate this information was repeated in English, though the only English I recall in the waiting room was my mother's addressed to me.

He was not Parisian but native to the city, perhaps to the street, even to the house, if I think of how the glass-shaded lamps and branched chandeliers must have followed an evolution from oil to kerosene to gas to electricity without changing shape or place. Rooms and passages were papered deep blue fading to green (the brighter oblong left by the removal of *The Doctor* was about the color of a teal), so that the time of day indoors was winter dusk, with pools of light like uncurtained windows. An assemblage of gilt-framed pictures began between the heron and swan doors with brisk scenes of biblical injustice—the casting-out of Hagar, the swindling of Esau—and moved along the hall with European history: Vercingetorix surrendering to the Romans, the earthquake at Lisbon, Queen Victoria looking exactly like a potato pancake receiving some dark and humble envoy; then, with a light over him to mark his importance, Napoléon III reviewing a regiment from a white horse. (The popularity of "Napoléon" as a Christian name did not connect with the first Bonaparte, as English Canadians supposed—when any thought was given to any matter concerning French Canadians at all—but with his nephew, the lesser Bonaparte, who had never divorced or insulted the Pope, and who had established clerical influence in the saddle as firmly as it now sat upon Quebec.) The sitting-room-converted-to-waiting-room had on display landmarks of Paris, identified in two languages:

> Le Petit Palais—The Petit Palais
> Place Vendôme—Place Vendôme
> Rue de la Paix—Rue de la Paix

as if the engraver had known they would find their way to a wall in Montreal.

Although he had trained in Paris, where, as our English doctor told my mother, leeches were still sold in pharmacies and babies died like flies, Chauchard was thought modern and forward-looking. He used the most advanced methods imported from the United States, or, as one would have said then, "from Boston," which meant both stylish and impeccably right. Ultraviolet irradiation was one, recommended for building up delicate children. I recall the black mask tied on, and the danger of blindness should one pull it off before being told. I owe him irradiation to the marrow and other sources of confusion: It was he who gave my mother the name of a convent where Jansenist discipline still had a foot on the neck of the twentieth century and where, as an added enchantment, I was certain not to hear a word of English. He never dreamed, I am sure, that I would be packed off there as a boarder from the age of four. Out of goodness and affection he gave me books to read—children's stories from nineteenth-century France which I hated and still detest. In these oppressive stories children were punished and punished hard for behavior that seemed in another century, above all on another continent, natural and right. I could never see the right-and-wrong over which they kept stumbling and only much later recognized it in European social fiddle-faddle—the trivial yardsticks that measure a man's character by the way he eats a boiled egg. The prose was stiff, a bit shrill, probably pitched too high for a North American ear. Even the bindings, a particularly ugly red, were repellent to me, while their gilt titles lent them the ceremonial quality of school prizes. I had plenty of English Victorian books, but the scolding could be got over, because there was no unfairness. Where there was, it was done away with as part of the plot. The authors were on the side of morality but also of the child. For a long time I imagined that most of my English books had been written by other children, but I never made that mistake with French; I saw these authors as large, scowling creatures with faces as flushed with crossness as the books' covers. Still, the books were presents, therefore important, offered without a word or a look Dr. Chauchard would not have bestowed on an adult. They had been his mother's; she lived in rooms at the top of the house, receiving her own friends, not often mingling with his. She must have let him have these treasures for a favored patient who did not understand the courtesy, even the sacrifice, until it was too late to say "Thank you." Another child's name—his mother's—was on the flyleaf; I seldom looked at it, concentrated as I was on my own. It is not simply rhetoric to say that I see him still—Fildes profile, white cuff, dark sleeve, writing the new dedication with a pen dipped in a blue inkwell, hand and book within the circle cast by the lamp on his desk. At home I would paste inside the front cover the plate my father had designed for me, which had "Linnet: Her Book" as ex libris, and the drawing of a stream flowing between grassy banks—his memory of the unhurried movement of England, no reflection of anything known to me in Quebec—bearing a single autumn leaf. Under the stream came the lines

Time, Time, which none can bind
While flowing fast leaves love
    behind.

The only child will usually give and lend its possessions
easily, having missed the sturdy training in rivalry and forced
sharing afforded by sisters and brothers, yet nothing would
have made me part willingly with any of the grim red books.
Grouped on a special shelf, seldom opened after the first reading, they were not reminders but a true fragment of his twilit
house, his swan and heron doors, Napoléon III so cunningly
lighted, "Le Petit Palais—The Petit Palais," and, finally, Dr.
Chauchard himself at the desk of his shadowy room writing
"*Pour ma chère petite Linnet*" in a book that had once belonged to another girl.

Now, how to account for the changed, stern, disapproving
Chauchard who in that same office gave me not a book but
a lecture beginning "Think of your unfortunate parents" and
ending "You owe them everything; it is your duty to love
them." He had just telephoned for my father to come and
fetch me. "How miserable they would be if anything ever
happened to you," he said. He spoke of my *petit Papa* and my
petite Maman with that fake diminution of authority characteristic of the Latin tongues which never works in English. I
sat on a chair still wearing outdoor clothes—navy reefer over
my convent uniform, HMS *Nelson* sailor hat held on by a
black elastic—neither his patient nor his guest at this dreadful crisis, wondering, What does he mean? For a long time
now my surprise visits to friends had been called, incorrectly,
"running away." Running away was one of the reasons my
parents gave when anyone asked why I had been walled up in
such a severe school at an early age. Dr. Chauchard, honored
by one of my visits, at once asked his office nurse, "Do her

parents know she's here?" Women are supposed to make dangerous patients for bachelor doctors; besotted little girls must seem even worse. But I was not besotted; I believed we were equals. It was he who had set up the equality, and for that reason I still think he should have invited me to remove my coat.

The only thing worth remarking about his dull little sermon is that it was in French. French was his language for medicine; I never heard him give an opinion in English. It was evidently the language to which he retreated if one became a nuisance, his back to a wall of white marble syntax. And when it came to filial devotion he was one with the red-covered books. Calling on my parents, not as my doctor but as their friend, he spoke another language. It was not merely English instead of French but the private dialect of a younger person who was playful, charming, who smoked cigarettes in a black-and-silver holder, looking round to see the effect of his puns and jokes. You could notice then, only then, that his black-currant eyes were never still.

The house he came to remained for a long time enormous in memory, though the few like it still standing—"still living," I nearly say—are narrow, with thin, steep staircases and close, high-ceilinged rooms. They were the work of Edinburgh architects and dated from when Montreal was a Scottish city; it had never been really English. A Saturday-evening gathering of several adults, one child, and a couple of dogs created a sort of tangle in the middle of the room—an entwining that was surely not of people's feet: In those days everyone sat straight. The women had to, because their girdles had hooks and stays. Men sat up out of habit, probably the habit of prosperity; the Depression created the physical slump, a change in posture to match the times. Perhaps desires and secrets and second thoughts threading from person to person, from bachelor to married woman, from mother of none to somebody's father, formed a cat's cradle—matted, invisible, and quite dangerous. Why else would Ruby, the latest homesick underpaid Newfoundland import, have kept tripping up as she lurched across the room with cups and glasses on a tray?

Transformed into jolly Uncle Raoul (his request), Dr. Chauchard would arrive with a good friend of his, divorced Mrs. Erskine, and a younger friend of both, named Paul-Armand. Paul-Armand was temporary, one of a sequence of young men who attended Mrs. Erskine as her bard, her personal laureate. His role did not outlive a certain stage of artless admiration; at the first sign of falling away, the first mouse squeak of disenchantment from him, a replacement was found. All of these young men were good-looking, well brought up, longing to be unconventional, and entirely innocent. Flanked by her pair of males, Mrs. Erskine would sway into the room, as graceful as a woman can be when she is boned from waist to thigh. She would keep on her long mole-skin coat, even though like all Canadian rooms this one was vastly overheated, explaining that she was chilly. This may have been an attempt to reduce the impression she gave of general largeness by suggesting an inner fragility. Presently the coat would come off, revealing a handwoven tea-cozy sort of garment—this at a time when every other woman was showing her knees. My mother sat with her legs crossed and one sandal dangling. Her hair had recently been shingled; she seemed to be groping for its lost comfortable warmth. Other persons, my father apart, are a dim choir muttering, "Isn't it past your bedtime?" My father sat back in a deep, chintz-covered chair and said hardly anything except for an occasional "Down" to his dogs.

In another season, in the country, my parents had other friends, summer friends, who drank old-fashioneds and danced to gramophone records out on the lawn. Winter friends were mostly coffee drinkers, who did what people do between wars and revolutions—sat in a circle and talked about revolutions and wars. The language was usually English, though not everyone was native to English. Mrs. Erskine commanded what she called "*good* French" and rather liked displaying it, but after a few sentences, which made those who could not understand French very fidgety and which annoyed the French Canadians present exactly in the way an affected accent will grate on Irish nerves, she would pick her way back to English. In mixed society, such little of it as existed, English seemed to be the social rule. It did not enter the mind of any English speaker that the French were at a constant disadvantage, like a team obliged to play all their matches away from home. Dr. Chauchard never addressed me in French here, not even when he would ask me to recite a French poem learned at my convent school. It began, "If I were a fly, Maman, I would steal a kiss from your lips." The nun in charge of memory work was fiddly about liaison, which produced an accidentally appropriate "*Si j'étaiszzzzzzzzune mouche, Maman.*" Dr. Chauchard never seemed to tire of this and may have thought it a reasonable declaration to make to one's mother.

It was a tactless rhyme, if you think of all the buzzing and stealing that went on in at least part of the winter circle, but I could not have known that. At least not consciously. Unconsciously, everyone under the age of ten knows everything. Under-ten can come into a room and sense at once everything felt, kept silent, held back in the way of love, hate, and desire, though he may not have the right words for such sentiments. It is part of the clairvoyant immunity to hypocrisy we are born with and that vanishes just before puberty. I knew, though no one had told me, that my mother was a bit foolish about Dr. Chauchard; that Mrs. Erskine would have turned cartwheels to get my father's attention but that even cartwheels would have failed; that Dr. Chauchard and Mrs. Erskine were somehow together but never went out alone. Paul-Armand was harder to place; too young to be a parent, he was a pest, a tease to someone smaller. His goading was never noticed, though my reaction to it, creeping behind his chair until I was in a position to punch him, brought an immediate response from the police: "Linnet, if you don't sit down I'm afraid you will have to go to your room." "If" and "I'm afraid" meant there was plenty of margin. Later: "Wouldn't you be happier if you just went to bed? No? Then get a book and sit down and read it." Presently, "Down, I said, sit down; did you hear what I've just said to you? I said, sit down, *down*." There came a point like convergent lines finally meeting where orders to dogs and instructions to children were given in the same voice. The only difference was that a dog got "Down, damn it," and, of course, no one ever swore at me.

This overlapping in one room of French and English, of Catholic and Protestant—my parents' way of being, and so to me life itself—was as unlikely, as unnatural to the Montreal climate as a school of tropical fish. Only later would I discover that most other people simply floated in mossy little ponds labeled "French and Catholic" or "English and Protestant," never wondering what it might be like to step ashore; or wondering, perhaps, but weighing up the danger. To be out of a pond is to be in unmapped territory. The earth might be flat; you could fall over the edge quite easily. My parents and their friends were, in their way, explorers. They had in common a fear of being bored, which is a fear one can afford to nourish in times of prosperity and peace. It makes for the most ruthless kind of exclusiveness, based as it is on the belief that anyone can be the richest of this or cleverest of that and still be the dullest dog that ever barked. I wince even now remembering those wretched once-only guests who were put on trial for a Saturday night and unanimously condemned. This heartlessness apart, the winter circle shared an outlook, a kind of humor, a certain vocabulary of the mind. No one made any of the standard Montreal statements, such as "What a lot of books you've got! Don't tell me you've read them," or "I hear you're some kind of artist. What do you really *do*?" Explorers like Dr. Chauchard and Mrs. Erskine and my mother and the rest recognized each other on sight; the recognition cut through disguisements of class, profession, religion, language, and even what poll takers call "other interests."

Once you have jumped out of a social enclosure, your eye is bound to be on a real, a geographical elsewhere; theirs seemed to consist of a few cities of Europe with agreeable-sounding names like Vienna and Venice. The United States consisted only of Boston and Florida then. Adults went to Florida for therapeutic reasons—for chronic bronchitis, to recover from operations, for the sake of mysterious maladies that had no names and were called in obituaries "a long illness bravely borne." Boston seemed to be an elegant little republic with its own parliament and flag. To English Montreal, cocooned in that other language nobody bothered to learn, the rest of the continent, Canada included, barely existed; travelers would disembark after long, sooty train trips expressing relief to be in the only city where there were decent restaurants and well-dressed women and where proper English could be heard. Elsewhere, then, became other people, and little groups would form where friends, to the tune of vast mutual admiration, could find a pleasing remoteness in each other. They resembled, in their yearnings, in their clinging together as a substitute for motion, in their craving for "someone to talk to," the kind of marginal social clans you find today in the capitals of Eastern Europe.

I was in the dining room cutting up magazines. My mother brought her coffee cup in, sat down, and said, "Promise me you will never be caught in a situation where you have to compete with a younger woman."

She must have been twenty-six at the very most; Mrs.

Erskine was well over thirty. I suppose she was appraising the amount of pickle Mrs. Erskine was in. They had become rivals. With her pale braids, her stately figure, her eyes the color of a stoneware teapot, Mrs. Erskine seemed to me like a white statue with features painted on. I had heard my mother praising her beauty, but for a child she was too large, too still. "Age has its points," my mother went on. "The longer your life goes on, the more chance it has to be interesting. Promise me that when you're thirty you'll have a lot to look back on."

My mother had on her side her comparative youth, her quickness, her somewhat giddy intelligence. She had been married, as she said, "for ever and ever" and was afraid nothing would ever happen to her again. Mrs. Erskine's chief advantage over my mother—being unmarried and available—was matched by an enviable biography. "Ah, don't ask me for my life's story now," she would cry, settling back to tell it. When the others broke into that sighing, singing recital of cities they went in for, repeating strings of names that sounded like sleigh bells (Venice, London, Paris, Rome), Mrs. Erskine would narrow her stoneware eyes and annihilate my mother with "But Charlotte, I've *been* to all those places, I've *seen* all those people." What, indeed, hadn't she seen—crown princes dragged out of Rolls-Royces by cursing mobs, duchesses clutching their tiaras while being raped by anarchists, strikers in England kicking innocent little Border terriers.

"...And as for the Hungarians and that Béla *Kun*, let me tell you...tore the uniforms right off the Red Cross *nurses*...made them dance the Charleston naked on top of *street*cars..."

"Linnet, wouldn't you be better off in your room?"

The fear of the horde was in all of them; it haunted even their jokes. "Bolshevik" was now "bolshie," to make it harmless. Petrograd had been their early youth; the Red years just after the war were still within earshot. They dreaded yet seemed drawn to tales of conspiracy and enormous might. The English among them were the first generation to have been raised on *The Wind in the Willows*. Their own Wild Wood was a dark political mystery; its rude inhabitants were still to be tamed. What was needed was a leader, a Badger. But when a Badger occurred they mistrusted him, too; my mother had impressed on me early that Mussolini was a "bad, wicked man." Fortunate Mrs. Erskine had seen "those people" from legation windows; she had, in another defeat for my mother, been married twice, each time to a diplomat. The word "diplomat" had greater cachet then than it has now. Earlier in the century a diplomat was believed to have attended universities in more than one country, to have two or three languages at his disposal and some slender notion of geography and history. He could read and write quite easily, had probably been born in wedlock, possessed tact and discretion, and led an exemplary private life. Obviously there were no more of these paragons then than there might be now, but fewer were needed, because there were only half as many capitals. Those who did exist spun round and round the world, used for all they were worth, until they became like those coats that outlast their buttons, linings, and pockets: Your diplomat, recalled from Bulgaria, by now a mere warp and woof, would be given a new silk lining, bone buttons, have his collar turned, and, after a quick reading of Norse myths, would be shipped to Scandinavia. Mrs. Erskine, twice wedded to examples of these freshened garments, had been everywhere—everywhere my mother longed to be.

"My *life*," said Mrs. Erskine. "Ah, Charlotte, don't ask me to tell you everything—you'd never believe it!" My mother asked, and believed, and died in her heart along with Mrs. Erskine's first husband, a Mr. Sparrow, shot to death in Berlin by a lunatic Russian refugee. (Out of the decency of his nature Mr. Sparrow had helped the refugee's husband emigrate accompanied by a woman Mr. Sparrow had taken to be the Russian man's wife.) In the hours that preceded his "going," as Mrs. Erskine termed his death, Mr. Sparrow had turned into a totally other person, quite common and gross. She had seen exactly how he would rise from the dead for his next incarnation. She had said, "Now then, Alfred, I think it has been a blissful marriage but perhaps not blissful enough. As I am the best part of your karma, we are going to start all over again in another existence." Mr. Sparrow, in his new coarse, uneducated voice, replied, "Believe you me, Bimbo, if I see you in another world, this time I'm making a detour." His last words—not what every woman hopes to hear, probably, but nothing in my mother's experience could come ankle-high to having a husband assassinated in Berlin by a crazy Russian. Mr. Erskine, the second husband, was not quite so interesting, for he merely "drank and drank and *drank*," and finally, unwittingly, provided grounds for divorce. Since in those days adultery was the only acceptable grounds, the divorce ended his ambitions and transformed Mrs. Erskine into someone déclassée; it was not done for a woman to spoil a man's career, and it was taken for granted that no man ever ruined his own. I am certain my mother did not see Mr. Sparrow as an ass and Mr. Erskine as a soak. They were men out of novels—half diplomat, half secret agent. The natural progress of such men was needed to drag women out of the dullness that seemed to be woman's fate.

There was also the matter of Mrs. Erskine's French: My mother could read and speak it but had nothing of her friend's intolerable fluency. Nor could my mother compete with her special status as the only English and Protestant girl of her generation to have attended French and Catholic schools. She had spent ten years with the Ursulines in Quebec City (languages took longer to learn in those days, when you were obliged to start by memorizing all the verbs) and had emerged with the chic little Ursuline lisp.

"Tell me again," my entranced mother would ask. "How do you say 'squab stuffed with sage dressing'?"

"Charlotte, I've told you and told you. *'Pouthin farthi au thauge.'* "

"Thankth," said my mother. Such was the humor of that period.

For a long time I would turn over like samples of dress material the reasons why I was sent off to a school where by all the rules of the world we lived in I did not belong. A sample that nearly matches is my mother's desire to tease Mrs. Erskine, perhaps to overtake her through me: If she had been unique in her generation, then I would be in mine. Unlikely as it sounds today, I believe that I was. At least I have never met another, just as no French-Canadian woman of my period can recall having sat in a classroom with any other English-speaking Protestant disguised in convent uniform. Mrs. Erskine, rising to the tease, warned that convents had gone downhill since the war and that the appalling French I spoke would be a handicap in Venice, London, Paris, Rome; if the Ursuline French of Quebec City was the best in the world after Tours, Montreal French was just barely a language.

How could my mother, so quick and sharp usually, have been drawn in by this? For a day or two my parents actually weighed the advantages of sending their very young daughter miles away, for no good reason. Why not even to France? "You know perfectly well why not. Because we can't afford it. Not that or anything like it."

Leaning forward in her chair as if words alone could not convince her listener, more like my mother than herself at this moment, Mrs. Erskine with her fingertips to her cheek, the other hand held palm outward, cried, "Ah, Angus, don't ask me for my life's story now!" This to my father, who barely knew other people had lives.

My father made this mysterious answer: "Yes, Frances, I

do see what you mean, but I have a family, and once you've got children you're never quite so free."

There was only one child, of course, and not often there, but in my parents' minds and by some miracle of fertility they had produced a whole tribe. At any second this tribe might rampage through the house, scribbling on the wallpaper, tearing up books, scratching gramophone records with a stolen diamond brooch. They dreaded mischief so much that I can only suppose them to have been quite disgraceful children.

"What's Linnet up to? She's awfully quiet."

"Sounds suspicious. Better go and look."

I would be found reading or painting or "building," which meant the elaboration of a foreign city called Marigold that spread and spread until it took up a third of my room and had to be cleared away when my back was turned, upon which, as relentless as a colony of beavers, I would start building again. To a visitor Marigold was a slum of empty boxes, serving trays, bottles, silver paper, overturned chairs, but these were streets and houses, churches and convents, restaurants and railway stations. The citizens of Marigold were cut out of magazines: Gloria Swanson was the Mother Superior, Herbert Hoover a convent gardener. Entirely villainous, they did their plotting and planning in an empty cigar box.

Whatever I was doing, I would be told to do something else immediately: I think they had both been brought up that way. "Go out and play in the snow" was a frequent interruption. Parents in bitter climates have a fixed idea about driving children out to be frozen. There was one sunken hour on January afternoons, just before the street lamps were lighted, that was the gray of true wretchedness, as if one's heart and stomach had turned into the same dull, cottony stuff as the sky; it was attached to a feeling of loss, of helpless sadness, unknown to children in other latitudes.

I was home weekends but by no means every weekend. Friday night was given to spoiling and rejoicing, but on Saturday I would hear, "When does she go back?"

"Not till tomorrow night."

Ruby, the homesick offshore import, sometimes sat in my room, just for company. She turned the radiator on so that you saw a wisp of steam from the overflow tap. A wicker basket of mending was on her lap; she wiped her eyes on my father's socks. I was not allowed to say to anyone "Go away," or anything like it. I heard her sniffles, her low, muttered grievances. Then she emerged from her impenetrable cloud of Newfoundland gloom to take an interest in the life of Marigold. She did not get down on the floor or in the way, but from her chair suggested some pretty good plots. Ruby was the inspirer of "The Insane Stepmother," "The Rich, Selfish Cousins," "The Death from Croup of Baby Sister" ("Is her face blue yet?" "No; in a minute"), and "The Broken Engagement," with its cast of three—rejected maiden, fickle lover, and chaperon. Paper dolls did the acting, the voices were ours. Ruby played the cast-off fiancée from the heart: "Don't chew men ever know what chew want?" Chaperon was a fine bossy part: "That's enough, now. Sit down; I said, *down*."

My parents said, "What does she see in Ruby?" They were cross and jealous. The jealousness was real. They did not drop their voices to say "When does she go back?" but were alert to signs of disaffection, and offended because I did not crave their company every minute. Once, when Mrs. Erskine, a bit of a fool probably, asked, "Who do you love best, your father or your mother?" and I apparently (I have no memory of it) answered, "Oh, I'm not really dying about anybody," it was recalled to me for a long time, as if I had set fire to the curtains or spat on the Union Jack.

"Think of your unfortunate parents," Dr. Chauchard had said in the sort of language that had no meaning to me, though I am sure it was authentic to him.

When he died and I read his obituary, I saw there had been still another voice. I was twenty and had not seen him since the age of nine. *The Doctor* and the red-covered books had been lost even before that, when during a major move from Montreal to a house in the country a number of things that belonged to me and that my parents were tired of seeing disappeared.

There were three separate death notices, as if to affirm that Chauchard had been three men. All three were in a French newspaper; he neither lived nor died in English. The first was a jumble of family names and syntax: "After a serene and happy life it has pleased our Lord to send for the soul of his faithful servant Raoul Étienne Chauchard, piously deceased in his native city in his fifty-first year after a short illness comforted by the sacraments of the Church." There followed a few particulars—the date and place of the funeral, and the names and addresses of the relatives making the announcement. The exact kinship of each was mentioned: sister, brother-in-law, uncle, nephew, cousin, second cousin.

The second obituary, somewhat longer, had been published by the medical association he belonged to; it described all the steps and stages of his career. There were strings of initials denoting awards and honors, ending with: "Dr. Chauchard had also been granted the Medal of Epidemics (Belgium)." Beneath this came the third notice: "The Arts and Letters Society of Quebec announces the irreparable loss of one of its founder members, the poet R. É. Chauchard." R. É. had published six volumes of verse, a book of critical essays, and a work referred to as "the immortal 'Progress,'" which did not seem to fall into a category or, perhaps, was too well known to readers to need identification.

That third notice was an earthquake, the collapse of the

cities we build over the past to cover seams and cracks we cannot account for. He must have been writing when my parents knew him. Why they neglected to speak of it is something too shameful to dwell on; he probably never mentioned it, knowing they would believe it impossible. French books were from France; English books from England or the United States. It would not have entered their minds that the languages they heard spoken around them could be written, too.

I met by accident years after Dr. Chauchard's death one of Mrs. Erskine's ex-minnesingers, now an elderly bachelor. His name was Louis. He had never heard of Paul-Armand, not even by rumor. He had not known my parents and was certain he had never accompanied Dr. Chauchard and Mrs. Erskine to our house. He said that when he met these two he had been fresh from a seminary, aged about nineteen, determined to live a life of ease and pleasure but not sure how to begin. Mrs. Erskine had by then bought and converted a farmhouse south of Montreal, where she wove carpets, hooked rugs, scraped and waxed old tables, kept bees, and bottled tons of pickled beets, preparing for some dark proletarian future should the mob—the horde, "those people"—take over after all. Louis knew the doctor only as the poet R. É. of the third notice. He had no knowledge of the Medal of Epidemics (Belgium) and could not explain it to me. I had found "Progress" by then, which turned out to be R. É.'s diary. I could not put faces to the X, Y, and Z that covered real names, nor could I discover any trace of my parents, let alone of *ma chère petite Linnet*. There were long thoughts about Mozart —people like that.

Louis told me of walking with Mrs. Erskine along a snowy road close to her farmhouse, she in a fur cape that came down to her boot tops and a fur bonnet that hid her braided hair. She talked about her unusual life and her two husbands and about what she now called "the predicament." She told him how she had never been asked to meet Madame Chauchard *mère* and how she had slowly come to realize that R. É. would never marry. She spoke of people who had drifted through the predicament, my mother among them, not singling her out as someone important, just as a wisp of cloud on the edge of the sky. "Poor Charlotte" was how Mrs. Erskine described the thin little target on which she had once trained her biggest guns. Yet "poor Charlotte"—not even an X in the diary, finally—had once been the heart of the play. The plot must have taken a full turning after she left the stage. Louis became a new young satellite, content to circle the powerful stars, to keep an eye on the predicament, which seemed to him flaming, sulfurous. Nobody ever told him what had taken place in the first and second acts.

Walking, he and Mrs. Erskine came to a railway track quite far from houses, and she turned to Louis and opened the fur cloak and said, smiling, *"Viens voir Mrs. Erskine."* (Owing to the Ursuline lisp this must have been "Mitheth Erthkine.") Without coyness or any more conversation she lay down—he said "on the track," but he must have meant near it, if you think of the ties. Folded into the cloak, Louis at last became part of a predicament. He decided that further experience could only fall short of it, and so he never married.

In this story about the cloak Mrs. Erskine is transmuted from the pale, affected statue I remember and takes on a polychrome life. She seems cheerful and careless, and I like her for that. Carelessness might explain her unreliable memory about Charlotte. And yet not all that careless: "She even knew the train times," said Louis. "She must have done it before." Still, on a sharp blue day, when some people were still in a dark classroom writing *"abyssus abyssum invocat"* all over their immortal souls, she, who had been through this and escaped with nothing worse than a lisp, had the sun, the snow, the wrap of fur, the bright sky, the risk. There is a raffish kind of nerve to her, the only nerve that matters.

For that one conversation Louis and I wondered what our

appearance on stage several scenes apart might make us to each other: If A was the daughter of B, and B rattled the foundations of C, and C, though cautious and lazy where women were concerned, was committed in a way to D, and D was forever trying to tell her life's story to E, the husband of B, and E had enough on his hands with B without taking on D, too, and if D decided to lie down on or near a railway track with F, then what are A and F? Nothing. Minor satellites floating out of orbit and out of order after the stars burned out. Mrs. Erskine reclaimed Dr. Chauchard but he never married anyone. Angus reclaimed Charlotte but he died soon after. Louis, another old bachelor, had that one good anecdote about the fur cloak. I lost even the engraving of *The Doctor*, spirited away quite shabbily, and I never saw Dr. Chauchard again or even tried to. What if I had turned up one day, aged eighteen or so, only to have him say to his nurse, "Does anyone know she's here?"

When I read the three obituaries it was the brass plate on the door I saw and "*Sur Rendez-vous.*" That means "No dropping in." After the warning came the shut heron door and the shut swan door and, at another remove, the desk with the circle of lamplight and R.É. himself, writing about X, Y, Z, and Mozart. A bit humdrum perhaps, a bit prosy, not nearly as good as his old winter Saturday self, but I am sure that it was his real voice, the voice that transcends this or that language. His French-speaking friends did not hear it for a long time (his first book of verse was not sold to anyone outside his immediate family), while his English-speaking friends never heard it at all. But I should have heard it then, at the start, standing on tiptoe to reach the doorbell, calling through the letter box every way I could think of, "I, me." I ought to have heard it when I was still under ten and had all my wits about me.

VOICES LOST IN SNOW

HALFWAY BETWEEN our two great wars, parents whose own early years had been shaped with Edwardian firmness were apt to lend a tone of finality to quite simple remarks: "Because I say so" was the answer to "Why?" and a child's response to "What did I just tell you?" could seldom be anything but "Not to"—not to say, do, touch, remove, go out, argue, reject, eat, pick up, open, shout, appear to sulk, appear to be cross. Dark riddles filled the corners of life because no enlightenment was thought required. Asking questions was "being tiresome," while persistent curiosity got one nowhere, at least nowhere of interest. How much has changed? Observe the drift of words descending from adult to child— the fall of personal questions, observations, unnecessary instructions. Before long the listener seems blanketed. He must hear the voice as authority muffled, a hum through snow. The tone has changed—it may be coaxing, even plaintive— but the words have barely altered. They still claim the ancient right-of-way through a young life.

"Well, old cock," said my father's friend Archie McEwen, meeting him one Saturday in Montreal. "How's Charlotte taking life in the country?" Apparently no one had expected my mother to accept the country in winter.

"Well, old cock," I repeated to a country neighbor, Mr. Bainwood. "How's life?" What do you suppose it meant to me, other than a kind of weather vane? Mr. Bainwood thought it over, then came round to our house and complained to my mother.

"It isn't blasphemy," she said, not letting him have much satisfaction from the complaint. Still, I had to apologize. "I'm sorry" was a ritual habit with even less meaning than "old cock." "Never say that again," my mother said after he had gone.

"Why not?"

"Because I've just told you not to."

"What does it mean?"

"Nothing."

It must have been after yet another "Nothing" that one summer's day I ran screaming around a garden, tore the heads off tulips, and—no, let another voice finish it; the only authentic voices I have belong to the dead: "...then she *ate* them."

It was my father's custom if he took me with him to visit a friend on Saturdays not to say where we were going. He was more taciturn than any man I have known since, but that wasn't all of it; being young, I was the last person to whom anyone owed an explanation. These Saturdays have turned into one whitish afternoon, a windless snowfall, a steep street. Two persons descend the street, stepping carefully. The child, reminded every day to keep her hands still, gesticulates wildly—there is the flash of a red mitten. I will never overtake this pair. Their voices are lost in snow.

We were living in what used to be called the country and is now a suburb of Montreal. On Saturdays my father and I came in together by train. I went to the doctor, the dentist, to my German lesson. After that I had to get back to Windsor station by myself and on time. My father gave me a boy's watch so that the dial would be good and large. I remember the No. 83 streetcar trundling downhill and myself, wondering if the watch was slow, asking strangers to tell me the hour. Inevitably—how could it have been otherwise?—after his death, which would not be long in coming, I would dream that someone important had taken a train without me. My route to the meeting place—deviated, betrayed by stopped clocks—was always downhill. As soon as I was old enough to understand from my reading of myths and legends that this journey was a pursuit of darkness, its terminal point a sunless underworld, the dream vanished.

Sometimes I would be taken along to lunch with one or another of my father's friends. He would meet the friend at Pauzé's for oysters or at Drury's or the Windsor Grill. The friend would more often than not be Scottish- or English-sounding, and they would talk as if I were invisible, as Archie McEwen had done, and eat what I thought of as English food—grilled kidneys, sweetbreads—which I was too finicky to touch. Both my parents had been made wretched as children by having food forced on them and so that particular torture was never inflicted on me. However, the manner in which I ate was subject to precise attention. My father disapproved of the North American custom that he called "spearing" (knife laid on the plate, fork in the right hand). My mother's eye was out for a straight back, invisible chewing, small mouthfuls, immobile silence during the interminable adult loafing over dessert. My mother did not care for food. If we were alone together, she would sit smoking and reading, sipping black coffee, her elbows used as props—a posture that would have called for instant banishment had I so much as tried it. Being constantly observed and corrected was like having a fly buzzing around one's plate. At Pauzé's, the only child, perhaps the only female, I sat up to an oak counter and ate oysters quite neatly, not knowing exactly what they were and certainly not that they were alive. They were served as in "The Walrus and the Carpenter," with bread and butter, pepper and vinegar. Dessert was a chocolate biscuit—plates of them stood at intervals along the counter. When my father and I ate alone, I was not required to say much, nor could I expect a great deal in the way of response. After I had been addressing him for minutes, sometimes he would suddenly come to life and I would know he had been elsewhere. "Of course I've been listening," he would protest, and he would repeat by way of proof the last few words of whatever it was I'd been saying. He was seldom present. I don't know where my father spent his waking life: just elsewhere.

What was he doing alone with a child? Where was his wife? In the country, reading. She read one book after another without looking up, without scraping away the frost on the windows. "The Russians, you know, the Russians," she said to her mother and me, glancing around in the drugged way adolescent readers have. "They put salt on the windowsills in winter." Yes, so they did, in the nineteenth century, in the boyhood of Turgenev, of Tolstoy. The salt absorbed the moisture between two sets of windows sealed shut for half the year. She must have been in a Russian country house at that moment, surrounded by a large Russian family, living out vast Russian complications. The flat white fields beyond her imaginary windows were like the flat white fields she would have observed if only she had looked out. She was myopic; the pupil when she had been reading seemed to be the whole of the eye. What age was she then? Twenty-seven, twenty-eight. Her husband had removed her to the country; now that they were there he seldom spoke. How young she seems to me now—half twenty-eight in perception and feeling, but with a husband, a child, a house, a life, an illiterate maid from the village whose life she confidently interfered with and mismanaged, a small zoo of animals she alternately cherished and forgot; and she was the daughter of such a sensible, truthful, pessimistic woman—pessimistic in the way women become when they settle for what actually exists.

Our rooms were not Russian—they were aired every day

and the salt became a great nuisance, blowing in on the floor.

"There, Charlotte, what did I tell you?" my grandmother said. This grandmother did not care for dreams or for children. If I sensed the first, I had no hint of the latter. Out of decency she kept it quiet, at least in a child's presence. She had the reputation, shared with a long-vanished nurse named Olivia, of being able to "do anything" with me, which merely meant an ability to provoke from a child behavior convenient for adults. It was she who taught me to eat in the Continental way, with both hands in sight at all times upon the table, and who made me sit at meals with books under my arms so I would learn not to stick out my elbows. I remember having accepted this nonsense from her without a trace of resentment. Like Olivia, she could make the most pointless sort of training seem a natural way of life. (I think that as discipline goes this must be the most dangerous form of all.) She was one of three godparents I had—the important one. It is impossible for me to enter the mind of this agnostic who taught me prayers, who had already shed every remnant of belief when she committed me at the font. I know that she married late and reluctantly; she would have preferred a life of solitude and independence, next to impossible for a woman in her time. She had the positive voice of the born teacher, sharp manners, quick blue eyes, and the square, massive figure common to both lines of her ancestry—the west of France, the north of Germany. When she said "There, Charlotte, what did I tell you?" without obtaining an answer, it summed up mother and daughter both.

My father's friend Malcolm Whitmore was the second godparent. He quarreled with my mother when she said something flippant about Mussolini, disappeared, died in Europe some years later, though perhaps not fighting for Franco, as my mother had it. She often rewrote other people's lives, providing them with suitable and harmonious endings. In her version of events you were supposed to die as you'd lived. He would write sometimes, asking me, "Have you been confirmed yet?" He had never really held a place and could not by dying leave a gap. The third godparent was a young woman named Georgie Henderson. She was my mother's choice, for a long time her confidante, partisan, and close sympathizer. Something happened, and they stopped seeing each other. Georgie was not her real name—it was Edna May. One of the reasons she had fallen out with my mother was that I had not been called Edna May too. Apparently, this had been promised.

Without saying where we were going, my father took me along to visit Georgie one Saturday afternoon.

"You didn't say you were bringing Linnet" was how she greeted him. We stood in the passage of a long, hot, high-ceilinged apartment, treading snow water into the rug.

He said, "Well, she is your godchild, and she has been ill."

My godmother shut the front door and leaned her back against it. It is in this surprisingly dramatic pose that I recall her. It would be unfair to repeat what I think I saw then, for she and I were to meet again once, only once, many years after this, and I might substitute a lined face for a smooth one and tough, large-knuckled hands for fingers that may have been delicate. One has to allow elbowroom in the account of a rival: "She must have had something" is how it generally goes, long after the initial "What can he see in her? He must be deaf and blind." Georgie, explained by my mother as being the natural daughter of Sarah Bernhardt and a stork, is only a shadow, a tracing, with long arms and legs and one of those slightly puggy faces with pulled-up eyes.

Her voice remains—the husky Virginia-tobacco whisper I associate with so many women of that generation, my parents' friends; it must have come of age in English Montreal around 1920, when girls began to cut their hair and to smoke. In middle life the voice would slide from low to harsh, and develop a chronic cough. For the moment it was fascinating to me—opposite in pitch and speed from my mother's, which was slightly too high and apt to break off, like that of a singer unable to sustain a long note.

It was true that I had been ill, but I don't think my godmother made much of it that afternoon, other than saying, "It's all very well to talk about that now, but I was certainly never told much, and as for that doctor, you ought to just hear what Ward thinks." Out of this whispered jumble my mother stood accused—of many transgressions, certainly, but chiefly of having discarded Dr. Ward Mackey, everyone's doctor and a family friend. At the time of my birth my mother had all at once decided she liked Ward Mackey better than anyone else and had asked him to choose a name for me. He could not think of one, or, rather, thought of too many, and finally consulted his own mother. She had always longed for a daughter, so that she could call her after the heroine of a novel by, I believe, Marie Corelli. The legend so often repeated to me goes on to tell that when I was seven weeks old my father suddenly asked, "What did you say her name was?"

"*Votre fille a frôlé la phtisie,*" the new doctor had said, the one who had now replaced Dr. Mackey. The new doctor was known to me as Uncle Raoul, though we were not related. This manner of declaring my brush with consumption was worlds away from Ward Mackey's "subject to bilious attacks." Mackey's objections to Uncle Raoul were neither envious nor personal, for Mackey was the sort of bachelor who could console himself with golf. The Protestant in him truly believed those other doctors to be poorly trained and superstitious, capable of recommending the pulling of teeth to cure tonsillitis, and of letting their patients cough to death or perish from septicemia just through Catholic fatalism.

What parent could fail to gasp and marvel at Uncle Raoul's

announcement? Any but either of mine. My mother could invent and produce better dramas any day; as for my father, his French wasn't all that good and he had to have it explained. Once he understood that I had grazed the edge of tuberculosis, he made his decision to remove us all to the country, which he had been wanting a reason to do for some time. He was, I think, attempting to isolate his wife, but by taking her out of the city he exposed her to a danger that, being English, he had never dreamed of: This was the heart-stopping cry of the steam train at night, sweeping across a frozen river, clattering on the ties of a wooden bridge. From our separate rooms my mother and I heard the unrivaled summons, the long, urgent, uniquely North American beckoning. She would follow and so would I, but separately, years and desires and destinations apart. I think that women once pledged in such a manner are more steadfast than men.

"*Frôler*" was the charmed word in that winter's story; it was a hand brushing the edge of folded silk, a leaf escaping a spiderweb. Being caught in the web would have meant staying in bed day and night in a place even worse than a convent school. Charlotte and Angus, whose lives had once seemed so enchanted, so fortunate and free that I could not imagine lesser persons so much as eating the same kind of toast for breakfast, had to share their lives with me, whether they wanted to or not—thanks to Uncle Raoul, who always supposed me to be their principal delight. I had been standing on one foot for months now, midway between "*frôler*" and "falling into," propped up by a psychosomatic guardian angel. Of course I could not stand that way forever; inevitably my health improved and before long I was declared out of danger and then restored—to the relief and pleasure of all except the patient.

"I'd like to see more of you than eyes and nose," said my godmother. "Take off your things." I offer this as an example of unnecessary instruction. Would anyone over the age of three prepare to spend the afternoon in a stifling room wrapped like a mummy in outdoor clothes? "She's smaller than she looks," Georgie remarked, as I began to emerge. This authentic godmother observation drives me to my only refuge, the insistence that she must have had something—he could not have been completely deaf and blind. Divested of hat, scarf, coat, overshoes, and leggings, grasping the handkerchief pressed in my hand so I would not interrupt later by asking for one, responding to my father's muttered "Fix your hair," struck by the command because it was he who had told me not to use "fix" in that sense, I was finally able to sit down next to him on a white sofa. My godmother occupied its twin. A low table stood between, bearing a decanter and glasses and a pile of magazines and, of course, Georgie's ashtrays; I think she smoked even more than my mother did.

On one of these sofas, during an earlier visit with my mother and father, the backs of my dangling feet had left a smudge of shoe polish. It may have been the last occasion when my mother and Georgie were ever together. Directed to stop humming and kicking, and perhaps bored with the conversation in which I was not expected to join, I had soon started up again.

"It doesn't matter," my godmother said, though you could tell she minded.

"Sit up," my father said to me.

"I am sitting up. What do you think I'm doing?" This was not answering but answering back; it is not an expression I ever heard from my father, but I am certain it stood like a stalled truck in Georgie's mind. She wore the look people put on when they are thinking, Now what are you spineless parents going to do about that?

"Oh, for God's sake, she's only a child," said my mother, as though that had ever been an excuse for anything.

Soon after the sofa-kicking incident she and Georgie moved into the hibernation known as "not speaking." This, the lingering condition of half my mother's friendships, usually followed her having said the very thing no one wanted to hear, such as "Who wants to be called Edna May, anyway?"

Once more in the hot pale room where there was nothing to do and nothing for children, I offended my godmother again, by pretending I had never seen her before. The spot I had kicked was pointed out to me, though, owing to new slipcovers, real evidence was missing. My father was proud of my quite surprising memory, of its long backward reach and the minutiae of detail I could describe. My failure now to shine in a domain where I was naturally gifted, that did not require lessons or create litter and noise, must have annoyed him. I also see that my guileless-seeming needling of my godmother was a close adaptation of how my mother could be, and I attribute it to a child's instinctive loyalty to the absent one. Giving me up, my godmother placed a silver dish of mint wafers where I could reach them—white, pink, and green, overlapping—and suggested I look at a magazine. Whatever the magazine was, I had probably seen it, for my mother subscribed to everything then. I may have turned the pages anyway, in case at home something had been censored for children. I felt and am certain I have not invented Georgie's disappointment at not seeing Angus alone. She disliked Charlotte now, and so I supposed he came to call by himself, having no quarrel of his own; he was still close to the slighted Ward Mackey.

My father and Georgie talked for a while—she using people's initials instead of their names, which my mother would not have done—and they drank what must have been sherry, if I think of the shape of the decanter. Then we left and went down to the street in a wood-paneled elevator that had sconce lights, as in a room. The end of the afternoon had a particular shade of color then, which is not tinted by distance or enhancement but has to do with how streets were lighted. Lamps were still gas, and their soft gradual blooming at dusk made the sky turn a peacock blue that slowly deepened to marine, then indigo. This uneven light falling in blurred pools gave the snow it touched a quality of phosphorescence, beyond which were night shadows in which no one lurked. There were few cars, little sound. A fresh snowfall would lie in the streets in a way that seemed natural. Sidewalks were dangerous, casually sanded; even on busy streets you found traces of the icy slides children's feet had made. The reddish brown of the stone houses, the curve and slope of the streets, the constantly changing sky were satisfactory in a way that I now realize must have been aesthetically comfortable. This is what I saw when I read "city" in a book; I had no means of knowing that "city" one day would also mean drab, filthy, flat, or that city blocks could turn into dull squares without mystery.

We crossed Sherbrooke Street, starting down to catch our train. My father walked everywhere in all weathers. Already mined, colonized by an enemy prepared to destroy what it fed on, fighting it with every wrong weapon, squandering strength he should have been storing, stifling pain in silence rather than speaking up while there might have been time, he gave an impression of sternness that was a shield against suffering. One day we heard a mob roaring four syllables over and over, and we turned and went down a different street. That sound was starkly terrifying, something a child might liken to the baying of wolves.

"What is it?"

"Howie Morenz."

"Who is it? Are they chasing him?"

"No, they like him," he said of the hockey player admired to the point of dementia. He seemed to stretch, as if trying to keep every bone in his body from touching a nerve; a look of helplessness such as I had never seen on a grown person gripped his face and he said this strange thing: "Crowds eat me. Noise eats me." The kind of physical pain that makes one seem rat's prey is summed up in my memory of this.

When we came abreast of the Ritz-Carlton after leaving Georgie's apartment, my father paused. The lights within at that time of day were golden and warm. If I barely knew what "hotel" meant, never having stayed in one, I connected the lights with other snowy afternoons, with stupefying adult conversation (Oh, those shut-in velvet-draped unaired low-voice problems!) compensated for by creamy bitter hot chocolate poured out of a pink-and-white china pot.

"You missed your gootay," he suddenly remembered. Established by my grandmother, "*goûter*" was the family word for tea. He often transformed French words, like putty, into shapes he could grasp. No, Georgie had not provided a *goûter*, other than the mint wafers, but it was not her fault—I had not been announced. Perhaps if I had not been so disagreeable with her, he might have proposed hot chocolate now, though I knew better than to ask. He merely pulled my scarf up over my nose and mouth, as if recalling something Uncle Raoul had advised. Breathing inside knitted wool was delicious—warm, moist, pungent when one had been sucking on mint candies, as now. He said, "You didn't enjoy your visit much."

"Not very," through red wool.

"No matter," he said. "You needn't see Georgie again unless you want to," and we walked on. He must have been smarting, for he liked me to be admired. When I was not being admired I was supposed to keep quiet. "You needn't see Georgie again" was also a private decision about himself. He was barely thirty-one and had a full winter to live after this one—little more. Why? "Because I say so." The answer seems to speak out of the lights, the stones, the snow; out of the crucial second when inner and outer forces join, and the environment becomes part of the enemy too.

Ward Mackey used to mention me as "Angus's precocious pain in the neck," which is better than nothing. Long after that afternoon, when I was about twenty, Mackey said to me,

"Georgie didn't play her cards well where he was concerned. There was a point where if she had just made one smart move she could have had him. Not for long, of course, but none of us knew that."

What cards, I wonder. The cards have another meaning for me—they mean a trip, a death, a letter, tomorrow, next year. I saw only one move that Saturday: My father placed a card faceup on the table and watched to see what Georgie made of it. She shrugged, let it rest. There she sits, looking puggy but capable, Angus waiting, the precocious pain in the neck turning pages, hoping to find something in the *National Geographic* harmful for children. I brush in memory against the spiderweb: What if she had picked it up, remarking in her smoky voice, "Yes, I can use that"? It was a low card, the kind that only a born gambler would risk as part of a long-term strategy. She would never have weakened a hand that way; she was not gambling but building. He took the card back and dropped his hand, and their long intermittent game came to an end. The card must have been the eight of clubs— "a female child."

IN YOUTH IS PLEASURE

MY FATHER DIED, then my grandmother; my mother was left, but we did not get on. I was probably disagreeable with anyone who felt entitled to give me instructions and advice. We seldom lived under the same roof, which was just as well. She had found me civil and amusing until I was ten, at which time I was said to have become pert and obstinate. She was impulsive, generous, in some ways better than most other people, but without any feeling for cause and effect; this made her at the least unpredictable and at the most a serious element of danger. I was fascinated by her, though she worried me; then all at once I lost interest. I was fifteen when this happened. I would forget to answer her letters and even to open them. It was not rejection or anything so violent as dislike but a simple indifference I cannot account for. It was much the way I would be later with men I fell out of love with, but I was too young to know that then. As for my mother, whatever I thought, felt, said, wrote, and wore had always been a positive source of exasperation. From time to time she attempted to alter the form, the outward shape at least, of the creature she thought she was modeling, but at last she came to the conclusion there must be something wrong with the clay. Her final unexpected upsurge of attention coincided with my abrupt unconcern: One may well have been the reason for the other.

It took the form of digging into my diaries and notebooks and it yielded, among other documents, a two-year-old poem,

Kiplingesque in its rhythms, entitled "Why I Am a Socialist." The first words of the first line were "You ask . . . ," then came a long answer. But it was not an answer to anything she'd wondered. Like all mothers—at least, all I have known—she was obsessed with the entirely private and possibly trivial matter of a daughter's virginity. Why I was a Socialist she rightly conceded to be none of her business. Still, she must have felt she had to say something, and the something was "You had better be clever, because you will never be pretty." My response was to take—take, not grab—the poem from her and tear it up. No voices were raised. I never mentioned the incident to anyone. That is how it was. We became, presently, mutually unconcerned. My detachment was put down to the coldness of my nature, hers to the exhaustion of trying to bring me up. It must have been a relief to her when, in the first half of Hitler's war, I slipped quietly and finally out of her life. I was now eighteen, and completely on my own. By "on my own" I don't mean a show of independence with Papa-Mama footing the bills: I mean that I was solely responsible for my economic survival and that no living person felt any duty toward me.

On a bright morning in June I arrived in Montreal, where I'd been born, from New York, where I had been living and going to school. My luggage was a small suitcase and an Edwardian picnic hamper—a preposterous piece of baggage my father had brought from England some twenty years before; it had been with me since childhood, when his death turned my life into a helpless migration. In my purse was a birth certificate and five American dollars, my total fortune, the parting gift of a Canadian actress in New York, who had taken me to see *Mayerling* before I got on the train. She was kind and good and terribly hard up, and she had no idea that apart from some loose change I had nothing more. The birth certificate, which testified I was Linnet Muir, daughter of Angus and of Charlotte, was my right of passage. I did not own a passport and possibly never had seen one. In those days there was almost no such thing as a "Canadian." You were Canadian-born, and a British subject, too, and you had a third label with no consular reality, like the racial tag that on Soviet passports will make a German of someone who has never been to Germany. In Canada you were also whatever your father happened to be, which in my case was English. He was half Scot, but English by birth, by mother, by instinct. I did not feel a scrap British or English, but I was not an American either. In American schools I had refused to salute the flag. My denial of that curiously Fascist-looking celebration, with the right arm stuck straight out, and my silence when the others intoned the trusting ". . . and justice for all" had never been thought offensive, only stubborn. Americans then were accustomed to gratitude from foreigners but did not demand it; they quite innocently could not imagine any country fit to live in except their own. If I could not recognize it, too bad for me. Besides, I was not a refugee—just someone from the backwoods. "You got schools in Canada?" I had been asked. "You got radios?" And once, from a teacher, "What do they major in up there? Basket weaving?"

My travel costume was a white piqué jacket and skirt that must have been crumpled and soot-flecked, for I had sat up all night. I was reading, I think, a novel by Sylvia Townsend Warner. My hair was thick and long. I wore my grandmother's wedding ring, which was too large, and which I would lose before long. I desperately wanted to look more than my age, which I had already started to give out as twenty-one. I was traveling light; my picnic hamper contained the poems and journals I had judged fit to accompany me into my new, unfettered existence, and some books I feared I might not find again in clerical Quebec—Zinoviev and Lenin's *Against the Stream*, and a few beige pamphlets from the Little Lenin Library, purchased secondhand in New York. I had a picture of Mayakovsky torn out of *Cloud in*

Trousers and one of Paddy Finucane, the Irish RAF fighter pilot, who was killed the following summer. I had not met either of these men, but I approved of them both very much. I had abandoned my beloved but cumbersome anthologies of American and English verse, confident that I had whatever I needed by heart. I knew every word of Stephen Vincent Benét's "Litany for Dictatorships" and "Notes to Be Left in a Cornerstone," and the other one that begins:

> They shot the Socialists at half-past five
> In the name of victorious Austria. . . .

I could begin anywhere and rush on in my mind to the end. "Notes . . ." was the New York I knew I would never have again, for there could be no journeying backward; the words "but I walked it young" were already a gate shut on a part of my life. The suitcase held only the fewest possible summer clothes. Everything else had been deposited at the various war-relief agencies of New York. In those days I made symbols out of everything, and I must have thought that by leaving a tartan skirt somewhere I was shedding past time. I remember one of those wartime agencies well because it was full of Canadian matrons. They wore pearl earrings like the Duchess of Kent's and seemed to be practicing her tiny smile. Brooches pinned to their cashmere cardigans carried some daft message about the Empire. I heard one of them exclaiming, "You don't expect me, a Britisher, to drink tea made with tea bags!" Good plain girls from the little German towns of Ontario, christened probably Wilma, Jean, and Irma, they had flowing eighteenth-century names like Georgiana and Arabella now. And the Americans, who came in with their arms full of every stitch they could spare, would urge them, the Canadian matrons, to stand fast on the cliffs, to fight the fight, to slug the enemy on the landing fields, to belt him one on the beaches, to keep going with whatever iron rations they could scrape up in Bronxville and Scarsdale; and the Canadians half shut their eyes and tipped their heads back like Gertrude Lawrence and said in thrilling Benita Hume accents that they would do that—indeed they would. I recorded "They're all trained nurses, actually. The Canadian ones have a good reputation. They managed to marry these American doctors."

Canada had been in Hitler's war from the very beginning, but America was still uneasily at peace. Recruiting had already begun; I had seen a departure from New York for Camp Stewart in Georgia, and some of the recruits' mothers crying and even screaming and trying to run alongside the train. The recruits were going off to drill with broomsticks because there weren't enough guns; they still wore old-fashioned headgear and were paid twenty-one dollars a month. There was a song about it: "For twenty-one dollars a day, once a month." As my own train crossed the border to Canada I expected to sense at once an air of calm and grit and dedication, but the only changes were from prosperous to shabby, from painted to unpainted, from smiling to dour. I was entering a poorer and a curiously empty country, where the faces of the people gave nothing away. The crossing was my sea change. I silently recited the vow I had been preparing for weeks: that I would never be helpless again and that I would not let anyone make a decision on my behalf.

When I got down from the train at Windsor station, a man sidled over to me. He had a cap on his head and a bitter Celtic face, with deep indentations along his cheeks, as if his back teeth were pulled. I thought he was asking a direction. He repeated his question, which was obscene. My arms were pinned by the weight of my hamper and suitcase. He brushed the back of his hand over my breasts, called me a name, and edged away. The murderous rage I felt and the revulsion that followed were old friends. They had for years been my reaction to what my diaries called "their hypocrisy." "They" was a world of sly and mumbling people, all of them older than myself. I must have substituted "hypocrisy" for every sort of aggression, because fright was a luxury I could not afford. What distressed me was my helplessness—I who had sworn only a few hours earlier that I'd not be vulnerable again. The man's gaunt face, his drunken breath, the flat voice which I assigned to the graduate of some Christian Brothers teaching establishment haunted me for a long time after that. "The man at Windsor station" would lurk in the windowless corridors of my nightmares; he would be the passenger, the only passenger, on a dark tram. The first sight of a city must be the measure for all second looks.

But it was not my first sight. I'd had ten years of it here—the first ten. After that, and before New York (in one sense, my deliverance), there had been a long spell of grief and shadow in an Ontario city, a place full of mean judgments and grudging minds, of paranoid Protestants and slovenly Catholics. To this day I cannot bear the sight of brick houses, or of a certain kind of empty treeless street on a Sunday afternoon. My memory of Montreal took shape while I was there. It was not a random jumble of rooms and summers and my mother singing "We've Come to See Miss Jenny Jones," but the faithful record of the true survivor. I retained, I rebuilt a superior civilization. In that drowned world, Sherbrooke Street seemed to be glittering and white; the vision of a house upon that street was so painful that I was obliged to banish it from the memorial. The small hot rooms of a summer cottage became enormous and cool. If I say that Cleopatra floated down the Chateauguay River, that the Winter Palace was stormed on Sherbrooke Street, that Trafalgar was fought on Lake St. Louis, I mean it naturally; they were the natural backgrounds of my exile and fidelity. I saw now at the far end of Windsor station—more foreign, echoing, and mysterious than any American station could be—a statue of Lord Mount Stephen, the founder of the Canadian Pacific, which everyone took to be a memorial to Edward VII. Angus, Charlotte, and the smaller Linnet had truly been: This was my proof; once upon a time my instructions had been to make my way to Windsor station should I ever be lost and to stand at the foot of Edward VII and wait for someone to find me.

I have forgotten to say that no one in Canada knew I was there. I looked up the number of the woman who had once been my nurse, but she had no telephone. I found her in a city directory, and with complete faith that "O. Carette" was indeed Olivia and that she would recall and welcome me I took a taxi to the east end of the city—the French end, the poor end. I was so sure of her that I did not ask the driver to wait (to take me where?) but dismissed him and climbed two flights of dark brown stairs inside a house that must have been built soon after Waterloo. That it was Olivia who came to the door, that the small gray-haired creature I recalled as dark and towering had to look up at me, that she unhesitatingly offered me shelter all seem as simple now as when I broke my fiver to settle the taxi. Believing that I was dead, having paid for years of Masses for the repose of my heretic soul, almost the first thing she said to me was *"Tu vis!"* I understood *"Tu es ici!"* We straightened it out later. She held both my hands and cried and called me *belle et grande.* *"Grande"* was good, for among American girls I'd seemed a shrimp. I did not see what there was to cry for; I was here. I was as naturally selfish with Olivia as if her sole reason for being was me. I stayed with her for a while and left when her affection for me made her possessive, and I think I neglected her. On her deathbed she told one of her daughters, the reliable one, to keep an eye on me forever. Olivia was the only person in the world who did not believe I could look after myself. Where she and I were concerned I remained under six.

Now, at no moment of this remarkable day did I feel anxious or worried or forlorn. The man at Windsor station could not really affect my view of the future. I had seen some of the worst of life, but I had no way of judging it or of knowing what the worst could be. I had a sensation of loud, ruthless power, like an enormous waterfall. The past, the part I would rather not have lived, became small and remote, a dark pinpoint. My only weapons until now had been secrecy and insolence. I had stopped running away from schools and situations when I finally understood that by becoming a name in a file, by attracting attention, I would merely prolong my stay in prison—I mean, the prison of childhood itself. My rebellions then consisted only in causing people who were physically larger and legally sovereign to lose their self-control, to become bleached with anger, to shake with such temper that they broke cups and glasses and bumped into chairs. From the malleable, sunny child Olivia said she remembered, I had become, according to later chroniclers, cold, snobbish, and presumptuous. "You need an iron hand, Linnet." I can still hear that melancholy voice, which belonged to a friend of my mother's. "If anybody ever marries you he'd better have an iron hand." After today I would never need to hear this, or anything approaching it, for the rest of my life.

And so that June morning and the drive through empty, sun-lit, wartime streets are even now like a roll of drums in the mind. My life was my own revolution—the tyrants deposed, the constitution wrenched from unwilling hands; I was, all by myself, the liberated crowd setting the palace on fire; I was the flags, the trees, the bannered windows, the flower-decked trains. The singing and the skyrockets of the 1848 I so trustingly believed would emerge out of the war were me, no one but me; and, as in the lyrical first days of any revolution, as in the first days of any love affair, there wasn't the whisper of a voice to tell me, "You might compromise."

If making virtue of necessity has ever had a meaning it must be here: for I was independent *inevitably*. There were good-hearted Americans who knew a bit of my story—as much as I wanted anyone to know—and who hoped I would swim and not drown, but from the moment I embarked on my journey I went on the dark side of the moon. "You seemed so sure of yourself," they would tell me, still troubled, long after this. In the cool journals I kept I noted that my survival meant nothing in the capitalist system; I was one of those not considered to be worth helping, saving, or even investigating. Thinking with care, I see this was true. What could I have turned into in another place? Why, a librarian at Omsk or a file clerk at Tomsk. Well, it hadn't happened that way; I had my private revolution and I settled in with Olivia in Montreal. Sink or swim? Of course I swam. Jobs were for the having; you could pick them up off the ground. Working for a living meant just what it says—a brisk necessity. It would be the least important fragment of my life until I had what I wanted. The cheek of it, I think now: Penniless, sleeping in a shed room behind the kitchen of Olivia's cold-water flat, still I pointed across the wooden balustrade in a long open office where I was being considered for employment and said, "But I won't sit there." Girls were "there," penned in like sheep. I did not think men better than women—only that they did more interesting work and got more money for it. In my journals I called other girls "Coolies." I did not know if life made them bearers or if they had been born with a natural gift for giving in. "Coolie" must have been the secret expression of one of my deepest fears. I see now that I had an immense conceit: I thought I occupied a world other people could scarcely envision, let alone attain. It involved giddy risks and changes, stepping off the edge blindfolded, one's hand on nothing more than a birth certificate and a five-dollar bill. At this time of sitting in judgment I was earning nine dollars a week (until I was told by someone that the local minimum wage was twelve, on which I left for greener fields) and washing my white piqué skirt at night and ironing at dawn, and coming home at all hours so I could pretend to Olivia I had dined. Part of this impermeable sureness that I needn't waver or doubt came out of my having lived in New York. The first time I ever heard people laughing in a cinema was there. I can still remember the wonder and excitement and amazement I felt. I was just under fourteen and I had never heard people expressing their feelings in a public place in my life. The easy reactions, the way a poignant moment caught them, held them still—all that was new. I had come there straight from Ontario, where the reaction to a love scene was a kind of unhappy giggling, while the image of a kitten or a baby induced a long flat "Aaaah," followed by shamed silence. You could imagine them blushing in the dark for having said that—just that "Aaaah." When I heard that open American laughter I thought I could be like these people too, but had been told not to be by everyone, beginning with Olivia: "*Pas si fort*" was something she repeated to me so often when I was small that my father had made a tease out of it, called "Passy four." From a tease it became oppressive too: "For the love of God, Linnet, passy four." What were these new people? Were they soft, too easily got at? I wondered that even then. Would a dictator have a field day here? Were they, as Canadian opinion had it, vulgar? Perhaps the notion of vulgarity came out of some incapacity on the part of the refined. Whatever they were, they couldn't all be daft; if they weren't I probably wasn't either. I supposed I stood as good a chance of being miserable here as anywhere, but at least I would not have to pretend to be someone else.

Now, of course there is much to be said on the other side: People who do not display what they feel have practical advantages. They can go away to be killed as if they didn't mind; they can see their sons off to war without a blink. Their upbringing is intended for a crisis. When it comes, they behave themselves. But it is murder in everyday life—truly murder. The dead of heart and spirit litter the landscape. Still, keeping a straight face makes life tolerable under stress. It makes *public* life tolerable—that is all I am saying; because in private people still got drunk, went after each other with bottles and knives, rang the police to complain that neighbors were sending poison gas over the transom, abandoned infant children and aged parents, wrote letters to newspapers in favor of corporal punishment, with inventive suggestions. When I came back to Canada that June, at least one thing had been settled: I knew that it was all right for people to laugh and cry and even to make asses of themselves. I had actually known people like that, had lived with them, and they were fine, mostly—not crazy at all. That was where a lot of my confidence came from when I began my journey into a new life and a dream past.

My father's death had been kept from me. I did not know its exact circumstances or even the date. He died when I was ten. At thirteen I was still expected to believe a fable about his being in England. I kept waiting for him to send for me, for my life was deeply wretched and I took it for granted he knew. Finally I began to suspect that death and silence can be one. How to be sure? Head-on questions got me nowhere. I had to create a situation in which some adult (not my mother, who was far too sharp) would lose all restraint and hurl the truth at me. It was easy: I was an artist at this. What I had not foreseen was the verbal violence of the scene or the effect it might have. The storm that seemed to break in my head, my need to maintain the pose of indifference ("What are you telling me that for? What makes you think I care?") were such a strain that I had physical reactions, like stigmata, which doctors would hopelessly treat on and off for years and which vanished when I became independent. The other change was that if anyone asked about my father I said, "Oh, he died." Now, in Montreal, I could confront the free adult world of falsehood and evasion on an equal footing; they would be forced to talk to me as they did to each other. Making appointments to meet my father's friends—Mr. Archie McEwen, Mr. Stephen Ross-Colby, Mr. Quentin Keller—I left my adult name, "Miss Muir." These were the men who eight, nine, ten years ago had asked, "Do you like your school?"—not knowing what else to say to children. I had curtsied to them and said, "Good night." I think what I wanted was special information about despair, but I should have known that would be taboo in a place where "like" and "don't like" were heavy emotional statements.

Archie McEwen, my father's best friend, or the man I mistook for that, kept me standing in his office on St. James Street West, he standing too, with his hands behind his back, and he said the following—not reconstructed or approximate but recalled, like "The religions of ancient Greece and Rome are extinct" or "O come, let us sing unto the Lord":

"Of course, Angus was a very sick man. I saw him walking along Sherbrooke Street. He must have just come out of hospital. He couldn't walk upright. He was using a stick. Inching along. His hair had turned gray. Nobody knew where Charlotte had got to, and we'd heard you were dead. He obviously wasn't long for this world either. He had too many troubles for any one man. I crossed the street because I didn't have the heart to shake hands with him. I felt terrible."

Savage? Reasonable? You can't tell, with those minds. Some recent threat had scared them. The Depression was too close, just at their heels. Archie McEwen did not ask where I was staying or where I had been for the last eight years; in fact, he asked only two questions. In response to the first I said, "She is married."

There came a gleam of interest—distant, amused: "So she decided to marry him, did she?"

My mother was highly visible; she had no secrets except unexpected ones. My father had nothing but. When he asked,

"Would you like to spend a year in England with your Aunt Dorothy?" I had no idea what he meant and I still don't. His only brother, Thomas, who was killed in 1918, had not been married; he'd had no sisters, that anyone knew. Those English mysteries used to be common. People came out to Canada because they did not want to think about the Thomases and Dorothys anymore. Angus was a solemn man, not much of a smiler. My mother, on the other hand—I won't begin to describe her; it would never end—smiled, talked, charmed anyone she didn't happen to be related to, swam in scandal like a partisan among the people. She made herself the central figure in loud, spectacular dramas which she played with the houselights on; you could see the audience too. That was her mistake; they kept their reactions, like their lovemaking, in the dark. You can imagine what she must have been in this world where everything was hushed, muffled, disguised: She must have seemed all they had by way of excitement, give or take a few elections and wars. It sounds like a story about the old and stale, but she and my father had been quite young eight and ten years before. The dying man creeping along Sherbrooke Street was thirty-two. First it was light chatter, then darker gossip, and then it went too far (*he* was ill and he couldn't hide it; *she* had a lover and didn't try); then suddenly it became tragic, and open tragedy was disallowed. And so Mr. Archie McEwen could stand in his office and without a trace of feeling on his narrow Lowland face—not unlike my father's in shape—he could say, "I crossed the street."

Stephen Ross-Colby, a bachelor, my father's painter chum: The smell of his studio on St. Mark Street was the smell of a personal myth. I said timidly, "Do you happen to have anything of his—a drawing or anything?" I was humble because I was on a private, personal terrain of vocation that made me shy even of the dead.

He said, "No, nothing. You could ask around. She junked a

lot of his stuff and he junked the rest when he thought he wouldn't survive. You might try..." He gave me a name or two. "It was all small stuff," said Ross-Colby. "He didn't do anything big." He hurried me out of the studio for a cup of coffee in a crowded place—the Honey Dew on St. Catherine Street, it must have been. Perhaps in the privacy of his studio I might have heard him thinking. Years after that he would try to call me "Lynn," which I never was, and himself "Steve." He'd come into his own as an artist by then, selling wash drawings of Canadian war graves, sun-splashed, wisteria mauve, lime green, with drifts of blossom across the name of the regiment; gained a reputation among the heartbroken women who bought these impersonations, had them framed— the only picture in the house. He painted the war memorial at Caen. ("Their name liveth forever.") His stones weren't stones but mauve bubbles—that is all I have against them. They floated off the page. My objection wasn't to "He didn't do anything big" but to Ross-Colby's way of turning the dead into thistledown. He said, much later, of that meeting, "I felt like a bastard, but I was broke, and I was afraid you'd put the bite on me."

Let me distribute demerits equally and tell about my father's literary Jewish friend, Mr. Quentin Keller. He was older than the others, perhaps by some twelve years. He had a whispery voice and a long pale face and a daughter older than I. "Bossy Wendy" I used to call her when, forced by her parents as I was by mine, Bossy Wendy had to take a whole afternoon of me. She had a room full of extraordinary toys, a miniature kitchen in which everything worked, of which all I recall her saying is "Don't touch." Wendy Keller had left Smith after her freshman year to marry the elder son of a Danish baron. Her father said to me, "There is only one thing you need to know and that is that your father was a gentleman."

Jackass was what I thought. Yes, Mr. Quentin Keller was a jackass. But he was a literary one, for he had once written a play called *Forbearance*, in which I'd had a role. I had bounded across the stage like a tennis ball, into the arms of a young woman dressed up like an old one, and cried my one line: "Here I am, Granny!" Of course, he did not make his living fiddling about with amateur theatricals; thanks to our meeting I had a good look at the inside of a conservative architect's private office—that was about all it brought me.

What were they so afraid of, I wondered. I had not yet seen that I was in a false position where they were concerned; being "Miss Muir" had not made equals of us but lent distance. I thought they had read my true passport, the invisible one we all carry, but I had neither the wealth nor the influence a provincial society requires to make a passport valid. My credentials were lopsided: The important half of the scales was still in the air. I needed enormous collateral security—fame, an alliance with a powerful family, the power of money itself. I remember how Archie McEwen, trying to place me in some sensible context, to give me a voucher so he could take me home and show me to his wife, perhaps, asked his second question: "Who inherited the—?"

"The what, Mr. McEwen?"

He had not, of course, read "Why I Am a Socialist." I did not believe in inherited property. "Who inherited the—?" would not cross my mind again for another ten years, and then it would be a drawer quickly opened and shut before demons could escape. To all three men the last eight years were like minutes; to me they had been several lives. Some of my confidence left me then. It came down to "Next time I'll know better," but would that be enough? I had been buffeted until now by other people's moods, principles, whims, tantrums; I had survived, but perhaps I had failed to grow some outer skin it was now too late to acquire. Olivia thought that; she was the only one. Olivia knew more about the limits of nerve than I did. Her knowledge came out of the clean, swept, orderly poverty that used to be tucked away in the corners of cities. It didn't spill out then, or give anyone a bad conscience. Nobody took its picture. Anyway, Olivia would not have sat for such a portrait. The fringed green rug she put over her treadle sewing machine was part of a personal fortune. On her mantelpiece stood a copper statuette of Voltaire in an armchair. It must have come down to her from some robustly anticlerical ancestor. "Who is he?" she said to me. "You've been to school in a foreign country." "A governor of New France," I replied. She knew Voltaire was the name of a bad man and she'd have thrown the figurine out, and it would have made one treasure less in the house. Olivia's maiden name was Ouvrardville, which was good in Quebec, but only really good if you were one of the rich ones. Because of her maiden name she did not want anyone ever to know she had worked for a family; she impressed this on me delicately—it was like trying to understand what a dragonfly wanted to tell. In the old days she had gone home every weekend, taking me with her if my parents felt my company was going to make Sunday a very long day. Now I understood what the weekends were about: Her daughters, Berthe and Marguerite, for whose sake she worked, were home from their convent schools Saturday and Sunday and had to be chaperoned. Her relatives pretended not to notice that Olivia was poor or even that she was widowed, for which she seemed grateful. The result of all this elegant sham was that Olivia did not say, "I was afraid you'd put the bite on me," or keep me standing. She dried her tears and asked if there was a trunk to follow. No? She made a pot of tea and spread a starched cloth on the kitchen table and we sat down to a breakfast of toast and honey. The honey tin was a ten-pounder decorated with bees the size of hornets. Lifting it for her, I remarked, "*C'est collant*," a word out of a frozen language that started to thaw when Olivia said, "*Tu vis!*"

On the advice of her confessor, who was to be my rival from now on, Olivia refused to tell me whatever she guessed or knew, and she was far too dignified to hint. Putting together the three men's woolly stories, I arrived at something about tuberculosis of the spine and a butchery of an operation. He started back to England to die there but either changed his mind or was too ill to begin the journey; at Quebec City, where he was to have taken ship, he shot himself in a public park at five o'clock in the morning. That was one version; another was that he died at sea and the gun was found in his luggage. The revolver figured in all three accounts. It was an officer's weapon from the Kaiser's war, that had belonged to his brother. Angus kept it at the back of a small drawer in the tall chest used for men's clothes and known in Canada as a highboy. In front of the revolver was a pigskin stud box and a pile of ironed handkerchiefs. Just describing that drawer dates it. How I happen to know the revolver was loaded and how I learned never to point a gun even in play is another story. I can tell you that I never again in my life looked inside a drawer that did not belong to me.

I know a woman whose father died, she thinks, in a concentration camp. Or was he shot in a schoolyard? Or hanged and thrown in a ditch? Were the ashes that arrived from some eastern plain his or another prisoner's? She invents different deaths. Her inventions have become her conversation at dinner parties. She takes on a child's voice and says, "My father died at Buchenwald." She chooses and rejects elements of the last act; one avoids mentioning death, shooting, capital punishment, cremation, deportation, even fathers. Her inventions are not thought neurotic or exhibitionist but something sanctioned by history. Peacetime casualties are not like that. They are lightning bolts out of a sunny sky that strike only one house. All around the ashy ruin lilacs blossom, leaves gleam. Speculation in public about the disaster would be indecent. Nothing remains but a silent, recurring puzzlement to the survivors: Why here and not there? Why this and not that? Before July was out I had settled his fate in my mind and I never varied: I thought he had died of homesickness; sickness for England was the consumption, the gun, the everything. "Everything" had to take it all in, for people in Canada then did not speak of irrational endings to life, and newspapers did not print that kind of news: This was because of the spiritual tragedy for Catholic families, and because the act had long been considered a criminal one in British law. If Catholic feelings were spared it gave the impression no one but Protestants ever went over the edge, which was unfair; and so the possibility was eliminated, and people came to a natural end in a running car in a closed garage, hanging from a rafter in the barn, in an icy lake with a canoe left to drift empty. Once I had made up my mind, the whole story somehow became none of my business: I had looked in a drawer that did not belong to me. More, if I was to live my own life I had to let go. I wrote in my journal that "they" had got him but would not get me, and after that there was scarcely ever a mention.

My dream past evaporated. Montreal, in memory, was a leafy citadel where I knew every tree. In reality I recognized nearly nothing and had to start from scratch. Sherbrooke Street had been the dream street, pure white. It was the avenue poor Angus descended leaning on a walking stick. It was a moat I was not allowed to cross alone; it was lined with gigantic spreading trees through which light fell like a rain of coins. One day, standing at a corner, waiting for the light to change, I understood that the Sherbrooke Street of my exile—my Mecca, my Jerusalem—was this. It had to be: There could not be two. It was *only* this. The limitless green where in a perpetual spring I had been taken to play was the campus of McGill University. A house, whose beauty had brought tears to my sleep, to which in sleep I'd returned to find it inhabited by ugly strangers, gypsies, was a narrow stone thing with a shop on the ground floor and offices above—if that was it, for there were several like it. Through the bare panes of what might have been the sitting room, with its deep private window seats, I saw neon strip-lighting along a ceiling. Reality, as always, was narrow and dull. And yet what dramatic things had taken place on this very corner: Once Satan had approached me—furry dark skin, claws, red eyes, the lot. He urged me to cross the street and I did, in front of a car that braked in time. I explained, "The Devil told me to." I had no idea until then that my parents did not believe what I was taught in my convent school. (Satan is not bilingual, by the way; he speaks Quebec French.) My parents had no God and therefore no Fallen Angel. I was scolded for lying, which was a thing my father detested, and which my mother regularly did but never forgave in others.

Why these two nonbelievers wanted a strong religious education for me is one of the mysteries. (Even in loss of faith they were unalike, for he was ex-Anglican and she was ex-Lutheran and that is not your same atheist—no, not at all.) "To make you tolerant" was a lame excuse, as was "French," for I spoke fluent French with Olivia, and I could read in two languages before I was four. Discipline might have been one reason—God knows, the nuns provided plenty of that—but according to Olivia I did not need any. It cannot have been for the quality of the teaching, which was lamentable. I suspect that it was something like sending a dog to a trainer (they were passionate in their concern for animals, especially dogs), but I am not certain it ever brought me to heel. The first of my schools, the worst, the darkest, was on Sherbrooke Street too. When I heard, years later, it had been demolished, it was like the burial of a witch. I had remembered it penitentiary size, but what I found myself looking at one day was simply a very large stone house. A crocodile of little girls emerged from the front gate and proceeded along the street—white-faced, black-clad, eyes cast down. I knew they were bored, fidgety, anxious, and probably hungry. I should have felt pity, but at eighteen all that came to me was thankfulness that I had been correct about one thing throughout my youth, which I now considered ended: Time had been on my side, faithfully, and unless you died you were always bound to escape.

BETWEEN ZERO AND ONE

W HEN I WAS young I thought that men had small lives of their own creation. I could not see why, born enfranchised, without the obstacles and constraints attendant on women, they set such close limits for themselves and why, once the limits had been reached, they seemed so taken aback. I could not tell much difference between a man aged thirty-six, about, and one forty or fifty; it was impossible to fix the borderline of this apparent disappointment. There was a space of life I used to call "between Zero and One" and then came a long mystery. I supposed that men came up to their wall, their terminal point, quite a long way after One. At that time I was nineteen and we were losing the war. The news broadcast in Canada was flatly optimistic, read out in the detached nasal voices de rigueur for the CBC. They were voices that seemed to be saying, "Good or bad, it can't affect *us*." I worked in a building belonging to the federal government—it was a heavy Victorian structure of the sort that exists on every continent, wherever the British thought they'd come to stay. This one had been made out of the reddish-brown Montreal stone that colors, in memory, the streets of my childhood and that architects have no use for now. The office was full of old soldiers from one war before: Ypres (pronounced "Wipers") and Vimy Ridge were real, as real as this minute, while Singapore, Pearl Harbor, Voronezh were the stuff of fiction. It seemed as if anything that befell the young, even dying, was bound to be trivial.

"Half of 'em'll never see any fighting," I often heard. "Anyway not like in the trenches." We did have one veteran from the current war—Mac Kirkconnell, who'd had a knock on the head during his training and was now good for nothing except civilian life. He and two others were the only men under thirty left in the place. The other two were physical crocks, which was why they were not in uniform (a question demented women sometimes asked them in the street). Mr. Tracy had been snow-blinded after looking out of a train window for most of a sunny February day; he had recovered part of his sight but had to wear mauve glasses even by electric light. He was nice but strange, infirm. Mr. Curran, reputed to have one kidney, one lung, and one testicle, and who was the subject of endless rhymes and ditties on that account, was not so nice: He had not wanted a girl in the office and had argued against my being employed. Now that I was there he simply pretended that he had won. There were about a dozen other men—older, old. I can see every face, hear every syllable, which evoked, for me, a street, a suburb, a kind of schooling. I could hear just out of someone's saying to me, "Say, Linnet, couja just gimme a hand here, please?" born here, born in Glasgow; immigrated early, late; raised in Montreal, no, farther west. I can see the rolled shirtsleeves, the braces, the eyeshades, the hunched shoulders, the elastic armbands, the paper cuffs they wore sometimes, the chopped-egg sandwiches in waxed paper, the apples, the oatmeal cookies ("Want any, Linnet? If you don't eat lunch nobody'll marry you"), the thermos flasks. Most of them lived thinly, paying for a bungalow, a duplex flat, a son's education: A good Protestant education was not to be had for nothing then. I remember a day of dark spring snowstorms, ourselves reflected on the black windows, the pools of warm light here and there, the green-shaded lamps, the dramatic hiss and gurgle of the radiators that always sounded like the background to some emotional outburst, the sudden slackening at the end of the afternoon when every molecule of oxygen in the room had turned into poison. Assistant Chief Engineer Macaulay came plodding softly along the wintry room and laid something down on my desk. It was a collection of snapshots of a naked woman prancing and skipping in what I took to be the backyard of his house out in Cartierville. In one she was in a baby carriage with her legs spread over the sides, pretending to drink out of an infant's bottle. The unknown that this represented was infinite. I also wondered what Mr. Macaulay wanted—he didn't say. He remarked, shifting from foot to foot, "Now, Linnet, they tell me you like modern art." I thought then, I think now, that the tunnel winters, the sudden darkness that April day, the years he'd had of this long green room, the knowledge that he would die and be buried "Assistant Chief Engineer Grade II" without having overtaken Chief Engineer McCreery had simply snapped the twig, the frail matchstick in the head that is all we have to keep us sensible.

Bertie Knox had a desk facing mine. He told the other men I'd gone red in the face when I saw Macaulay's fat-arsed wife. (He hadn't seen *that* one; I had turned it over, like a bad card.) The men teased me for blushing, and they said, "Wait till you get married, Linnet, you haven't done with shocks." Bertie Knox had been in this very office since the age of twelve. The walls had been a good solid gray then—not this drawing-room green. The men hadn't been pampered and coddled, either. There wasn't even a water cooler. You were fined for smoking, fined for lateness, fined for sick leave. He had worked the old ten-hour day and given every cent to his mother. Once he pinched a dime of it and his mother went for him. He locked himself in a cupboard. His mother took the door off its hinges and beat him blue with a wooden hanger. During the Depression, married, down to half pay, four kids in the house, he had shoveled snow for twenty cents an hour. "And none the worse for it," he would always wind up. Most of the men seemed to have been raised in hardship by stern, desperate parents. What struck me was the good they thought it had done them (I had yet to meet an adult man with a poor opinion of himself) and their desire to impose the same broken fortunes on other people, particularly on the young—though not their own young, of course. There was a touch of sadness, a touch of envy to it, too. Bertie Knox had seen Mr. Macaulay and Mr. McCreery come in as Engineers Grade II, wet behind the ears, puffed up with their new degrees, "just a couple more college punks." He said that engineering was the world's most despised profession, occupied mainly by human apes. Instead of a degree he had a photograph of himself in full kilt, Highland Light Infantry, 1917: He had gone "home," to a completely unknown Old Country, and joined up there. "Will you just look at that lad?" he would plead. "Do they come like him today? By God, they do not!" Bertie Knox could imitate any tone and accent, including mine. He could do a CBC announcer droning, "The British have ah taken ah Tobruk," when we knew perfectly well the Germans had. (One good thing about the men was that when anything seemed hopeless they talked nonsense. The native traits of pessimism and constant grumbling returned only when there was nothing to grumble about.) Bertie Knox had a wooden leg, which he showed me; it was dressed in a maroon sock with clocks up the sides and a buckled garter. He had a collection of robust bawdy songs—as everyone (all the men, I mean) had in Canada, unless they were pretending—which I copied in a notebook, verse upon verse, with the necessary indications: Tune—"On, Wisconsin!"; Tune—"Men of Harlech"; Tune— "We Gather Together to Ask the Lord's Blessing." Sometimes he took the notebook and corrected a word here and there. It doesn't follow that he was a cheerful person. He laughed a lot but he never smiled. I don't think he liked anyone, really.

The men were statisticians, draftsmen, civil engineers. Painted on the frosted glass of the office door was

REVIEW AND DEVELOPMENT
RESEARCH AND EXPANSION
OF
WARTIME INDUSTRY
"REGIONAL AND URBAN"

The office had been called something else up until September 1939; according to Bertie Knox they were still doing the same work as before, and not much of it. "It looks good," he said. "It sounds good. What is its meaning? Sweet bugger all." A few girls equipped with rackety typewriters and adding machines sat grouped at the far end of the room, separated from the men by a balustrade. I was the first woman ever permitted to work on the men's side of this fence. A pigeon among the cats was how it sometimes felt. My title was "aide." Today it would be something like "trainee." I was totally unqualified for this or any other kind of work and had been taken on almost at my own insistence that they could not do without me.

"Yes, I know all about that," I had replied, to everything.

"Well, I *suppose* it's all right," said Chief Engineer. The hiring of girls usually fell to a stout grim woman called "Supervisor," but I was not coming in as a typist. He had never interviewed a girl before and he was plainly uncomfortable, asking me questions with all the men straining to hear. There were no young men left on account of the war, and the office did need someone. But what if they trained me, he said, at great cost and expense to the government, and what if I then did the dreadful thing girls were reputed to do, which was to go off and get married? It would mean a great waste of time and money just when there was a war on.

I was engaged, but not nearly ready for the next step. In

any case, I told him, even if I did marry I would need to go on working, for my husband would more than likely be sent overseas. What Chief Engineer did not know was that I was a minor with almost no possibility of obtaining parental consent. Barring some bright idea, I could not do much of anything until I was twenty-one. For this interview I had pinned back my long hair; I wore a hat, gloves, earrings, and I folded my hands on my purse in a conscious imitation of older women. I did not mind the interview, or the furtively staring men. I was shy, but not self-conscious. Efforts made not to turn a young girl's head—part of an education I had encountered at every stage and in every sort of school—had succeeded in making me invisible to myself. My only commercial asset was that I knew French, but French was of no professional use to anyone in Canada then—not even to French Canadians; one might as well have been fluent in Pushtu. Nevertheless I listed it on my application form, along with a very dodgy "German" (private lessons between the ages of eight and ten) and an entirely impudent "Russian": I was attending Russian evening classes at McGill, for reasons having mainly to do with what I believed to be the world's political future. I recorded my age as twenty-two, hoping to be given a grade and a salary that would correspond. There were no psychological or aptitude tests; you were taken at your word and lasted according to performance. There was no social security and only the loosest sort of pension plan; hiring and firing involved no more paperwork than a typed letter—sometimes not even that. I had an unmistakably Montreal accent of a kind now almost extinct, but my having attended school in the United States gave me a useful vagueness of background.

And so, in an ambience of doubt, apprehension, foreboding, incipient danger, and plain hostility, for the first time in the history of the office a girl was allowed to sit with the men. And it was here, at the desk facing Bertie Knox's, on the only uncomfortable chair in the room, that I felt for the first time that almost palpable atmosphere of sexual curiosity, sexual resentment, and sexual fear that the presence of a woman can create where she is not wanted. If part of the resentment vanished when it became clear that I did not know what I was doing, the feeling that women were "trouble" never disappeared. However, some of the men were fathers of daughters, and they quickly saw that I was nothing like twenty-two. Some of them helped me then, and one man, Hughie Pryor, an engineer, actually stayed late to do some of my work when I fell behind.

Had I known exactly what I was about, I might not have remained for more than a day. Older, more experienced, I'd have called it a dull place. The men were rotting quietly until pension time. They kept to a slow English-rooted civil-service pace; no one wasted office time openly, but no one produced much, either. Although they could squabble like hens over mislaid pencils, windows open or shut, borrowed triangles, special and sacred pen nibs used for tracing maps, there was a truce about zeal. The fact is that I did not know the office was dull. It was so new to me, so strange, such another climate, that even to flow with the sluggish tide training men and women into the heart of the city each day was a repeated experiment I sensed, noted, recorded, as if I were being allowed to be part of something that was not really mine. The smell of the building was of school—of chalk, dust, plaster, varnish, beeswax. Victorian, Edwardian, and early Georgian oil portraits of Canadian captains of industry, fleshed-out pirate faces, adorned the staircase and halls—a daily reminder that there are two races, those who tread on people's lives, and the others. The latest date on any of the portraits was about 1925: I suppose photography had taken over. Also by then the great fortunes had been established

131

and the surviving pirates were retired, replete and titled, usually to England. Having had both French and English schooling in Quebec, I knew that these pink-cheeked marauders were what English-speaking children were led to admire (without much hope of emulation, for the feast was over). They were men of patriotism and of action; we owed them everything. They were in a positive, constructive way a part of the Empire and of the Crown; this was a good thing. In a French education veneration was withheld from anyone except the dead and defeated, ranging from General Montcalm expiring at his last battle to a large galaxy of maimed and crippled saints. Deprivation of the senses, mortification of mind and body were imposed, encouraged, for phantom reasons—something to do with a tragic past and a deep fear of life itself. Montreal was a city where the greater part of the population were wrapped in myths and sustained by belief in magic. I had been to school with little girls who walked in their sleep and had visions; the nuns who had taught me seemed at ease with the dead. I think of them even now as strange, dead, punishing creatures who neither ate nor breathed nor slept. The one who broke one of my fingers with a ruler was surely a spirit without a mind, tormented, acting in the vengeful driven way of homeless ghosts. In an English school visions would have been smartly dealt with—cold showers, the parents summoned, at the least a good stiff talking-to. These two populations, these two tribes, knew nothing whatever about each other. In the very poorest part of the east end of the city, apparitions were commonplace; one lived among a mixture of men and women and their imaginings. I would never have believed then that anything could ever stir them from their dark dreams. The men in the portraits were ghosts of a kind, too; they also seemed to be saying, "Too late, too late for you," and of course in a sense so it was: It was too late for anyone else to import Chinese and Irish coolie labor and wring a railway out of them. That had already been done.

Once I said to half-blind Mr. Tracy, "Things can't just stay this way."

"Change is always for the worse" was his reply. His own father had lost all his money in the Depression, ten years before; perhaps he meant that.

I climbed to the office in a slow reassuring elevator with iron grille doors, sharing it with inexpressive women and men—clearly, the trodden-on. No matter how familiar our faces became, we never spoke. The only sound, apart from the creaking cable, was the gasping and choking of a poor man who had been gassed at the Somme and whose lungs were said to be in shreds. He had an old man's pale eyes and wore a high stiff collar and stared straight before him, like everyone else. Some of the men in my office had been wounded, too, but they made it sound pleasant. Bertie Knox said he had hobbled on one leg and crutches in the 1918 Allied victory parade in Paris. According to him, when his decimated regiment followed their Highland music up the Champs-Élysées, every pretty girl in Paris had been along the curb, fighting the police and screaming and trying to get at Bertie Knox and take him home.

"It was the kilts set 'em off," said Bertie Knox. "That and the wounds. And the Jocks played it up for all they was worth, bashing the very buggery out of the drums." "Jocks" were Scots in those days—nothing more.

Any mention of that older war could bring the men to life, but it had been done with for more than twenty years now. Why didn't they move, walk, stretch, run? Each of them seemed to inhabit an invisible square; the square was shared with *my* desk, *my* graph paper, *my* elastic bands. The contents of the square were tested each morning: The drawers of my own desk—do they still open and shut? My desk lamp—does it still turn on and off? Have my special coat hanger, my favorite nibs, my drinking glass, my calendar, my children's pictures, my ashtray, the one I brought from

133

home, been tampered with during the night? Sometimes one glimpsed another world, like an extra room ("It was my young daughter made my lunch today"—said with a dismissive shrug, lest it be taken for boasting) or a wish outdistanced, reduced, shrunken, trailing somewhere in the mind: "I often thought I wanted..." "Something I wouldn't have minded having..." Easily angry, easily offended, underpaid, at the mercy of accidents—an illness in the family could wipe out a life's savings—still they'd have resisted change for the better. Change was double-edged; it might mean improving people with funny names, letting them get uppity. What they had instead were marks of privilege—a blind sureness that they were superior in every way to French Canadians, whom in some strange fashion they neither heard nor saw (a lack of interest that was doubly and triply returned); they had the certainty they'd never be called on to share a washroom or a drawing board or to exchange the time of day with anyone "funny" (applications from such people, in those days, would have been quietly set aside); most important of all, perhaps, they had the distinction of the individual hand towel. These towels, as stiff as boards, reeking of chloride bleach, were distributed once a week by a boy pushing a trolley. They were distributed to men, but not even to *all* men. The sanctioned carried them to the washroom, aired and dried them on the backs of chairs, kept them folded in a special drawer. Assimilated into a male world, I had one too. The stenographers and typists had to make do with paper towels that scratched when new and dissolved when damp. Any mistake or oversight on towel day was a source of outrage: "Why the bejesus do I get a torn one three times running? You'd think I didn't count for anything round here." It seemed a true distress; someday some simple carelessness might turn out to be the final curse: They were like that prisoner of Mussolini, shut up for life, who burst into tears because the soup was cold. When I received presents of candy I used to bring them in for the staff; these wartime chocolates tasted of candle wax but were much appreciated nonetheless. I had to be careful to whom I handed the box first: I could not begin with girls, which I'd have thought natural, because Supervisor did not brook interruptions. I would transfer the top layer to the lid of the box for the girls, for later on, and then consider the men. A trinity of them occupied glass cubicles. One was diabetic; another was Mr. Tracy, who, a gentle alcoholic, did not care for sweets; and the third was Mr. Curran. Skipping all three I would start with Chief Engineer McCreery and descend by way of Assistant Chief Engineers Grade I and then II; I approached them by educational standards, those with degrees from McGill and Queen's—Queen's first—to, finally, the technicians. By that time the caramels and nougats had all been eaten and nothing left but squashy orange and vanilla creams nobody liked. Then, then, oh God, who was to receive the affront of the last chocolate, the one reposing among crumbs and fluted paper casings? Sometimes I was cowardly and left the box adrift on a drawing board with a murmured "Pass it along, would you?"

I was deeply happy. It was one of the periods of inexplicable grace when every day is a new parcel one unwraps, layer on layer of tissue paper covering bits of crystal, scraps of words in a foreign language, pure white stones. I spent my lunch hours writing in notebooks, which I kept locked in my desk. The men never bothered me, apart from trying to feed me little pieces of cake. They were all sad when I began to smoke—I remember that. I could write without hearing anyone, but poetry was leaving me. It was not an abrupt removal but like a recurring tide whose high-water mark recedes inch by inch. Presently I was deep inland and the sea was gone. I would mourn it much later: It was such a gentle separation at the time that I scarcely noticed. I had notebooks stuffed with streets and people: My journals were full of "but what he *really* must have meant was . . ." There were endless political puzzles I tried to solve by comparing one thing with another, but of course nothing matched; I had not lost my adolescent habit of private, passionate manifestos. If politics was nothing but chess—Mr. Tracy's ways of sliding out of conviction—K was surely Social Justice and Q Extreme Morality. I was certain of this, and that after the war—unless we were completely swallowed up, like those Canadian battalions at Hong Kong—K and Q would envelop the world. Having no one to listen to, I could not have a thought without writing it down. There were pages and pages of dead butterflies, wings without motion or lift. I began to ration my writing, for fear I would dream through life as my father had done. I was afraid I had inherited a poisoned gene from him, a vocation without a gift. He had spent his own short time like a priest in charge of a relic, forever expecting the blessed blood to liquefy. I had no assurance I was not the same. I was so like him in some ways that a man once stopped me in front of the Bell Telephone building on Beaver Hall Hill and said, "Could you possibly be Angus Muir's sister?" That is how years telescope in men's minds. That particular place must be the windiest in Montreal, for I remember dust and ragged papers blowing in whirlpools and that I had to hold my hair. I said, "No, I'm not," without explaining that I was not his sister but his daughter. I had heard people say, referring to me but not knowing who I was, "He had a daughter, but apparently she died." We couldn't *both* be dead. Having come down on the side of life, I kept my distance. Writing now had to occupy an enormous space. I had lived in New York until a year before and there were things I was sick with missing. There was no theater, no music; there was one museum of art with not much in it. There was not even a free public lending library in the sense of the meaning that would have been given the words "free public lending library" in Toronto or New York. The municipal library was considered a sinister joke. There was a persistent, apocryphal story among English

Canadians that an American philanthropic foundation (the Carnegie was usually mentioned) had offered to establish a free public lending library on condition that its contents were not to be censored by the provincial government of Quebec or by the Catholic Church, and that the offer had been turned down. The story may not have been true but its persistence shows the political and cultural climate of Montreal then. Educated French Canadians summed it up in shorter form: Their story was that when you looked up "Darwin" in the card index of the Bibliothèque de Montréal you found "See anti-Darwin." A Canadian actress I knew in New York sent me the first published text of *The Skin of Our Teeth*. I wrote imploring her to tell me everything about the production—the costumes, the staging, the voices. I've never seen it performed—not read it since the end of the war. I've been told that it doesn't hold, that it is not rooted in anything specific. It was then; its Ice Age was Fascism. I read it the year of Dieppe, in a year when "Russia" meant "Leningrad," when Malta could be neither fed nor defended. The Japanese were anywhere they wanted to be. Vast areas of the world were covered with silence and ice. One morning I read a little notice in the *Gazette* that Miss Margaret Urn would be taking auditions for the Canadian Broadcasting Corporation. I presented myself during my lunch hour with *The Skin of Our Teeth* and a manuscript one-act play of my own, in case. I had expected to find queues of applicants but I was the only one. Miss Urn received me in a small room of a dingy office suite on St. Catherine Street. We sat down on opposite sides of a table. I was rendered shy by her bearing, which had a head-mistress quality, and perplexed by her accent—it was the voice any North American actor will pick up after six months of looking for work in the West End, but I did not know that. I opened *The Skin of Our Teeth* and began to read. It was floating rather than reading, for I had much of it by heart. When I read "Have you milked the mammoth?" Miss Urn stopped me. She reached over the table and placed her hand on the page.

"My dear child, what is this rubbish?" she said.

I stammered, "It is a . . . a play in New York."

Oh, fool. The worst thing to say. If only I had said, "Tallulah Bankhead," adding swiftly, "London, before the war." Or, better, "An Edwardian farce. Queen Alexandra, deaf though she was, much appreciated the joke about the separation of m and n." "A play in New York" evoked a look Canada was making me familiar with: amusement, fastidious withdrawal, gentle disdain. What a strange city to have a play in, she might have been thinking.

"Try reading this," she said.

I shall forget everything about the war except that at the worst point of it I was asked to read *Dear Octopus*. If Miss Urn had never heard of Thornton Wilder I had never heard of Dodie Smith. I read what I took to be parody. Presently it dawned on me these were meant to be real people. I broke up laughing because of Sabina, Fascism, the Ice Age that was perhaps upon us, because of the one-act play still in my purse. She took the book away from me and closed it and said I would, or would not, be hearing from her.

Now there was excitement in the office: A second woman had been brought in. Mrs. Ireland was her name. She had an advanced degree in accountancy and she was preparing a doctorate in some branch of mathematics none of the men were familiar with. She was about thirty-two. Her hair was glossy and dark; she wore it in braids that became a rich mahogany color when they caught the light. I admired her hair, but the rest of her was angry-looking—flushed cheeks, red hands and arms. The scarf around her throat looked as though it had been wound and tied in a fury. She tossed a paper on my desk and said, "Check this. I'm in a hurry." Chief Engineer looked up, looked at her, looked down. A play within the play, a subplot, came to life; I felt it exactly as children can sense a situation they have no name for. In the afternoon she said, "Haven't you done that yet?" She had a positive, hammering sort of voice. It must have carried as far as the portraits in the hall. Chief Engineer unrolled a large map showing the mineral resources of eastern Canada and got behind it. Mrs. Ireland called, to the room in general, "Well, is she supposed to be working for me or isn't she?" Oh? I opened the bottom drawer of my desk, unlocked the middle drawer, began to pack up my personal affairs. I saw that I'd need a taxi: I had about three pounds of manuscripts and notes, and what seemed to amount to a wardrobe. In those days girls wore white gloves to work; I had two extra pairs of these, and a makeup kit, and extra shoes. I began filling my wastebasket with superfluous cargo. The room had gone silent: I can still see Bertie Knox's ratty little eyes judging, summing up, taking the measure of this new force. Mr. Tracy, in his mauve glasses, hands in his pockets, came strolling out of his office; it was a sort of booth, with frosted-glass panels that did not go up to the ceiling. He must have heard the shouting and then the quiet. He and Mr. Curran and Mr. Elwitt, the diabetic one, were higher in rank than Chief Engineer, higher than Office Manager; they could have eaten Supervisor for tea and no one would dare complain. He came along easily—I never knew him to rush. I remember now that Chief Engineer called him "Young Tracy," because of his father; "Old Tracy"—the real Tracy, so to speak—was the one who'd gone bust in the Depression. That was why Young Tracy had this job. He wasn't all that qualified, really; not so different from me. He sat down on Bertie Knox's desk with his back to him.

"Well, bolshie," he said to me. This was a long joke: it had to do with my political views, as he saw them, and it was also a reference to a character in an English comic called "Pip and

Squeak" that he and I had both read as children—we'd discussed it once. Pip and Squeak were a dog and a penguin. They had a son called Wilfred, who was a rabbit. Bolshie seemed to be a sort of acquaintance. He went around carrying one of those round black bombs with a sputtering fuse. He had a dog, I think—a dog with whiskers. I had told Mr. Tracy how modern educators were opposed to "Pip and Squeak." They thought that more than one generation of us had been badly misled by the unusual family unit of dog, penguin, and rabbit. It was argued that millions of children had grown up believing that if a dog made advances to a female penguin she would produce a rabbit. "Not a *rabbit*," said Mr. Tracy reasonably. "*Wilfred*."

I truly liked him. He must have thought I was going to say something now, if only to rise to the tease about "bolshie," but I was in the grip of that dazzling anger that is a form of snow blindness, too. I could not speak, and anyway didn't want to. I could only go on examining a pencil to see if it was company property or mine—as if that mattered. "Are you taking the day off or trying to leave me?" he said. I can feel that tense listening of men pretending to work. "I was looking over your application form," he said. "D'you know that your father knew my father? Yep. A long time ago. My father took it into his head to commission a mural for a plant in Sorel. Brave thing to do. Nobody did anything like that. Your father said it wasn't up his street. Suggested some other guy. My old man took the *two* of them down to Sorel. Did a lot of clowning around, but the Depression was just starting, so the idea fell through. My old man enjoyed it, though."

"Clowning around" could not possibly have been my father, but then the whole thing was so astonishing. "I should have mentioned it to you when you first came in," he said, "but I didn't realize it myself. There must be a million people called Muir; I happened to be looking at your form because apparently you're due for a raise." He whistled something for a second or two, then laughed and said, "Nobody ever quits around here. It can't be done. It upsets the delicate balance between labor and government. You don't want to do that. What do you want to do that for?"

"Mr. Curran doesn't like me."

"Mr. Curran is a brilliant man," he said. "Why, if you knew Curran's whole story you'd"—he paused—"you'd stretch out the hand of friendship."

"I've been asking and asking for a chair that doesn't wobble."

"Take the day off," he said. "Go to a movie or something. Tomorrow we'll start over." His life must have been like that. "You know, there's a war on. We're all needed. Mrs. Ireland has been brought here from . . ."

"From Trahnah," said Mrs. Ireland.

"Yes, from Toronto, to do important work. I'll see something gets done about that chair."

He stood up, hands in his pockets, slouching, really; gave an affable nod all round. The men didn't see; their noses were almost touching their work. He strolled back to his glass cubicle, whistling softly. The feeling in the room was like the sight of a curtain raised by the wind now sinking softly.

"Oh, Holy Hannah!" Mrs. Ireland burst out. "I thought this was supposed to be a wartime agency!"

No one replied. *My father knew your father. I'll see something gets done about that chair.* So that is how it works among men. To be noted, examined, compared.

Meanwhile I picked up the paper she'd tossed on my desk hours before and saw that it was an actuarial equation. I waited until the men had stopped being aware of us and took it over and told her I could not read it, let alone check it. It had obviously been some kind of test.

She said, "Well, it was too much to hope for. I have to single-handedly work out some wartime overtime pensions plan taking into account the cost of living and the earnest hope that the Canadian dollar won't sink." And I was to have been her assistant. I began to admire the genius someone—Assistant Chief Engineer Macaulay, perhaps—had obviously seen in me. Mrs. Ireland went on, "I gather after this little comic opera we've just witnessed that you're the blue-eyed girl around here." (Need I say that I'd hear this often? That the rumor I was Mr. Tracy's mistress now had firm hold on the feminine element in the room—though it never gained all the men—particularly on the biddies, the two or three old girls loafing along to retirement, in comfortable corsets that gave them a sort of picket fence around the middle? That the obscene anonymous notes I sometimes found on my desk—and at once unfairly blamed on Bertie Knox—were the first proof I had that prolonged virginity can be the mother of invention?) "You can have your desk put next to mine," said Mrs. Ireland. "I'll try to dig some good out of you."

But I had no intention of being mined by Mrs. Ireland. Remembering what Mr. Tracy had said about the hand of friendship I told her, truthfully, that it would be a waste for her and for me. My name was down to do documentary-film work, for which I thought I'd be better suited; I was to be told as soon as a vacancy occurred.

"Then you'll have a new girl," I said. "You can teach her whatever you like."

"*Girl!*" She could not keep her voice down, ever. "There'll not be a girl in this office again, if I have a say. Girls make me sick, sore, and weary."

I thought about that for a long time. I had believed it was only because of the men that girls were parked like third-class immigrants at the far end of the room—the darkest part, away from the windows—with the indignity of being watched by Supervisor, whose whole function was just that. But there, up on the life raft, stepping on girls' fingers, was Mrs. Ireland, too. If that was so, why didn't Mrs. Ireland get along with the men, and why did they positively and openly hate her—openly especially after Mr. Tracy's extraordinary and instructive sorting out of power?

"What blinking idiot would ever marry *her*?" said Bertie Knox. "Ten to one she's not married at all. Ireland must be her maiden name. She thinks the 'Mrs.' sounds good." I began to wonder if she was not a little daft sometimes: She used to talk to herself; quite a lot of it was about me.

"You can't run a wartime agency with *that* going on," she'd say loudly. "That" meant poor Mr. Tracy and me. Or else she would declare that it was unpatriotic of me to be drawing a man's salary. Here I think the men agreed. The salary was seventy-five dollars a month, which was less than a man's if he was doing the same work. The men had often hinted it was a lot for a girl. Girls had no expenses; they lived at home. Money paid them was a sort of handout. When I protested that I had the same expenses as any bachelor and did not live at home, it was countered by a reasonable "Where you live is up to you." They looked on girls as parasites of a kind, always being taken to restaurants and fed by men. They calculated the cost of probable outings, even to the Laura Secord chocolates I might be given, and rang the total as a casual profit to me. Bertie Knox used to sing, "I think that I shall never see a dame refuse a meal that's free." Mrs. Ireland said that all this money would be better spent on soldiers who were dying, on buying war bonds and plasma, on the purchase of tanks and Spitfires. "When I think of parents scrimping to send their sons to college!" she would conclude. All this was floods of clear water; I could not give it a shape. I kept wondering what she expected me to *do*, for that at least would throw a shadow on the water, but then she dropped me for a time in favor of another crusade, this one against Bertie Knox's singing. He had always sung. His voice conveyed rakish parodies of hymns and marches to every corner of the room. Most of the songs were well known; they came back to us from the troops, were either simple and rowdy or expressed a deep skepticism about the war, its aims and purposes, the way it was being conducted, and about the girls they had left at home. It was hard to shut Bertie Knox up: He had been around for a long time. Mrs. Ireland said she had not had the education she'd had to come here and listen to foul language. Now absolutely and flatly forbidden by Chief Engineer to sing any ribald song *plainly*, Bertie Knox managed with umptee-um syllables as best he could. He became Mrs. Ireland's counterpoint.

"I know there's a shortage of men," Mrs. Ireland would suddenly burst out.

"Oh umptee tum titty," sang Bertie Knox.

"And that after this war it will be still worse. . . ."

"Ti umpty dum diddy."

"There'll hardly be a man left in the world worth his salt. . . ."

"Tee umpty tum tumpty."

"But what I do not see . . ."

"Tee diddle dee dum."

"Is why a totally unqualified girl . . ."

"Tum tittle umpty tumpty."

"Should be subsidized by the taxpayers of this country . . ."

"Pum pum tee umpty pumpee."

"Just because her father failed to paint . . ."

"Oh umpty tumpty tumpty."

"A mural down in . . ."

"Tee umpty dum dum."

"Sorel."

"Tum tum, oh, dum dum, oh, pum pum, oh, oh, uuuum."

"Subsidized" stung, for I worked hard. Having no training I had no shortcuts. There were few mechanical shortcuts of any kind. The engineers used slide rules, and the machines might baffle today because of their simplicity. As for a computer, I would not have guessed what it might do or even look like. Facts were recorded on paper and stored in files and summarized by doing sums and displayed in some orderly fashion on graphs. I sat with one elbow on my desk, my left hand concealed in my hair. No one could see that I was counting on my fingers, in units of five and ten. The system by twelves would have finished me; luckily no one mentioned it. Numbers were a sunken world; they were a seascape from which perfect continents might emerge at any minute. I never saw more than their outline. I was caught on Zero. If zero meant Zero, how could you begin a graph on nothing? How could anything under zero be anything but Zero too? I spoke to Mr. Tracy: What occupied the space between Zero and One? It must be something arbitrary, not in the natural order of numbers. If One was solid ground, why not begin with One? Before One there was what? Thin air? Thin air must be Something. He said kindly, "Don't worry your head," and if I had continued would certainly have added, "Take the day off." Chief Engineer McCreery often had to remind me, "But we're not *paying* you to think!" If that was so, were we all being paid not to think? At the next place I worked things were even worse. It was another government agency, called Dominion Film Center—my first brush with the creative life. Here one was handed a folded thought like a shapeless school uniform and told, "There, wear that." Everyone had it on, regardless of fit. It was one step on: "We're not paying you to think about whatever you are thinking." I often considered approaching Mrs. Ireland, but she would not accept even a candy from me, let alone a question. "There's a war on" had been her discouraging refusal of a Life Saver once.

The men by now had found out about her husband. He had left school at Junior Fourth (Grade Seven) and "done nothing to improve himself." He was a Pole. She was ashamed of having a name that ended in "ski" and used her maiden name; Bertie Knox hadn't been far off. Thinking of it now, I realize she might not have been ashamed but only aware that the "ski" name on her application could have relegated it to a bottom drawer. Where did the men get their information, I wonder. Old "ski" was a lush who drank her paycheck and sometimes beat her up; the scarves she wound around her neck were meant to cover bruises.

That she was unhappily married I think did not surprise me. What impressed me was that so many of the men were too. I had become engaged to be married, for the third time. There was a slight overlapping of two, by which I mean that the one in Halifax did not know I was also going to marry the one from the West. To the men, who could not follow my life as closely as they'd have wanted—I gave out next to nothing—it seemed like a long betrothal to some puppy in uniform, whom they had never seen, and whose Christian name kept changing. One of my reasons for discretion was that I was still underage. Until now I had been using my minority as an escape hatch, the way a married man will use his wife—for "Ursula will never divorce" I substituted "My mother will never consent." Once I had made up my mind I simply began looking for roads around the obstacle; it was this search, in fact, that made me realize I must be serious. No one, no one at all, knew what I was up to, or what my entirely apocryphal emancipation would consist of; all that the men knew was that this time it did look as if I was going through with it. They took me aside, one after the other, and said, "Don't do it, Linnet. Don't do it." Bertie Knox said, "Once you're in it, you're in it, kiddo." I can't remember any man ever criticizing his own wife—it is something men don't often do, anywhere—but the warning I had was this: Marriage was a watershed that transformed sweet, cheerful, affectionate girls into, well, their own mothers. Once a girl had caught (their word) a husband she became a whiner, a snooper, a killjoy, a wet blanket, a grouch, and a bully. What I gleaned out of this was that it seemed hard on the men. But then even Mrs. Ireland, who never said a word to me, declared, "I think it's terrible." She said it was insane for me to marry someone on his way overseas, to tie up my youth, to live like a widow without a widow's moral status. Why were she and I standing together, side by side, looking out the window at a gray sky, at pigeons, at a streetcar grinding up the steep street? We could never possibly have stood close, talking in low voices. And yet there she is; there I am with Mrs. Ireland. For once she kept her voice down. She looked out—not at me. She said the worst thing of all. Remembering it, I see the unwashed windowpane. She said, "Don't you girls ever know when you're well off? Now you've got no one to lie to you, to belittle you, to make a fool of you, to stab you in the back." But we were different—different ages, different women, two lines of a graph that could never cross.

Mostly when people say "I know exactly how I felt" it can't be true, but here I am sure—sure of Mrs. Ireland and the window and of what she said. The recollection has something to do with the blackest kind of terror, as stunning as the bolts of happiness that strike for no reason. This blackness, this darkening, was not wholly Mrs. Ireland, no; I think it had to do with the men, with squares and walls and limits and numbers. How do you stand if you stand upon Zero? What will the passage be like between Zero and One? And what will happen at One? Yes, what will happen?

VARIETIES OF EXILE

IN THE THIRD summer of the war I began to meet refugees. There were large numbers of them in Montreal—to me a source of infinite wonder. I could not get enough of them. They came straight out of the twilit Socialist-literary landscape of my reading and my desires. I saw them as prophets of a promised social order that was to consist of justice, equality, art, personal relations, courage, generosity. Each of them—Belgian, French, Catholic German, Socialist German, Jewish German, Czech—was a book I tried to read from start to finish. My dictionaries were films, poems, novels, Lenin, Freud. That the refugees tended to hate one another seemed no more than a deplorable accident. Nationalist pigheadedness, that chronic, wasting, and apparently incurable disease, was known to me only on Canadian terms and I did not always recognize its symptoms. Anything I could not decipher I turned into fiction, which was my way of untangling knots. At the office where I worked I now spent my lunch hour writing stories about people in exile. I tried to see Montreal as an Austrian might see it and to feel whatever he felt. I was entirely at home with foreigners, which is not surprising—the home was all in my head. They were the only people I had met until now who believed, as I did, that our victory would prove to be a tidal wave nothing could stop. What I did not know was how many of them hoped and expected their neighbors to be washed away too.

I was nineteen and for the third time in a year engaged to

be married. What I craved at this point was not love, or romance, or a life added to mine, but conversation, which was harder to find. I knew by now that a man in love does not necessarily have anything interesting to say: If he has, he keeps it for other men. Men in Canada did not talk much to women and hardly at all to young ones. The impetus of love—of infatuation, rather—brought on a kind of conversation I saw no reason to pursue. A remark such as "I can't live without you" made the speaker sound not only half-witted to me but almost truly, literally, insane. There is a girl in a Stefan Zweig novel who says to her lover, "Is that all?" I had pondered this carefully many years before, for I supposed it had something unexpected to do with sex. Now I gave it another meaning, which was that where women were concerned men were satisfied with next to nothing. If every woman was a situation, she was somehow always the same situation, and what was expected from the woman—the situation—was so limited it was insulting. I had a large opinion of what I could do and provide, yet it came down to "Is that all? Is that all you expect?" Being promised to one person after another was turning into a perpetual state of hesitation and refusal: I was not used to hesitating over anything and so I supposed I must be wrong. The men in my office had warned me of the dangers of turning into a married woman; if this caution affected me it was only because it coincided with a misgiving of my own. My private name for married women was Red Queens. They looked to me like the Red Queen in *Through the Looking-Glass*, chasing after other people and minding their business for them. To get out of the heat that summer I had taken a room outside Montreal in an area called simply "the Lakeshore." In those days the Lakeshore was a string of verdant towns with next to no traffic. Dandelions grew in the pavement cracks. The streets were thickly shaded. A fragrance I have never forgotten of mown grass and leaf smoke drifted from yard to yard. As I walked to my commuters' train early in the morning I saw kids still in their pajamas digging holes in the lawns and Red Queen wives wearing housecoats. They stuck their heads out of screen doors and yelled instructions—to husbands, to children, to dogs, to postmen, to a neighbor's child. How could I be sure I wouldn't sound that way—so shrill, so discontented? As for a family, the promise of children all stamped with the same face, cast in the same genetic mold, seemed a cruel waste of possibilities. I would never have voiced this to anyone, for it would have been thought unnatural, even monstrous. When I was very young, under seven, my plan for the future had been to live in every country of the world and have a child in each. I had confided it: With adult adroitness my listener led me on. How many children? Oh, one to a country. And what would you do with them? Travel in trains. How would they go to school? I hate schools. How will they learn to read and write, then? They'll know already. What would you live on? It will all be free. That's not very sensible, is it? Why not? As a result of this idyll, of my divulgence of it, I was kept under watch for a time and my pocket money taken away lest I save it up and sail to a tropical island (where because of the Swiss Family Robinson I proposed to begin) long before the onset of puberty. I think no one realized I had not even a nebulous idea of how children sprang to life. I merely knew two persons were required for a ritual I believed had to continue for nine months, and which I imagined in the nature of a long card game with mysterious rules. When I was finally "told"—accurately, as it turned out—I was offended at being asked to believe something so unreasonable, which could not be true because I had never come across it in books. This trust in the printed word seems all the more remarkable when I remember that I thought children's books were written by other children. Probably at nineteen I was still dim about relevant dates, plain facts, brass tacks, consistent reasoning. Perhaps I was still hoping for magic card games to short-circuit every sort of common sense—common sense is only an admission we don't know much. I know that I wanted to marry this third man but that I didn't want to be anybody's Red Queen.

The commuters on the Montreal train never spoke much to each other. The mystifying and meaningless "Hot enough for you?" was about the extent of it. If I noticed one man more than the anonymous others it was only because he looked so hopelessly English, so unable or unwilling to concede to anything, even the climate. Once, walking a few steps behind him, I saw him turn into the drive of a stone house, one of the few old French-Canadian houses in that particular town. The choice of houses seemed to me peculiarly English too—though not, of course, what French Canadians call "English," for that includes plain Canadians, Irish, Swedes, anything you like not natively French. I looked again at the house and at the straight back going along the drive. His wife was on her knees holding a pair of edging shears. He stopped to greet her. She glanced up and said something in a carrying British voice so wild and miserable, so resentful, so intensely disagreeable that it could not have been the tag end of a morning quarrel; no, it was the thunderclap of some new engagement. After a second he went on up the walk, and in another I was out of earshot. I was persuaded that he had seen me; I don't know why. I also thought it must have been humiliating for him to have had a witness.

Which of us spoke first? It could not have been him and it most certainly could not have been me. There must have been a collision, for there we are, speaking, on a station platform. It is early morning, already hot. I see once again, without surprise, that he is not dressed for the climate.

He said he had often wondered what I was reading. I said I was reading "all the Russians." He said I really ought to read Arthur Waley. I had never heard of Arthur Waley. Similar signaling takes place between galaxies rushing apart in the outer heavens. He said he would bring me a book by Arthur Waley the next day.

"Please don't. I'm careless with books. Look at the shape this one's in." It was the truth. "All the Russians" were being published in a uniform edition with flag-red covers, on grayish paper, with microscopic print. The words were jammed together; you could not have put a pin between the lines. It was one of those cheap editions I think we were supposed to be sending the troops in order to cheer them up. Left in the grass beside a tennis court *The Possessed* now curved like a shell. A white streak ran down the middle of the shell. The rest of the cover had turned pink. That was nothing, he said. All I needed to do was dampen the cover with a sponge and put a weight on the book. *The Wallet of Kai Lung* had been to Ceylon with him and had survived. Whatever bait "Ceylon" may have been caught nothing. Army? Civil service? I did not take it up. Anyway I thought I could guess.

"You'd better not bring a book for nothing. I don't always take this train."

He had probably noticed me every morning. The mixture of reserve and obstinacy that next crossed his face I see still. He smiled, oh, not too much: I'd have turned my back on a grin. He said, "I forgot to . . . Frank Cairns."

"Muir. Linnet Muir." Reluctantly.

The thing is, I knew all about him. He was, one, married and, two, too old. But there was also three: Frank Cairns was stamped, labeled, ticketed by his tie (club? regiment? school?); by his voice, manner, haircut, suit; by the impression he gave of being stranded in a jungle, waiting for a rescue party—from England, of course. He belonged to a species of British immigrant known as remittance men. Their obsolescence began on 3 September 1939 and by 8 May 1945 they were extinct. I knew about them from having had one in the family. Frank Cairns worked in a brokerage house—he told me later—but he probably did not need a job, at least not for a living. It must have been a way of ordering time, a flight from idleness, perhaps a means of getting out of the house.

The institution of the remittance man was British, its genesis a chemical structure of family pride, class insanity, and imperial holdings that seemed impervious to fission but in the end turned out to be more fragile than anyone thought. Like all superfluous and marginal persons, remittance men were characters in a plot. The plot began with a fixed scene, an immutable first chapter, which described a powerful father's taking umbrage at his son's misconduct and ordering him out of the country. The pound was then one to five dollars, and there were vast British territories everywhere you looked. Hordes of young men who had somehow offended their parents were shipped out, golden deportees, to Canada, South Africa, New Zealand, Singapore. They were reluctant pioneers, totally lacking any sense of adventure or desire to see that particular world. An income—the remittance—was provided on a standing banker's order, with one string attached: "Keep out of England." For the second chapter the plot allowed a choice of six crimes as reasons for banishment: Conflict over the choice of a profession—the son wants to be a tap dancer. Gambling and debts—he has been barred from Monte Carlo. Dud checks—"I won't press a charge, sir, but see that the young rascal is kept out of harm's way." Marriage with a girl from the wrong walk of life—"Young man, you have made your bed!" Fathering an illegitimate child: ". . . and broken your mother's heart." Homosexuality, if discovered: Too grave for even a lecture—it was a criminal offense.

This is the plot of the romance: This is what everyone repeated and what the remittance man believed of himself. Obviously, it is a load of codswallop. A man legally of age could marry the tattooed woman in a circus, be arrested for check-bouncing or for soliciting boys in Green Park, be obliged to recognize his by-blow and even to wed its mother, become a ponce or a professional wrestler, and still remain where he was born. All he needed to do was eschew the remittance and tell his papa to go to hell. Even at nineteen the plot was a story I wouldn't buy. The truth came down to something just as dramatic but boring to tell: a classic struggle for dominance with two protagonists—strong father, pliant son. It was also a male battle. No son was ever sent into exile by his mother, and no one has ever heard of a remittance *woman*. Yet daughters got into scrapes nearly as often as their brothers. Having no idea what money was, they ran up debts easily. Sometimes, out of ignorance of another sort, they dared to dispose of their own virginity, thus wrecking their value on the marriage market and becoming family charges for life. Accoucheurs had to be bribed to perform abortions; or else the daughters were dispatched to Austria and Switzerland to have babies they would never hear of again. A daughter's disgrace was long, expensive, and hard to conceal, yet no one dreamed of sending her thousands of miles away and forever: On the contrary, she became her father's unpaid servant, social secretary, dog walker, companion, sick nurse. Holding on to a daughter, dismissing a son were relatively easy: It depended on having tamely delinquent children, or a thunderous personality no child would dare to challenge, and on the weapon of money—bait or weapon, as you like.

Banished young, as a rule, the remittance man (the RM, in my private vocabulary) drifted for the rest of his life, never quite sounding or looking like anyone around him, seldom raising a family or pursuing an occupation (so much for the "choice of profession" legend)—remote, dreamy, bored. Those who never married often became low-key drunks. The remittance was usually ample without being handsome, but enough to keep one from doing a hand's turn; in any case few remittance men were fit to do much of anything, being well schooled but half educated, in that specifically English way, as well as markedly unaggressive and totally uncompetitive, which would have meant early death in the New World for anyone without an income. They were like children waiting for the school vacation so that they could go home, except that at home nobody wanted them: The nursery had been turned into a billiards room and Nanny dismissed. They were parted from mothers they rarely mentioned, whom in some way they blended with a Rupert Brooke memory of England, of the mother country, of the Old Country as everyone at home grew old. Often as not the payoff, the keep-away black-mail funds, came out of the mother's marriage settlement— out of the capital her own father had agreed to settle upon her unborn children during the wear and tear of Edwardian en-gagement negotiations. The son disgraced would never see more than a fixed income from this; he was cut off from a share of inheritance by his contract of exile. There were cases where the remittance ended abruptly with the mother's death, but that was considered a bad arrangement. Usually the allowance continued for the exile's lifetime and stopped when he died. No provision was made for his dependents, if he had them, and because of his own subject attitude to money he was unlikely to have made any himself. The in-come reverted to his sisters and brothers, to an estate, to a cat-and-dog hospital—whatever his father had decreed on some black angry day long before.

Whatever these sons had done their punishment was surely a cruel and singular one, invented for naughty children by a cosmic headmaster taking over for God: They were obliged to live over and over until they died the first separation from home, and the incomparable trauma of rejection. Yes, they were like children, perpetually on their way to a harsh school; they were eight years of age and sent "home" from India to childhoods of secret grieving among strangers. And this wound, this amputation, they would mercilessly inflict on their own children when the time came—on sons always, on daughters sometimes—persuaded that early heartbreak was right because it was British, hampered only by the financial limit set for banishment: It costs money to get rid of your young.

And how they admired their fathers, those helpless sons! They spoke of them with so much admiration, with such a depth of awe: Only in memory can such voices still exist, the calm English voice on a summer night—a Canadian night so alien to the speaker—insisting, with sudden firmness, with a pause between words, "My ... father ... once ... said ... to ... me ... ," and here would follow something utterly trivial, some advice about choosing a motorcar or training a dog. To the Canadian grandchildren the unknown grandfather was seven feet tall with a beard like George V, while the grandmother came through weepy and prissy and not very interesting. It was the father's Father, never met, never heard, who made Heaven and Earth and Eve and Adam. The father in Canada seemed no more than an apostle transmitting a paternal message from the Father in England—the Father of us all. It was, however, rare for a remittance man to marry, rarer still to have any children; how could he become a father when he had never stopped being a son?

If the scattered freemasonry of offspring the remittance man left behind, all adult to elderly now, had anything in common it must have been their degree of incompetence. They were raised to behave well in situations that might never occur, trained to become genteel poor on continents where even the concept of genteel poverty has never existed. They were brought up with plenty of books and music and private lessons, a nurse sometimes, in a household where certain small luxuries were deemed essential—a way of life that, in North America at least, was supposed to be built on a sunken concrete base of money; otherwise you were British con men, a breed of gypsy, and a bad example.

Now, your remittance man was apt to find this assumption quite funny. The one place he would never take seriously was the place he was in. The identification of prominent local families with the name of a product, a commodity, would be his running joke: "The Allseeds are sugar, the Bilges are coal, the Cumquats are cough medicine, the Doldrums are coffins, the Earwigs are saucepans, the Fustians are timber, the Grindstones are beer." But his young, once they came up against it, were bound to observe that their concrete base was the dandelion fluff of a banker's order, their commodity nothing but "life in England before 1914," which was not negotiable. Also, the constant, nagging "What does your father really *do*?" could amount to persecution.

"Mr. Bainwood wants to know what you do."

"Damned inquisitive of him."

Silence. Signs of annoyance. Laughter sometimes. Or something silly: "What do *you* do when you aren't asking questions?"

No remittance man's child that I know of ever attended a university, though care was taken over the choice of schools. There they would be, at eighteen and nineteen, the boys wearing raincoats in the coldest weather, the girls with their hair ribbons and hand-knits and their innocently irritating English voices, well read, musical, versed in history, probably because they had been taught that the past is better than now, and somewhere else better than here. They must have been the only English-Canadian children to speak French casually, as a matter of course. Untidy, unpunctual, imperially tactless, they drifted into work that had to be "interesting," "creative," never demeaning, and where—unless they'd had the advantage of a rough time and enough nous to draw a line against the past—they seldom lasted. There was one in every public relations firm, one to a radio station, two to a publisher—forgetting appointments, losing contracts, jamming typewriters, sabotaging telephones, apologizing in accents it would have taken elocution lessons to change, so strong had been paternal pressure against the hard Canadian r, not to mention other vocables:

"A-t-e is *et*, darling, not *ate*."

"I can't say *et*. Only farmers say it."

"Perhaps here, but you won't always be here."

Of course the children were guilt-drenched, wondering which of the six traditional crimes they ought to pin on their father, what his secret was, what his past included, why he had been made an outcast. The answer was quite often "Nothing, no reason," but it meant too much to be unraveled and knit up. The saddest were those unwise enough to look into the families who had caused so much inherited woe. For the family was often as not smaller potatoes than the children had thought, and their father's romantic crime had been just the inability to sit for an examination, to stay at a university, to handle an allowance, to gain a toehold in any profession, or even to decide what he wanted to do—an ineptitude so maddening to live with that the Father preferred to shell out forever rather than watch his heir fall apart before his eyes. The male line, then, was a ghost story. A mother's vitality would be needed to create ectoplasm, to make the ghost offspring visible. Unfortunately the exiles were apt to marry absent-minded women whose skirts are covered with dog hairs—the drooping, bewildered British-Canadian mouse, who counts on tea leaves to tell her "what will happen when Edward goes." None of us is ever saved entirely, but even an erratic and alarming maternal vitality could turn out to be better than none.

Frank Cairns was childless, which I thought wise of him. He had been to Ceylon, gone back to England with a stiff case of homesickness disguised as malaria, married, and been shipped smartly out again, this time to Montreal. He was a neat, I think rather a small, man, with a straight part in his hair and a quick, brisk walk. He noticed I was engaged. I did not reply. I told him I had been in New York, had come back about a year ago, and missed "different things." He seemed to approve. "You can't make a move here," he said more than once. I was not sure what he meant. If he had been only the person I have described I'd have started taking an earlier train to be rid of him. But Frank Cairns was something new, unique of his kind, and almost as good as a refugee, for he was a Socialist. At least he said he was. He said he had never voted anywhere but that if he ever in the future happened to be in England when there was an election he would certainly vote Labour. His Socialism did not fit anything else about him, and seemed to depend for its life on the memory of talks he'd once had with a friend whom he described as brilliant, philosophical, farseeing, and just. I thought, Like Christ, but did not know Frank Cairns well enough to say so. The non-believer I had become was sometimes dogged by the child whose nightly request had been "Gentle Jesus, meek and mild, look upon a little child," and I sometimes got into ferocious arguments with her, as well as with other people. I was too curious about Frank Cairns to wish to quarrel over religion— at any rate not at the beginning. He talked about his friend without seeming able to share him. He never mentioned his name. I had to fill in the blank part of this conversation without help; I made the friend a high-ranking civil servant in Ceylon, older than anyone—which might have meant forty-two—an intellectual revolutionary who could work the future out on paper, like arithmetic.

Wherever his opinions came from, Frank Cairns was the first person ever to talk to me about the English poor. They seemed to be a race, different in kind from other English. He showed me old copies of *Picture Post* he must have saved up from the Depression. In our hot summer train, where everyone was starched and ironed and washed and fed, we considered slum doorways and the faces of women at the breaking point. They looked like Lenin's "remnants of nations" except that there were too many of them for a remnant. I thought of my mother and her long preoccupation with the fate of the Scottsboro Boys. My mother had read and mooned and fretted about the Scottsboro case, while I tried to turn her attention to something urgent, such as that my school uniform was now torn in three places. It is quite possible that my mother had seldom seen a black except on railway trains. (If I say "black" it is only because it is expected. It was a rude and offensive term in my childhood and I would not have been allowed to use it. "Black" was the sort of thing South Africans said.) Had Frank Cairns actually seen those *Picture Post* faces, I wondered. His home, his England, was every other remittance man's—the one I called "Christopher-Robin-land" and had sworn to keep away from. He hated Churchill, I remember, but I was used to hearing that. No man who remembered the Dardanelles really trusted him. Younger men (I am speaking of the handful I knew who had any opinion at all) were not usually irritated by his rhetoric until they got into uniform.

Once in a book I lent him he found a scrap of paper on which I had written the title of a story I was writing, "The Socialist RM," and some scrawls in, luckily, a private shorthand of mine. A perilous moment: "remittance man" was a term of abuse all over the Commonwealth and Empire.

"What is it?" he asked. "Resident Magistrate?"

"It might be Royal Marine. Royal Mail. I honestly don't remember. I can't read my own writing sometimes." The last sentence was true.

His Socialism was unlike a Czech's or a German's; though he believed that one should fight hard for social change, there was a hopelessness about it, an almost moral belief that improving their material circumstances would get the downtrodden nowhere. At the same time, he thought the poor *were* happy, that they had some strange secret of happiness—

161

the way people often think all Italians are happy because they have large families. I wondered if he really believed that a man with no prospects and no teeth in his head was spiritually better off than Frank Cairns and why, in that case, Frank Cairns did not let him alone with his underfed children and his native good nature. This was a British left-wing paradox I was often to encounter later on. What it seemed to amount to was leaving people more or less as they were, though he did speak about basic principles and the spread of education. It sounded dull. I was Russian-minded; I read Russian books, listened to Russian music. After Russia came Germany and Central Europe—that was where the real mystery and political excitement lay. His Webbs and his Fabians were plodding and gray. I saw the men with thick mustaches, wearing heavy boots, sharing lumpy meals with moral women. In the books he brought me I continued to find his absent friend. He produced Housman and Hardy (I could not read either), Siegfried Sassoon and Edmund Blunden, H.G. Wells and Bernard Shaw. The friend was probably a Scot—Frank Cairns admired them. The Scots of Canada, to me, stood for all that was narrow, grasping, at a standstill. How I distrusted those granite bankers who thought it was sinful to smoke! I was wrong, he told me. The true Scots were full of poetry and political passion. I said, "Are you sure?" and turned his friend into a native of Aberdeen and a graduate from Edinburgh. I also began a new notebook: "Scottish Labour Party. Keir Hardie. Others." This was better than the Webbs but still not as good as Rosa Luxemburg.

It was Frank Cairns who said to me "Life has no point," without emphasis, in response to some ignorant assumption of mine. This was his true voice. I recall the sidelong glance, the lizard's eye that some men develop as they grow old or when they have too much to hide. I was no good with ages. I cannot place him even today. Early thirties, probably. What else did he tell me? That "Scotch" was the proper term and

"Scots" an example of a genteelism overtaking the original. That unless the English surmounted their class obsessions with speech and accent Britain would not survive in the world after the war. His remedy (or his friend's) was having everyone go to the same schools. He surprised me even more by saying, "I would never live in England, not as it is now."

"Where, then?"

"Nowhere. I don't know."

"What about Russia? They all go to the same schools."

"Good Lord," said Frank Cairns.

He was inhabited by a familiar who spoke through him, provided him with jolting outbursts but not a whole thought. Perhaps that silent coming and going was the way people stayed in each other's lives when they were apart. What Frank Cairns was to me was a curio cabinet. I took everything out of the cabinet, piece by piece, examined the objects, set them down. Such situations, riddled with ambiguity, I would blunder about with for a long time until I learned to be careful.

The husband of the woman from whom I rented my summer room played golf every weekend. On one of those August nights when no one can sleep and the sky is nearly bright enough to read by, I took to the backyard and found him trying to cool off with a glass of beer. He remembered he had offered to give me golf lessons. I did not wish to learn, but did not say so. His wife spoke up from a deck chair: "You've never offered to teach me, I notice." She then compounded the error by telling me everyone was talking about me and the married man on the train. The next day I took the Käthe Kollwitz prints down from the walls of my room and moved back to Montreal without an explanation. Frank Cairns and I met once more that summer to return some books. That was all. When he called me at my office late in November, I said, "Who?"

He came into the coffee shop at Windsor station, where I was waiting. He was in uniform. I had not noticed he was good-looking before. It was not something I noticed in men. He was a first lieutenant. I disapproved: "Couldn't they make you a private?"

"Too old," he said. "As it is I am too old for my rank." I thought he just meant he might be promoted faster because of that.

"You don't look old." I at once regretted this personal remark, the first he had heard from me. Indeed, he had shed most of his adult life. He must have seemed as young as this when he started out to Ceylon. The uniform was his visa to England; no one could shut him away now. His face was radiant, open: He was halfway there. This glimpse of a purpose astonished me; why should a uniform make the change he'd been unable to make alone? He was not the first soldier I saw transfigured but he was the first to affect me.

He kept smiling and staring at me. I hoped he was not going to make a personal remark in exchange for mine. He said, "That tam makes you look, I don't know, Canadian. I've always thought of you as English. I still think England is where you might be happy."

"I'm happy here. You said you'd never live there."

"It would be a good place for you," he said. "Well, well, we shall see."

He would see nothing. My evolution was like freaky weather then: A few months, a few weeks even, were the equivalent of long second thoughts later on. I was in a completely other climate. I no longer missed New York and "different things." I had become patriotic. Canadian patriotism is always anti-American in part, and feeds upon anecdotes. American tourists were beginning to arrive in Montreal looking for anything expensive or hard to find in the United States; when they could not buy rationed food such as meat and butter, or unrationed things such as nylon stockings (because they did not exist), they complained of ingratitude. This was because Canada was thought to be a recipient of American charity and on the other end of Lend-Lease. Canadians were, and are, enormously touchy. Great umbrage had been taken over a story that was going around in the States about Americans who had been soaked for black-market butter in Montreal; when they got back across the border they opened the package and found the butter stamped "Gift of the American People." This fable persisted throughout the war and turned up in print. An American friend saw it in, I think, Westbrook Pegler's column and wrote asking me if it was true. I composed a letter I meant to send to *The New York Times*, demolishing the butter story. I kept rewriting and reshaping it, trying to achieve a balance between crippling irony and a calm review of events. I never posted it, finally, because my grandmother appeared to me in a dream and said that only fools wrote to newspapers.

Our coffee was tepid, the saucers slopped. He complained, and the waitress asked if we knew there was a war on. "Christ, what a bloody awful country this is," he said.

I wanted to say, "Then why are you with a Canadian regiment?" I provided my own answer: "They pay more than the Brits." We were actually quarreling in my head, and on such a mean level. I began to tear up a paper napkin and to cry.

"I have missed you," he remarked, but quite happily; you could tell the need for missing was over. I had scarcely thought of him at all. I kept taking more and more napkins out of the container on the table and blotting my face and tearing the paper up. He must be the only man I ever cried about in a public place. I hardly knew him. He was not embarrassed, as a Canadian would have been, but looked all the happier. The glances we got from other tables were full of understanding. Everything gave the wrong impression—his uniform, my engagement ring, my tears. I told him I was going to be married.

"Nonsense," he said.

"I'm serious."

"You seem awfully young."

"I'll soon be twenty." A slip. I had told him I was older. It amazed me to remember how young I had been only the summer before. "But I won't actually be a married woman," I said, "because I hate everything about them. Another thing I won't be and that's the sensitive housewife—the one who listens to Brahms while she does the ironing and reads all the new books still in their jackets."

"No, don't be a sensitive housewife," he said.

He gave me *The Wallet of Kai Lung* and *Kai Lung's Golden Hours*, which had been in Ceylon with him and had survived.

Did we write to each other? That's what I can't remember. I was careless then; I kept moving on. Also I really did, that time, get married. My husband was posted three days afterward to an American base in the Aleutian Islands—I have forgotten why. Eight months later he returned for a brief embarkation leave and then went overseas. I had dreaded coming in to my office after my wedding for fear the men I worked with would tease me. But the mixture of war and separation recalled old stories of their own experiences, in the First World War. Also I had been transformed into someone with a French surname, which gave them pause.

"Does he—uh—speak any French?"

"Not a word. He's from the West." Ah. "But he ought to. His father is French." Oh.

I had disappeared for no more than four days, but I was Mrs. Something now, not young Linnet. They spoke about me as "she," and not "Linnet" or "the kid." I wondered what they saw when they looked at me. In every head bent over a desk or a drawing board there was an opinion about women; expressed, it sounded either prurient or coarse, but I still cannot believe that is all there was to it. I know I shocked them profoundly once by saying that a wartime ditty popular with the troops, "Rock me to sleep, Sergeant-Major, tuck me in my little bed," was innocently homosexual. That I could have such a turn of thought, that I could use such an expression, that I even knew it existed seemed scandalous to them. "You read too damned much," I was told. Oddly enough, they had never minded my hearing any of the several versions of the song, some of which were unspeakable; all they objected to was my unfeminine remark. When I married they gave me a suitcase, and when I left for good they bought me a Victory Bond. I had scrupulously noted every detail of the office, and the building it was in, yet only a few months later I would walk by it without remembering I had ever been inside, and it occurs to me only now that I never saw any of them again.

I was still a minor, but emancipated by marriage. I did not need to ask parental consent for anything or worry about being brought down on the wing. I realized how anxious I had been once the need for that particular anxiety was over. A friend in New York married to a psychiatrist had sent me a letter saying I had her permission to marry. She did not describe herself as a relative or state anything untrue—she just addressed herself to whom it may concern, said that as far as *she* was concerned I could get married, and signed. She did not tell her husband, in case he tried to put things right out of principle, and I mentioned to no one that the letter was legal taradiddle and carried about as much weight as a library card. I mention this to show what essential paperwork sometimes amounts to. My husband, aged twenty-four, had become my legal guardian under Quebec's preposterous Napoleonic law, but he never knew that. When he went overseas he asked me not to join any political party, which I hadn't thought of doing, and not to enlist in the Army or the Air Force. The second he vanished I tried to join the Wrens, which had not been on the list only because it slipped his mind. Joining one of the services had never been among my plans and projects—it was he who accidentally put the idea in my head. I now decided I would turn up overseas, having made it there on my own, but I got no further than the enlistment requirements, which included "... of the white race only." This barrier turned out to be true of nearly all the navies of the Commonwealth countries. I supposed everyone must have wanted it that way, for I never heard it questioned. I was only beginning to hear the first rumblings of hypocrisy on our side—the right side; the wrong side seemed to be guilty of every sin humanly possible except simulation of virtue. I put the blame for the racial barrier on Churchill, who certainly *knew*, and had known since the First World War; I believed that Roosevelt, Stalin, Chiang Kai-shek, and de Gaulle did not know, and that should it ever come to their attention they would be as shocked as I was.

Instead of enlisting I passed the St. John Ambulance first-aid certificate, which made me a useful person in case of total war. The Killed-Wounded-Missing columns of the afternoon paper were now my daily reading. It became a habit so steadfast that I would automatically look for victims even after the war ended. The summer of the Scottish Labour Party, Keir Hardie, and Others fell behind, as well as a younger, discarded Linnet. I lighted ferocious autos-da-fé. Nothing could live except present time. In the ever-new present I read one day that Major Francis Cairns had died of wounds in Italy. Who remembers now the shock of the known name? It was like a flat white light. One felt apart from everyone, isolated. The field of vision drew in. Then, before one could lose consciousness, vision expanded, light and shadow moved, voices pierced through. One's heart, which had stopped, beat hard enough to make a room shudder. All this would occupy about a second. The next second was inhabited by disbelief. I saw him in uniform, so happy, halfway there, and myself making a spectacle of us, tearing a paper napkin. I was happy for him that he would never need to return to the commuting train and the loneliness and be forced to relive his own past. I wanted to write a casual letter saying so. One's impulse was always to write to the dead. Nobody knew I knew him, and in Canada it was not done to speak of the missing. I forgot him. He went under. I was doing a new sort of work and sharing a house with another girl whose husband was also overseas. Montreal had become a completely other city. I was no longer attracted to refugees. They were going through a process called "integrating." Some changed their names. Others applied for citizenship. A refugee eating cornflakes was of no further interest. The house I now lived in contained a fireplace, in which I burned all my stories about Czech and German anti-Fascists. In the picnic hamper I used for storing journals and notebooks I found a manila envelope marked "Lakeshore." It contained several versions of "The Socialist RM" and a few other things that sounded as if they were translated from the Russian by Constance Garnett. I also found a brief novel I had no memory of having written, about a Scot from Aberdeen, a left-wing civil servant in Ceylon—a man from somewhere, living elsewhere, confident that another world was entirely possible, since he had got it all down. It had shape, density, voice, but I destroyed it too. I never felt guilt about forgetting the dead or the living, but I minded about that one manuscript for a time. All this business of putting life through a sieve and then discarding it was another variety of exile; I knew that even then, but it seemed quite right and perfectly natural.

1933

ABOUT A YEAR after the death of M. Carette, his three survivors—Berthe and her little sister, Marie, and their mother—
had to leave the comfortable flat over the furniture store in
Rue Saint-Denis and move to a smaller place. They were not
destitute: There was the insurance and the money from the
sale of the store, but the man who had bought the store from
the estate had not yet paid and they had to be careful.

Some of the lamps and end tables and upholstered chairs
were sent to relatives, to be returned when the little girls
grew up and got married. The rest of their things were carried
by two small, bent men to the second floor of a stone house
in Rue Cherrier near the Institute for the Deaf and Dumb.
The men used an old horse and an open cart for the removal.
They told Mme. Carette that they had never worked outside
that quarter; they knew only some forty streets of Montreal
but knew them thoroughly. On moving day, soft snow, like
graying lace, fell. A patched tarpaulin protected the Carettes'
wine-red sofa with its border of silk fringe, the children's
brass bedstead, their mother's walnut bed with the carved
scallop shells, and the round oak table, smaller than the old
one, at which they would now eat their meals. Mme. Carette
told Berthe that her days of entertaining and cooking for
guests were over. She was just twenty-seven.

They waited for the moving men in their new home, in
scrubbed, empty rooms. They had already spread sheets of *La
Presse* over the floors, in case the men tracked in snow. The

curtains were hung, the cream-colored blinds pulled halfway down the sash windows. Coal had been delivered and was piled in the lean-to shed behind the kitchen. The range and the squat, round heater in the dining room issued tidal waves of dense metallic warmth.

The old place was at no distance. Parc Lafontaine, where the children had often been taken to play, was just along the street. By walking an extra few minutes, Mme. Carette could patronize the same butcher and grocer as before. The same horse-drawn sleighs would bring bread, milk, and coal to the door. Still, the quiet stone houses, the absence of heavy traffic and shops made Rue Cherrier seem like a foreign country.

Change, death, absence—the adult mysteries—kept the children awake. From their new bedroom they heard the clang of the first streetcar at dawn—a thrilling chord, metal on metal, that faded slowly. They would have jumped up and dressed at once, but to their mother this was still the middle of the night. Presently, a new, continuous sound moved in the waking streets, like a murmur of leaves. From the confused rustle broke distinct impressions: an alarm clock, a man speaking, someone's radio. Marie wanted to talk and sing. Berthe had to invent stories to keep her quiet. Once she had placed her hand over Marie's mouth and been cruelly bitten.

They slept on a horsehair mattress, which had a summer and a winter side, and was turned twice a year. The beautiful stitching at the edge of the sheets and pillows was their mother's work. She had begun to sew her trousseau at the age of eleven; her early life was spent in preparation for a wedding. Above the girls' bed hung a gilt crucifix with a withered spray of box hedge that passed for the Easter palms of Jerusalem.

Marie was afraid to go to the bathroom alone after dark. Berthe asked if she expected to see their father's ghost, but Marie could not say: She did not yet know whether a ghost and the dark meant the same thing. Berthe was obliged to get up at night and accompany her along the passage. The hall light shone out of a blue glass tulip set upon a column painted to look like marble. Berthe could just reach it on tiptoe; Marie not at all.

Marie would have left the bathroom door open for company, but Berthe knew that such intimacy was improper. Although her First Communion was being delayed because Mme. Carette wanted the two sisters to come to the altar together, she had been to practice confession. Unfortunately, she had soon run out of invented sins. Her confessor seemed to think there should be more: He asked if she and her little sister had ever been in a bathroom with the door shut, and warned her of grievous fault.

On their way back to bed, Berthe unhooked a calendar on which was a picture of a family of rabbits riding a toboggan. She pretended to read stories about the rabbits and presently both she and Marie fell asleep.

They never saw their mother wearing a bathrobe. As soon as Mme. Carette got up she dressed herself in clothes that were in the colors of half mourning—mauve, dove gray. Her fair hair was brushed straight and subdued under a net. She took a brush to everything—hair, floors, the children's elbows, the kitchen chairs. Her scent was of Baby's Own soap and Florida Water. When she bent to kiss the children, a cameo dangled from a chain. She trained the girls not to lie, or point, or gobble their food, or show their legs above the knee, or leave fingerprints on windowpanes, or handle the parlor curtains—the slightest touch could crease the lace, she said. They learned to say in English, "I don't understand" and "I don't know" and "No, thank you." That was all the English anyone needed between Rue Saint-Denis and Parc Lafontaine.

In the dining room, where she kept her sewing machine, Mme. Carette held the treadle still, rested a hand on the stopped wheel. "What are you doing in the parlor?" she called. "Are you touching the curtains?" Marie had been spitting on the window and drawing her finger through the spit. Berthe, trying to clean the mess with her flannelette petticoat, said, "Marie's just been standing here saying 'Saint Marguerite, pray for us.' "

Downstairs lived M. Grosjean, the landlord, with his Irish wife and an Airedale named Arno. Arno understood English and French; Mme. Grosjean could only speak English. She loved Arno and was afraid he would run away: He was a restless dog who liked to be doing something all the time. Sometimes M. Grosjean took him to Parc Lafontaine and they played at retrieving a collapsed and bitten tennis ball. Arno was trained to obey both *"Cherchez!"* and "Go fetch it!" but he paid attention to neither. He ran with the ball and Mme. Grosjean had to chase him.

Mme. Grosjean stood outside the house on the back step, just under the Carettes' kitchen window, holding Arno's supper. She wailed, "Arno, where have you got to?" M. Grosjean had probably taken Arno for a walk. He made it a point never to say where he was going: He did not think it a good thing to let women know much.

Mme. Grosjean and Mme. Carette were the same age, but they never became friends. Mme. Carette would say no more than a few negative things in English ("No, thank you" and "I don't know" and "I don't understand") and Mme. Grosjean could not work up the conversation. Mme. Carette had a word with Berthe about Irish marriages: An Irish marriage, while not to be sought, need not be scorned. The Irish were not English. God had sent them to Canada to keep people from marrying Protestants.

That winter the girls wore white leggings and mittens, knitted by their mother, and coats and hats of white rabbit fur. Each of them carried a rabbit muff. Marie cried when Berthe had to go to school. On Sunday afternoons they played with Arno and M. Grosjean. He tried to take their picture but it wasn't easy. The girls stood on the front steps, hand in hand, mitten to mitten, while Arno was harnessed to a sled with curved runners. The red harness had once been worn by another Airedale, Ruby, who was smarter even than Arno.

M. Grosjean wanted Marie to sit down on the sled, hold the reins, and look sideways at the camera. Marie clung to Berthe's coat. She was afraid that Arno would bolt into the Rue Saint-Denis, where there were streetcars. M. Grosjean lifted her off the sled and tried the picture a different way, with Berthe pretending to drive and Marie standing face-to-face with Arno. As soon as he set Marie on her feet, she began to scream. Her feet were cold. She wanted to be carried. Her nose ran; she felt humiliated. He got out his handkerchief, checked green and white, and wiped her whole face rather hard.

Just then his wife came to the front door with a dish of macaroni and cut-up sausages for Arno. She had thrown a sweater over her cotton housecoat; she was someone who never felt the cold. A gust of wind lifted her loose hair. M. Grosjean told her that the kid was no picnic. Berthe, picking up English fast, could not have repeated his exact words, but she knew what they meant.

Mme. Carette was still waiting for the money from the sale of the store. A brother-in-law helped with the rent, sending every month a generous postal order from Fall River. It was Mme. Carette's belief that God would work a miracle, allowing her to pay it all back. In the meantime, she did fine sewing. Once she was hired to sew a trousseau, working all day in the home of the bride-to-be. As the date of the wedding drew near she had to stay overnight.

Mme. Grosjean looked after the children. They sat in her front parlor, eating fried-egg sandwiches and drinking cream soda (it did not matter if they dropped crumbs) while she played a record of a man singing, "Dear one, the world is waiting for the sunrise."

Berthe asked, in French, "What is he saying?" Mme. Grosjean answered in English, "A well-known Irish tenor."

When Mme. Carette came home the next day, she gave the girls a hot bath, in case Mme. Grosjean had neglected their elbows and heels. She took Berthe in her arms and said she must never tell anyone their mother had left the house to sew for strangers. When she grew up, she must not refer to her mother as a seamstress, but say instead, "My mother was clever with her hands."

That night, when they were all three having supper in the kitchen, she looked at Berthe and said, "You have beautiful hair." She sounded so tired and stern that Marie, eating mashed potatoes and gravy, with a napkin under her chin, thought Berthe must be getting a scolding. She opened her mouth wide and started to howl. Mme. Carette just said, "Marie, don't cry with your mouth full."

Downstairs, Mme. Grosjean set up her evening chant, calling for Arno. "Oh, where have you got to?" she wailed to the empty backyard.

"The dog is the only thing keeping those two together," said Mme. Carette. "But a dog isn't the same as a child. A dog doesn't look after its masters in their old age. We shall see what happens to the marriage after Arno dies." No sooner had she said this than she covered her mouth and spoke through her fingers: "God forgive my unkind thoughts." She propped her arms on each side of her plate, as the girls were forbidden to do, and let her face slide into her hands.

Berthe took this to mean that Arno was doomed. Only a calamity about to engulf them all could explain her mother's elbows on the table. She got down from her chair and tried to pull her mother's hands apart, and kiss her face. Her own tears ran into her long hair, down onto her starched piqué collar. She felt tears along her nose and inside her ears. Even while she sobbed out words of hope and comfort (Arno would never die) and promises of reassuring behavior (she and Marie would always be good) she wondered how tears could flow in so many directions at once.

Of course, M. Grosjean did not know that all the female creatures in his house were frightened and lonely, calling and weeping. He was in Parc Lafontaine with Arno, trying to play go-fetch-it in the dark.

THE CHOSEN HUSBAND

In 1949, a year that contained no other news of value, Mme. Carette came into a legacy of eighteen thousand dollars from a brother-in-law who had done well in Fall River. She had suspected him of being a Freemason, as well as of other offenses, none of them trifling, and so she did not make a show of bringing out his photograph; instead, she asked her daughters, Berthe and Marie, to mention him in their prayers. They may have, for a while. The girls were twenty-two and twenty, and Berthe, the elder, hardly prayed at all.

The first thing that Mme. Carette did was to acquire a better address. Until now she had kept the Montreal habit of changing her rented quarters every few seasons, a conversation with a landlord serving as warranty, rent paid in cash. This time she was summoned by appointment to a rental agency to sign a two-year lease. She had taken the first floor of a stone house around the corner from the church of Saint Louis de France. This was her old parish (she held to the network of streets near Parc Lafontaine) but a glorious strand of it, Rue Saint-Hubert.

Before her inheritance Mme. Carette had crept to church, eyes lowered; had sat where she was unlikely to disturb anyone whose life seemed more fortunate, therefore more deserving, than her own. She had not so much prayed as petitioned. Now she ran a glove along the pew to see if it was dusted, straightened the unread pamphlets that called for more vocations for missionary service in Africa, told a confessor that, like all the prosperous, she was probably without fault. When the holy-water font looked mossy, she called the parish priest and had words with his housekeeper, even though scrubbing the church was not her job. She still prayed every day for the repose of her late husband, and the unlikelier rest of his Freemason brother, but a tone of briskness caused her own words to rattle in her head. Church was a hushed annex to home. She prayed to insist upon the refinement of some request, and instead of giving thanks simply acknowledged that matters used to be worse.

Her daughter Berthe had been quick to point out that Rue Saint-Hubert was in decline. Otherwise, how could the Carettes afford to live here? (Berthe worked in an office and was able to pay half the rent.) A family of foreigners were installed across the road. A seamstress had placed a sign in a ground-floor window—a sure symptom of decay. True, but Mme. Carette had as near neighbors a retired opera singer and the first cousins of a city councillor—calm, courteous people who had never been on relief. A few blocks north stood the mayor's private dwelling, with a lamppost on each side of his front door. (During the recent war the mayor had been interned, like an enemy alien. No one quite remembered why. Mme. Carette believed that he had refused an invitation to Buckingham Palace, and that the English had it in for him. Berthe had been told that he had tried to annex Montreal to the state of New York and that someone had minded. Marie, who spoke to strangers on the bus, once came home with a story about Fascist views; but as she could not spell "Fascist," and did not know if it was a kind of landscape or something to eat, no one took her seriously. The mayor had eventually been released, was promptly reelected, and continued to add luster to Rue Saint-Hubert.)

Mme. Carette looked out upon long façades of whitish stone, windowpanes with beveled edges that threw rainbows. In her childhood this was how notaries and pharmacists had lived, before they began to copy the English taste for freestanding houses, blank lawns, ornamental willows, leashed dogs. She recalled a moneyed aunt and uncle, a family of well-dressed, soft-spoken children, heard the echo of a French more accurately expressed than her own. She had tried to imitate the peculiarity of every syllable, sounded like a plucked string, had tried to make her little girls speak that way. But they had rebelled, refused, said it made them laughed at.

When she had nothing to request, or was tired of repeating the same reminders, she shut her eyes and imagined her funeral. She was barely forty-five, but a long widowhood strictly observed had kept her childish, not youthful. She saw the rosary twined round her hands, the vigil, the candles perfectly still, the hillock of wreaths. Until the stunning message from Fall River, death had been her small talk. She had never left the subject, once entered, without asking, "And what will happen then to my poor little Marie?" Nobody had ever taken the question seriously except her Uncle Gildas. This was during their first Christmas dinner on Rue Saint-Hubert. He said that Marie should pray for guidance, the sooner the better. God had no patience with last-minute appeals. (Uncle Gildas was an elderly priest with limited social opportunities, though his niece believed him to have wide and worldly connections.)

"Prayer can fail," said Berthe, testing him.

Instead of berating her he said calmly, "In that case, Berthe can look after her little sister."

She considered him, old and eating slowly. His cassock exhaled some strong cleaning fluid—tetrachloride; he lived in a rest home, and nuns took care of him.

Marie was dressed in one of Berthe's castoffs—marine-blue velvet with a lace collar. Mme. Carette wore a gray-white dress Berthe thought she had seen all her life. In her first year of employment Berthe had saved enough for a dyed rabbit coat. She also had an electric seal, and was on her way to sheared raccoon. "Marie had better get married," she said.

Mme. Carette still felt cruelly the want of a husband, someone—not a daughter—to help her up the step of a streetcar, read *La Presse* and tell her what was in it, lay down the law to Berthe. When Berthe was in adolescence, laughing and whispering and not telling her mother the joke, Mme. Carette had asked Uncle Gildas to speak as a father. He sat in the parlor, in a plush chair, all boots and cassock, knees apart and a hand on each knee, and questioned Berthe about her dreams. She said she had never in her life dreamed anything. Uncle Gildas replied that anyone with a good conscience could dream events pleasing to God; he himself had been doing it for years. God kept the dreams of every living person on record, like great rolls of film. He could have them projected whenever he wanted. Montreal girls, notoriously virtuous, had his favor, but only up to a point. He forgave, but never forgot. He was the embodiment of endless time— though one should not take "embodiment" literally. Eternal remorse in a pit of flames was the same to him as a rap on the fingers with the sharp edge of a ruler. Marie, hearing this, had fainted dead away. That was the power of Uncle Gildas.

Nowadays, shrunken and always hungry, he lived in retirement, had waxed linoleum on his floor, no carpet, ate tapioca soup two or three times a week. He would have stayed in bed all day, but the nuns who ran the place looked upon illness as fatigue, fatigue as shirking. He was not tired or lazy; he had nothing to get up for. The view from his window was a screen of trees. When Mme. Carette came to visit—a long streetcar ride, then a bus—she had just the trees to look at: She could not stare at her uncle the whole time. The trees put out of sight a busy commercial garage. It might have distracted him to watch trucks backing out, perhaps to witness a bloodless accident. In the morning he went downstairs to the chapel, ate breakfast, sat on his bed after it was made. Or crossed the gleaming floor to a small table, folded back the oilcloth cover, read the first sentence of a memoir he was writing for his great-nieces: "I was born in Montreal, on the 22nd of May, 1869, of pious Christian parents, connected to Montreal families for whom streets and bridges have been named." Or shuffled out to the varnished corridor, where there was a pay phone. He liked dialing, but out of long discipline never did without a reason.

Soon after Christmas Mme. Carette came to see him, wearing Berthe's velvet boots with tassels, Berthe's dyed rabbit coat, and a feather turban of her own. Instead of praying for guidance Marie had fallen in love with one of the Greeks who were starting to move into their part of Montreal. There had never been a foreigner in the family, let alone a pagan. Her uncle interrupted to remark that Greeks were usually Christians, though of the wrong kind for Marie. Mme. Carette implored him to find someone, not a Greek, of the right kind: sober, established, Catholic, French-speaking, natively Canadian. "Not Canadian from New England," she said, showing a brief ingratitude to Fall River. She left a store of nickels, so that he could ring her whenever he liked.

Louis Driscoll, French in all but name, called on Marie for the first time on the twelfth of April, 1950. Patches of dirty snow still lay against the curb. The trees on Rue Saint-Hubert looked dark and brittle, as though winter had killed them at last. From behind the parlor curtain, unseen from the street, the Carette women watched him coming along from the bus stop. To meet Marie he had put on a beige tweed overcoat, loosely belted, a beige scarf, a bottle-green snap-brim fedora, crêpe-soled shoes, pigskin gloves. His trousers were sharply pressed, a shade darker than the hat. Under his left arm he held close a parcel in white paper, the size and shape of a two-pound box of Laura Secord chocolates. He stopped frequently to consult the house numbers (blue and white, set rather high, Montreal style), which he compared with a slip of paper brought close to his eyes.

It was too bad that he had to wear glasses; the Carettes were not prepared for that, or for the fringe of ginger hair below his hat. Uncle Gildas had said he was of distinguished appearance. He came from Moncton, New Brunswick, and was employed at the head office of a pulp-and-paper concern. His age was twenty-six. Berthe thought that he must be a failed seminarist; they were the only Catholic bachelors Uncle Gildas knew.

Peering at their front door, he walked into a puddle of slush. Mme. Carette wondered if Marie's children were going to be nearsighted. "How can we be sure he's the right man?" she said.

"Who else could he be?" Berthe replied. What did he want with Marie? Uncle Gildas could not have promised much in her name, apart from a pliant nature. There could never be a meeting in a notary's office to discuss a dowry, unless you counted some plates and furniture. The old man may have frightened Louis, reminded him that prolonged celibacy—except among the clergy—is displeasing to God. Marie is poor, he must have said, though honorably connected. She will feel grateful to you all her life.

Their front steps were painted pearl gray, to match the building stone. Louis's face, upturned, was the color of wood ash. Climbing the stair, ringing the front doorbell could change his life in a way he did not wholly desire. Probably he wanted a woman without sin or risk or coaxing or remorse; but did he want her enough to warrant setting up a household? A man with a memory as transient as his, who could read an address thirty times and still let it drift, might forget to come to the wedding. He crumpled the slip of paper, pushed it inside a tweed pocket, withdrew a large handkerchief, blew his nose.

Mme. Carette swayed back from the curtain as though a stone had been flung. She concluded some private thought by addressing Marie: "... although I will feel better on my deathbed if I know you are in your own home." Louis meanwhile kicked the bottom step, getting rid of snow stuck to his shoes. (Rustics kicked and stamped. Marie's Greek had wiped his feet.) Still he hesitated, sliding a last pale look in the direction of buses and streetcars. Then, as he might have turned a gun on himself, he climbed five steps and pressed his finger to the bell.

"Somebody has to let him in," said Mme. Carette.

"Marie," said Berthe.

"It wouldn't seem right. She's never met him."

He stood quite near, where the top step broadened to a small platform level with the window. They could have leaned out, introduced him to Marie. Marie at this moment seemed to think he would do; at least, she showed no sign of distaste, such as pushing out her lower lip or crumpling her chin. Perhaps she had been getting ready to drop her Greek: Mme. Carette had warned her that she would have to be a servant to his mother, and eat peculiar food. "He's never asked me to," said Marie, and that was part of the trouble. He hadn't asked anything. For her twenty-first birthday he had given her a locket on a chain and a box from Maitland's, the West End confectioner, containing twenty-one chocolate mice. "He loves me," said Marie. She kept counting the mice and would not let anyone eat them.

In the end it was Berthe who admitted Louis, accepted the gift of chocolates on behalf of Marie, showed him where to leave his hat and coat. She approved of the clean white shirt, the jacket of a tweed similar to the coat but lighter in weight, the tie with a pattern of storm-tossed sailboats. Before shaking hands he removed his glasses, which had misted over, and wiped them dry. His eyes meeting the bright evening at the window (Marie was still there, but with her back to the street) flashed ultramarine. Mme. Carette hoped Marie's children would inherit that color.

He took Marie's yielding hand and let it drop. Freed of the introduction, she pried open the lid of the candy box and said, distinctly, "No mice." He seemed not to hear, or may have thought she was pleased to see he had not played a practical joke. Berthe showed him to the plush armchair, directly underneath a chandelier studded with lightbulbs. From this chair Uncle Gildas had explained the whims of God; against its linen antimacassar the Greek had recently rested his head.

Around Louis's crêpe soles pools of snow water formed. Berthe glanced at her mother, meaning that she was not to mind; but Mme. Carette was trying to remember where Berthe had said that she and Marie were to sit. (On the sofa, facing Louis.) Berthe chose a gilt upright chair, from which she could rise easily to pass refreshments. These were laid out on a marble-topped console: vanilla wafers, iced sultana cake, maple fudge, marshmallow biscuits, soft drinks. Behind the sofa a large pier glass reflected Louis in the armchair and the top of Mme. Carette's head. Berthe could tell from her mother's posture, head tilted, hands clasped, that she was silently asking Louis to trust her. She leaned forward and asked him if he was an only child. Berthe closed her eyes. When she opened them, nothing had changed except that Marie was eating chocolates. Louis seemed to be reflecting on his status.

He was the oldest of seven, he finally said. The others were Joseph, Raymond, Vincent, Francis, Rose, and Claire. French was their first language, in a way. But, then, so was English. A certain Louis Joseph Raymond Driscoll, Irish, veteran of Waterloo on the decent side, proscribed in England and Ireland as a result, had come out to Canada and grafted on pure French stock a number of noble traits: bright, wavy hair, a talent for public speaking, another for social aplomb. In every generation of Driscolls, there had to be a Louis, a

Joseph, a Raymond. (Berthe and her mother exchanged a look. He wanted three sons.)

His French was slow and muffled, as though strained through wool. He used English words, or French words in an English way. Mme. Carette lifted her shoulders and parted her clasped hands as if to say, "Never mind, English is better than Greek." At least, they could be certain that the Driscolls were Catholic. In August his father and mother were making the Holy Year pilgrimage to Rome.

Rome was beyond their imagining, though all three Carettes had been to Maine and Old Orchard Beach. Louis hoped to spend a vacation in Old Orchard (in response to an ardent question from Mme. Carette), but he had more feeling for Quebec City. His father's people had entered Canada by way of Quebec.

"The French part of the family?" said Mme. Carette.

"Yes, yes," said Berthe, touching her mother's arm.

Berthe had been to Quebec City, said Mme. Carette. She was brilliant, reliable, fully bilingual. Her office promoted her every January. They were always sending her away on company business. She knew Plattsburgh, Saranac Lake. In Quebec City, at lunch at the Château Frontenac, she had seen well-known politicians stuffing down oysters and fresh lobster, at taxpayers' expense.

Louis's glance tried to cross Berthe's, as he might have sought out and welcomed a second man in the room. Berthe reached past Mme. Carette to take the candy box away from Marie. She nudged her mother with her elbow.

"The first time I ever saw Old Orchard," Mme. Carette resumed, smoothing the bodice of her dress, "I was sorry I had not gone there on my honeymoon." She paused, watching Louis accept a chocolate. "My husband and I went to Fall River. He had a brother in the lumber business."

At the mention of lumber, Louis took on a set, bulldog look. Berthe wondered if the pulp-and-paper firm had gone bankrupt. Her thoughts rushed to Uncle Gildas—how she would have it out with him, not leave it to her mother, if he had failed to examine Louis's prospects. But then Louis began to cough and had to cover his mouth. He was in trouble with a caramel. The Carettes looked away, so that he could strangle unobserved. "How dark it is," said Berthe, to let him think he could not be seen. Marie got up, with a hiss and rustle of taffeta skirt, and switched on the twin floor lamps with their cerise silk shades.

"There," she seemed to be saying to Berthe. "Have I done the right thing? Is this what you wanted?"

Louis still coughed, but weakly. He moved his fingers, like a child made to wave good-bye. Mme. Carette wondered how many contagious children's diseases he had survived; in a large family everything made the rounds. His eyes, perhaps seeking shade, moved across the brown wallpaper flecked with gold and stopped at the only familiar sight in the room—his reflection in the pier glass. He sat up straighter and quite definitely swallowed. He took a long drink of ginger ale. "When Irish eyes are smiling," he said, in English, as if to himself. "When Irish eyes are smiling. There's a lot to be said for that. A lot to be said."

Of course he was at a loss, astray in an armchair, with the Carettes watching like friendly judges. When he reached for another chocolate, they looked to see if his nails were clean. When he crossed his legs, they examined his socks. They were fixing their first impression of the stranger who might take Marie away, give her a modern kitchen, children to bring up, a muskrat coat, a charge account at Dupuis Frères department store, a holiday in Maine. Louis continued to examine his bright Driscoll hair, the small nose along which his glasses slid. Holding the glasses in place with a finger, he answered Mme. Carette: His father was a dental surgeon, with a degree from Pennsylvania. It was the only degree worth mentioning. Before settling into a dentist's chair the patient should always read the writing on the wall. His mother was born Lucarne, a big name in Moncton. She could still get into her wedding dress. Everything was so conveniently arranged at home—cavernous washing machine, giant vacuum cleaner—that she seldom went out. When she did, she wore a two-strand cultured-pearl necklace and a coat and hat of Persian lamb.

The Carettes could not match this, though they were related to families for whom bridges were named. Mme. Carette sat on the edge of the sofa, ankles together. Gentility was the brace that kept her upright. She had once been a young widow, hard pressed, had needed to sew for money. Berthe recalled a stricter, an unsmiling mother, straining over pleats and tucks for clients who reneged on pennies. She wore the neutral shades of half mourning, the whitish grays of Rue Saint-Hubert, as though everything had to be used up—even remnants of grief.

Mme. Carette tried to imagine Louis's mother. She might one day have to sell the pearls; even a dentist trained in Pennsylvania could leave behind disorder and debts. Whatever happened, she said to Louis, she would remain in this flat. Even after the girls were married. She would rather beg on the steps of the parish church than intrude upon a young marriage. When her last, dreadful illness made itself known, she would creep away to the Hôtel Dieu and die without a murmur. On the other hand, the street seemed to be filling up with foreigners. She might have to move.

Berthe and Marie were dressed alike, as if to confound Louis, force him to choose the true princess. Leaving the sight of his face in the mirror, puzzled by death and old age, he took notice of the two moiré skirts, organdy blouses, patent-leather belts. "I can't get over those twins of yours," he said to Mme. Carette. "I just can't get over them."

Once, Berthe had tried Marie in her own office—easy work, taking messages when the switchboard was closed.

She knew just enough English for that. After two weeks the office manager, Mr. Macfarlane, had said to Berthe, "Your sister is an angel, but angels aren't in demand at Prestige Central Burners."

It was the combination of fair hair and dark eyes, the enchanting misalliance, that gave Marie the look of an angel. She played with the locket the Greek had given her, twisting and unwinding the chain. What did she owe her Greek? Fidelity? An explanation? He was punctual and polite, had never laid a hand on her, in temper or eagerness, had traveled a long way by streetcar to bring back the mice. True, said Berthe, reviewing his good points, while Louis ate the last of the fudge. It was true about the mice, but he should have become more than "Marie's Greek." In the life of a penniless unmarried young woman, there was no room for a man merely in love. He ought to have presented himself as *something*: Marie's future.

In May true spring came, moist and hot. Berthe brought home new dress patterns and yards of flowered rayon and piqué. Louis called three evenings a week, at seven o'clock, after the supper dishes were cleared away. They played hearts in the dining room, drank Salada tea, brewed black, with plenty of sugar and cream, ate éclairs and mille-feuilles from Celentano, the bakery on Avenue Mont Royal. (Celentano had been called something else for years now, but Mme. Carette did not take notice of change of that kind, and did not care to have it pointed out.) Louis, eating coffee éclairs one after another, told stories set in Moncton that showed off his family. Marie wore a blue dress with a red collar, once Berthe's, and a red barrette in her hair. Berthe, a master player, held back to let Louis win. Mme. Carette listened to Louis, kept some of his stories, discarded others, garnering information useful to Marie. Marie picked up cards at random, disrupting the game. Louis's French was not as woolly as before, but he had somewhere acquired a common Montreal accent. Mme. Carette wondered who his friends were and how Marie's children would sound.

They began to invite him to meals. He arrived at half past five, straight from work, and was served at once. Mme. Carette told Berthe that she hoped he washed his hands at the office, because he never did here. They used the blue-willow-pattern china that would go to Marie. One evening, when the tablecloth had been folded and put away, and the teacups and cards distributed, he mentioned marriage—not his own, or to anyone in particular, but as a way of life. Mme. Carette broke in to say that she had been widowed at Louis's age. She recalled what it had been like to have a husband she could consult and admire. "Marriage means children," she said, looking fondly at her own. She would not be alone during her long, final illness. The girls would take her in. She would not be a burden; a couch would do for a bed.

Louis said he was tired of the game. He dropped his hand and spread the cards in an arc.

"So many hearts," said Mme. Carette, admiringly.

"Let me see." Marie had to stand: there was a large teapot in the way. "Ace, queen, ten, eight, five . . . a wedding." Before Berthe's foot reached her ankle, she managed to ask, sincerely, if anyone close to him was getting married this year.

Mme. Carette considered Marie as good as engaged. She bought a quantity of embroidery floss and began the ornamentation of guest towels and tea towels, place mats and pillow slips. Marie ran her finger over the pretty monogram with its intricate frill of vine leaves. Her mind, which had sunk into hibernation when she accepted Louis and forgot her Greek, awoke and plagued her with a nightmare. "I became a nun" was all she told her mother. Mme. Carette wished it were true. Actually, the dream had stopped short of vows. Barefoot, naked under a robe of coarse brown wool, she moved along an aisle in and out of squares of sunlight. At the altar they were waiting to shear her hair. A strange man—not Uncle Gildas, not Louis, not the Greek—got up out of a pew and stood barring her way. The rough gown turned out to be frail protection. All that kept the dream from sliding into blasphemy and abomination was Marie's entire unacquaintance, awake or asleep, with what could happen next.

Because Marie did not like to be alone in the dark, she and Berthe still shared a room. Their childhood bed had been taken away and supplanted by twin beds with quilted satin headboards. Berthe had to sleep on three pillows, because the aluminum hair curlers she wore ground into her scalp. First thing every morning, she clipped on her pearl earrings, sat up, and unwound the curlers, which she handed one by one to Marie. Marie put her own hair up and kept it that way until suppertime.

In the dark, her face turned to the heap of pillows dimly seen, Marie told Berthe about the incident in the chapel. If dreams are life's opposite, what did it mean? Berthe saw that there was more to it than Marie was able to say. Speaking softly, so that their mother would not hear, she tried to tell Marie about men—what they were like and what they wanted. Marie suggested that she and Berthe enter a cloistered convent together, now, while there was still time. Berthe supposed that she had in mind the famous Martin sisters of Lisieux, in France, most of them Carmelites and one a saint. She touched her own temple, meaning that Marie had gone soft in the brain. Marie did not see; if she had, she would have thought that Berthe was easing a curler. Berthe reminded Marie that she was marked out not for sainthood in France but for marriage in Montreal. Berthe had a salary and occasional travel. Mme. Carette had her Fall River bounty. Marie, if she put her mind to it, could have a lifetime of love.

"Is Louis love?" said Marie.

There were girls ready to line up in the rain for Louis, said Berthe.

"What girls?" said Marie, perplexed rather than disbelieving.

"Montreal girls," said Berthe. "The girls who cry with envy when you and Louis walk down the street."

"We have never walked down a street," said Marie.

The third of June was Louis's birthday. He arrived wearing a new seersucker suit. The Carettes offered three monogrammed hemstitched handkerchiefs—he was always polishing his glasses or mopping his face. Mme. Carette had prepared a meal he particularly favored—roast pork and coconut layer cake. The sun was still high. His birthday unwound in a steady, blazing afternoon. He suddenly put his knife and fork down and said that if he ever decided to get married he would need more than his annual bonus to pay for the honeymoon. He would have to buy carpets, lamps, a refrigerator. People talked lightly of marriage without considering the cost for the groom. Priests urged the married condition on bachelors—priests, who did not know the price of eight ounces of tea.

"Some brides bring lamps and lampshades," said Mme. Carette. "A glass-front bookcase. Even the books to put in it." Her husband had owned a furniture shop on Rue Saint-Denis. Household goods earmarked for Berthe and Marie had been stored with relatives for some twenty years, waxed and polished and free of dust. "An oak table that seats fourteen," she said, and stopped with that. Berthe had forbidden her to draw up an inventory. They were not bartering Marie.

"Some girls have money," said Marie. Her savings—eighteen dollars—were in a drawer of her mother's old treadle sewing machine.

A spasm crossed Louis's face; he often choked on his food.

Berthe knew more about men than Marie—more than her mother, who knew only how children come about. Mr. Ryder, of Berthe's office, would stand in the corridor, letting elevators go by, waiting for a chance to squeeze in next to Berthe. Mr. Sexton had offered her money, a regular allowance, if she would go out with him every Friday, the night of his Legion meeting. Mr. Macfarlane had left a lewd poem on her desk, then a note of apology, then a poem even worse than the first. Mr. Wright-Ashburton had offered to leave his wife—for, of course, they had wives, Mr. Ryder, Mr. Sexton, Mr. Macfarlane, none of whom she had ever encouraged, and Mr. Wright-Ashburton, with whom she had been to Plattsburgh and Saranac Lake, and whose private behavior she had described, kneeling, in remote parishes, where the confessor could not have known her by voice.

When Berthe accepted Mr. Wright-Ashburton's raving proposal to leave his wife, saying that Irene probably knew about them anyway, would be thankful to have it in the clear, his face had wavered with fright, like a face seen underwater—rippling, uncontrolled. Berthe had to tell him she hadn't meant it. She could not marry a divorced man. On Louis's face she saw that same quivering dismay. He was afraid of Marie, of her docility, her monogrammed towels, her dependence, her glass-front bookcase. Having seen this, Berthe was not surprised when he gave no further sign of life until the twenty-fifth of June.

During his absence the guilt and darkness of rejection filled every corner of the flat. There was not a room that did not speak of humiliation—oh, not because Louis had dropped Marie but because the Carettes had honored and welcomed a clodhopper, a cheapjack, a ginger-haired nobody. Mme. Carette and Marie made many telephone calls to his office, with a variety of names and voices, to be told every time he was not at his desk. One morning Berthe, on her way to work, saw someone very like him hurrying into Windsor station. By the time she had struggled out of her crowded streetcar, he was gone. She followed him into the great concourse and looked at the times of the different trains and saw where they were going. A trapped sparrow fluttered under the glass roof. She recalled an expression of Louis's, uneasy and roguish, when he had told Berthe that Marie did not understand the facts of life. (This in English, over the table, as if Mme. Carette and Marie could not follow.) When Berthe asked what these facts might be, he had tried to cross her glance, as on that first evening, one man to another. She was not a man; she had looked away.

Mme. Carette went on embroidering baskets of flowers, ivy leaves, hunched over her work, head down. Marie decided to find a job as a receptionist in a beauty salon. It would be pleasant work in clean surroundings. A girl she had talked to on the bus earned fourteen dollars a week. Marie would give her mother eight and keep six. She did not need Louis, she said, and she was sure she could never love him.

"No one expected you to love him," said her mother, without looking up.

On the morning of the twenty-fifth of June he rang the front doorbell. Marie was eating breakfast in the kitchen, wearing Berthe's aluminum curlers under a mauve chiffon scarf, and Berthe's mauve-and-black kimono. He stood in the middle of the room, refusing offers of tea, and said that the whole world was engulfed in war. Marie looked out the kitchen window, at bare yards and storage sheds.

"Not there," said Louis. "In Korea."

Marie and her mother had never heard of the place. Mme. Carette took it for granted that the British had started something again. She said, "They can't take you, Louis, because of your eyesight." Louis replied that this time they would take everybody, bachelors first. A few married men might be allowed to make themselves useful at home. Mme. Carette put her arms around him. "You are my son now," she said. "I'll never let them ship you to England. You can hide in our coal shed." Marie had not understood that the mention of war was a marriage proposal, but her mother had grasped it at once. She wanted to call Berthe and tell her to come home immediately, but Louis was in a hurry to publish the banns. Marie retired to the bedroom and changed into Berthe's white sharkskin sundress and jacket and toeless white suede shoes. She smoothed Berthe's suntan makeup on her legs, hoping that her mother would not see she was not wearing stockings. She combed out her hair, put on lipstick and earrings, and butterfly sunglasses belonging to Berthe. Then, for the first time, she and Louis together walked down the front steps to the street.

At Marie's parish church they found other couples standing about, waiting for advice. They had heard the news and decided to get married at once. Marie and Louis held hands, as though they had been engaged for a long time. She hoped no one would notice that she had no engagement ring. Unfortunately, their banns could not be posted until July, or the marriage take place until August. His parents would not be present to bless them: At the very day and hour of the ceremony they would be on their way to Rome.

The next day, Louis went to a jeweler on Rue Saint-Denis, recommended by Mme. Carette, but he was out of engagement rings. He had sold every last one that day. Louis did not look anywhere else; Mme. Carette had said he was the only man she trusted. Louis's mother sent rings by registered mail. They had been taken from the hand of her dead sister, who had wanted them passed on to her son, but the son had vanished into Springfield and no longer sent Christmas cards. Mme. Carette shook her own wedding dress out of tissue paper and made a few adjustments so that it would fit Marie. Since the war it had become impossible to find silk of that quality.

Waiting for August, Louis called on Marie every day. They rode the streetcar up to Avenue Mont Royal to eat barbecued chicken. (One evening Marie let her engagement ring fall into a crack of the corrugated floor of the tram, and a number of strangers told her to be careful, or she would lose her man, too.) The chicken arrived on a bed of chips, in a wicker basket. Louis showed Marie how to eat barbecue without a knife and fork. Fortunately, Mme. Carette was not there to watch Marie gnawing on a bone. She was sewing the rest of the trousseau and had no time to act as chaperone.

Berthe's office sent her to Buffalo for a long weekend. She brought back match folders from Polish and German restaurants, an ashtray on which was written "Buffalo Hofbrau," and a number of articles that were much cheaper down there, such as nylon stockings. Marie asked if they still ate with knives and forks in Buffalo, or if they had caught up to Montreal. Alone together, Mme. Carette and Berthe sat in the kitchen and gossiped about Louis. The white summer curtains were up; the coal-and-wood range was covered with clean white oilcloth. Berthe had a new kimono—white, with red pagodas on the sleeves. She propped her new red mules on the oven door. She smoked now, and carried everywhere the Buffalo Hofbrau ashtray. Mme. Carette made Berthe promise not to smoke in front of Uncle Gildas, or in the street, or at Marie's wedding reception, or in the front parlor, where the smell might get into the curtains. Sometimes they had just tea and toast and Celentano pastry for supper. When Berthe ate a coffee éclair, she said, "Here's one Louis won't get."

The bright evenings of suppers and card games slid into the past, and by August seemed long ago. Louis said to Marie, "We knew how to have a good time. People don't enjoy themselves anymore." He believed that the other customers in the barbecue restaurant had secret, nagging troubles. Waiting for the wicker basket of chicken, he held Marie's hand and stared at men who might be Greeks. He tried to tell her what had been on his mind between the third and twenty-fifth of June, but Marie did not care, and he gave up. They came to their first important agreement: Neither of them wanted the blue-willow-pattern plates. Louis said he would ask his parents to start them off with six place settings of English Rose. She seemed still to be listening, and so he told her that the name of her parish church, Saint Louis de France, had always seemed to him to be a personal sign of some kind: An obscure force must have guided him to Rue Saint-Hubert and Marie. Her soft brown eyes never wavered. They forgot about Uncle Gildas, and whatever it was Uncle Gildas had said to frighten them.

Louis and Marie were married on the third Saturday of August, with flowers from an earlier wedding banked along the altar rail, and two other wedding parties waiting at the back of the church. Berthe supposed that Marie, by accepting the ring of a dead woman and wearing the gown of another woman widowed at twenty-six, was calling down the blackest kind of misfortune. She remembered her innocent nakedness under the robe of frieze. Marie had no debts. She owed Louis nothing. She had saved him from a long journey to a foreign place, perhaps even from dying. As he placed the unlucky ring on her finger, Berthe wept. She knew that some of the people looking on—Uncle Gildas, or Joseph and Raymond Driscoll, amazing in their ginger likeness—were mistaking her for a jealous older sister, longing to be in Marie's place.

Marie, now Mme. Driscoll, turned to Berthe and smiled, as she used to when they were children. Once again, the smile said, "Have I done the right thing? Is this what you wanted?" "Yes, yes," said Berthe silently, but she went on crying. Marie had always turned to Berthe; she had started to walk because she wanted to be with Berthe. She had been standing, holding on to a kitchen chair, and she suddenly smiled and let go. Later, when Marie was three, and in the habit of taking her clothes off and showing what must never be seen, Mme. Carette locked her into the storage shed behind the kitchen. Berthe knelt on her side of the door, sobbing, calling, "Don't be afraid, Marie. Berthe is here." Mme. Carette relented and unlocked the door, and there was Marie, wearing just her undershirt, smiling for Berthe.

Leading her mother, Berthe approached the altar rail. Marie seemed contented; for Berthe, that was good enough. She kissed her sister, and kissed the chosen husband. He had not separated them but would be a long incident in their lives. Among the pictures that were taken on the church steps, there is one of Louis with an arm around each sister and the sisters trying to clasp hands behind his back.

The wedding party walked in a procession down the steps and around the corner: another impression in black-and-white. The August pavement burned under the women's thin soles. Their fine clothes were too hot. Children playing in the road broke into applause when they saw Marie. She waved her left hand, showing the ring. The children were still French-Canadian; so were the neighbors, out on their balconies to look at Marie. Three yellow leaves fell—white, in a photograph. One of the Driscoll boys raced ahead and brought the party to a stop. There is Marie, who does not yet understand that she is leaving home, and confident Louis, so soon to have knowledge of her bewildering ignorance.

Berthe saw the street as if she were bent over the box camera, trying to keep the frame straight. It was an important picture, like a precise instrument of measurement: so much duty, so much love, so much reckless safety—the distance between last April and now. She thought, It had to be done. They began to walk again. Mme. Carette realized for the first time what she and Uncle Gildas and Berthe had brought about: the unredeemable loss of Marie. She said to Berthe, "Wait until I am dead before you get married. You can marry a widower. They make good husbands." Berthe was nearly twenty-four, just at the limit. She had turned away so many attractive prospects, with no explanation, and had frightened so many others with her skill at cards and her quick blue eyes that word had spread, and she was not solicited as before.

Berthe and Marie slipped away from the reception—moved, that is, from the parlor to the bedroom—so that Berthe could help her sister pack. It turned out that Mme. Carette had done the packing. Marie had never had to fill a suitcase, and would not have known what to put in first. For a time, they sat on the edge of a bed, talking in whispers. Berthe smoked, holding the Buffalo Hofbrau ashtray. She showed Marie a black lacquer cigarette lighter she had not shown her mother. Marie had started to change her clothes; she was just in her slip. She looked at the lighter on all sides and handed it back. Louis was taking her to the Château Frontenac, in Quebec City, for three nights—the equivalent of ten days in Old Orchard, he had said. After that, they would go straight to the duplex property, quite far north on Boulevard Pie IX, that his father was helping him buy. "I'll call you tomorrow morning," said Marie, for whom tomorrow was still the same thing as today. If Uncle Gildas had been at Berthe's mercy, she would have held his head underwater. Then she thought, Why blame him? She and Marie were Montreal girls, not trained to accompany heroes, or to hold out for dreams, but just to be patient.

FROM CLOUD TO CLOUD

THE FAMILY'S EXPERIENCE of Raymond was like a long railway journey with a constantly shifting point of view. His mother and aunt were of a generation for whom travel had meant trains—slow trips there and back, with an intense engagement in eating, or a game of cards with strangers, interrupted by a flash of celestial light from the frozen and sunstruck St. Lawrence. Then came the dark brown slums of the approach to Montreal, the signal to get one's luggage down from the rack.

To make a short story shorter, his Aunt Berthe (she worked in an office full of English Canadians) would have said Raymond was Heaven and Hell. Mother and aunt, the two sisters had thought they never could love anyone more than Raymond; then, all at once, he seemed to his aunt so steadily imperfect, so rigid in his failings, that the changing prospect of his moods, decisions, needs, life ceased to draw her attention.

He'd had a father, of course—had him until he was eighteen, even though it was Raymond's practice to grumble that he had been raised, badly, by women. His last memories of his father must surely have been Louis dying of emphysema, upright in the white-painted wicker chair, in blazing forbidden sunlight, mangling a forbidden cigar. The partially flagged backyard had no shade in it—just two yellow fringed umbrellas that filtered the blue of July and made it bilious. Louis could not sit in their bogus shadow, said it made him sweat. Behind the umbrellas was the kitchen entrance to a duplex dwelling of stucco and brick, late 1940s in style—a cube with varnished doors—at the northern end of Boulevard Pie IX. "Remember that your father owned his own home," said Louis; also, "When we first moved up here, you could still see vacant lots. It depressed your mother. She wasn't used to an open view."

Where Raymond's sandbox had been stood a granite bird-bath with three aluminum birds the size of pigeons perched on the rim—the gift from Louis's firm when he had to take early retirement, because he was so ill. He already owned a gold watch. He told Raymond exactly where to find the watch in his desk—in which drawer. Raymond sat cross-legged on the grass and practiced flipping a vegetable knife; his mother had found and disposed of his commando dagger. His father could draw breath but had to pause before he spoke. Waiting for strength, he looked up at the sky, at a moon in sunlight, pale and transparent—a memory of dozens of other waning moons. (It was the summer of the moon walk. Raymond's mother still mentions this, as though it had exerted a tidal influence on her affairs.)

The silent intermissions, his gaze upturned, made it seem as if Louis were seeking divine assistance. Actually, he knew everything he wished to say. So did Raymond. Raymond—even his aunt will not deny it—showed respect. He never once remarked, "I've heard this before," or uttered the timeless, frantic snub of the young, "I know, I know, I *know*."

His father said, "There have always been good jobs in Boston," "Never forget your French, because it would break your mother's heart," "One of these days you're going to have to cut your hair," "Marry a Catholic, but not just any Catholic," "With a name like Raymond Joseph Driscoll you can go anywhere in the world," "That autograph album of mine is worth a fortune. Hang on to it. It will always get you out of a tight spot."

In his lifetime Louis wrote to hockey players and film stars and local politicians, and quite often received an answer. Raymond as a child watched him cutting out the signature and pasting it in a deep blue leather-bound book. Now that Raymond is settled in Florida, trying to build a career in the motel business, his whole life is a tight spot. He finds it hard to credit that the album is worth nothing. Unfortunately, it is so. Most of the signatures were facsimiles, or had been dashed off by a secretary. The few authentic autographs were of names too obscure to matter. The half dozen that Louis purchased from a specialized dealer on Peel Street, since driven out of business, were certified fakes. Louis kept "Joseph Stalin" and "Harry S Truman" in a locked drawer, telling Marie, his wife, that if Canada was ever occupied by one of the two great powers, or by both at once, she would be able to barter her way to safety.

Raymond had a thin mane of russet hair that covered his profile when he bent over to retrieve the knife. He wore circus-rodeo gear, silver and white. Louis couldn't stand the sight of his son's clothes; in his dying crankiness he gave some away. Raymond stored his favorite outfits at his aunt's place. She lived in a second-story walk-up, with front and back balconies, a long, cool hall, three bedrooms, on the west side of Parc Lafontaine. She was unmarried and did not need all that space; she enjoyed just walking from room to room. Louis spoke to Raymond in English, so that he would be able to make his way in the world. He wanted him to go to an English commercial school, where he might meet people who would be useful to him later on. Raymond's aunt said that her English was better than Louis's: his "th" sometimes slipped into "d." Louis, panting, mentioned to Raymond that Berthe, for all her pretensions, was not as well off property-wise as her sister and brother-in-law, though she seemed to have more money to throw around. "Low rent in any crummy neighborhood—that's her creed," said Raymond's father. In

his last, bad, bitter days, he seemed to be brooding over
Berthe, compared her career with his own, said she had an in-
born craving for sleeping with married men. But before he
died he took every word back, said she had been a good friend
to him, was an example for other women, though not necessarily married women. He wanted her to keep an eye on
Marie and Raymond—he said he felt as if he were leaving
behind two helpless children, one eighteen, the other in her
forties, along with the two cars, the valuable autograph album, the gold watch, and the paid-up house.

Louis also left a handwritten inconvenient request to be
buried in New Brunswick, where he came from, rather than
in Montreal. Raymond's mother hid the message behind a
sofa cushion, where it would be discovered during some future heavy cleaning. She could not bring herself to tear it
up. They buried Louis in Notre Dame des Neiges cemetery,
where Marie intended to join him, not too soon. She ordered
a bilingual inscription on the gravestone, because he had spoken English at the office and French to her.

Raymond in those days spoke French and English, too,
with a crack in each. His English belonged to a subdivision
of Catholic Montreal—a bit Irish-sounding but thinner than
any tone you might hear in Dublin. His French vocabulary
was drawn from conversations with his mother and aunt, and
should have been full of tenderness. He did not know what he
wanted to be. "If I ever write, I'm going to write a book about
the family," he told his aunt the day of Louis's funeral, looking at the relatives in their black unnatural clothes, soaking
up heat. It was the first time he had ever said this, and most
likely the last. Poor Raymond could barely scrawl a letter,
couldn't spell. He didn't mind learning, but he hated to be
taught. After he left home, Berthe and Marie scarcely had the
sight of his handwriting. They had his voice over the telephone, calling from different American places (they thought
of Vietnam as an American place) with a gradually altered

accent. His French filled up with English, as with a deposit of pebbles and sand, and in English he became not quite a stranger: Even years later he still said "palm" to rhyme with "jam."

Raymond behaved correctly at the funeral, holding his mother's arm, seeing that everyone had a word with her, causing those relatives who did not know him well to remark that he was his father all over again. He was dressed in a dark suit, bought in a hurry, and one of Louis's ties. He had not worn a tie since the last family funeral; Berthe had to fasten the knot. He let her give his hair a light trim, so that it cleared his shoulders.

Marie would not hold a reception: The mourners had to settle for a kiss or a handshake beside the open grave. Louis's people, some of whom had come a long way, were starting back with the pieces of a break beyond mending. Marie didn't care: Her family feelings had narrowed to Raymond and Berthe. After the funeral, Raymond drove the two sisters to Berthe's flat. He sat with his mother at the kitchen table and watched Berthe cutting up a cold chicken. Marie kept on her funeral hat, a black straw pillbox with a wisp of veil. No one said much. The chicken was not enough for Raymond, so Berthe got out the ham she had baked the night before in case Marie changed her mind about inviting the relatives. She put the whole thing down in front of him, and he hacked pieces off and ate with his fingers. Marie said, "You wouldn't dare do that if your father could see you," because she had to say something. She and Berthe knew he was having a bad time.

When he finished, they moved down the hall to Berthe's living room. She opened the doors to both balconies, to invite a crossbreeze. The heated air touched the looped white curtain without stirring a fold of it. Raymond took off his jacket and tie. The women had already removed their black

stockings. Respect for Louis kept them from making themselves entirely comfortable. They had nothing in particular to
do for the rest of the day. Berthe had taken time off from the
office, and Marie was afraid to go home. She believed that
some essence of Louis, not quite a ghost, was in their house
on Boulevard Pie IX, testing locks, turning door handles, sliding drawers open, handling Marie's poor muddled household
accounts, ascertaining once and for all the exact amount of
money owed by Marie to Berthe. (Berthe had always been
good for a small loan toward the end of the month. She had
shown Marie how to entangle the books, so that Louis need
never know.)

Raymond stretched out on Berthe's pale green sofa, with a
pile of cushions under his head. "Raymond, watch where you
put your feet," said his mother.

"It doesn't matter," said Berthe. "Not today."

"I don't want you to wish we weren't here," said Marie.
"After we've moved in, I mean. You'll never know we're in
the house. Raymond, ask Aunt Berthe for an ashtray."

"There's one right beside him," said Berthe.

"I won't let Raymond put his feet all over the furniture,"
said Marie. "Not after today. If you don't want us, all you
have to do is say."

"I have said," said Berthe, at which Raymond turned his
head and looked at her intently.

Tears flooded Marie's eyes at the improbable vision of
Berthe ordering her nearest relatives, newly bereaved, to
pack and go. "We're going to be happy, because we love each
other," she said.

"Have you asked Raymond where he wants to live?" said
Berthe.

"Raymond wants whatever his mother wants," said Marie.
"He'll be nice. I promise. He'll take the garbage down. Won't
you, Raymond? You'll take the garbage out every night for
Aunt Berthe?"

"Not every night," said his aunt. "Twice a week. Don't cry. Louis wouldn't want to see you in tears."

A quiver of shyness touched all three. Louis returned to memory in superior guise, bringing guidance, advice. "Papa wouldn't mind if we watched the news," said Raymond.

For less than a minute they stared at a swaying carpet of jungle green, filmed from a helicopter, and heard a French voice with a Montreal accent describe events in a place the sisters intended never to visit. Raymond jumped to an English channel, without asking if anyone minded. He was the male head of the family now; in any case, they had always given in. Vietnam in English appeared firmly grounded, with a Canadian sergeant in the Marine Corps—shorn, cropped, gray-eyed, at ease. He spoke to Raymond, saying that it was all right for a Canadian to enlist in a foreign army.

"Who cares?" said Marie, fatally. English on television always put her to sleep. She leaned back in her armchair and began very gently to snore. Berthe removed Marie's glasses and her hat, and covered her bare legs with a lace quilt. Even in the warmest weather she could wake up feeling chilled and unloved. She fainted easily; it was her understanding that the blood in her arms and legs congealed, leaving her brain unattended. She seemed content with this explanation and did not seek another.

Raymond sat up, knocking over the pile of cushions. He gathered his hair into a topknot and held it fast. "They send you to San Diego," he said. What was he seeing, really? Pacific surf? A parade in sunlight? Berthe should have asked.

When Marie came to, yawning and sighing, Berthe was putting color on her nails (she had removed it for the funeral) and Raymond was eating chocolate cake, watching Rod Laver. He had taken off his shirt, shoes, and socks. "Laver's the greatest man in the modern world," he said.

"Ah, Raymond," said his mother. "You've already forgotten your father."

As Marie had promised, he carried the garbage out, making a good impression on the Portuguese family who lived downstairs. (Louis, who would not speak to strangers, had made no impression at all.) At five o'clock the next morning, Berthe's neighbor, up because he had an early delivery at his fruit store, saw Raymond throw a duffel kit into his mother's car and drive away. His hair was tied back with a white leather thong. He wore one of his rodeo outfits and a pair of white boots.

Before leaving Berthe's flat he had rifled her handbag, forgotten on a kitchen chair—a century before, when they assembled for the funeral feast. Before leaving Montreal he made a long detour to say good-bye to his old home. He was not afraid of ghosts, and he had already invented a father who was going to approve of everything he did. In Louis's desk he found the gold watch and one or two documents he knew he would need—among them the birth certificate that showed him eighteen. He took away as a last impression the yellowed grass in the backyard. Nothing had been watered since Louis's death.

Berthe has often wondered what the Marines in the recruiting office down in Plattsburgh made of Raymond, all silver and white, with that lank brick-dust hair and the thin, cracked English. Nothing, probably: They must have expected civilians to resemble fake performers. There was always someone straggling down from Montreal. It was like joining the Foreign Legion. After his first telephone call, Berthe said to Marie, "At least we know where he is," but it was not so; they never quite knew. He did not go to San Diego: A military rule of geography splits the continent. He had enlisted east of the Mississippi, and so he was sent for training to Parris Island. The Canadian Marine had forgotten to mention that possibility. Berthe bought a number of road maps, so that she could look up these new names. The Mississippi seemed to stop dead at Minneapolis. It had nothing to do with Canada. Raymond should have turned the car around and driven home. (Instead, he left it parked in Plattsburgh. He could not remember, later, the name of the street.)

He has never been back. His excuse used to be that he had nowhere to stay in Montreal. Marie sold the duplex and moved in with Berthe. The last thing he wanted to see on vacation was another standard motel unit, and he knew Berthe wouldn't have him in the house.

He enlisted for four years, then another three. Marie looked upon him as a prisoner, in time to be released. Released honorably? Yes, or he would not have been allowed to settle in Florida: He was still a Canadian in 1976; he could easily have been deported. When he became an American citizen and called Marie, expecting congratulations, she told him that 98 percent of the world's forest fires were started by Americans. It was all she could think of to say. He has been down there ever since, moving like a pendulum between Hollywood North and Hollywood Beach, Fort Lauderdale and the stretch of Miami known as Little Quebec, from the number of French Canadians who spend holidays there. They have their own newspaper, their own radio station and television channel, they import Montreal barbecue. Hearing their voices sometimes irritates him, sometimes makes him homesick for the summer of 1969, for the ease with which he jumped from cloud to cloud.

Marie still believes that "Parris Island" was one of Raymond's famous spelling mistakes. He must have spent part of his early youth, the least knowable, in a place called Paris, South Carolina. She often wonders about other mothers and sons, and whether children feel any of the pain they inflict. Berthe thinks of how easy it must have been for Raymond to leave, with the sun freshly risen, slanting along side streets, here and there front steps sluiced and dark, the sky not yet a burning glass. He must have supposed the rest of his life was going to be like that. When she and Marie ransacked the house on Boulevard Pie IX, looking for clues, imagining he'd left a letter, left some love, they kept the shades drawn, as if there were another presence in the rooms, tired of daylight.

FLORIDA

Berthe carette's sister, Marie, spent eight Christ-mases of her life in Florida, where her son was establishing a future in the motel industry. Every time Marie went down she found Raymond starting over in a new place: His motels seemed to die on his hands. She used to come back to Montreal riddled with static electricity. Berthe couldn't hand her a teaspoon without receiving a shock, like a small silver bullet. Her sister believed the current was generated by a chemical change that occurred as she flew out of Fort Lauderdale toward a wet, dark, snowy city.

Marie had been living with Berthe ever since 1969, the year her husband died. She still expected what Berthe thought of as husband service: flights met, cabs hailed, doors held, tips attended to. Berthe had to take the bus out to Dorval Airport, with Marie's second-best fur coat over her arm and her high-heeled boots in a plastic bag. Through a glass barrier she could watch her sister gliding through customs, dressed in a new outfit of some sherbet tone—strawberry, lemon-peach—with everything matching, sometimes even her hair. She knew that Marie had been careful to tear the American store and union labels out of the clothes and sew in Canadian ones, in case customs asked her to strip.

"Don't tell me it's still winter," Marie would wail, kissing Berthe as if she had been away for months rather than just a few days. Guiding Marie's arms into the second-best-mink sleeves (paws and piecework), Berthe would get the first of the silvery shocks.

One year, when her son, Raymond, had fallen in love with a divorced woman twice his age (it didn't last), Marie arrived home crackling, exchanging sparks with everything she touched. When she ate a peppermint she felt it detonating in her mouth. Berthe had placed a pot of flowering paper-white narcissi on Marie's dressing table, a welcome-home present reflected on and on in the three mirrors. Marie shuffled along the carpeted passage, still in her boots. She had on her Florida manner, pretending she was in Berthe's flat by mistake. As soon as she saw the plant, she went straight over and gave it a kiss. The flower absorbed a charge and hurled it back. Berthe examined the spot on Marie's lip where the shock had struck. She could find nothing, no trace. Nevertheless Marie applied an ice cube.

She waited until midnight before calling Raymond, to get the benefit of the lower rate. His line was tied up until two: He said the police had been in, investigating a rumor. Marie told about the plant. He made her repeat the story twice, then said she had built up a reserve of static by standing on a shag rug with her boots on. She was not properly grounded when she approached the flower.

"Raymond could have done more with his life," said Marie, hanging up. Berthe, who was still awake, thought he had done all he could, given his brains and character. She did not say so: She never mentioned her nephew, never asked about his health. He had left home young, and caused a lot of grief and trouble.

On Marie's eighth visit, Raymond met her at the airport with a skinny woman he said was his wife. She had dark blond hair and one of those unset permanents, all corkscrews. Marie looked at her, and looked away. Raymond explained that he had moved back to Hollywood North. Marie said she didn't care, as long as she had somewhere to lay her head.

They left the terminal in silence. Outside, she said, "What's this car? Japanese? Your father liked a Buick."

"It belongs to Mimi," he said.

Marie got in front, next to Raymond, and the skinny woman climbed in behind. Marie said to Raymond in French, "You haven't told me her name."

"Well, I have, of course. I introduced you. Mimi."

"Mimi isn't a name."

"It's hers," he said.

"It can't be. It's always short for something—for Michèle. Did you ever hear of a Saint Mimi? She's not a divorced woman, is she? You were married in church?"

"In a kind of church," he said. "She belongs to a Christian movement."

Marie knew what that meant: pagan rites. "You haven't joined this thing—this movement?"

"I don't want to join anything," he said. "But it has changed my life."

Marie tried to consider this in an orderly way, going over in her mind the parts of Raymond's life that wanted changing. "What sort of woman would marry an only son without his mother's blessing?" she said.

"Mom," said Raymond, switching to English, and perhaps forgetting she hated to be called this. "She's twenty-nine. I'm thirty-three."

"What's her maiden name?" said Marie.

"Ask her," he said. "I didn't marry her family."

Marie eased the seat belt and turned around, smiling. The woman had her eyes shut. She seemed to be praying. Her skin was freckled, pale for the climate; perhaps she had come to one of the oases of the heart where there are no extremes of weather. As for Raymond, he was sharp and dry, with a high, feverish forehead. His past had evaporated. It annoyed him to have to speak French. On one of his mother's other visits he had criticized her Montreal accent, said he had heard better

French in the streets of Saigon. He lit a cigarette, but before she could say, "Your father died of emphysema," threw it out.

Mimi, perhaps made patient by prayer, spoke up: "I am happy to welcome any mother of Raymond's. May we spend a peaceful and mutually enriching Christmas." Her voice moved on a strained, single note, like a soprano recitative. Shyness, Marie thought. She stole a second look. Her eyes, now open, were pale blue, with stubby black lashes. She seemed all at once beguiling and anxious, hoping to be forgiven before having mentioned the sin. A good point, but not good enough to make her a Catholic.

Raymond carried Marie's luggage to a decent room with cream walls and tangerine curtains and spread. The motel looked clean and prosperous, but so had the others. Mimi had gone off on business of her own. ("I'm feeling sick," she had said, getting out of the car, with one freckled hand on her stomach and the other against her throat.)

"She'll be all right," he told Marie.

Alone with Marie, he called her *Maman*, drew her to the window, showed her a Canadian flag flying next to the Stars and Stripes. The place was full of Canadians, he said. They stole like raccoons. One couple had even made off with the bathroom faucets. "Nice-looking people, too."

"Your father never ran down his own kind," said Marie. She did not mean to start an argument but to point out certain limits. He checked the towels, counted the hangers, raised (or lowered; she could not tell) the air-conditioning. He turned his back while she changed into her hibiscus-patterned chiffon, in case they were going out. In a mirror he watched her buckling her red sandals. Berthe's Christmas present.

"Mimi is the first woman I ever met who reminded me of you," he said. Marie let that pass. They walked arm in arm across the parking lot, and he pointed out different things that might interest her—Quebec license plates, a couple of dying palms. On the floor of the lobby lay a furled spruce tree, with its branches still tied. Raymond prodded the tree with his running shoe. It had been here for a week, he said, and it was already shedding. Perhaps Marie and Mimi would like to trim it.

"Trim it with what?" said Marie. Every year, for seven years, she had bought decorations, which Raymond had always thrown out with the tree.

"*I* don't know," he said. "Mimi wants me to set it up on a mirror."

Marie wondered what Raymond's title in this place might be. "Manager," he'd said, but he and Mimi lived like caretakers in an inconvenient arrangement of rooms off the lobby. To get to their kitchen, which was also a storage place for beer and soft drinks, Marie had to squeeze behind the front desk. Every door had a peephole and chain lock. Whenever a bell rang in the lobby Raymond looked carefully before undoing the lock. Another couple worked here, too, he explained, but they were off for Christmas.

The three ate dinner in the kitchen, hemmed in by boxes and crates. Marie asked for an apron, to protect her chiffon. Mimi did not own one, and seemed astonished at the request. She had prepared plain shrimp and boiled rice and plain fruit salad. No wonder Raymond was drying up. Marie showed them pictures of Berthe's Christmas tree, this year red and gold.

Mimi looked for a long time at a snapshot of Berthe, holding a glass, sitting with her legs crossed and her skirt perhaps a bit high. "What's in the glass?" she said.

"Gin does my sister a lot of good," said Marie. She had not enjoyed her shrimp, washed down with some diet drink.

"I'm surprised she never got married," said Mimi. "How old is she? Fifty-something? She still looks good, physically and mentally."

"I am surprised," said Marie, in French. "I am surprised at the turn of this conversation."

"Mimi isn't criticizing Aunt Berthe," said Raymond. "It's a compliment."

Marie turned to Mimi. "My sister never had to get married. She's always made good money. She buys her own fur coats."

Mimi did not know about Berthe, assistant office manager at Prestige Central Burners—a multinational with tentacles in two cities, one of them Cleveland. Last year Mr. Linden from the Cleveland office had invited Berthe out to dinner. His wife had left him; he was getting over the loss. Berthe intended to tell him she had made a lifetime commitment to the firm, with no leftover devotion. She suggested the Ritz-Carlton—she had been there once before, and had a favorite table. During dinner they talked about the different ways of cooking trout, and the bewildering architectural changes taking place in Cleveland and Montreal. Berthe mentioned that whenever a landmark was torn down people said, "It's as bad as Cleveland." It was hard to reconcile the need for progress with the claims of tradition. Mr. Linden said that tradition was flexible.

"I like the way you think," he said. "If only you had been a man, Miss Carette, with your intellect, and your powers of synthesis, you might have gone . . . ," and he pointed to the glass bowl of blueberry trifle on the dessert trolley, as if to say, "even farther."

The next day Berthe drew on her retirement savings account and made a down payment on a mink coat (pastel, fully let out) and wore the coat to work. That was her answer. Marie admired this counterstroke more than any feat of history. She wanted Mimi to admire it, too, but she was tired after the flight, and the shock of Raymond's marriage, and the parched, disappointing meal. Halfway through the story her English thinned out.

"What's she saying?" said Mimi. "This man gave her a coat?"

"It's too bad it couldn't have worked out better for Aunt Berthe," said Raymond. "A widower on the executive level. Well, not exactly a widower, but objectively the same thing. Aunt Berthe still looks great. You heard what Mimi said."

"Berthe doesn't need a widower," said Marie. "She can sit on her front balcony and watch widowers running in Parc Lafontaine any Sunday. There's no room in the flat for a widower. All the closets are full. In the spare-room closet there are things belonging to you, Raymond. That beautiful white rodeo belt with the silver buckle Aunt Berthe gave you for your fourteenth birthday. It cost Berthe thirty dollars, in dollars of that time, when the Canadian was worth more than the American."

"Ten cents more," said Raymond.

"Ten cents of another era," said Marie. "Like eighty cents today."

"Aunt Berthe can move if she feels crowded," he said. "Or she can just send me the belt." He spoke to Mimi. "People in Montreal move more often than in any other city in the world. I can show you figures. My father wasn't a Montrealer, so we always lived in just the one house. *Maman* sold it when he died."

"I wouldn't mind seeing that house," said Mimi, as though challenging Marie to produce it.

"Why should Berthe move?" said Marie. "First you want to tie her up with a stranger, then you want to throw her out of her home. She's got a three-bedroom place for a rent you wouldn't believe. She'd be crazy to let it go. It's easier to find a millionaire with clean habits than my sister's kind of flat."

"People don't get married to have three bedrooms," said Mimi, still holding Berthe's picture. "They get married for love and company."

"I am company," said Marie. "I love my sister, and my sister loves me."

"Do you think I married Raymond for *space*?" said Mimi.

217

Raymond said something in English. Marie did not know what it meant, but it sounded disgusting. "Raymond," she said. "Apologize to your wife."

"Don't talk to him," said Mimi. "You're only working him up."

"Don't you dare knock your chair over," said his mother. "Raymond! If you go out that door, I won't be here when you get back."

The two women sat quietly after the door slammed. Then Mimi picked up the fallen chair. "That's the real Raymond," she said. "That's Raymond, in public and private. I don't blame any man's mother for the way the man turns out."

"He had hair like wheat," said Marie. "It turned that rusty color when he was three. He had the face of an angel. It's the first time I've ever seen him like this. Of course, he has never been married before."

"He'll be lying on the bed now, sulking," said Mimi. "I'm not used to that. I hadn't been married before, either." She began rinsing plates at the sink. The slit of a window overlooked cars and the stricken palms. Tears ran down her cheeks. She tried to blot them on her arm. "I think he wants to leave me."

"So what if he does leave," said Marie, looking in vain for a clean dish towel. "A bad, disobedient boy. He ran away to Vietnam. The last man in our family. He should have been thinking about having sons instead of traveling around. Raymond's father was called Louis. My father's name was Odilon. Odilon-Louis—that's a nice name for a boy. It goes in any language."

"In my family we just have girls," said Mimi.

"Another thing Raymond did," said Marie. "He stole his father's gold watch. Then he lost it. Just took it and lost it."

"Raymond never lost that watch," said Mimi. "He probably sold it to two or three different people. Raymond will always be Raymond. I'm having a baby. Did he tell you that?"

"He didn't have to," said Marie. "I guessed it when we were in the car. Don't cry anymore. They can hear. The baby can hear you."

"He's already heard plenty from Raymond."

Marie's English died. "Look," she said, struggling. "This baby has a grandmother. He's got Berthe. *You've* got Berthe. Never mind Raymond."

"He'll need a father image," said Mimi. "Not just a lot of women."

"Raymond had one," said Marie. "He still joined the Marines."

"He or she," said Mimi. "I don't want to know. I want the surprise. I hope he likes me. She. It feels like a girl."

"It would be good to know in advance," said Marie. "Just for the shopping—to know what to buy. Do you want to save the rest of the shrimp or throw it out?"

"Save it," said Mimi. "Raymond hardly ate anything. He'll be hungry later on."

"That bad boy," said Marie. "I don't care if he never eats again. He'll find out what it's like, alone in the world. Without his mother. Without his aunt. Without his wife. Without his baby."

"I don't want him to be alone," said Mimi, showing Marie her streaked face, the sad little curls stuck to her wet cheeks. "He hasn't actually gone anywhere. I just said I thought he was thinking about it."

Marie tried to remember some of the English Berthe used. When she was talking to people from her office, Berthe would say, "All in good time," and "No way he can do that," and "Count on me," and "Not to worry."

"He won't leave you," said Marie. "No way I'll let him do that. Count on me." Her elbow brushed against the handle of the refrigerator door; she felt a silvery spark through the chiffon sleeve. This was the first time such a thing had happened in Florida; it was like an approving message from

Berthe. Mimi wiped her hands on a paper towel and turned to Marie.

"Be careful," said Marie, enfolding Raymond's wife and Raymond's baby. "Be careful the baby doesn't get a shock. Everything around here is electric. I'm electric. We'll have to be careful from now on. We've got to make sure we're grounded." She had gone into French, but it didn't matter. The baby could hear, and knew what she meant.

LET IT PASS

WELL INTO HER nineties, my aunt continues to send me news of people in Montreal I've had no trouble forgetting. When I open a letter of hers, a shower of clippings falls out, along with her reminders: "Steve! Mrs. Christopher Shrew was Nancy Pervious. Was dying to marry you. Good thing you got away." Or "Peter Delorme. Nice boy until he got into politics. Leaves three fine sons."

At some point she must have mentioned Carlotta Peel, the daughter of my former wife, but I'd no idea what the girl looked like or even what age she might be until she turned up on my doorstep, uninvited, in the South of France. It was an August day, in a season of drought. A layer of dust like fine salt covered the fading gardens. Brittle plane leaves blew into the corners of the terrace. The hotter the day, the grayer the sea. The sun beat through a thin grayish layer of haze that resembled the tail of a dust storm. I was reading a new book, which I had taken to be the secret diaries of General Georges Boulanger. He was the French Minister of War who might have thrown over the Third Republic, if he'd put his mind to it, and finally dismayed his admirers by committing suicide on his mistress's grave. I had read steadily from the downfall of Louis Napoleon until about 1890, almost the end, surprised that someone I'd classed as a featherhead had shown so much wit and grace, when I looked again at the author's notes and realized I was reading a work of fiction. I dropped the book face down and began composing letters to the author and his publisher asking for the return of my hundred and sixty-nine francs. Someone called my name. By then I was asleep and dreaming. I was at a christening, and a stranger suddenly handed me about a dozen prayer books. The infant at the font began to wail, a sort of mewing. The clergyman rang a bell for silence. The child's mother said, "Steve! Steve Burnet!" I said, "For Christ's sake, I'm holding all these bloody books!"

I woke up and went round to the front of the house, and found a tall child (child to me; Carlotta considered herself a young woman) with sleepy dark eyes. She wore a kind of uniform of white cotton, with a long buttoned tunic, and with her narrow shoulders and cinnamon summer skin she could have been Indian. I remember that the first things she said were on a rising note: "Steve Burnet? You knew my mother?" —which meant nothing until she added, "My mother, Lily?" At that I saw a resemblance, though not to recollections of Lily; rather, to Carlotta's maternal grandmother, my late, crazy mother-in-law, anchored in memory as Old Lady Quale. Between Carlotta and me arose Mrs. Quale's owlish staring and head of sleek black hair. Lily's girl was a fragment of that ancient lump of righteousness—saner, probably; certainly prettier; perhaps more commonplace. As for Lily, I had not set eyes on her since she was twenty-three.

My life since that early capsizal had been sparsely and prudently occupied by married women in no hurry to leave their husbands. Indeed, the introduction of divorce into Italy had caused me to close down a six-year-old story. (It was managed without racking debate. A Canadian diplomat, evenhanded by nature, one of the rare foreigners to whom the French have not taken immediate and weighty dislike, I was invited to observe voting practices in the Society Islands. I obtained a long leave of absence, rented my summer house in France to a Belgian opposite number, loitered in the South Pacific as long as my means allowed, and spent an undue amount of time drawing up my conclusions. When eventually one summer I returned to Europe, it was to find Sandra dismissing men as a form of *agitazione* and studying to become a breeder of white Pekinese.)

My aunt believed that a distaste for restless and unclaimed women had me moored in a careful system of ways and means, keeping a blameless married woman friend around to act as hostess and accompany me to concerts and funerals, and pursuing invisible affairs with other men's wives. In other words (this is still my aunt speaking), I was no different from any trifling, piffling male with a wife and girlfriends and a deck of ready stories. No woman was supposed to bring me more than she could pack and remove on short notice. It was my aunt's opinion that I had too much regard for what was likely to happen. I thought she was wrong, and that I expected nearly nothing.

No matter where I was posted, whether abroad or back in Ottawa, I usually managed to spend a brief summer vacation in France. There I dispensed with women altogether, caught up on my reading, and tried to write a book. I meant it to be a summary of recent times, with my experiences and judgment used tactfully, never intrusively, as a binding thread. I would have called it "My Century," but the title had already been employed by a celebrated Polish poet. Every year at high summer, I was driven to unpack my Hermes, set it on the marble table in the shadiest part of the terrace, roll in a sheet of Extra Strong, and type "Chapter 1." I could see a tamed and orderly design of streams and rivulets (early youth, intellectual awakening) feeding a tranquil river that debouched into a limpid sea. Unfortunately, it wanted only a few minutes for the sea to churn up and disgorge a ton of dead fish. Most people considered great were in reality only average; middling masters I held in contempt; as for amateurs in any field, I saw no reason why they should not be airlifted to Mongolia and left to forage. Obviously, this was of no interest to anyone except cranks; yet I felt no spite, no disappointment, no envy of younger men. I had done nearly everything I wanted, and had been as successful as my aunt had hoped.

After half an hour I would push the typewriter aside, open a thick notebook, uncap the gold Parker I was given years ago for having passed, unexpectedly well, an examination in political science, and write, "Chapter 1." Then I would cap the pen and stare at the Mediterranean, wondering if the wisp of darkness on the horizon could be a mirage projection of Corsica.

Apart from this activity I ate breakfast and lunch at home, went down for a swim early, when no one was around, played some tennis at a court up near the railway station, and dined with elderly neighbors. At the end of a few weeks I bolted the window shutters, disconnected and locked up the telephone (so that burglars would not be tempted to make long-distance calls), and returned to the wrack and low tide of my profession.

Not long ago, I sold the house where Carlotta came to look for me. The wreckers may have saved some of the tiles from the terrace floor, with their worn pattern of olive leaves. It used to be reached by a downhill flight of steps from a noisy highway. The steps continued almost all the way to the sea and came to a stop at a hedge of scarred cactus, bounding a narrow and stony public beach. Prewar cottages and villas descended the slope, with the stairs as common thoroughfare. My terrace overlooked a particularly ugly and derelict cottage; for years I had tried to buy it from its greedy absentee owner, so that I might have it razed and a garden put there instead. Unfortunately, while I was lingering in the Tuamotu Archipelago, trying to give Sandra enough rope, my Belgian tenant had met the asking price, and now maintained the wreck as a picturesque eyesore. That summer, it was occupied by his niece, Irma Baes, an amateur artist of great stamina and enthusiasm.

There was a gate at the top of the steps, kept locked. The postman no longer included us in his rounds. This, and the shape and variety of aerials on every rooftop, and the installation of Irma Baes, were the most remarkable changes on my side of the gate. Beyond it nearly everything had altered.

"I just jiggled the lock," said Carlotta, when I asked how she'd got inside. There was a taxi up on the road, with an eight-kilometer fare on its meter, which was still ticking over. She had no money, she said—no cash, that is; just a lot of traveler's checks. She talked in the accents of modern Montreal—accents that render the speaker unplaceable except within vast regional boundaries. One would have guessed she was not from Mississippi or California, not much else. Lily had had the old Quebec-Irish inflection.

I settled the cab, locked the iron gate, and fastened the chain bolt; it could be removed by reaching through iron bars, but no matter. Carlotta meantime had carried the telephone outside and lay prone on the warm terrace, talking to Lily, or perhaps to some transatlantic drifter she had picked up and turned into an intimate friend. I wondered if she knew enough French to deal with a local operator and to reverse charges. I am sure I was not niggardly, but I would be retiring before long on a tight pension; my personal capital, scrupulously amassed, judiciously invested, might need a long stretch. In my family, old people seemed to hang on forever, exacting and hale. My parents lasted nearly a century, offering to the brink of speechlessness their unsolicited advice.

Carlotta said, "Kiss, kiss," and "Bye," and "O.K., I'll tell him that." She smiled up at me and said, "It's all right for me to stay here, Steve. I mean, if it's all right with you. Just two days. I'm going to Paris, but my mother's friends can't take me right away. Their place is full up."

Only a few women still called me Steve. She was using

inherited form. When I was much younger, around the time when Lily ran away with Mr. Chadwick's gardener, I changed my signature from "Steven B. Burnet" to "S. Blake Burnet" and became, I thought, a different person. Old school friends went on saying "Burney," but new acquaintances took it for granted my name must be Blake. I was just twenty-five, the age when new acquaintances gradually begin to fill one's life.

I was not accustomed to addressing recumbent adolescents. I wished Carlotta would stand or at least sit up. I said the first thing that came into my head: "Do you mean to say that your family let you come to France without making any arrangements for you?" I kept back a question just as insistent: how it was that Lily knew I still had this house. My aunt and her parents had once been settled in the same town, Châtelroux, just south of Montreal, but several significant streets apart. The Quales were rooted in Catholic, English-speaking, bungalow territory. Most Catholics were French Canadian. The Quales and their kind seemed wedged like a piece from the wrong puzzle between English Protestants and French Catholics, matching neither in coloration or design. (The Quales were probably capable of making great sacrifices, my aunt had once said. They had eked out a year of boarding school for their unaccountable daughter.)

"No," said Carlotta, trailing scorn for elderly hebetude. She had just spent a week with a couple in Monaco, people her stepfather knew. The lady was nice, but the man had tried.

"Tried what?"

"Just tried. I had to lock my bedroom door." She raised an arm, as though signaling, and imitated turning a key.

"Where do these people live?"

"I just told you. In Monaco. They've got a house, and a sort of dried-up garden. There was no water in the shower half the time."

"Where was his wife while you were locking your door?"

"In the Princess Grace Hospital," she said, without a dot of hesitation. "She got a bleeding ulcer from some stuff she drank."

"What kind of stuff?"

"Some sort of cleaning fluid."

"I must speak to your mother," I said. "Where is she? In Montreal?"

Carlotta got to her feet. I was confronted by myself in her opaque dark glasses. "Not in summer. In summer they're mostly in Vermont. Anyway, I've just talked to her."

"I've only your word for it."

A harsh thing to say to someone young, but she answered equally, "When I called them from Monaco, they said if I couldn't find you I was to fly home. So I said I'd found you. Anyway, my stepfather's going to call you. You never gave me a chance to say. He's waiting for midnight. He never calls before midnight, except on business."

"How did you get away from the house? Didn't that man try to stop you?"

"I stayed in my room till he went to the bank. Then the cleaning lady came. She helped me get a taxi."

"Who told you he'd gone to the bank?"

"That's where he works."

"Get me the number in Vermont," I said.

"They'll only tell you what I've already told you," she said. "You'll see."

Her stepfather, Benjamin Harrower, answered. He had an agreeable voice, English sliding into American; a clergyman's voice. I had no idea what Harrower did. Someone had told my aunt he was an immigrant entrepreneur who ran a tourist bureau. "It's a terrible imposition," he said. "We're very grateful to you. You've heard the story. Carlotta sounded pretty upset."

"I'm glad she had my address."

"Well, no, she didn't. Lily told her to find out if your

number was listed, and to let us know. She told Carlotta not to call you, to let us handle it from here."

"She didn't call. She just drove straight over in a taxi. Eight kilometers."

"She's never been away, not without Lily and me. She thinks adults are always where they're supposed to be."

"How long is she going to be homeless?"

"Just three days." One more than Carlotta had said. "If it's a nuisance, would you just put her on a return flight? We don't want her to be on her own. She's still awfully young, though she doesn't believe it."

"We don't need to send her back. Not for the sake of three days. I'm leaving myself at the end of the week."

"She's a good kid." Harrower seemed to be waiting for me to confirm the opinion. "She should have called collect. I suppose it's too late to do anything about it now."

I tried to entertain Carlotta, although her youth bored me, and her belief that she was here to learn and that I could teach made me sententious and prosy. On her second day, we went to a Fellini festival in Nice, saw two movies, had lunch in a courtyard. Carlotta had promised her mother not to eat meat or fish in France. While I searched the menu, she glanced past me, over my shoulder.

Presently she said, "Steve, there's a really sick bird in a cage on the kitchen windowsill. It doesn't like the hot sun. I'll bet they haven't changed its water. The kitchen doesn't look too clean, either. Maybe somebody ought to report the restaurant." Then, "Look at the two gays over there, eating fish soup. My stepfather says they mean the end of civilization as we know it. He says they caused the fall of Rome. The gays."

Her maternal grandfather, Ernie Quale, quit the Montreal police force to become a private detective, making a special pursuit of divorce cases. He used to set up false evidence of adultery or stalk real lovers until he caught them in bed. Once he tried to blackmail a Quebec politician, and got the lobes of his ears slit. That was before Carlotta's time; almost before mine.

In the evening, I took her along to a dinner party. Carlotta excepted, the youngest person at the table was sixty-one. The oldest ninety-four. A few of them had known Lily. There was Victor de Stentor, who had kept his hair and teeth and eyesight but lost his eyebrows; Watt Chadwick, a novelist Carlotta had not heard of but whose work she now gallantly proposed to read in its entirety; a couple of antique dealers, husband and wife, who traded in the furniture heirs try to sell off in a hurry. Across from Carlotta sat a retired American naval officer who had lost an arm and had to have his meat cut. Americans seldom washed up along this fragment of coast. His neighbors referred to him as "the Admiral," and had never bothered to decide if he was Bessel, Biesel, or Beisel, while the antique dealers called him Ivor instead of Ira. Next to him, attentive to his requirements, was the former wife of a French minister of state. More as chatter than conversation, she announced to the table that her ex-husband was threatening to bring legal action against her for continuing to use his name.

Carlotta, whose French was better than fair, said she should never have given up her own name. Taking another name was like signing a brief for slavery. Carlotta had been in France nine days now—long enough to know the whole male-female business was due for an overhauling.

Ira Biesel looked at me and said, "Lily's daughter?," as if he could hardly believe it.

"Lily is my mother," said Carlotta, "but Steve isn't my father. At least, I don't think so." She seemed so startled, hurt almost, when we laughed that I wondered what nonsense was taking its slow course through the child's head. To Victor de Stentor, sitting beside her, she said, "I'm a committed vegetarian," and, holding a slice of roast beef between knife and fork, deftly removed it to his plate. I wanted to ask why she had helped herself to something she had no intention of eating, but remembered with some thankfulness that she was not mine, and that she was probably too old to be checked in public.

Later, as we left the party and climbed a number of steps to my house, she said, "I enjoyed that. I really did. You can learn a lot from older people. In Monaco, we just watched TV."

We brought books to breakfast, as if we had been living together for a long time.

"Why do you call this a terrace?" Carlotta said.

"What would you call it?"

"More like a deck, but not exactly. I like to get things right."

Irma Baes, already at grips with creation, waved from her garden. In only five weeks, progressing well beyond the symbolic hurdle of my "Chapter 1," she had completed the freestanding structures Quaternion I, II, and III, and was pasting sequins one by one on the naked framework of IV. Irma belonged to the subversive, incompetent forces whose mission it is to make art useless. Her work, which I believe she unloaded on loyal friends, could not be got inside any normal dwelling except by dint of pulling down a wall and part of the roof. Cultural authorities the world over were prepared to encourage her by means of grants; indulgent relations were disposed to gamble on her future. I suppose it was a sign that I had lived a long time and seen a great deal that everything meant to reflect the era seemed out of date. Try to tell them it's already been done, I thought. (I had told her; her eyes filled with tears.) I had reached the step of the staircase from which one cannot estimate age; I could only look down and think, Young. I'd have put Irma at thirty-odd. When her present grant, or her uncle's patience, ran out, and she had to go back to the hardboiled and standpat world of filling out new application forms ("Age? Shows? Group? Single? Sponsors?"), something would need to be done with her summer's work. There was no possible way the structures could be carried up to the road without smashing some of my windows. No van, no hired truck, no container could hold the complete Quaternion. Perhaps it could be conveyed the other way, beyond the cactus hedge, and burned on the beach.

"I like her hair," said Carlotta, waving back. "That's its natural color. I asked her. It's a natural streak effect." Carlotta dropped her voice. "You know? She had this racing-car driver who loved her? He went into a canal in Belgium and drowned. He could drive, but he couldn't swim."

"I've heard the story."

"So now she just has her art."

"Loved her" was surely fictitious, like her bogus facade of art. I thought she invented both to explain her solitude. Her tragedy, if she had one, was her own unwieldy enthusiasm. She was like a puppy bounding against one's legs. One wanted to throw a stick far out in the water; anything to keep her away. I did not say so; in any case, Carlotta had gone back to her book.

"There was a French queen who threw her lovers out of a tower," she said presently. "The tower's been wrecked, so I won't be able to see it when I go to Paris."

Any likeness of purpose between Queen Jeanne and Lily must have escaped her, and I certainly did not try to sow one in her mind. From hints and attitudes, I had already discovered that she looked upon her mother as a classic case of pre-liberation womanhood, stumbling from man to man in search of the love and support no man can give, except when it suits him. In a way, it was true. In another, a man repeatedly flung out of a tower may lie for a long time *hors de combat*, of no help to anyone.

Carlotta did not expect conversation, except in the form of informative remarks or answers to questions. It made her a comfortable companion. She said, "What's your book about?"

"It's a guide to local landmarks." I proposed to drive that morning to a Saracen fortress, restored a great number of times and now refurbished more or less as it may have looked in the seventeenth century. I asked Carlotta if she'd like that.

"Are there people living there?"

"I don't think so. Not now."

"Could we take Irma? She never goes anywhere."

"Miss Baes has her art."

She carried our breakfast dishes to the kitchen, rinsed them, helped me fasten the shutters—we were going to be out for much of the day—and found a hiding place for the telephone so ingenious that, later, she could not remember where it was. (Wrapped in a pajama top, under a pillow.)

We drove inland, on winding mountain roads. She may have felt homesick, for she began to talk about her mother and stepfather—what they liked and approved of, how they lived, where they went for holidays. I did not respond, not directly; there was no question of my discussing Lily with her child. However, by the time we reached the castle, some two hours later, I decided I could not go on behaving as though I had scarcely known her at all.

"The first time I ever came up here was with your mother," I said. "We hadn't been married long. Five weeks, I think."

There was a parking lot for tourists, now. We left my rented Peugeot and started up an unpaved avenue, between lines of yellowing shade trees, chestnut and oak.

"She never mentioned any castles," said Carlotta. "She just remembers a kind of shack, and a beach with a lot of seaweed."

"The shack, as you call it, is my present house. The terrace used to be the kitchen floor."

"Did you buy it because it reminded you of somebody? I mean, you wanted . . ." She paused. "Like, if you kept the house, this person might come back to it?"

"I bought it because it was unbelievably cheap. The only deal I've ever made in my life."

She looked up, first at me, then at the faded leaves. "What's wrong with the trees? It can't be pollution. We're practically on top of a mountain."

"The European tree disease—virus and mystery." Actually, it was as much as anyone knew.

"Who do they belong to?"

"The trees? I've never thought about it. The state, I suppose."

"Which state?"

"France. You're still in France."

"I know *that*. Only France isn't a state. It's a country. Vermont is a state. Florida's a state. They ought to be fined for not looking after their trees. The French, I mean."

The castle, which we could now see clearly, had died long before, gutted by neglect. Then, restored, its spirit had been gutted, this time by the presence of tourists. Every stone in the tower and battlements had been quarried early in this century, when an American couple had bestowed imagination and money on a ruin. I wondered if I had a duty to inform Carlotta, for whom the whole of past time could be contained in a doll house, immeasurable periods crammed under a small roof. "It hasn't the charm of the lovely places along the Loire," I began, as though Carlotta might care; as if she knew where the Loire was. I was leading round to the tricky question of fakery; tricky because Carlotta was young. I wondered if, in dealing with the young, illusion wasn't safer ground. "Here in the South, castles were really fortresses. When there was no more need for a fortress, it was allowed to crumble. Villagers hauled the stones away and stabled their goats in whatever remained."

She took off her sunglasses, perhaps to make sure I was telling the truth. I had treated her to a two-hour drive over terrible roads, with the Mediterranean revealed in greens and grays rather than shades of sapphire as we climbed. She could have been at the beach, learning from Irma. She said, "Who built this one?"

I gave up on restorations and said, "The Saracens."

"They should have paved their driveway. You could twist an ankle."

"Your mother liked the view." What else? "We came up by bus, I recall. We were too broke to rent a car." I said this, I hope, not sentimentally. By no means did I ever wish to visit anything with Lily again.

Mrs. Benjamin Harrower: I still owned books with "Lily Burnet" on the flyleaf. Once, some twenty years ago, I had received a Christmas card signed "Ken and Lily Peel." Peel was second consort, companion to Lily's middle reign. He must have taken over some of the Christmas grind that year, using an old address book of Lily's, so dazed and uninterested he no longer recognized "Steve Burnet" as a chapter heading in Lily's life. I had examined his handwriting, which I was seeing for the first time. It was stingy and defensive, nothing like his face.

My mind, as a rule shut against Lily's fortunes, let in remembered chitchat about the way Peel was supposed to have died. They say he got up on a dark winter morning, still drunk from the night before, stumbled, hit his head on a rocking chair, died at once. It is hard to die by falling on a chair. He must have died on his feet and keeled over. Harrower was edging his way out of Lily's kingdom, too, if one could trust Carlotta's register of events.

"Ben's got this nonfunctioning spleen," she had told me during the drive. "He's a very sick man. His father made a lot of money, in scales, but Ben knew the whole personal-enterprise thing was over, so he didn't carry on the business."

I supposed I was hearing a new jargon, with "in scales" replacing "in spades." Was that it? "No, Steve," said Carlotta, giving me a firm, governessy look. "Scales. What you weigh yourself on. Anyway, he made a good banker. But his spleen was overmedicated, and it just ran down."

"The man in Monaco," I said, "the one who works in a bank. Is he an associate of Ben's?"

"He reports to Ben," she said, using the diffident tone reserved for a royal connection. I was surprised at how quickly she'd picked up a European mannerism. "It's not really a bank, more an investment thing. Ben took early retirement so he could write a book about his experiences. Like, how he was born in the middle class and just stayed there. It's a question of your own individual will power. I can't explain it like he does. He's very, very convincing. But now he'll never write that book. He depends on my mother for everything. She has to keep track of what he eats and drinks—how many Martinis, at what time of day. He drinks Martinis. He's that generation."

So was I, but I did not want to engage a topic as intimate as age. Carlotta was fifteen, the product of some mindless flurry on the part of Lily before entering the peace of the menopause. During her Burnet epoch, she had avoided even conversation about having children. She was afraid any child of hers might take after her own parents, the one slit-eared, the other a destroy-the-heretics-and-let-God-sort-it-out Inquisitor.

Ben Harrower, his father in scales. From his tone of voice, I'd guessed a liberal clergyman with a working fireplace in his study. He'd bought the house in Vermont after Canada adopted the metric system, Carlotta said. He believed metric was an invention of the K.G.B. The minds of Russians could not adapt to miles, pounds, Fahrenheit temperature; for that reason, the Soviet Union was unlikely to invade the United States. "He could hardly believe it when China went metric," said Carlotta. "Last winter he and Mummy went to England and the BBC was giving the temperature in Celsius. He was born over there, so you can imagine how he felt." She was utterly free from malice or mockery, saying this; at such a remove from the Quales, even from me, that the distance could not be measured under any system.

"Who does this whole place actually belong to?" said Carlotta. We stood in the last thin patch of shade at the end of the road. Before us, in white sunlight, a drawbridge stretched over the dry bed of a moat. "Does it belong to France? I mean, the state?" She edged a dented Pepsi can aside with her shoe, and shifted her light weight to the other foot—Lily's old sign of concentration.

"Some part of the state," I said. "Some ministry or other. It used to be owned by a family who had a sardine-canning monopoly." I was not making fun of her; it was so.

She took this for a fair answer, remarking only that her mother would not let them eat tinned fish.

"So you do eat some fish at home? Meat, too?"

"Ben got poisoning in Hong Kong," she said. "So now we're careful."

Refuse littered the ditch: crumpled bags, bent straws, stubs of entry tickets. There was a child's toy monkey and a toothbrush. I wondered if the sardine connection had anything to do with a large fish someone had drawn on the planks of the bridge. Perhaps there was a more subtle reason for it, a revival of early Christian symbolism, a devious way of saying, "Pagans, go home." But as we drew nearer I saw that it was the approximate representation of a phallus. In the north of Europe, a graffito of that sort would indicate defiance and unrest; in the south, it probably signified the hope of a steady birth rate. Or just somebody boasting, I decided, noticing a chalked telephone number.

"They ought to arrest all those people," said Carlotta, looking where I looked.

"The sardine canners bought the castle from the de Stentor family," I said, glad to have a ready topic. "Victor is a connection of theirs, much removed. A junior branch. I've often wondered if he has any real claim on the name. You met him at dinner last night."

"He's fat," said Carlotta. "Victor. He wanted to take me to a casino, but you have to be eighteen to get in. They ask to see your passport. I wouldn't have gone with him anyway. He's a very old man. He shouldn't be running round to casinos. He might have a stroke, or something."

"He had no business inviting you anywhere."

"I know. I was still tired after the movies in Nice, and then Irma gave me an art lesson." I was silent. "So?" she said. "Victor lived up here?"

"Some of his relatives. Before them, there was a Cuban. He gave extravagant masked balls and parties. There are people still living down here who can remember the music, the dancers, the thousands of candles."

"Where does a Cuban get that kind of money?" She answered her own question: "Vice."

I started to say, "Long, long before Fidel Castro," but to Carlotta no such time existed. The repeated collapse and inflation of events continued to perplex me, even though I had once written a thesis on Talleyrand and published a number of afterthoughts. Since the arrival of Carlotta, the flattened present, the engorged past had scarcely quit my mind. They were like a cartoon drawing of a snake that has swallowed history whole. I said, "Before the Cuban, an American couple named Primage paid for extensive repairs. They didn't own the place and never lived here. One wonders how they got up the hill. Mules and a guide, I suppose."

"Why did they bother?" said Carlotta. "It came off their taxes?"

"Income tax barely existed. Americans were like that. They loved France and wanted the French to love them. They hadn't yet worked out that France and the French are entirely different."

"The state wouldn't get a cent out of me," said Carlotta. "You saw those trees?"

The cost of admittance was seven times greater than in Lily's day. "You could get in cheaper," said Carlotta. "Have you got a senior card?"

"I am not sixty-five."

"I'm sorry. I thought Mummy said you'd retired."

I wondered where Lily picked up her information. For years I had been turning my back on anyone likely to say, "I've met your ex-wife." Sometimes I still came across a couple by the name of Lapwing, Harry and Edith, who had been young and hard up in France with Lily and me. Edie and Lily had gone to the same Catholic school; that was the connection. It was a wives' story, with the women ("the girls," we had said then) whispering and laughing and trading stories about the men. The Lapwings now lived out West and were entirely taken up by their own affairs—university machinations, mostly.

Carlotta stopped to consider four rusted cannons in the flagged courtyard. She said, "They ought to be boiled down, or whatever it is you do with weapons. My mother's a committed pacifist. She won't even let Ben keep a gun in the house."

"They were brought here during the French Revolution," I said. "Never used. They can't hurt anyone." She still seemed troubled. Revolution? Soviet walkabout? Will miles, gallons, Fahrenheit temperature hold the line? "Long before that time," I said—thinking, The vaguer the better; less alarming for the child—"the castle belonged to the tax collector for a powerful local count. There was an ancient line of counts in the region, older than the French royal family. They spoke a dialect you can still hear in one or two villages."

"I guess it's a pretty old place," said Carlotta neutrally.

Guides and touring groups packed the stone entrance hall, which was brighter and cleaner than I remembered. The guides wore badges—"English," "Français," "Deutsch," "Italiano"—and looked, to me, too young to know about anything. As for the visitors, they resembled nothing so much as migrant labor waiting to board one of those long trains with dirty windows. Like migrants, they hung on to radios, cameras, extra clothes for a change of weather, plastic bags of fruit and chocolate, newspapers. Most of these articles had to be left at a cloakroom, after fierce argument. A "No Tipping" sign stood propped behind a saucer set out for tips. Tourists responded by unloading small change from foreign countries. Carlotta's shoulder-strap bag held only Kleenex and her passport. During the drive, she had got out her passport and examined it, frowning over the facts of her birth date and height. She was dressed in white shorts, a blue shirt, running shoes, and wore around her neck a gold heart on a chain.

In Lily's day, women tourists had dressed in flowered nylon blouses, pleated white skirts, white nylon cardigans with pearl buttons. I recalled a man in a gleaming white shirt, sleeves rolled to reveal a tattoo of peacock blue—a long number, like the number of a freight car. Outside, he and his wife took pictures of each other, then asked me to take pictures of them. They sat down on the dry grass, after searching in vain for a sign saying they mustn't. They put their heads close together and smiled up at me. The moat was fed by a shallow stream. Some people sat along the edge, which was high and straight, like the bank of a canal, and let their legs dangle. The legs and thighs even of young people looked veined and pale. Everyone over here had seemed like that, to me—bruised, pallid, glancing around to look for rules and prohibitions.

Carlotta said, "Let's stay with the French group. We'll learn more." I wondered if it would be interesting or instructive to describe my tour with Lily, and the man in the white shirt, and how it had been thought bad taste to flaunt that kind of tattoo. The sight affected people; some young men and women had had their tattoo effaced by means of plastic surgery, out of regard for the feelings of strangers.

"Steve," said Carlotta. "I want to ask you something. Why wasn't Irma at that dinner last night?"

"Miss Baes doesn't know many people. This is her first summer down here."

"All the more reason to ask her. She's nice. We talked a long time. She showed me her work."

"You could hardly fail to see it."

"She's got some little stuff inside. She makes things out of paper."

"We don't seem to know many artists."

"You could know her."

"We are probably too old to interest Miss Baes. You made the remark that Victor was an old man."

"You're around the same age as Ben and Mummy," said Carlotta. She may have thought I was feeling hurt over the business of the senior card.

Lily had wanted to know if the fee went to the sardine canners. She had soft fair hair, pale skin; was allergic to sunlight; wore a limp straw hat tied on with a colored scarf. She had on that day new rope-soled shoes, bought at a local market.

Half the fee went to the canners, half to the state, said the guide. He was a veteran of the First World War, wore all his ribbons. Lily said that seemed reasonable. Some tourists nodded, agreeing. Sharing was a popular concept. A woman with a Central European accent said, quite loudly, that the whole thing should go to the state, thus to the people. The man with the tattoo whispered something to his wife. They seemed troubled. They had known at least one state that deserved absolutely nothing.

Swallows darted round the tower at the time of Lily. The moat, brown and still, reflected long flanks of stone, threw sparks of reflected sunlight on dark portraits and tapestries. The canning family kept a suite of private rooms, one or two of which could be inspected from the doorway. Chain ropes prevented visitors from wandering inside. Lily slipped to the front line of tourists, without actually pushing, as artlessly as a child. She saw a television set and one book, a paperback about flying saucers. It was quite tattered, as if every fish canner in the world had read it in turn. This was a rich period for space apparitions. There was an uneasy feeling—not quite a fear; something more prickly and insistent—that superior creatures were on their way to judge us and might go back with a poor report.

I peered in over heads and shoulders. The visitors were looking hard at the television set; there were only a few around. This one was fitted into a walnut cabinet, both doors of which stood wide. Upon the glassy screen shone a square of yellow light, the reflection of the west window. I had not made up my mind about television. Lily knew that, and wondered what she should think. Was it a legitimate household object? Should it be left naked, or concealed in some other piece of furniture, brought out when there was ballet dancing to watch? As there was a ballet program on television about once a year, and a short one at that, perhaps to have a set of one's own was a selfish extravagance—especially now, when there was so much talk about sharing.

Lily made her way back to me, stretched to her top height—in new shoes, making an allowance for rope soles, five feet three—and pointed out that these people had not only a fish-canning monopoly and a suite of rooms in a rebuilt Saracen fortress but the walnut cabinet and all it contained. A reproach? I was a graduate student living on a grant and an allowance my Aunt Elspeth gave me. I should not have been married at all. My parents were Anglican medical missionaries in China. They were elderly and poor, had married at an age when they expected to be spared God's gift of offspring. My mother, delivered of me (God's last word on the subject), had gone straight back to Shanghai. The first face I remember is my aunt's.

"This is the long gallery, where the conspirators were hanged." Our guide spoke to no one but Lily. Her eyes were hazel with golden flecks. The sun shining in at the west window made them look transparent, pale gold. She did not ask about the conspiracy: her whole outlook was naturally conniving. Plots and quiet skirmishes had led to her present state of development. The guide continued to stare at her, helplessly, caught on the rapt, sunstruck way she looked back. The interlaced initials over the fireplace were the count's tax collector's, he told her. When the count confiscated the castle, out of greed and envy, he had the tax collector hanged in this room, facing north, so that his cipher, now ruined root and branch, was the last thing he saw before his blood turned dark. "As dark as the blood of a bedbug," said the guide, as though he had been hanged and revived any number of times.

Carlotta said she could not understand one word our guide was saying. She knew French; she'd had straight A's in French. But her French was an international, no-accent linguistic utensil. This fellow had an accent. To prove her point, she told me in no-accent French what she thought of four tapestries depicting Wisdom, Virtue, Sobriety, and King Solomon greeting the Queen of Sheba: the colors were like mud, and the whole thing needed to be dry-cleaned.

An English group now crowded into the room, jostling the French and bringing all movement to a stop. We heard, in a tinny kind of English, "The graffiti scraped into the walls are not for the eyes of every member of the family." Carlotta giggled and covered her mouth with both hands. "However," the voice went on, exceedingly careful, "the curtain can be drawn aside for a small extra fee." Through spread fingers Carlotta said to me, "That thing on the bridge? They can see it for nothing." For some reason the French guide thought that Carlotta was laughing at him. He held himself as straight as if he were on review, and spoke coldly: "In the bedroom of the countess, draperies and bed hangings are covered with plastic. Some visitors, in the past, came here with scissors and tried to cut off pieces of silk, for souvenirs." Carlotta thought she had been criticized, and would not look. "Scissors," she repeated, just to herself.

Lily had been fast to see that the arms embroidered on the valance belonged to the count's mistress. "Showing what men can get away with," she had said. She had marched over to a portrait of the mistress as Artemis, with a breast showing, then examined the countess looking like her everyday self—crabbed, deceived, forty. There should have been a mirror so that Lily could compare her face with the faces of those other two. Instead there was a glass case holding the count's plans for rebuilding what he was soon, recklessly, to tear down. Unfortunately, he ran out of funds—hadn't stopped to think that only his dead collector had known how to raise money.

"Who wants to know about these people?" Lily had said. She meant that my subject, history, was just the record of simple-minded careers. Her life, necessarily remote from public interest, would nonetheless be clear, rapid, strong.

Our tickets had allowed a climb to the top of the tower. From a windblown height we looked at a new village built out of the dark stone quarried in the region. The main street was as wide as a square, to allow for tourist cars and buses.

243

Lily struggled to ask me something: The houses were all copies of old houses, weren't they? Could people live good lives in a false setting?

I watched a truck carrying blocks of stone as it tried to back and turn on a dirt road. "I think most people are pleased just to have four walls and a roof."

"I know that."

I tried again. Did she mean that the bareness and coldness of a dead past had no power to comfort the present? This time, I had overshot. Still, I was paying attention, and she leaned against my arm, gratefully—a light, slight pressure. Then she turned and ran down the winding staircase with one motion, like a dancer.

At the bottom of the steps was a black-painted door. She waited for me to catch up before touching the handle. Behind us, a guide called that we were looking at the tomb of a local poet, not yet part of the tour. On the grave, a rose bloomed and shed. Askew on a heap of masonry—the rubble of a chapel—a sign read "Please do not stand on the main altar when taking photographs." Roses and honeysuckle clung to the sign. Around this oasis a gardener moved, clipping box hedge. A lavender-edged walk led nowhere. A sprinkler turned lopsidedly on a blanket-size lawn.

"Do you remember 'The Secret Garden'?" Lily said.

"My aunt tried to read it to me."

"Could we have something like this? I don't mean a whole castle. Just a garden."

"It's not for sale."

"The whole of Europe is for sale."

I wondered where she was getting this. Lapwing's wife had gone sour on France. She was sick of cooking on a coal-and-wood stove and hauling ashes.

I didn't want to own anything. It was my Aunt Elspeth who advanced the money for the house where I spent my honeymoon—the whole of my marriage, really. At first I went on renting it for holidays. The rent gradually rose from eight to twenty-four dollars a month. The owner decided to sell because he thought our part of the coast would never be developed, and my aunt came over to see what it was worth. There was no trace of Lily by then, apart from some damp, spotted books she had drawn from English libraries and blithely inscribed with her own name. I had kept meaning to take them back, but I was not often there. As the British colonies dwindled, the libraries closed. The libraries were often run by parish committees attached to churches in the diocese of Gibraltar. For some of my neighbors, the whole of the western Mediterranean was just a bishop's district.

Five thousand dollars: not much of a buy—a seaside wreck with a view over another damaged roof. All the same, said my aunt, her hand shading her eyes, there was the sea. "When you start to earn money, Steve, you should buy that other place and tear it down." She wanted me to have something. If it could not be Lily, let it be a tumbledown house.

Lily never needed to own an inch of Europe. She could make it up. She began to invent her own Europe from the time she learned to read. There were no mermaids in Canadian waters; no one rode to Canterbury. She had to invent something or perish from disappointment. She imagined a place where trees were enchanted, stones turned into frogs, frogs into princes. Later, she seemed to be inventing Bach and Mozart, then a host of people who lived with Bach and Mozart easily, so that she could keep good company in her mind. Sometimes I hear a dash of Lily's music over a radio and I wish I were still young—twenty-four would do—and could find Lily's inventions, and watch her trying to live in them again.

I would like to provide the justice lacking in her biography. I would like to say that she married an Italian composer-conductor. A German novelist-essayist-political thinker. An Argentinian playwright-designer-poet-revolutionary: nothing harebrained—a fellow respected, consulted by chancellors and presidents. Better still, the billionaire grandson of some Methodist grocer, generous toward the arts and all his wives. But she married me, young and broke and hardworking (Lily's transcription: immature and tightfisted); left me for a nineteen-year-old English vagabond employed to work in the garden of an ambiguous bachelor neighbor; surfaced in Montreal as Mrs. Ken Peel; lived in a series of tidy and overheated apartments; had Carlotta and sent her to one of the Catholic schools she had once professed to despise. After the rocking-chair disaster she married Harrower, got the income, the travel, the friends in Paris and Monaco, with or without magic. (According to Carlotta, Lily's chronicler, Harrower had been in the background for some time, "chasing after Mummy.")

When she finally deserted me, in the southern house, the elements of my work in plastic bags to protect them from the seeping rain, I thought she might have waited, might have found the place more to her liking with the roof tiled. She had nothing against Talleyrand, even took a bus to Nice to look things up in the municipal library, so that she and I could talk as equals. Came back with the news that Talleyrand was the father of Eugène Delacroix.

I had to tell her that history is contrary in position to gossip. What offended her? That I wouldn't play games with my work? I think it must have been then she decided I might not turn into an ambassador (she was miles ahead of me) but a teacher of history at some boggy university. She saw herself driving children to basketball practice. Saw a row of tiny shoes, cleaned with liquid whitener, on a kitchen windowsill, drying in the sun. Saw icicles dripping and snowy backyards.

I was ready for university at fifteen, won a gold medal for history two years later. My photograph was in the Montreal *Star*. When an interviewer on CJAD said I looked like F. Scott Fitzgerald, everyone my Aunt Elspeth knew tried to find Fitzgerald's books. Most of the work was out of print, and French translations were banned in Quebec. (Not that anyone in my aunt's circle could have read them.) My aunt owned two novels and a collection of short stories which she would not lend: she had the habit of underlining, and she did not want outsiders to know her private thoughts and feelings. Besides, the books were hallowed now, in some way connected to my prospects.

At twenty-four, the best the prodigy had to say was that history isn't gossip. Was that my whole mind? When Lily asked me that, I saw I had hurt her feelings. I apologized. She said, "It doesn't matter what you're sorry about. You're still the same man." I thought she was being unreasonable because she was a woman. We were sitting half turned away from each other on the stony beach. We had expected the French South to be something like Florida, but the sky was wet flannel and we wore sweaters over sweaters.

My aunt never liked my engagement to Lily: she saw Catholic entrapment, a soul floundering in the Vatican net. She still spent most of the year in Châtelroux. Some of the furniture in her house was supposed to have been brought north by ancestors who'd refused the American Revolution. Family legends had them walking all the way from Virginia, carrying chairs on their heads.

Engaged to Lily, I sat in my aunt's green-and-white kitchen, at a table drawn up to the window. There was a crust of spring snow on the sill, melting in the sun. I had a room in Montreal, near the university. I came down on weekends whenever I could, whenever Lily was not available. She had a job in Montreal, secretary to a dentist in the Medical Arts Building. Quale relatives in one of the suburbs—Verdun, I think—kept an eye on her. She must have been twenty-two, but her family pretended she was fourteen and still a virgin.

My aunt was making pancakes. She walked back and forth between stove and table; I'd never known her as restless. She said that if I really meant to marry the Quale girl the marriage had to work. Catholics won't divorce. (It couldn't fail, I knew—buttering pancakes, smiling.) Let me tell you what women won't stand for, she said. They don't want to be deprived of sex or money. One or the other, if it can't be helped, but never both. Well, sometimes even both, so long as there is no public humiliation. "Such as the husband's spending a lot of money on another woman," she said.

She had mentioned two subjects, sex and money, that until now she had pretended did not exist. I had just been made an honorary member of a closed society—the association of women who stop talking when a man (or child) comes into the room.

About money: I had none—not yet—but Lily knew. Later, I tried to remember if I had ever neglected her or tried to make a fool of her. The public teasing to which Harry Lapwing subjected his wife disgusted me. No; what went wrong had nothing to do with either of the things my aunt had mentioned. Lily must have seen me—my mind, my life, my future, my Europe—as a swindle. She began to enjoy long conversations with Watt Chadwick's gardener. He had thin yellow hair, was drifting, desperate, homesick. Told her he was a music student, that gardening was destroying his hands. Talked about the glories of England: he must have glossed over Oliver Cromwell. One day the two blond truants plodded up the hill to the railway station. "Leaving everything," said Mr. Chadwick, when he came over to cry about it. (Such tears! No woman could have inspired them.) In fact, they had left nothing but two men who could not even comfort each other.

Carlotta looked with strengthened disgust at her surroundings —the flagged courtyard and rusted cannons. The tour was over. "We were ripped off," she said. "We never got up the tower, and the German guide told his group a lot more."

"It's just the language," I said. "It sounds like more."

"I've never been anywhere important. I need to know the

right things." So that was the trouble. I made her tell me some of the places she had been to—New York, Boston, Jamaica, Bermuda—and tried to explain why they mattered. Her parents had never taken her really away, she said, shaking her head. Ben and Lily went to England, or Japan, or those other, great destinations, during the school term, when there were out-of-season rates.

She seemed dejected beyond any cause I could think of. Perhaps she was hungry. "We'll stop somewhere for lunch on the way back," I said, remembering all the places Lily and I could never afford. We were half across the bridge (the graffito by now trodden to a blur) when I saw Victor de Stentor and Irma Baes get to their feet out of some dry stubble behind the trees and start down the avenue, hand in hand.

My first reaction was to draw Carlotta's attention away from the pair. Her remarks in the restaurant in Nice had shown her to be a dangerous girl, inquisitive and censorious. She carried, intact, deeply buried, a moral legacy from the Quales. There was also her terrible, shadeless social goodness. She would be capable of telling Irma, "You shouldn't be holding hands with that old Victor. You could do a lot better. Why, he even tried to take *me* out. He'd try anything."

It was I who was thinking this, not Carlotta. On second thought, I was not sure Irma could do better, or that she could do anything at all. A long line of good-looking women came before her in Victor's life. She had nothing to show but a bogus affair with a dead driver. Had she been to Victor's house? Did he invite her to dinner parties without the rest of us? He still had the same drab yellow villa on Cap Martin where Lily had dined, believing herself in Riviera society. The gravel lawn was the same, except that occasionally a truckload of fresh stones was raked over the old. By way of a garden he had two stubby palm trees, like leafy cigars. He still kept as servants clandestine foreigners, who led a stealthy, watchful, and perhaps half-starved existence. (For as long as

I'd known him, Victor offered his guests the same dinner of roast chicken with saffron rice, which he ate contentedly, often explaining that saffron contained every wholesome element required for the nutrition of rich and poor.) In the old days, they had been Italians and Yugoslavs; now they were likely to be Tamil or Pakistani.

The house had seemed strange to Lily and me. It was furnished with Edwardian oddments, bought on the cheap just after the war, when a number of villas and their contents were sold up. Some of the owners were too old to pick up a way of life so changed; some could not afford to. Foamy, gauzy curtains used to blow in and out the dining-room windows, which simply means there were no screens. Mosquito bites on Lily's thin skin swelled like hives. She mentioned screens once, at one of his dinner parties, and everyone laughed. People laughed at screens in all those civilized places that abounded in flying, stinging, poisonous insects.

Victor made his servants spray the dining room with a substance now banned in the industrial world, although stocks of it remain on other continents, left behind by industrial developers. The servants used large cans with pump handles. They bumped into one another, not looking where they were going. Lily and I inhaled the stuff, ate it and drank it (it fell in droplets over the saffron rice and into our wine); Lily rubbed it over her arms and neck.

I'm reminded of Lily whenever I read about DDT and how our generation stocked it in our bodies. Nobody knows the specific harm it may have caused; it is just there, in me and in Lily—all we have left that is still alike. In powdered form it was a palliative against fleas and lice. (Nothing killed the French strains.) Fleas and lice were the mid-century European plague, Divine castigation for sex among strangers. It was Lily who first noticed that when European men had nothing in particular to do, were just standing idle, they scratched themselves, in a dreamy, somnolent way. At first, she sup-

posed their clothes were too tight. She wanted my opinion:
I was supposed to know about Europe, because my Aunt
Elspeth had taken me to England when I was a child. But the
Burnets and Copes (my aunt was a widowed Mrs. Cope) did
not consider England to be a part of Europe. I could not tell
Lily a thing about the clothes of European men. She had to
find out for herself.

What she found out kept her faithful, at least for a time.
Lapwing's wife, of wide and casual experience, told her that
the men were more entertaining than North Americans, but
conceited, grudge-bearing, and dirty. Edie Lapwing used to go
down to the harbor at night and make close investigations in
the shelter of beached fishing boats.

"So long as her hobby lets Lapwing get on with his work,"
I said, when Lily told me, though it was not the way I felt
about men and women and marriage. I wished Lily could find
a line of interest apart from Edie and Edie's men, but I wasn't
sure if I should say it. I did not want her to turn from DDT to
Talleyrand. Her interests might be trivial, but they were not
inconvenient. "I don't think you've picked a very pleasant
subject," I said. It was the way I'd been brought up to show
disapproval—qualifying, modifying. She laughed, and said her
research was as valuable as mine. She knew as much about
the acquired resistance of French fleas as I did about French
history. Of course, there was less to learn, and her only source
of inquiry was Edie.

Victor was never attracted by Lily's frail beauty. Her ab-
solute personal poverty (he had antennae for that) canceled
any sexual pull. He believed, and told me, that she would
fade out before thirty. He was separated from a wife of his
own, Angelica, who lived down in Genoa. You have to be grim
and rich to put up with that climate, and, in fact, all the
Genoese I got to know (I had a stretch of career in Italy) were
grim and rich. The rich, engaged in the struggles of richness,
always choose a gray and flinty climate to do their struggling

in: Hamburg, Milan, Lyons. The laws of Italy still forbade divorce. Victor could easily have convinced a French court that Angelica had deserted him, but it suited his hugger-mugger business arrangements to have an extra, legal domicile in another country. A separation agreement did not prevent him from giving Angelica's address as his own. The agreement itself caused nothing more disruptive than fitful grappling over household goods. Once, Angelica came over while Victor was giving a dinner party and took the dining-room furnishings away. His guests were still at their drinks, in the stiff, ugly salon across the hall. They pretended not to see (he favored the British colony)—all but Lily, who held her glass of Campari in both hands and stood in the doorway and stared.

It was our first sight of Angelica. She carried in a crocodile attaché case an Italian court order, signed by a relative of hers, and six copies of a permit to carry the stuff over the frontier, duty-free. She came in a van, which she made the driver park straight across the front door, as in a police raid. Lily took an inventory of her red dress, tightly belted, her hat of glossy red straw, the nail polish that was the exact color of the hat. Her hair, the yellow of nasturtiums, was longer than Lily's. She dragged a stepladder out of the kitchen, kicked off her thin red sandals, climbed in bare feet. (The table had already been removed, the carpet rolled up and hoisted aboard the van.)

Angelica examined the chandelier, seeing if it could be taken down, while Victor, at the foot of the ladder, observed with unabashed displeasure his wife's naked legs. "Angelica, this is undignified," he said. She said the equivalent of "What is dignity?," but in language more violent and personal, and started to unscrew the light bulbs. (Lily reminded me later that Victor never stopped scratching the back of his neck.) He finally gave up, left her there, and took his party of seven to a restaurant, where he paid with a check that may have been dud: he made a great show of waving his signature dry and advised the headwaiter to have it framed.

Angelica still lives in Genoa; Victor will never retire. He continues to deal in crumbling property—villas with their shutters askew, their gardens crowded with those wild shrubs that bear clusters of spines. Two dead villas, side by side, razed to make way for an apartment block, or a small shopping center and parking space. Most clearances were completed about fifteen years ago. Victor's operations consist of mopping up. For a long time he looked at our enclave of shabby villas and saw them reduced to a framed photograph of southern decay hanging on the wall of the "Old Riviera" room at some local museum. In place of houses he envisioned three or four different things, all tall and white, inspired by the look of Beirut when it was still a good place for real estate.

Now here was Victor, with no eyebrows left, forever married to Angelica, venturing to replace the dead racing-car driver who haunted poor Irma's imagination. He was proposing a neck that, so far, no one had broken. He may even have promised never to die, thinking it would please her—although, I suspect now, it is not at all what women want.

Watching the two make their way hand in hand down the road, I experienced love's opposite, which is resentment. Neither of them possessed the least qualification for being loved. Irma had never been able to stir up friendship. Some people had imitated her Belgian accent; the Admiral swore she had tried to entangle him in a conversation about art (he was too smart to be caught), and that when she mentioned the Bauhaus he had understood "the bowwows." I was not so unjust as to think she and Victor deserved each other. He was still the man at the foot of the ladder, scratching his neck and pleading for dignity. Irma was no more a pirate than most of the rest of us; she would have clutched the chandelier and said, "Help me! I'm falling!" She was a sad little amateur, failed before she was launched. Nevertheless, love's opposite reflected Irma's vision of Victor. She turned to him there in the road, and it was like watching a tree burst into wild blossom because a saint had touched it. Now my mind changed in a second. She was too good for Victor de Stentor. I believed the story of the lover drowned in the canal: brave, disinterested, superior to Victor. For the sake of his memory, I would have seen Victor dead, bloated, devoured by crabs.

"Let me show you where the Cuban used to hold concerts of chamber music for his guests," I said, guiding Carlotta a few steps toward a bleak terrace surrounded by a broken balustrade patched with concrete.

"Is this old?"

"Some of it. Try and imagine the music, the moonlight, the stiff wind that rises at about ten o'clock, the audience quietly freezing on their gilt chairs. Vladimir de Pachmann played here. He was a great favorite at that time."

"What did he play?"

"He played Chopin on a grand piano, and every so often he stopped playing and cried."

"We listen to a lot of music at home. My mother likes it."

"I know. It used to be music with meals. I can never see a lamb chop without hearing Mozart."

"You shouldn't get into those habits—looking at a chop and thinking about Mozart. It comes from living alone." Strangers had joined us, believing the terrace must be part of a tour. "Steve," said Carlotta. "Let's go. The sun's very hot. You ought to have a hat on."

On the road she made me walk in shade. The other pair had disappeared. Victor was probably making his pitch about turning our small community into a contemporary instrument for living, once we'd accepted generous compensation. At least the two were safe from prying, if not from each other. Seeing the worst ahead for them did not make me feel on high ground. I held Carlotta's arm for a second. She said, "Why don't you buy a car and just leave it here? It would be cheaper than renting one."

"I'm here only a few weeks a year."

"Like, how many?"

"Three, four. Sometimes six. It depends. I'm wondering where to take you to lunch."

"It's really nice of you," she said.

"To think about lunch?"

"Yes, and to show me all these different things, and take the time to explain. A lot of men wouldn't be bothered."

"I'm sure most of them would," I said, to round off the subject.

"Mmm. Ya. Men." From Lily's daughter, three profound philosophical statements; but she was Ken Peel's child, too.

The last time I ever saw Ken Peel was on a June afternoon, just before Lily and I got married and sailed to France. He stood on the threshold of his sporting-goods store, hands in his pockets, rocking slightly in his white-and-tan shoes, sniffing the air of downtown Montreal. I was walking west along St. Catherine Street, on my way to see an Italian movie the Church was trying to have banned in Quebec. I could make out the hand-lettered sign Peel hung on the door when he had better things to do than sell gym kits: "BACH IN 20 MIN." (Either that sign announced a perpetually postponed concert, my aunt once said, or it showed Mr. Peel was careless about everything.)

I supposed he must have been seeing off one of his married women friends: such was his reputation. At that moment the wife of a titled Austrian exile, or a jailed union leader, or a night-club waiter (there was no bias to his adventures) might be combing her hair in a taxi, trying to pull together a credible story about the way she'd spent the afternoon. Perhaps she was one of the stiff, tough, powdered Anglo-Montreal women I encountered at cocktail parties when I was roped in as escort for my aunt. I could see her, Peel's *petite dame*, surveying the room with slightly pouched eyes, hand clamped on a gin-and-tonic, thin line of scarlet lipstick, one of the famous Montreal hats sitting square, no one at the party even close to guessing she had recently been treated with some insolence on Peel's storage-room couch.

Peel, face tilted, smiling at the sky, might have recognized me as an occasional customer. I had never paid by check, so he had no reason to remember my name. I have probably altered my recollection of that moment, changed its shape, refined it, as I still sometimes will tinker with shreds of a dream. It seems to me that I drew level with the store window, then turned and bolted across the street. I think that I saw, or was given to see, with a dream's narrowed focus, a black-and-white postcard image of Lily on the edge of Peel's couch, drawing on a stocking. For the first time I noticed how much she resembled the young Marlene, the Weimar Dietrich: the same half-shut eyes, the same dreamy and invulnerable gaze. She slid into the stocking, one perfect leg outstretched, the other bent and bare.

Actually, Lily was already dressed, waiting in the shadow of the store for Peel to give her the all-clear. She moved nearer the hot, bright street, and must have observed me, dodging behind a streetcar. I think I glanced back; either that or a whole city block swung round. Lily, wearing a hat of white straw and a white dress amazingly uncrumpled, slid past Peel and ran straight into traffic, calling, "Steve! Steve!" Peel took his hands out of his pockets; perhaps his way of showing surprise. I think now (I have been thinking it over for years) that she saw me turn round, and knew I knew. So, better to brazen it out.

I slowed down, stopped, examined a display of garden furniture in a store window. She ran on tiptoe, shuffling, the way women used to run in spike heels; caught up; grabbed me by the sleeve. Part of my mind had fallen into darkness. I could not recall having ever loved her. The Dietrich-like image dissolved, was replaced by one of Ken Peel, in heightened tones, wearing the trusting smile of the natural con artist. That face was the stamp of his Montreal generation, distributed unevenly among all ranks and classes of English-speaking males, as luck is thinly or thickly spread.

My next immediate feeling was snobbish relief that Peel was nobody's friend, and the incident could be contained. But then it occurred to me that the people I knew had already come to some conclusion about Lily. A girl who could glide out of the late-afternoon shadows of Peel's place had the habit of dark doorways.

Her hand rested lightly on my arm. She explained what she was doing on St. Catherine Street—buying a birthday present. (I was about to be twenty-four.) "A new tennis racquet," she said—the last thing in the world I needed just then.

We went to the movie, and I appraised the nervous, then confident way she held my hand. She must have been saying to herself, "I was wrong. He doesn't know." Until today we had read each other's thoughts. Telepathic marvels, un-matched coincidences fed our conversation. Now the flow of one mind into another seemed to me unhealthy, unwise. I prayed never to stand revealed to anyone again. The film was about a pregnant woman in an Italian village who believes she has been seduced by a messenger from Heaven. Lily had a lapsed Catholic's glibness on such matters, and did not bother to lower her voice. The cinema was nearly empty, so that her remarks carried. First a woman said, "Would you mind?," then a man called, "Ah, shut your face!"

We left and walked along to a German restaurant called The Old Mill, and had beer and Wiener schnitzels. The film had reminded Lily of the boarding school, accursed and de-spised, to which Old Lady Quale had consigned her when she was trying to get Lily away from boys; specifically, from me. I knew most of the stories, but I let her talk. She looked past me, with the soft bright stare that took in everything.

Why didn't I challenge her? Because she might have lied,

accused me of being jealous, of following her all round the city, always trying to catch her out. She might swear she had never been inside Peel's store; rather, only once, to inquire about racquets. I had no method, no system, for coming to terms with Lily. My aunt never lied—she had never been frightened—and my parents lived in a barren climate of the truth at any cost. Lily occupied a terrain more lush and changeable, but she had been brought up by dangerous people.

I began to wonder if I could be sure. Perhaps she had been walking by, had happened to glance in the shopwindow, seen the very thing, stepped inside to have a word with Mr. Peel. She was nothing to Peel except Miss L. Quale, secretary to a dentist in the Medical Arts Building. I had to ask myself if I wanted to live with Lily or without her: I had always been with Lily. When I was much younger, had won prizes, had my looks compared to F. Scott Fitzgerald's, I had studied my face, without vanity, wondering if my overpraised and temperate character held some other essence—more charming, more devious, even weak. In my aunt's copy of "All the Sad Young Men" I had found an underscored passage about the end of love, the end of April; never the same love twice; "let it pass." My aunt must have recognized her own stoic yearning for my late uncle, young Lieut. Cope. I knew nothing about him, except for a sepia studio portrait in First World War uniform.

Lily ate three bites of schnitzel. We traded plates, and I finished it off. She drank a sip of beer, pushed the glass across, took my empty one. I was coming out of darkness, ready to listen to her again. She said how much she owed me, how much she had learned from me. Without me, she would never have known about European movies, Anna Magnani, Vittorio De Sica. She might have been like her own mother—ignorant, bigoted, probably mad. I didn't answer. I think she believed it: I know at the time I thought it was true.

We were married in Christ Church Cathedral, east of where the European cinema and the German restaurant and Peel's old store used to be. All effaced; never replaced. The Quales would not attend the wedding, because it was in an Anglican church. My parents sent a letter from China and managed to congratulate me without mentioning Lily. (The Maoists were about to send them packing.) My aunt was there, wearing a great many layers of clothing for the tropical day. All that linen and silk must have been a kind of armor. I had wanted Lily to be given a token of family jewelry. It wasn't exactly the czarist imperial treasure, but a pin or a ring might have made Lily feel welcome and secure. My aunt did not think such a gesture was required or even sensible; she did not expect the marriage to last. For the same reason, she would have preferred a civil ceremony to all these reckless promises to God, but in Quebec only religious rites were allowed. She kissed Lily on the cheek, then suddenly relented, removed the seed-pearl brooch fastened to her jacket, and pinned it on Lily's dress.

Lily and I sailed to France on a Polish freighter. The Lapwings were already installed in a Mediterranean hovel, on the most decrepit street of an ancient quarter. An open sewer ran under their windows. Lapwing never noticed; he sat indoors, working out a community of purpose between William Morris and St. Paul that so far had escaped academic notice. In a letter to Lily, Edie had described how their neighbors threw garbage out their windows and stoned stray cats and dogs. She was not complaining but felt relieved to be at last confronted with the real world. The Lapwings did not think we were ready for the kind of life that underlies appearances, and so they had leased for us a more conventional dwelling, close to bus routes. There was a view over the sea. It would cost us eight dollars a month. (The Lapwings were paying six.)

On the second day out Lily curled up and was deathly seasick. Then she seemed to be bleeding to death. The ship's doctor took me aside and said, "We can call it an accident. Don't worry. You are young, you can have other children."

I said, "It's a mistake." Lily could not have been pregnant: I had taken the greatest care. I never wanted my aunt to be able to say Lily had trapped me by being cunning and Catholic and fertile. I was not the son of missionaries for nothing: I saw the incident as a clean sweep, the falsehood washed away, the pagan wrenched from old customs, blood sacrifice of the convert—Lily converted to me, entirely.

Though slight of figure, she was very strong. Her health improved quickly. She told me over and again about the life we would have together, and the happiness that would carry us. But I imagined she was thinking, He doesn't know, and I said to myself, Well, let it pass. In the shack above the sea I heard, "He doesn't know," more and more faintly, and Lily must have heard a dying, a fading, a whispering "Let it pass." She had more sense than any man, so she cut the sound.

IN A WAR

WHEN LILY QUALE was fourteen, stockings were hard to come by, because we were in a war and factories were dressing soldiers. She colored her bare legs with pancake makeup, some of which always rubbed off on the edge of her skirt. Recently she had taken up with a Polish girl, a few years older, twice expelled from convent schools. She taught Lily how to draw a fake seam with eyebrow pencil and explained a few other matters usually left obscure in Catholic Quebec.

Lily's mother showed a cold face to the girl who knew such a lot. She didn't think well of me, either, although I knew hardly anything that might interest Lily.

"You and Lily are too big to be natural company for each other now," her mother said one Saturday afternoon, when Lily and I were sitting in the Quales' kitchen, on the excuse of doing homework. I was a year ahead, writing an essay on how railways helped the Industrial Revolution, while Lily tried to disentangle the reasons for the American Civil War. We barely knew that Canada had a history. "She ought to be with a girl her own age," Mrs. Quale went on, "and you, Steve, you'd be better off with another boy. And I don't want the two of you going upstairs to study in Leo's room unless I'm in the house."

That was how adults saw things then: simply. Catholic-Protestant stories, all bad luck, lay strewn around us, the rocks and bricks of separation. Why let anything go too far between two kids who were bound to separate? The town we lived in straggled along both sides of the Châtelroux River. There was no core to the place except a huddle of stores around the French church, with its aluminum-painted roof and spire. The Quales were in bungalow territory, Catholic and English-speaking—everyone's minority. The last thing they looked for was trouble. My aunt had a house on the opposite shore, facing the river. We had a dock and a rowboat and a canoe. We had French-Canadian neighbors, working a strip farm, and English-Canadian acquaintances living in houses like ours, farther down the road, toward the bridge and railway station. We had a wide lawn and an enclosed backyard, and a low hedge of shrubs with red berries, and a covered gallery running around three sides of the house. We did not keep a cat, because my aunt thought cats were hypocrites, and we gave up keeping a dog after Snowy drowned and Rex was poisoned. My parents were Anglican missionaries in China; my Aunt Elspeth was bringing me up.

I knew even then that Mrs. Quale was mistaken about Lily. She could never have wanted a close girlfriend. The Polish chum was just a handbook she studied for expertise. Lily kept a large pond stocked with social possibilities, nearly all boys, and thought nothing of calling me on a Saturday if some other happy chance had let her down. My aunt, hearing my end of the negotiation, would dub me a human jellyfish; but one of the things adults forget is how complete younger people seem to one another, how individual and clearly defined. It is the grown person who looks evasive and blurry, who needs to improvise. Lily to me was without shadow: I took it for granted she worked her arrangements with hook and reel. My easygoing response was more toughly snobbish, and so more injurious to Lily, than my aunt could guess. Probably, I thought well of myself for letting Leo Quale's little sister get away with murder.

Before that time, when I was still in seventh grade—in those days known as Junior Fourth—my aunt remarked that it would be good for someone like me, raised by a woman, to have a stalwart figure of some kind to look up to. I thought about Lily, and the scale of her nerve, and how she learned the uses of gall from watching her brother Leo, and I said, "You mean like Leo Quale?"

"Leo has certain qualities," said my aunt, as if he had barely escaped hanging. "It was more a gentleman I had in mind—say, like Mr. Coleman."

She was defining a stage of growth as well as a caste. It is true that at fifteen Leo was too advanced to make a friend of me, but he was still too immature to offer paternal advice about sexual prudence and financial restraint. (My aunt actually believed fathers can do this.) She began to think well of him later that year, after running out of other models for me. To my aunt the male nature was expected to combine the qualities of an Anglo-Canadian bank manager and a British war poet, which means to say a dead one. Folded inside the masculine psyche there had to be a bright yearning to suffocate face down in a flooded trench, to bleed from wounds inflicted by England's enemies, even to be done in by a septic flea bite, if a patriotic case could be made against the flea.

Leo showed that eagerness to perish: enlist, ship overseas, never be heard from again. He was heavy and blond, a kind of Viking, one of the thick ones, out of dark small parents, Glasgow Irish on both sides. It had taken him six years to flounder through his last three grades, and he was now becalmed in eighth. He could read, he could even work complicated sums in his head, but he could not write a complete sentence. My aunt blamed his school, which also happened to be mine: Leo should have had Catholic teachers. All these years he had felt bewildered, unwanted, could not focus his intelligence. A memory of Leo—placid, sleepy, too big for his desk—stands next to my aunt's appraisal.

After school and all day Saturday he delivered groceries to English customers, on both sides of the river. Sometimes he made four or five trips along the same street—particularly Fridays, when there was a rush on beer. Quebec was the only part of Canada where beer could be sold by a grocer, instead of in a government liquor store. We owed the privilege to the twists and snarls of Catholic morality, said my aunt, who drank only sherry.

Leo and my aunt were expecting a war, well ahead of world leaders. "Ah, it'll come, all right," he would assure her, lowering a box of provisions from his shoulder to the kitchen table. "And we'll be in it. Don't you worry, Mrs. Cope. We need a good old war to sort us out."

"I'm afraid you're right, Leo. War brings out the best in men and nations, but we have to remember the fallen and the missing, and sometimes there is injustice, too."

"It's them or us," said Leo. "England forever!" He sounded a bit crazy. He couldn't have heard it at home: his father hated the English.

What did my aunt mean by "missing," I used to wonder. How did you know you were missed: I had never missed my parents, and their letters showed no longing to see me but simply told me to be good. People in Châtelroux, when they talked about the last war or the next, said, "You've got to die sometime." In St. George's Anglican Church my aunt and I droned in unison that we believed in the resurrection of the body, though common evidence spoke against such a thing. Leo may have seen a brief future in the Army as an improvement over the immediate prospect, stuck in a classroom where he was a head taller than his teacher. Perhaps he was just exercising his native talent for saying whatever might appeal. He once boasted to my aunt that, at thirteen, he had tried to join the Mac-Paps—the Mackenzie-Papineau Battalion, the Canadians fighting Franco. It was no more preposterous than his father's claim to have played rugby for Ireland: Mr. Quale was built like a jockey and had never been outside Quebec.

You expected people like the Quales to be undersized.

They descended from immigrants known to other British in-
comers as "Glasgow runts." The term has vanished: it takes
only two generations, no time in real time, to acquire strong
teeth and large hands and feet and a long backbone. Only
aversions and fears, the stuff of racial memory, are handed
down intact.

To recall the Quales around their supper table, with the
radio turned right up, three or four saucepans bubbling on
the stove, everyone eating something different, Mr. Quale
yelling back at the radio during the news broadcast, laying
down the law on England, or Quebec politics, or the Spanish
Loyalists ("Every last man a louse" did for them all) is to
see in deep perspective the Gorbals of Glasgow, where their
parents had started out, and farther away, thin on the horizon, the trampling of Ireland. Mr. and Mrs. Quale belong to
the first race of Irish, black-haired, driven underground, their
great gods shrunk to leprechauns. Leo is the Norse marauder,
hopelessly astray in the dark. Lily seems delicate, at least to
the eye, with pale fine hair: a recent prototype, if you count
in centuries.

Weekdays Mr. Quale got up at five and took the train to
Montreal, where he was a plainclothes officer on the police
force. He did not know French but could cause the arrest
of people who did not understand English. Usually he came
back in the middle of the afternoon and sat on a bench outside the railway station reading the Montreal *Star* until about
five, the Quales' suppertime. Their neighbors said Old Lady
Quale gave him no peace to read the crime news at home. She
thought a husband was supposed to keep moving, emptying
the water pan under the icebox, examining for short circuits
the loops of wiring that hung in fronds all over the house.

She had eyes that were fierce and round, and with her flat
face and little beaked nose made me think of an owl. She
screamed at children who walked on her lumpy, dried-up
flower beds, at drivers who parked delivery vans in front of

34

her door; but there were days on end when she had nothing to say, and peered out of some private darkness to the light. Then, all at once normal again, in whatever degree any Quale normality could amount to, she would start to predict the family future. It was as if she had been granted a vision during her silent trance. Lily was going to be in trouble at an early age. ("In trouble" meant unmarried and pregnant. As Lily was believed not to know how pregnancy started, the prophecy had to be left to drift, like a canoe with nobody in it.) Leo could expect a career of panhandling in downtown Montreal. Mr. Quale was sure to be fired from the police force, for inertia, while Mrs. Quale was promised an old age of taking in washing.

Hearing it, the children went on eating their supper, unmoved. Family conversation usually slanted in a single direction. "You'll see I was right!" and "Believe you me, one day you'll wish you'd listened!" and the shadowy, the mysterious "Remember me when the time comes." Unlike most parents on their street, the Quales did not beat their children, but they kept saying they ought to, and that the kids were asking for it. Any day now Mrs. Quale would take the broom to them and Mr. Quale start swinging the buckle end of his belt. Leo believed it might happen, though he could have knocked his father down with a shove; Lily, who was intelligent, did not.

Mr. Mitchell Coleman, elected by my aunt to be an example for me, had to resign from the prep school in Montreal where he taught English and art. She passed on the news in a cluster of baffling remarks: it was a great shock to his friends, he had betrayed a trust, he had to live with his conscience, only God could judge, and he would never set foot here again.

I thought he had pilfered something. It was the worst I could imagine as adult bad behavior. My aunt had a friend who borrowed small objects. (We never said "stole.") Her husband would go through her handbag at night and find an ivory carving, a butter knife, a china soap dish. I was not expected to have opinions about grown people. Once, I had imitated Mr. Coleman's way of standing in front of a bookcase, reading titles in an undertone, and my aunt had reproached me for mocking a man of moral worth, whose very friendship confirmed our own decency. Now she was in a close predicament, needing to let me know he had fallen and at once describing and concealing the nature of the fall.

Dilemmas of upbringing were often referred to my father, whose delayed seaborne answer was likely to be "Have it out with him." Having it out terrified her. She gave me a glass of ginger ale and three squares of cocoa fudge on a bread plate and made me sit down in the parlor, facing her but at a distance. I ate the fudge, then the crumbs. Meanwhile she said that Mr. Coleman's badness was an example of reality. Until now, "reality" had meant having no money. In her way she was as deft at dealing out a bleak future as any parent across the river. Poverty and high principle seemed to occupy the same terrain—to my mind, a vacant lot. I knew some of the discourse by heart: my father was unlikely to amass any capital out in China; one day I might have nothing to fall back on but a clean reputation. Better to run out of worldly goods than the world's good opinion, she said, never having been faced with the choice.

What was she trying to tell me? She knew, but wished she had a man there to take over the notes and deliver the lecture. It was for my benefit that she invited so many inspirational male figures to meals. Her generation of women attached no secondary meaning to "confirmed bachelor" or "not the marrying kind." Some men got along without a wife. English novels were full of them. Occasionally one of those bluff and taciturn heroes got tired of eating cold suppers and let himself be overtaken by a fresh-faced, no-nonsense country girl.

That was fiction: in the real world homosexuality was a criminal offense, liable to a sentence in a penitentiary. For that reason, scores of thoroughly unmarriageable men had to let themselves be seen as a catch, without getting caught. My aunt was a social godsend, for she was attractive and kind, a widow who did not want to remarry ("Steven wouldn't like it"), and, apparently, bleached of desire. At least, she sent none of those coded messages over the female telegraph, meant to be deciphered only by selected men. Or, perhaps she sent explicit signals and was puzzled because no answer came. Or, owing to the amazing boundlessness of ambiguity, may have received more replies than anyone guessed.

At the time I am telling about, she was calm and cheerful, wore her glossy hair parted in the middle, had a supply of single acquaintances described as brainy, therefore harmless, masculine by denomination and ego, willing to take the train or drive down from Montreal, receive one glass of dark sherry, eat a well-done roast and Yorkshire pudding, and put up with me.

Boyd McAllister arrived in a roadster that had the shine and color of a new chestnut. I climbed into the rumble seat, by way of a step the size of a piano pedal, and he took me for a spin along the river. My aunt shamed me by calling, "Don't fall in!" Ray Archer turned up slightly drunk, wearing a kilt, and got just his food: no sherry. Later, my aunt said he had no right to a clan tartan, not even on his mother's side. Herbie Dunn, just back from London, had seen Jack Buchanan singing and dancing, wearing a top hat. He gave my aunt a Buchanan record, "I'm in a Dancing Mood." We played it on the gramophone and he showed us some steps.

"Now, Steven, watch Mr. Dunn," my aunt said, as if this, too, were part of a virile education.

But the pleasures of adults are unbecoming. I looked out the parlor window, to the road and the river. More people walked than drove. There were French-Canadian boys dressed for Sunday, stiff and buttoned-up, and a few Anglos throwing sticks for their dogs. The English had on comfortable weekend clothes. To the French, they looked like hand-me-downs. "If you didn't know who they were, you'd hand them a nickel," our farmer neighbor once said. The river was the color of thin maple syrup. On the far side, in a spread of bungalows, was my Protestant school and the deep Catholic mystery of Lily and Leo.

In those days people owned just a few clothes, no more than they needed. A garment was part of one's singularity. Our teachers put on the same things day after day—the same dress, the same shoes, the same crumpled suit. Leo *was* his plaid shirt and navy-blue sweater, Lily her red coat and knitted leggings. She pulled the leggings off when she got to school, revealing white cotton stockings, and draped them over the radiator, along with other snowy outfits. We were four grades to a room; the smell of the class was of wool drying. Whenever Lily tore her white stockings or got them dirty her crazy mother would scream, "I'll whip you, Lily Quale, I swear to God!," but Lily took no notice.

Mitchell Coleman came to Sunday dinner in blazer and flannels, a white shirt, and a striped tie, gray and maroon. He probably had been cautioned from childhood to be neat and clean, even where it didn't show, in case he got knocked down by a streetcar and had to be carried to the Royal Victoria Hospital and undressed by strangers. With his exactly combed sandy hair, his jacket and trousers uncreased even after a train ride, he was ready for every kind of accident except the one he ran into.

I make him sound set and congealed, but he was in his early twenties, a local poet of the schoolmaster breed. He offered my aunt stapled, mimeographed editions of his work— long spans of verse in which Canada sprawled forbiddingly (nothing enticing about the national posture) between two bleak alternatives, the United States and the frozen North. I realize now that he was an early nationalist, a term that would have been as meaningless to my aunt as "reality" was to me. Her Canada was a satellite planet, reflecting the fire of English wars, English kings and queens, English habits and ways. My uncle had been killed at Ypres. The men she summoned to dinner matched in age the young officer in the sepia photograph in her bedroom.

Alone with me, in mock after-dinner conversation, Mr. Coleman looked elderly and oppressive. My aunt would leave us so that he could tell me about ideals heritable by men—apparently a richer legacy than any endowed on women. I could hear her in the dining room, clearing the table. She would not come to my rescue until it was time for Mr. Coleman to catch a train back to Montreal. He lived in a two-room apartment in the basement of a stone house on Bishop Street. His windows were just under the ceiling: looking up, he could watch the boots and shoes of strangers going by. It cost him twenty-two dollars a month, which my aunt said was high. That was all we knew about his private arrangements.

The instant she left the room he would stand up, facing the bookcase, with his back to me.

"Read Dickens?"

"Aunt Elspeth reads 'A Christmas Carol.' "

"Aloud, at Christmas?"

"Yes, sir."

"Read Kipling?"

"When we have to."

"At school?"

"Yes, sir."

"You've read the Henty books, I suppose?"

"We've got some that used to belong to my uncle."

"Good. They're good stuff. Read any poetry?"

"When we have to."

"What do they make you read? British? American? Any Canadian?"

"I wouldn't know, sir."

He told my aunt that bringing civilization to children was like throwing rose petals at a moving target.

"Some of the petals stick," she said. "I'm sure some do." She looked at me, as if wishing I would stop dodging.

If optimism is the prime requirement for teaching, she was a born educator. Mr. Coleman seemed to attract defeat and may have been in the wrong line altogether, on several counts. For one thing, whatever the scope of his personal adventures, he absolutely hated small boys. But when my aunt unfolded his disgrace, or thought she had, small boys were on her mind. She wanted to know if he had ever made a clear, coarse suggestion while standing in her parlor, reeling off names of authors. I did not know what she was getting at, and was merely thankful to hear he was never coming back. Her assurance that his failure was God's business meant that one more fragment of disorder had been added to the mess in Heaven.

"It may be for the best that it has come to light," she said, encouraging me to speak up. It was her second attempt, after the dead try over cocoa fudge. This time I was pushing a lawnmower around the backyard, earning my allowance. She sat on the back step, on a straw cushion usually kept in the hammock.

"Are you just as glad?"

"What about?"

"About not having to see Mitchell Coleman anymore."

I was just as glad, which condemned him. On his last visit he had sneered at her taste in books.

"She's reading Depression novels," he had said. "And now this thing." He pulled it off the shelf. " 'The Case of Sergeant Grischa.' Not a lady's book. I'd like to know how it got here, right next to"—he paused to make certain—" 'To the Lighthouse.' "

"Leo Quale read it," I said. "He says it's the best book anybody ever wrote."

"Do you know what it's about?"

"Yes. He told me. They shoot him."

"Your friend Leo?"

"No, the sergeant. He's supposed to be a deserter, so they shoot him."

"Don't take it to heart. It's only a story. Most of us die in bed."

He sounded simpler, easier—too late. My side of the exchange closed down. It was all right with me if we hated each other, as long as my aunt didn't know.

Better a reticent kid than one suddenly cold. He sensed the change—he was not a teacher for nothing—and began to speak at random, as if we shared the same tastes and the same age: "Arnold Zweig. I wonder if he and that other Zweig are brothers, like the two Manns." Did he really think I could tell him? "She's read it, too," he said, showing me how the book fell open in his hands.

Later on, I discovered it opened to passages that my aunt, or Leo, may have liked in particular. The core of her mind, or Leo's, contained more anxiety than anyone guessed. One of the two had lingered over the short truth that death means dying. Only someone with great denseness of spirit needs to be reminded, so I suppose the steady reader to have been Leo.

Released from eighth grade, Leo became free to carry groceries full time. He set a box down in our kitchen and made the remark that we seemed to live on cereal. His habit of uttering one pointless thing after the other had my aunt believing he had plenty to say but lacked a sense of direction.

"Your parents must be paying Catholic-school tax, Leo," she said to him. "Why weren't you in a Catholic school?"

"You have to take a bus. My sister Lily pukes in buses."

"There are two Catholic schools here in the town."

"They're both French."

"What of it? It isn't too late for Lily to change. She could learn French, and she'd be with her own kind. We often see the little Chartrand girls going by, wearing their uniforms. They look so sweet, all in black."

Leo stared at the demented lady who did not know there were Catholics and Catholics. He made a stab at saner conversation, and asked if this was an old house.

"Fairly old," said my aunt, smiling. She did not want to make the tenant of a raw bungalow feel ill at ease.

"About a hundred years?"

"Perhaps more."

"Did you always live here?"

"It was a summer home," said my aunt. "But when I had Steven—I mean when Steven came to stay with me—I decided to bring him up in a house instead of an apartment."

"We move a lot," he said—I think with pride.

The Quales were not rich or poor enough to stay put. They kept packing and unpacking their bedsteads and their chamber pots and the family washtub. Each move was decided for the better, but they still had to pump cold water and cross a backyard to a privy. There was the same glassed-in cube of a veranda around the front door and storm porch at the back. The storm porch, a storage shed made of unpainted planks, was meant for brooms and pails, old newspapers, overshoes, rubber boots, stray scarves and mittens, jam jars without lids, hockey sticks. It was the place where the Quales shed snow from their outdoor clothes and where Leo sat down on a broken chair to take off his skates.

Sometimes when he got up in the morning, Mr. Quale would find a hobo sleeping on the floor, under a strip of carpet. "God alone keeps tramps from freezing to death," he would say aloud, as he heated the rest of last night's soup for the man. No one was ever turned away: the magic of retribution could transform any workingman into a vagrant. While the stranger drank his soup, Mr. Quale pretended to sort newspapers, so he wouldn't make off with the bowl. If Lily came out, with her nightgown stuffed inside her woollen leggings, and her coat around her shoulders, on her way to the privy, Mr. Quale would order her back to her room until the man had disappeared. Sitting on the edge of her bed, she could hear them exchanging neutral opinions about good and bad times. The only thing Mr. Quale ever offered, other than soup, was a pair of old skates that hung by their tied laces from a rusty nail.

"Can you use these skates?" he would ask.

"I don't think so. Thanks all the same."

In every Châtelroux household there were skates that seemed to have arrived on their own, and that no one could wear. Ours were attached to the lock of a shutter. Every so often my aunt unhooked the skates and examined them. "Steven, are you sure they aren't yours?"

"They're miles too big."

"Well, they certainly don't belong to me."

"Somebody must have left them behind."

"I suppose so. I wish he'd come and take them back."

She tried to fob them off on Leo. He took one look and said, "Gurruls'."

"Girls' skates, Leo? Are you sure? Perhaps your mother could try wearing them, or Lily. Lily would have to grow into them, of course."

"Lily doesn't wear black skates. Only white."

Another day, she tried to get him to take home an assortment of piano scores, and seemed astonished to hear the Quales had no piano.

"Why not, Leo? Don't you like music?"

"My dad likes that Gershwing," he said, after a pause.

It is the only time I can ever remember my aunt's seeming foolish to me. She was pink in the face, ready to lead him by the hand through Gershwin to Bach. I bring to mind her flushed forehead and the excitement in the room, tension I was still too young to be able to measure, generated by the presence of the town dunce, unteachable and dying to go to war. Mr. Coleman had been right about her reading; Leo entered her imagination on the same wave as the Depression. For a while she decided the poor were to be joined, or imitated, rather than tided over. Leo was not offended; he did not know he was poor. The Quales were better off than most of their neighbors.

My aunt began to say that a taste of family life, of the warm, untidy kind that Leo surely enjoyed, might be good for me. She often sent me to the Quales' house with a grocery list for Leo, when she could as easily have called the store. A sheltered boy had much to learn from a brave, older boy already making his own way, she said; but all I learned, tagging after someone too big and too different, was that I had it in me to resent my aunt. I couldn't hate her. She wasn't a mean woman, not even strict by nature. She was trying to make up for the absence of a man's firm guidance.

Their family life seemed to me fierce and mournful. Between Leo and his mother lay something cold, like cold poison. On one of her dark days I watched Mrs. Quale putting Leo's plaid shirt through the hand wringer, clamped on the edge of the sink.

"On top of that," she said, perhaps to herself, not to me, "he had to take his time getting born. Arse first, as if he had all the leisure in the world. In no hurry. Didn't care about *me*. They said, 'Come on, Mrs. Q., make an effort, you don't want him to strangle.' He was blue in the face, when they finally saw he had a face. Didn't get oxygen. That's why. No oxygen. Nurse said, 'So don't be surprised if he stays pretty dim from the neck up.'"

Pursuing his cultural awakening, my aunt led Leo past the dining room, where he stopped to stare at an engraved portrait of Sir Walter Scott, but before he could ask who it was, and his age, she ushered him through to the parlor, showed him books, and said, "You may borrow anything."

His hand went straight to "The Case of Sergeant Grischa," which he may have taken to be a detective story. He kept it, I think, about three months, returned it, then asked to have it again.

Much later, Lily told me about the first time he brought the book to supper and propped it in front of his plate. He had been reading it some five weeks.

"What're you wasting time on now?" said his mother.

"Let the boy read," said Mr. Quale. "It's education."

Mrs. Quale had nothing against that. She believed in education but was not sure how it was obtained.

"Well, what is it?" said Mr. Quale. "Answer your mother when she speaks to you."

"Book I borrowed from Mrs. Cope."

"Take it back," his father said. "They'll be saying you stole it."

"Tell me, Leo," said Lily. "Tell me what it's about." She was so crazy about reading that she read the stuff on calendars. "I'll read to you, Leo. I've finished eating. Do you want me to read to you?"

Lily was the favorite: they didn't mind letting her read. When she could not pronounce a word, she skipped the whole line. The radio news, tuned to the pitch of Mrs. Quale's voice when she raised it, ran alongside Lily's tone, which was soft and unsteady. Mrs. Quale soon grew sick and tired of hearing Lily, and she could not figure out what sort of army the sergeant belonged to. Mr. Quale became impatient, too. He shouted that in his day deserters were stood up and shot, and that was the end of it. They didn't drag their existence on for dozens of pages. Mrs. Quale said it would do Leo a lot more good if he read to Lily. They did try it that way, several evenings, but he didn't enjoy it, and for the others he was too slow. He finally finished the book, on his own, and was the only one in the family who knew the deserter was stood up and shot.

Leo had his tonsils and adenoids out and walked home an hour later, bleeding into a towel. His small mother was with him, holding on to his sleeve. The cuts became infected, and he nearly died. When he was said to be out of danger, my aunt made me go and see him. She sent two jars of grape jelly, wrapped in leftover Christmas paper, and a note of encouragement, signed, "(Mrs.) Elizabeth B. Cope."

My first surprise was that they were humbly glad to see me—the shrimpy parents, and Lily, wearing just her petticoat, her hair all suds. (Rumor had it that Catholics never washed.)

"Get some clothes on you," her father said. "There's company."

Leo was getting royal treatment, propped up in his parents' double bed with an embroidered pillow stuffed behind his neck. A number of unsorted social facts were shed from my person as I accepted his invitation to sit down at the foot of the bed.

He said, "Well, sport," in a husky whisper, and moved his legs to allow me more room. I hardly dared look at him—I was not sure how to deal with my advancement to family friend—and stared instead at the pattern of daisies and asters on the pillow case. On a table next to the bed was a white enamel basin with a towel over it. He said they were giving him emetics, so he would throw up the rest of the infection.

"Well, sport," he said again, meaning, I think, that extra conversation was up to me. The room was dark, ferociously heated by a kerosene stove. A stylized design of birch leaves, or sunflower petals, had been carved in the stove lid, to serve as vents. The heat and brilliance of the flame had turned the stove into a magic lantern: the whole ceiling was covered with ornamentation, hugely magnified, in quivering red and blue. Lily came in and sat down, combing her wet hair. She had buttoned on a gray cardigan belonging to her father, which fitted her like a coat. She said, "You're fine, Leo," because she still thought he might be dying.

Leo changed the position of his feet. I took it for a hint and got straight off the bed. He said, "Come again, sport," and that rounded off the visit.

In March he put his clothes on, and found that everything he owned was short in the legs and sleeves. He had to duck under the frame doorway between the kitchen and storm porch. He did not return to work at once but did odd jobs around the house, getting his strength back. My aunt had a new delivery boy, Doug Bagshaw. He kept his tips, coppers and nickels, in a baking-powder tin. He liked to weigh the tin in his hand and make the coins jingle. My aunt did not try to draw him out, and never once said he or the Bagshaws might be good for me. When she referred to the old days, before Leo was taken so ill, it was to mention Herbie Dunn and his kind gift of the Jack Buchanan record. She recalled other Buchanan songs—"Two Little Bluebirds" and "A Cup of Coffee, a Sandwich, and You"—which she hummed for me. Buchanan was so tall, and his top hat made him so much taller, that he had trouble finding suitable dance partners. Saying this, she drew herself up, even straighter than before.

"I'm the general, you can be Grischa, the rest of you are soldiers." That was Lily, marshaling her troops of little girls on the soggy spring lawn. There had been a freeze, then a thaw, then a new fall of spring snow. The game was a mixture of hide-and-seek and tag, with two teams drawn up, as in red rover or run sheep run. Anyone on the wrong side, the army that wasn't Lily's, could be shot on sight. "Grischa" was leader of a team, the equivalent of being a general. The victims lay down and got their coats wet.

Leo had been sweeping the front walk. Now he stood leaning on his broom, eating jujubes out of a paper bag. There was only one other boy, Vince Whitton, aged six. His sister, Beryl, wasn't allowed to play in the street unless she agreed to take him with her.

Vince said, "One other time, I was over here and some person gave us some jujubes," but Leo never made a move.

My aunt had sent me across the river after school to find out if Leo was ever going to work for the grocer again; it would be her last show of interest in the Quales. I stood, neither claimed nor discarded, doing nothing in particular, watching Lily in her red coat.

Just then Mr. Quale came along the street and up the walk Leo had cleared of snow. He wore a wool cap and a long gray scarf. He said to Leo, "How do you stand all that jabbering?," meaning the little girls, excited and shrill.

Nothing is so numbing as an unexpected audience. The soldiers started to pick lumps of snow from each other's coats. Mr. Quale nodded his head, as if it were on a wire spring, and took his cold pipe out of his pocket. He pointed the stem at the girls, then at us, and said, "And bear this in mind, lads. You can't ever do a bloody thing with them."

Now Mrs. Quale appeared on the doorstep. She held up a white stocking so we could see the hole in it, and called, "I'll thrash you, Lily Quale—I swear to God!"

Vince Whitton started to wail: "Beryl, I want to go home."

"Go home, then."

"Not without you."

"Glory, wouldn't I be glad to see the last of you," his sister said.

When the war came Leo waited to be the right age; then he enlisted and left Châtelroux. His mother baked coconut biscuits and marble cake, which she posted to him in a tin box. He brought the box back empty when he came on leave. They talked about different things to eat. She had an old, stained, illustrated cookbook they looked at together, and Leo would pick out what he wanted for supper. No more of everybody eating something different: the others had to settle for Leo's choice.

Lily and I commuted to high schools in Montreal. We took the same train in the morning but did not sit together. Girls sat with girls, boys with boys. Sometimes in the afternoon we saw each other in Windsor Station. The Quales had moved to a two-story, semi-detached house made of orange brick. A steep, narrow staircase rose out of the living room. It was the first thing you saw when you came in. Mrs. Quale waxed the steps and kept them very clean, and never missed a chance to say "upstairs." There was a bathroom and an indoor toilet. They were buying the house inch by inch.

Leo's room contained a large bed with a candlewick spread and a varnished desk, in case he had something to write. The desk and the counterpane were the first things Mrs. Quale ever had delivered from Eaton's. No sooner were they moved upstairs than he went away, leaving behind his civilian life and his life altogether. On that wartime Saturday when I sat doing homework with Lily, Leo had got to Halifax with his regiment and was waiting to embark. His bed was always made up, Lily told me. Mrs. Quale, who now loved Leo best, had heard about embarkation leaves that occurred twice, sons and husbands who came back after having said good-bye. She thought she might see Leo, late at night, under the light in the porch, carrying his kit. Some women dreaded any hitch in the slow process of separation. It was impossible to speak the same brave words twice. Some said they would as soon face a ghost as a man seen off back a few days later but somehow different in look and manner, already remote.

When Mrs. Quale would let us, we used Leo's desk. In the kitchen our books got stained, because Mrs. Quale kept wiping the table oilcloth with a soapy rag, part of an old undershirt of Leo's. Upstairs we were obliged to sit at opposite ends of the desk, so our knees wouldn't touch. Mrs. Quale would look in, bringing us something to eat or drink, or just making sure we hadn't stirred from our chairs. Once, I re-member, she said, "Who's winning?" as though "education" were another of Lily's games, one for which Leo had never found the knack.

Lily tried again: "How about letting us work in Leo's room?"

"You heard me. Not unless I'm in the house."

"You are in the house."

Mrs. Quale replied that we were to keep away from the stairs altogether. She was here, yes, but not for long. She sounded as if she had finally decided to quit her home and family, but she was just taking an embroidered tray run-ner over to Mrs. Bagshaw's, because of next day's Sodality sale. The sale was for the benefit of Catholic missions: my father's rivals.

"Steve," she said, "either you go home right away or you promise you'll stay where you are, by the window, where the neighbors can see you."

In their new kitchen hung a mirror with a frame of grained pitch pine—just for decoration. No one had to wash or shave in the kitchen sink. Mrs. Quale pinned a blue feather to her hat, then stared at it.

"Keep the feather on, Mum," said Lily. "It looks lovely." But Mrs. Quale could not decide.

Five minutes after her mother had gone out the front door, Lily said, "It would be better upstairs. We can't even spread our things out here—there's so much stuff on the table, ketchup and mustard and that. And I hate the noise of that kitchen clock. It's like a hammer."

"She said to stay near the window."

"Dad stops work at noon Saturdays, but he never gets in before five. Mum will be having tea with the other ladies."

"She might want to come back, just to see where you

are," I said. "She may change her mind about wearing the feather."

"No, not now. She'd have done it right away." The clock was a china plate with a pattern of windmills. The arms of the tallest windmill told the time. She looked up; we both did. "Don't bother to bring all your books," she said. "Just what you'll be needing."

Upstairs we started one thing, then another. There wasn't much to it; we never got beyond high fever. I wanted to pull down the blind, but Lily said it would draw the neighbors' attention. She folded the bedspread—her mother's pride. She must have made a mistake about the family timetable, for we suddenly heard Mr. Quale at the front door. We were on our feet and presentable by the time he reached the kitchen and dropped something—a newspaper, probably—on the table. He got a bottle out of the icebox and poured himself a beer, capped the bottle, put it back. There was a moment of silence: he may have picked up the blue feather lying on the drainboard, wondering what it was doing there. Or he may have noticed the books we'd left behind, or heard us moving around, talking in whispers. He plodded to the foot of the stairs and called, "Who's home?"

Lily pulled the coverlet over the sheets and smoothed it. We started down the staircase and met him, almost at the top.

"Want me to get your tea, Dad?" she said.

"I'm all right." He did not acknowledge me.

Lily collected the rest of my books from the kitchen. I held them flat on my chest, like a shield. She came with me along the river road, up the wooden steps to the bridge, and about halfway across. The Montreal train rushed by and the whole bridge shook; we had to stop and hold on to the railing. As the noise faded, in a thinning mist of steam and soot, she said, "Leo's gone for good. I've said good-bye to him. I know it. Dad's already starting to say I'm all they've got, and

Leo isn't even overseas. I'm not all they've got. They've got their new house."

When Lily arrived home her mother was waiting in the doorway. She smacked Lily's face twice, and Mr. Quale came running out of the kitchen, shouting something. He stopped to unbuckle his belt. Lily thought, God in Heaven, is he going to take all his clothes off, and she backed off and went down the front step and stood in the street. Her father came no farther than the veranda, because of the neighbors. He had his belt in his hand and looked as if he had just got up. They stared at each other, with the length of the front walk between them. Then he threaded the belt back on and said, "Have I ever laid a hand on you? But just you keep out of my way, now. Stay out of my way. That's what I want to tell you." His voice was so steady and quiet that Lily began to cry.

He had looked in Leo's room and seen nothing—and he was a policeman who later became a detective, specializing in divorces and evidence of adultery. When his wife came home the first thing she did was turn back the bedspread, and she found makeup from Lily's bare legs all over the sheet.

The Quales came to my aunt's house that night, carrying a leather grip. My aunt, sensing something, told me to go to my room. I was too big to be ordered that way, exactly, but I went upstairs and lay on the floor and listened through the iron grille of the hot-air register. I could hear Mrs. Quale telling my aunt how I had played them false and destroyed their daughter.

My aunt made an astonishing reply: "You have let that girl run wild. It's a wonder nothing worse has ever happened. She roams all over town on Leo's bike, talking to strangers. She has been seen near the highway, talking to men in cars. She has been seen with a gang, Lily the only girl, throwing stones at people in canoes."

The stone-throwing incident had occurred when Lily was eleven. My aunt was not trying to excuse me but simply was upholding the tradition that made girls responsible for their own virtue. I was guilty of having disobeyed Lily's mother—nothing more.

"Put that thing away," my aunt said, sharply, next.

The Quales had opened the leather bag and were attempting to unfold the evidence. "It's the sheet," said Mr. Quale—his only remark.

"I believe you. Please put it away."

"Don't you look down on us," said Mrs. Quale. "We've got our only son in the service. Lily's always been head of her class. We own most of the home we live in. My husband has an honored position on the police force. Mr. Quale has never walked a beat."

Did my aunt smile? Something made Mrs. Quale break into full-throated weeping—nothing like my aunt's rare, silent tears. It was a comic-strip bawling, Katzenjammer roars of "Wah!" and "Ooh." My aunt said, "I know, I know," and offered to make tea. Soon after that I heard the Quales leave.

My aunt did not let me think I was innocent. The only reason she did not send me away to school, as she wanted to, was that my father could not afford the fees. She was saving her own money to put me through university. In the meantime, it would be good if I were to show common sense and gratitude. I had never heard her say I was supposed to be grateful for anything: for a time, it put a wall of shyness between us. The Quales, stretching their means to the limit, shut Lily up with nuns, in one of the places from which her Polish friend had been expelled. I went on commuting, but without a sight of Lily.

Windsor Station was full of soldiers, and there was a brownish, bleak kind of light on winter afternoons. Once I saw Lily's Polish friend. She was a tender blonde, dimpled, with small blue eyes—something like Leo's. I noticed her wedding ring, and said, "Is your husband going overseas?"

"Oh, no," she said. "Morrie's got a heart. I mean, he's cardiac. I'm not here for anything in particular. I just came over with my girlfriend." I had shot past her in height. She had to look up, as Leo's mother did to Leo. Her girlfriend, talking to a knot of airmen in the shadows of the station, was unknown to me. Lily's friend seemed to be weighing the advantages of spending any more time in my company, but she must have spent more than I remember: it was she who told me what happened after Lily got home that other afternoon. She was a good-natured girl but restless, as if nothing had yet been settled, in spite of the wedding ring. She wrote me off, abruptly, and turned away. I took that for a good sign. I would not have known how to end the conversation. Something in my manner spoke for me, and would always ease me out of awkward times. So I thought.

"Aren't you Steven Burnet?" Mitchell Coleman looked wholly different as a soldier: younger, for one thing. The lumpy uniform, the thick boots, the close-cut hair, brought him near to Leo in age and manner. Even in the unprepossessing uniform he seemed neat and spruce, still ready to be knocked unconscious and undressed by strangers—all that was left of his former self.

He gave me a slow look and probably surmised, correctly, that I had known him at once but would never have approached him. "I barely recognized you," he said. "You're twice your old height. But there's still a look—a family look, I suppose. More of an expression than an arrangement of features." I did not know what to make of a personal observation of that kind. I wondered if he meant to criticize my aunt's appearance, or mine. "How old can you be now?"

"I'm still going to high school."

"They tried to teach me how to make Army training films," he said. "But documentary movies are a string of lies. I decided not to sit the war out." He did not ask for news of his old friend; the trusted friend who had dropped him, without a word of explanation, without hearing his side of the case. "Well," he said. "For King and country, eh?" and there was not a hint or a glance to let me know whether he was being ironic. He shouldered his kit, and we shook hands.

He's only a corporal, like Leo, I said to myself. At his age he should at least be a captain.

When she was playing at war, Lily made medals out of silver paper. Her soldiers, pronounced dead, got up to receive a decoration. They said, "I've got mud on my coat. I'm going to catch it at home. Somebody, help me get the mud off."

In that war, or one like it, Vince Whitton begins to whine: "Beryl, my feet are getting cold. I'm hungry. I have to go to the bathroom."

"You can pee your pants, for all I care."

He stops sniveling for a minute, and moves closer to Leo; leaves the girls to be with the men. Mr. Quale points the stem of his pipe, that time or another, and says, "You can't do a bloody thing with them." The players freeze. They stand, hardly breathing, small creatures in an open field, hoping they have become the white of the snow around them and the hawk will leave them alone.

Leo's death made two of the English newspapers in Montreal. My aunt sent Mrs. Quale a note. Looking back, she felt that the Quales had never been suited to the occasion; in short, they had done me no good whatever. I had learned nothing from Leo or his family—"poor Leo," he had become. In a sense, they had ceased even to be a family, with Leo gone and Lily away from home, under close surveillance. Once, she said, "The worst mistake I ever made was when I let you chase around after Leo"—which shows how blameless her life must have been.

THE CONCERT PARTY

ONCE, LONG AGO, for just a few minutes I tried to pretend I was Harry Lapwing. Not that I admired him or hoped to become a minor Lapwing; in fact, my distaste was so overloaded that it seemed to add weight to other troubles I was piling up then, at twenty-five. I thought that if I could not keep my feelings cordial I might at least try to flatten them out, and I remembered advice my Aunt Elspeth had given me: "Put yourself in the other fellow's place, Steve. It saves wear."

I was in the South of France, walking along a quay battered by autumn waves, as low in mind as I was ever likely to be. My marriage had dropped from a height. There weren't two pieces left I could fit together. Lapwing wasn't to blame, yet I kept wanting to hold him responsible for something. Why? I still don't know. I said to myself, O.K., imagine your name is Harry Lapwing. Harry Lapwing. You are a prairie Socialist, a William Morris scholar. All your life this will make you appear boring and dull. When you went to England in the late forties and said you were Canadian, and Socialist, and working on aspects of William Morris, people got a stiff, trapped look, as if you were about to read them a poem. You had the same conversation twenty-seven times, once for each year of your life:

"Which part of Canada are you from?"

"I was born in Manitoba."

"We have cousins in Victoria."

"I've never been out there."

"I believe it's quite pretty."

"I wouldn't know. Anyway, I haven't much eye."

One day, in France, at a shabby Mediterranean resort called Rivebelle (you had gone there because it was cheap) someone said, "I'd say you've got quite an eye—very much so," looking straight at Edie, your wife.

The speaker was a tall, slouched man with straight black hair, pale skin, and a limp. (It turned out that some kid at the beach had gouged him behind the knee with the point of a sunshade.) You met in the airless, shadowed salon of a Victorian villa, where an English novelist had invited everyone he could think of—friends and neighbors and strangers picked up in cafés—to hear a protégé of his playing Scriabin and Schubert through the hottest hours of the day.

You took one look at the ashy stranger and labeled him "the mooch." He had already said he was a playwright. No one had asked, but in those days, the late Truman era, travelers from North America felt bound to explain why they weren't back home and on the job. It seemed all right for a playwright to drift through Europe. You pictured him sitting in airports, taking down dialogue.

He had said, "What part of Canada are you from?"

You weren't expecting this, because he sounded as if he came from some part of Canada, too. He should have known before asking that your answer could be brief and direct or cautious and reserved; you might say, "That's hard to explain," or even "I'm not sure what you mean." You were so startled, in fact, that you missed four lines of the usual exchange and replied, "I wouldn't know. Anyway, I don't have much eye."

He said, "I'd say you've got quite an eye . . ." and then turned to Edie: "How about you?"

"Oh, I'm not from any part of anything," Edie said. "My people came from Poland."

Now, you have already told her not to say this without

also mentioning that her father was big in cement. At that time Poland just meant Polack. Chopin was dead. History hadn't got round to John Paul II. She looked over your head at the big guy, the mooch. Fergus Bray was his name; the accent you had spotted but couldn't place was Cape Breton Island. So that he wasn't asking the usual empty question (empty because for most people virtually any answer was bound to be unrevealing) but making a social remark—the only social remark he will ever address to you.

You are not tall. Your head is large—not abnormally but remarkably. Once, at the beach, someone placed a child's life belt with an inflated toy sea horse on your head, and it sat there, like Cleopatra's diadem. Your wife laughed, with her mouth wide open, uncovering a few of the iron fillings they plugged kids' teeth with during the Depression. You said, "Ah, that's enough, Edie," but your voice lacked authority. The first time you ever heard a recording of your own voice, you couldn't figure out who that squeaker might be. Some showoff in London said you had a voice like H. G. Wells'—all but the accent. You have no objection to sounding like Wells. Your voice is the product of two or three generations of advanced university education, not made for bawling orders.

Today, nearly forty years later, no one would dare crown you with a sea-horse life belt or criticize your voice. You are Dr. Lapwing, recently retired as president of a prairie university called Osier, after having been for a long time the head of its English department. You still travel and publish. You have been presented to the Queen, and have lunched with a prime minister. He urged you to accept a cigar, and frowned with displeasure when you started to smoke.

To the Queen you said, ". . . and I also write books."

"Oh?" said Her Majesty. "And do you earn a great deal of money from writing books?"

You started to give your opinion of the academic publishing crisis, but there were a number of other persons waiting, and the Queen was obliged to turn away. You found this exchange dazzling. For ten minutes you became a monarchist, until you discovered that Her Majesty often asks the same question: "Do you earn a great deal of money with your poems, vaulting poles, copper mines, music scores?" The reason for the question must be that the answer cannot drag much beyond "Yes" or "No." "Do you like writing books?" might bring on a full paragraph, and there isn't time. You are proud that you tried to furnish a complete and truthful answer. You are once more anti-monarchist, and will not be taken in a second time.

The subject of your studies is still William Morris. Your metaphor is "frontiers." You have published a number of volumes that elegantly combine your two preoccupations: "William Morris: Frontiers of Indifference." "Continuity of a Frontier: The Young William Morris." "Widening Frontiers: The Role of the Divine in William Morris." "Secondary Transformations in William Morris: A Double Frontier."

When you and Edie shook hands with the mooch for the first time, you were on a grant, pursuing your first Morris mirage. To be allowed to pursue anything for a year was a singular honor; grants were hard to come by. While you wrote and reflected, your books and papers spread over the kitchen table in the two-room dwelling you had rented in the oldest part of Rivebelle, your wife sat across from you, reading a novel. There was nowhere else for her to sit; the bedroom gave on a narrow medieval alley. You could not very well ask Edie to spend her life in the dark, or send her into the streets to be stared at by yokels. She didn't object to the staring, but it disturbed you. You couldn't concentrate, knowing that she was out there, alone, with men trying to guess what she looked like with her clothes off.

What was she reading? Not the thick, gray, cementlike Prix Goncourt novel you had chosen, had even cut the pages of, for her. You looked, and saw a French translation of

"Forever Amber." She had been taught to read French by nuns—another problem; she was too Polish Catholic for your enlightened friends, and too flighty about religion to count as a mystic. To intellectual Protestants, she seemed to be one more lapsed Catholic without guilt or conviction.

"You shouldn't be reading that. It's trash."

"It's not trash. It's a classic. The woman in the bookstore said so. It's published in a classics series."

"Maybe in France. Nowhere else in the civilized world."

"Well, it's their own business, isn't it? It's French."

"Edie, it's American. There was even a movie."

"When?"

"I don't know. Last year. Five years ago. It's the kind of movie I wouldn't be caught dead at."

"Neither would I," said Edie staunchly.

"Only the French would call that a classic."

"Then what are we doing here?"

"Have you forgotten London? The bedbugs?"

"At least there was a scale in the room."

Oh, yes; she used to scramble out of bed in London saying, "If you have the right kind of experience, it makes you lose weight." The great innocence of her, crouched on the scale; hands on her knees, trying to read the British system. The best you could think of to say was "You'll catch cold."

"What's a stone?" she would ask, frowning.

"I've already told you. It's either seven or eleven or fourteen pounds."

"Whatever it is, I haven't lost anything."

For no reason you knew, she suddenly stopped washing your nylon shirts in the kitchen sink and letting them drip in melancholy folds on *France-Soir*. You will never again see a French newspaper without imagining it blistered, as sallow in color as the shirts. The words "nylon shirt" will remind you of a French municipal-bonds scandal, a page-one story of the time. She ceased to shop, light the fire in the coal-and-wood stove (the only kind of stove in your French kitchen), cook anything decent, wash the plates, carry out the ashes and garbage. She came to bed late, when she thought you had gone to sleep, put out her cigarette at your request, and hung on to her book, her thumb between the pages, while you tried to make love to her.

One night, speaking of Fergus Bray, you said, "Could you sleep with a creep like him?"

"Who, the mooch? I might, if he'd let me smoke."

With this man she made a monkey of you, crossed one of your favorite figures of speech ("frontiers") and vanished into Franco's Spain. You, of course, will not set foot in Franco territory—not even to reclaim your lazy, commonplace, ignorant, Polack, lower-middle-class, gorgeous rose garden of a wife. Not for the moment.

I am twenty-seven, you say to yourself. She is nearly twenty-nine. When I am only thirty-eight, she will be pushing forty, and fat and apathetic. Those blond Slavs turn into pumpkins.

Well, she is gone. Look at it this way: you can work in peace, cross a few frontiers of your own, visit the places your political development requires—Latvia, Estonia, Poland. You join a French touring group, with a guide moonlighting from a celebrated language institute in Paris. (He doesn't know Polish, it turns out; Edie might have been useful.) You make your Eastern rounds, eyes keen for the cultural flowering some of your friends have described to you. You see quite a bit of the beet harvest in Silesia, and return by way of London. At Canada House, you sign a fraudulent statement declaring the loss of your passport, and receive a new one. The idea is to get rid of every trace of your Socialist visas. Nothing has changed in the past few weeks. Your wife is still in Madrid. You know, now, that she has an address on Calle de Hortaleza, and that Fergus Bray has a wife named Monica in Glace Bay, Nova Scotia.

Your new passport announces, as the old one did, that a Canadian citizen is a British subject. You object, once again, to the high-handed assumption that a citizen doesn't care what he is called. You would like to cross the words out with indelible ink, but the willful defacement of a piece of government property, following close on to a false statement made under oath, won't do your career any good should it come to light. Besides, you may need the Brits. Canada still refuses to recognize the Franco regime. There is no embassy, no consulate in Madrid, just a man in an office trying to sell Canadian wheat. What if Fergus Bray belts you on the nose, breaks your glasses? You can always ring the British doorbell and ask for justice and revenge.

You pocket the clean passport and embark on a train journey requiring three changes. In Madrid you find Edie bedraggled, worn out, ready to be rescued. She is barelegged, with canvas sandals tied on her feet. The mooch has pawned her wedding ring and sold her shoes in the flea market. You discover that she has been supporting the bastard—she who never found your generous grant enough for two, who used to go shopping with the francs you had carefully counted into her hand and return with nothing but a few tomatoes. Her beauty has coarsened, which gives you faith in abstract justice. You remind yourself that you are not groveling before this woman; you are taking her back, greasy hair, chapped skin, skinny legs, and all. Even the superb breasts seem lower and flatter, as well as you can tell under the cheap cotton dress she has on.

The mooch is out, prowling the city. "He does that a lot," she says.

You choose a clean, reasonable restaurant and buy her a meal. With the first course (garlic soup) her beauty returns. While you talk, quietly, without a trace of rebuke, she goes on eating. She is listening, probably, but this steady gluttonous attention to food seems the equivalent of keeping her thumb between the pages of "Forever Amber." Color floods her cheeks and forehead. She finishes a portion of stewed chicken, licks her fingers, sweeps back her tangled hair. She seems much as before—cheerful, patient, glowing, just a little distracted.

Already, men at other tables are starting to glance at her—not just the Latins, who will stare at anyone, but decent tourists, the good kind, Swedes, Swiss, whose own wives are clean, smart, have better table manners. These men are gazing at Edie the way the mooch did that first time, when she looked back at him over your head. You think of Susanna and the Elders. You can't tell her to cover up: the dress is a gunnysack, nothing shows. You tell yourself that something must be showing.

All this on a bowl of soup, a helping of chicken, two glasses of wine. "I'm sure I look terrible," she says. If she could, she would curl up on her chair and go to sleep. You cannot allow her to sleep, even in imagination. There is too much to discuss. She resists discussion. The two of you were apart, now you are back together. That seems to be all she wants to hear. She sighs, as if you were keeping her from something she craves (sleep?), and says, "It's all right, Harry. Whatever it is you've done, I forgive you. I'll never throw anything up to you. I've never held a grudge in my life."

In plain terms, this is not a recollection but the memory of one, riddled with mistakes of false time and with hindsight. When Lapwing lost and found his wife, the Queen was a princess, John Paul II was barely out of a seminary, and Lapwing was edging crabwise toward his William Morris œuvre—for some reason, by way of a study of St. Paul. Stories about the passport fraud and how Fergus Bray is supposed to have sold Edie's shoes had not begun to circulate. Lapwing's try at engaging Her Majesty in conversation—a favorite academic anecdote, perhaps of doubtful authenticity—was made some thirty years later.

Osier, when Lapwing started teaching, was a one-building college, designed by a nostalgic Old Country architect to reproduce a Glasgow train shed. In the library hung a map of Ulster and a photograph of Princess May of Teck on her wedding day; on the shelves was a history of England, in fifteen volumes, but none of Canada—or, indeed, of any part of North America. There were bound copies of *Maclean's*, loose copies of *The Saturday Evening Post*, and a row of prewar British novels in brown, plum, and deep-blue bindings, reinforced with tape—the legacy of an alumnus who had gone away to die in Bermuda. From the front windows, Lapwing could see mud and a provincial highway; from the back, a basketball court and the staff parking lot. Visiting Soviet agricultural experts were always shown round the lot, so that they could count the spoils of democracy. Lapwing was the second Canadian-educated teacher ever to be hired; the first, Miss Mary MacLeod, a brilliant Old Testament scholar, taught Nutrition and Health. She and Lapwing shared Kraft-cheese sandwiches and subversive minority conversation. After skinning alive the rest of the staff, Miss MacLeod would remember Universal Vision and say it was probably better to have a lot of Brits than a lot of Americans. Americans would never last a winter up here. They were too rich and spoiled.

In the nineteen-sixties, a worldwide tide of euphoric prosperity and love of country reached Osier, dislodging the British. When the tide receded, it was discovered that their places had been taken by teachers from Colorado, Wyoming, and Montana, who could stand the winters. By the seventies, Osier had buried Nutrition and Health (Miss MacLeod was recycled into Language Structure), invented a graduate-studies program, had the grounds landscaped—with vast undulating lawns that, owing to drought and the nature of the soil, soon took on the shade and texture of Virginia tobacco—

ceased to offer tenure to the foreign-born, and was able to call itself a university.

Around this time I was invited to Osier twice, to deliver a guest lecture on Talleyrand and to receive an honorary degree. On the second occasion, Lapwing, wearing the maroon gown Osier had adopted in a further essay at smartening up, prodded my arm with his knuckle and whispered, "We both made it, eh, Burnet?"

To Lapwing I was simply an Easterner, Anglo-Quebec—a permanent indictment. Like many English-Canadians brought up to consider French an inferior dialect, visited on hotel maids and unprincipled politicians, he had taken up the cause of Quebec after nationalism became a vanguard idea and moved over from right to left. His loyalties, once he defined them, traveled easily: I remember a year when he and his wife would not eat lettuce grown in Ontario because agricultural workers in California were on strike. With the same constancy, he now dismissed as a racist any Easterner from as far down the seaboard as Maryland whose birth and surroundings caused him to speak English.

Our wives were friends; that was what threw us into each other's company for a year, in France. Some of the external, convivial life of men fades when they get married, except in places like Saudi Arabia. I can think of no friendship I could have maintained where another woman, the friend's wife or girlfriend, was uncongenial to Lily. Lapwing and I were both graduate students, stretching out grants and scholarships, for the first time in our lives responsible for someone else. That was what we had in common, and it was not enough. Left to ourselves, we could not have discussed a book or a movie or a civil war. He thought I was supercilious and rich; thought it when I was in my early twenties, and hard up for money, and unsure about most things. What I thought about him I probably never brought into focus, until the day I felt overburdened by dislike. I had been raised by my widowed aunt, cautioned to find in myself opinions that could be repeated without embarrassing anyone; that were not displeasing to God; on the whole, that saved wear.

In France, once we started to know people, we were often invited all four together, as a social unit. We went to dinner in rooms where there were eight layers of wallpaper, and for tea and drinks around cracked ornamental pools (Rivebelle had been badly shelled only a few years before), and Lapwing told strangers the story of his life; rather, what he thought about his life. He had been born into a tough-minded, hard-working, well-educated family. Saying so, he brought all other conversation to a standstill. It was like being stalled in an open, snowy plain, with nothing left to remind you of culture and its advantages but legends of the Lapwings—how they had studied and struggled, with what ease they had passed exams in medicine and law, how Dr. Porter Lapwing had discovered a cheap and ready antidote for wasp venom. (He blew cigar smoke on the sting.)

We met a novelist, Watt Chadwick, who invited us, all four, to a concert. None of us had known a writer before, and we observed him at first uneasily—wondering if he was going to store up detractory stuff about us—then with interest, trying to surmise if he wrote in longhand or on a typewriter, worked in the morning or the afternoon, and where he got his ideas. At the back of our wondering was the notion that writing novels was not a job for a man—a prejudice from which we had to exclude Dickens and others, and which we presently overcame. The conflict was more grueling for Lapwing, whose aim was to teach literature at a university. Mr. Chadwick's family had built a villa in Rivebelle in the eighteen-eighties which he still occupied much of the year. He was regarded highly in the local British colony, where his books were lent and passed around until the bindings collapsed. Newcomers are always disposed to enter into local snobberies: the invitation delighted and flattered us.

"He finds us good-looking and interesting," Lily said to me, seriously, when we talked it over. Lapwing must have risen as an exception in her mind, because she added, "And Harry has lots to say."

Rivebelle was a sleepy place that woke up once a year for a festival of chamber music. The concerts were held in a square overlooking the harbor, a whole side of it open to a view of the sea. The entire coastal strip as far as the other side of Nice had been annexed to Italy, until about a year prior to the shelling I've mentioned, and the military commander of the region had shown more aptitude for improving the town than for fortifying its beaches. No one remembers his name or knows what became of him: his memorial is the Rivebelle square. He had the medieval houses on its south boundary torn down (their inhabitants were quartered God knows where) and set his engineering corps to build a curving staircase of stone, mosaic, and stucco, with a pattern of "V"s for "Viva" and "M"s for "Mussolini," to link the square and the harbor. In the meantime children went down to the shore and paddled in shallow water, careful not to catch their feet in a few strands of barbed wire. The commander did not believe an attack could come from that direction. Perhaps he thought it would never come at all.

On concert nights Lily and I often leaned on the low wall that replaced the vanished houses and watched, as they drifted up and down the steps and trod on the "V"s, visitors in evening dress. They did not look rich, as we understood the word, but indefinably beyond that. Their French, English, German, and Italian were not quite the same as the languages we heard on the beaches, spoken by tourists who smacked their children and buried the remains of pizzas in the sand. To me they looked a bit like extras in prewar films about Paris or Vienna, but Lily studied their clothes and manner. There was a difference between pulling out a mauled pack of cigarettes and opening a heavy cigarette case: the movement of hand and wrist was not the same. She noticed all that. She once said, leaning on the wall, that there was something unfinished about us, the Burnets and Lapwings. We had packed for our year abroad as if the world were a lakeside summer cottage. I still couldn't see myself removing my squashed Camels to a heavy case and snapping it open, like a gigolo.

"You've never seen a gigolo," said Lily. And, almost regretfully, "Neither have I."

She dressed with particular attention to detail for Mr. Chadwick's evening, in clothes I had never noticed before. Edie gave her a silk blouse that had got too tight. Lily wore it the way Italian girls did, with the collar raised and the sleeves pushed up and the buttons undone as far as she dared. I wondered about the crinoline skirt and the heart-shaped locket on a gold chain.

"They're from Mrs. Biesel," Lily said. "She went to a lot of trouble. She even shortened the skirt." The Biesels were an American couple who had rented a house that Queen Alexandra was supposed to have stayed in, seeking relief from her chronic rheumatism and the presence of Edward VII. Mr. Biesel, a former naval officer who had lost an arm in the North Africa landings, was known locally as the Admiral, though I don't think it was his rank. Mr. Chadwick always said, "Admiral Bessel." He often had trouble with names, probably because he had to make up so many.

The Biesels attracted gossip and rumors, simply by being American: if twenty British residents made up a colony, two Americans were a mysterious invasion. Some people believed the Admiral reported to Washington on Rivebelle affairs: there were a couple of diplomats' widows and an ex-military man who had run a tin-pot regiment for a sheikh or an emir. Others knew for certain that Americans who cooperated with the Central Intelligence Agency were let off paying income tax. Mr. Chadwick often dined and played bridge at Villa

Delizia, but he had said to Lily and me, "I'm careful what I say. With Admiral Bessel, you never can tell."

He had invited a fifth guest to the concert—David Ogdoad, his part-time gardener, aged about nineteen, a student of music and an early drifter. His working agreement with Mr. Chadwick allowed him to use the piano, providing Mr. Chadwick was not at the same moment trying to write a novel upstairs. The piano was an ancient Pleyel that had belonged to Mr. Chadwick's mother; it was kept in a room called the winter salon, which jutted like a promontory from the rest of the house, with shuttered windows along two sides and a pair of French doors that were always locked. No one knew, and perhaps Mr. Chadwick had forgotten, if he kept the shutters closed because his mother had liked to play the piano in the dark or if he did not want sunlight further to fade and mar the old sofas and rugs. Here, from time to time, when Mr. Chadwick was out to lunch or dinner, or, for the time being, did not know what to do next with "Guy" and "Roderick" and "Marie-Louise," David would sit among a small woodland of deprived rubber plants and labor at getting the notes right. He was surprisingly painstaking for someone said to have a restless nature but badly in need of a teacher and a better instrument: the Pleyel had not been tuned since before the war.

Now, of course Mr. Chadwick could have managed all this differently. He could have made David an allowance instead of paying token wages; introduced David to his friends as an equal; found him a teacher, had the piano restored, or bought a new one; built a music studio in the garden. Why not? Male couples abounded on this part of the coast. There were distinguished precedents, who let themselves be photographed and interviewed. Mr. Maugham lived not far away. But Mr. Chadwick was smaller literary stuff, and he didn't want the gossip. The concert outing was a social trial balloon. Any of Mr. Chadwick's friends, seeing the six of us, were supposed to say, "Watt has invited a party of young people," and not the fatal, the final, "Watt has started going out with his gardener."

Mr. Chadwick had not been able to book six seats together, which was all to the good: it meant there was no chance of my having to sit next to Lapwing. He was opposed on principle to the performance of music and liked to say so while it was going on, and his habit of punching one in the arm to underscore his opinions always made me feel angry and helpless. I sat with Lily in the second row, with the Lapwings and Mr. Chadwick and his gardener just behind. The front row was kept for honored guests. Mr. Chadwick pointed them out to Edie: the local mayor, and Jean Cocteau, and some elderly Bavarian princesses.

People applauded as Cocteau was shown to his seat. He was all in white, with bright quick eyes. The Bavarians were stout and dignified, in blue or pink satin, with white fur stoles.

"How do you get to be a Bavarian princess?" I heard Edie say.

"You could be born one," said Mr. Chadwick. He kept his voice low, like a radio announcer describing an opera. "Or you could marry a Bavarian prince."

"What about the fantastic-looking Italians?" said Edie. "At the end of the row. The earrings! Those diamonds are diamonds."

Mr. Chadwick was willing to give the wearer of the earrings a niche in Italian nobility.

"Big money from Milan," said Lapwing, as if he knew all about both. "Cheese exporters." His tone became suspicious, accusing almost: "Do you actually know Cocteau?"

"I have met M. Cocteau," said Mr. Chadwick. "I make a distinction between meeting and knowing, particularly with someone so celebrated."

"That applause for him just now—was it ironic?"

I could imagine Lapwing holding his glasses on his blob of a nose, pressing his knuckle between his eyes. I felt responsible, the way you always do when a compatriot is making a fool of himself.

Of course not, Mr. Chadwick replied. Cocteau was adored in Rivebelle, where he had decorated an abandoned chapel, now used for weddings. It made everyone happy to know he was here, the guest of the town, and that the violinist Christian Ferras would soon emerge from the church, and that the weather could be trusted—no mistral, no tramontane to carry the notes away, no threat of rain.

I think he said some of this for David, so that David would be appreciative even if he could not be content, showing David he had reason upon reason for staying with Mr. Chadwick; for at any moment David might say he had had enough and was going home. Not home to Mr. Chadwick's villa, where he was said to occupy a wretched room—a nineteenth-century servant's room—but home to England. And here was the start of Mr. Chadwick's dilemma—his riddle that went round and round and came back to the same point: What if David stopped playing gardener and was moved into the best spare bedroom—the room with Monet-like water lilies on three walls? What would be his claim on the room? What could he be called? Mr. Chadwick's adopted nephew? His gifted young friend? And how to explain the shift from watering the agapanthus to spending the morning at the piano and the afternoon on the beach?

"Do you know who the three most attractive men in the world are?" said Edie all of a sudden. "I'll tell you. Cary Grant, Ali Khan, and Prince Philip."

None of the three looked even remotely like Lapwing. I glanced at Lily, expecting a flash of complicity.

Instead she said softly, "Pablo Picasso, Isaac Stern, Juan Fangio."

"What about them?"

"The most attractive."

"Who's Fangio? You mean the racing driver? Have you ever seen him?"

"Just his pictures."

"I can't see what they've got in common."

"Great, dark eyes," said Lily.

I suppressed the mention that I did not have great, dark eyes, and decided that what she really must have meant was nerve and genius. I knew by now that nerve comes and goes, with no relation to circumstance; as for genius, I had never been near it. Probably genius grew stately and fat or gaunt and haunted, lost its hair, married the wrong person, died in its sleep. David Ogdoad, of whom I was still barely aware except as a problem belonging to Mr. Chadwick, had been described—by Mr. Chadwick, of course—as a potential genius. (I never heard his name again after that year.) He had small, gray eyes, and with his mouth shut looked like a whippet—something about the way he stretched his neck.

A string orchestra filed onstage, to grateful applause (the musicians were half an hour late), and an eerie hush settled over the square. For the next hour or so, both Lapwings held still.

At intermission Mr. Chadwick tried to persuade us to remain in our seats; he seemed afraid of losing us—or perhaps just of losing David—in the shuffling crowd. Some people were making for a bar across the square, others struggled in the opposite direction, toward the church. I imagined Christian Ferras and the other musicians at bay in the vestry, their hands cramped from signing programs. David was already in the aisle, next to Lily.

"The intermission lasts a whole hour," said Lapwing, lifting his glasses and bringing the program close to his face. "Why don't we just say we'll meet at the bar?"

"And I'll look after Mr. Chadwick," said Edie, taking him by the arm. But it was not Edie he wanted.

303

Lily turned to David, smiling. She loved being carried along by this crowd of players from old black-and-white movies, hearing the different languages mingling and overlapping.

"Glorious, isn't he?" said David, about Ferras.

Lily answered something I could not hear but took to be more enthusiastic small talk, and slipped a hand under her collar, fingering the gold chain. As we edged past the cheaper seats, she said, "This is where Steve and I usually sit. It's so far back that you don't see the musicians. We're very grateful to Mr. Chadwick for tonight." No one could say she had undermined David's sense of thankfulness; he had been given a spring and summer in the South, and it hadn't cost him a centime. I thought we should not discuss Mr. Chadwick with David at all, but my reasons were confused and obscure. I believed David liked Lily because she took him seriously as a musician and not as someone's gardener. I thought the constant company of an older, nervous man must be stifling, even though I could not imagine him with a young one: he wanted to be looked after and to be rebellious, all at once. The natural companion for David was someone like Lily—attractive, and charming, and married to another man. I knew he was restless and had talked to her about London. That was all I thought I knew.

At the grocery store that served as theater bar, wine and French gin and whiskey and soft drinks were being dispensed, at triple price. The wine was sour and undrinkable. David asked for tonic; Lily and I usually had Cokes. The French she had learned in her Catholic boarding school allowed her to negotiate this, timidly. She liked ordering, enjoyed taking over sometimes, but Mr. Chadwick had corrected her Canadian accent and made her shy. David, merely impressed, asked if she had been educated in Switzerland.

The possibility of becoming a different person must have occurred to her. She picked up the bottle of tonic, as if she had never heard of Coca-Cola, still less ordered it, and demanded a glass. No more straws; no more drinking from bottles. She then handed David a tepid Coke, and he was too struck by love to do anything but swallow it down.

Lapwing in only a few minutes had managed to summon and consume large quantities of wine. His private reasoning had Mr. Chadwick paying for everything: after all, he had brought Lapwing up here to be belabored by Mozart. Edie, who had somehow lost Mr. Chadwick, was drinking wine, too. I noticed that Lily wanted me to foot the bill: the small wave of her hand was an imperial gesture. Distancing herself from me, the graduate of a Swiss finishing school forgot we had no money, or nearly none. I fished a wad of francs out of my pocket and dropped them on the counter. Lapwing punched me twice on the shoulder, perhaps his way of showing thanks.

"I don't know about you," he said, "but I'm one of those people for whom music is wave after wave of disjointed noise." He made "those people" sound like a superior selection.

Mr. Chadwick, last to arrive, looked crumpled and mortified, as if he had been put through some indignity. All I could do was offer him a drink. He looked silently and rather desperately at the grocery shelves, the cans of green peas, the cartons leaking sugar, the French gin with the false label.

"It's very kind of you," he said.

Lily and Edie linked arms and started back toward the church. They wanted to see the musicians at close quarters. Mr. Chadwick had recaptured David, which left me saddled with Lapwing.

"I don't have primitive anti-Catholic feelings," said Lapwing. "Edie was a Catholic, of course, being a Pole. A middle-class Pole. I encouraged her to keep it up. A woman should have a moral basis, especially if she doesn't have an intellectual one. Is Lily still Catholic?"

"It's her business." We had been over this ground before.

"And you?"

"I'm not anything."

"You must have started out as something. We all do."

"My parents are Anglican missionaries," I said. "I'm nothing in particular."

"I'm sorry to hear that," Lapwing said.

"Why?"

I hoped he would say he didn't know, which would have raised him a notch. Instead he drank the wine left in Edie's glass and hurried after the two women.

In the bright church, where every light had been turned on and banks of votive candles blazed, our wives wandered from saint to saint. Edie had tied a bolero jacket around her head. The two were behaving like little girls, laughing and giggling, displaying ex-Catholic behavior of a particular kind, making it known that they took nothing in this place seriously but that they were perfectly at home. Lapwing responded with Protestant prudence and gravity, making the remark that Lily should cover her hair. I looked around and saw no red glow, no Presence. For the sake of the concert the church had been turned into a public hall; in any case, what Lily chose to do was her business. Either God existed and was not offended by women and their hair or He did not; it came to the same thing.

Mr. Chadwick was telling David about design and decoration. He pointed to the ceiling and to the floor. I heard him say some interesting things about the original pagan site, the Roman shrine, the early Christian chapel, and the present rickety Baroque—a piece of nonsense, he said. Lapwing and I, stranded under a nineteenth-century portrayal of St. Paul, given the face of a hanging judge, kept up an exchange that to an outsider might have resembled conversation. I was so hard up for something to say that I translated the inscription under the picture: "St. Paul, Apostle to the Gentiles, put to death as a martyr in Rome, A.D. 67."

"I've been working on him," Lapwing said. "I've written

a lot of stuff." He tipped his head to look at the portrait, frowning. "Saul is the name, of course. The whole thing is a fake. The whole story."

"What do you mean? He never existed?"

"Oh, he existed, all right. Saul existed. But that seizure on the road to Damascus can be explained in medical terms of our time." Lapwing paused, and then said rather formally, "I've got doctors in the family. I've read the books. There's a condition called eclampsia. Toxemia of pregnancy, in other words. Say Lily was pregnant—say she was carrying the bacteria of diphtheria, or typhoid, or even tetanus. . . ."

"Why couldn't it be Edie?"

"O.K., then, Edie. I'm not superstitious. I don't imagine the gods are up there listening, waiting for me to make a slip. Say it's Edie. Well, she could have these seizures, she could hallucinate. I'm not saying it's a common condition. I'm not saying it often happens in the civilized world. I'm saying it could have happened in very early A.D."

"Only if Paul was a pregnant woman."

"Men show female symptoms. It's been known to happen— the male equivalent of hysterical pregnancy. Oh, not deliberately. I'm not saying it's common behavior. I don't want you to misquote me, if you decide to research my topic. I'm only saying that Saul, Paul, was on his way to Damascus, probably to be treated by a renowned physician, and he had this convulsion. He heard a voice. You know the voice I mean." Lapwing dropped his tone, as though nothing to do with Christianity should ever be mentioned in a church. "He hallucinated. It was a mystical hallucination. In other words, he did a Joan of Arc."

It was impossible to say if Lapwing was trying to be funny. I thought it safer to follow along: "If it's true, it could account for his hostility to women. He had to share a condition he wasn't born to."

"I've gone into that. If you ever research my premise,

remember I've gone into everything. I think I may drop it, actually. It won't get me far. There's no demand."

"I don't see the complete field," I said. That sounded all right—inoffensive.

"Well, literature. But I may have strayed. I may be over the line." He dropped his gaze from the portrait to me, but still had to look up. "I don't really want to say more."

I think he was afraid I might encroach on his idea, try to pick his brain. I assured him that I was committed to French history and politics, but even that may have seemed too close, and he turned away to look for Edie, to find out for certain what she was doing, and ask her to stop.

Mr. Chadwick had found the evening so successful that he decided on a bolder social move: David must give a piano recital in the villa, with a distinguished audience in attendance. A reception would follow—white-wine cup, petits fours—after which some of us would be taken to a restaurant, as Mr. Chadwick's guests, for a dinner in David's honor. The event was meant to be a long jump in his progress from gardener to favored house guest.

He was let off gardening duty and spent much of his time now at the Biesels', where they offered him a cool room with a piano in it and left him in peace. Meanwhile the winter salon was torn apart and cleaned, dustcovers were removed from the sofas, the windows and shutters opened and washed and sealed tight again. The expert brought in from Nice to restore the Pleyel had a hard time putting it to rights, and asked for an extra fee. Mr. Chadwick would not give it, and for a time it looked as if there would be no recital at all. Mrs. Biesel quietly intervened and paid the difference. Mr. Chadwick never knew. One result of the conflict and its solution, apart from the piano's having been fixed, was that Mr. Chadwick began to tell stories about how he had, in the past, showed great firmness with workmen and tradesmen. They were boring stories, but, as Lily said, it was better than hearing the stories about his mother.

It seemed to me that the recital could end in nothing but disgrace and ridicule. I wondered why David went along with the idea.

"Amateurs have a lot of self-confidence," said Mrs. Biesel, when I asked what she thought. "A professional would be scared." I had come round to her house to call for Lily: she was spending a lot of time there, too, encouraging David.

Mrs. Biesel had a soft Southern voice and was not always easy to understand. (I was amazed when I discovered that to Mr. Chadwick all North Americans sounded alike.) I recall Mrs. Biesel with her head to one side, poised to listen, and her curved way of sitting, as if she were too tall and too thin for most chairs. I could say she was like a Modigliani, but it's too easy, and I am not sure I had heard of Modigliani then. The Biesels were rich, by which I mean that they had always lived with money, and when they spent any they always gave themselves a moral excuse. The day Lily decided she wanted to go to London without me, the Biesels paid her way. They saw morality on that occasion as a matter of happiness, Lily's in particular. Any suggestion that they might have conspired to harm and deceive was below their view of human nature. Conversation on the subject soon became like a long talk in a dream, with no words remembered, just an impression of things intended.

Mr. Chadwick pored over stacks of yellowed sheet music his mother had kept in a rosewood Canterbury. He wanted David to play short pieces with frequent changes in mood. "None of your all-Schubert," he said. "It just puts people to sleep."

Mrs. Biesel supplied printed programs on thick ivory paper. We were supposed to keep them as souvenirs, but the printer had left off the date. She apologized to Mr. Chadwick, as though it were her own fault. (It is curious how David was overlooked; the recital seemed to have become a social arrangement between Mrs. Biesel and Mr. Chadwick.) Mr. Chadwick ran his eye down the page and said, "But he's not doing the Debussy. He's doing the Ravel."

"It's a long, hard program," said Mrs. Biesel, in just above a whisper. "It might have been easier if he had simply worked up some Bach."

At three o'clock on one of the hottest afternoons since the start of recorded temperatures, David sat down to the restored Pleyel. On the end wall behind him was a large Helleu drawing of Mr. Chadwick's mother playing the piano, with her head thrown back and a bunch of violets tied to her wrist. The winter carpets, rolled up and stacked next to the fireplace, smelled of old dust and moth repellent. Still Mr. Chadwick would not let the room be aired. To open the windows meant letting in heat. "You must all sit very still," he announced, as David got ready to start. "It's moving about, stirring up the atmosphere, that makes one feel warm."

Who was there? Mr. Chadwick's friends and neighbors, and a number of people I suspect he brought in on short acquaintance. I remember his doctor, a dour Alsatian who had the complete confidence of the British colony; he had acquired a few reassuring expressions in English, such as "It's just a little chill on the liver" and "Port's the thing." People liked that. When I think of the Canadians in the winter salon—the Lapwings, and Lily and me, and Fergus Bray, and an acquaintance of Lapwing's called Michael Hagen-Beck—it occurs to me that abroad, outside embassy premises or official functions, I never saw that many in one room again. Hagen-Beck was an elderly-looking undergraduate of nineteen or twenty, dressed in scant European-style shorts, a khaki shirt, knee socks, and gym shoes. Near the end of the recital, he walked out of the house and did not come back.

Lily mooned at David, as she had at Christian Ferras. I

supposed it must be her way of contemplating musicians. There was nothing wrong with it; I had just never thought of her as a mooner of any kind. Once she sprang from her chair and pushed open a shutter: the room was so dim that David had to strain to read the music. Mr. Chadwick left the shutter ajar, but latched the window once more, murmuring again his objection to stirring up the atmosphere.

During the Chopin Edie went to sleep, wearing one of those triangular smiles that convey infinite secret satisfaction. Her husband wiped his forehead with a cotton scarf he took out of her handbag and returned carefully, without waking her up. I had the feeling they got along better when one of them was unconscious. He adjusted his glasses and frowned at a gilt Buddha sitting in front of the cold fireplace, as if he were trying to assess its place in Mr. Chadwick's spiritual universe. During the pause between the Chopin and the Albéniz, he unlocked the French doors, left them wide, and went out to the baking terrace, half covered by the branches of a jacaranda; into the hot shade of the tree he dragged a wrought-iron chair and a chintz-covered pillow (the chair looked as if it had not been moved since the reign of Edward VII), making a great scraping sound over the flagstones. The scraping blended with the first bars of the Albéniz; those of us in the salon who were still awake pretended not to hear.

I envied Lapwing, settled comfortably in iron and chintz, in the path of a breeze, however tepid, with trumpet-shaped blue flowers falling on his neck and shoulders. He seemed to be sizing up over the chalkier blue of a plumbago hedge the private beach and white umbrellas of the Pratincole, Rivebelle's only smart hotel—surviving evidence that this part of the coast had been fashionable before the war. In an open court couples were dancing to a windup gramophone, as they did every day at this hour. We could hear one of those tinny French voices, all vivacity, but with an important ingredient missing—true vitality, I think—singing an old

American show tune with sentimental French lyrics: *pour toi, pour moi, pour toujours.* It reminded me of home, all but the words, and finally I recognized a song my aunt had on a record, with "She Didn't Say 'Yes'" on the other side. Perhaps she used to dance to it, before she decided to save her energy for bringing me up. I remembered just some of the words: "new luck, new love." I wondered if there was any sense to them—if luck and love ever changed course after moving on. Mr. Chadwick was old enough to know, but it wasn't a thing I could ask.

Lapwing sat between two currents of music. Perhaps he didn't hear: the Pratincole had his whole attention. Our wives longed to dance, just once, in that open court, under the great white awning, among the lemon trees in tubs, and to drink champagne mixed with something at the white-and-chromium bar, but we could not afford so much as a Pratincole drink of water. I don't know how, but Lapwing had gained the impression that Mr. Chadwick was taking us for dinner there. He sat at his ease under the jacaranda, choosing his table. (A later review of events had Lapwing urging Hagen-Beck to join us for dinner, even though his share of the day was supposed to end with the petits fours: a story that Lapwing continued to evoke years after in order to deny it.)

The rest of us sat indoors, silent and sweating. We seemed to be suffocating under layers of dark-green gauze, what with the closed shutters, and the vines pressing on them, and the verd-antique incrustation in the ancient bronze ornaments and candelabra. The air that came in from the terrace, now that Lapwing had opened the French doors, was like the emanation from a furnace, and the sealed windows cut off any hope of a crossbreeze. Mrs. Biesel fanned herself with a program, when she was not using it to beat time. Fergus Bray slid from his sofa to the marble floor and lay stretched, propped on an elbow. I noticed he had concealed under the sofa a full tumbler of whiskey, which he quietly sipped. Once, sinking into a deep sleep and pulling myself up just in time, I caught sight of Lapwing leaning into the room, with his eyes and glasses glittering, looking—in memory—like the jealous husband he was about to become.

If a flash of prophecy could occur to two men who have no use for each other, he and I would have shared the revelation that our wives were soon to travel—his to Madrid with one of that day's guests, mine to London on the same train as our host's gardener and friend. (It was Mrs. Biesel's opinion that Lily had just wanted company on the train.) Mentioning two capital cities makes their adventure sound remote, tinged with fiction, like so many shabby events that occur in foreign parts. If I could say that Lily had skipped to Detroit and Edie to Moose Jaw, leaving Lapwing and me stranded in a motel, we would come out of it like a couple of gulls. But "Madrid," and "London," and "the Mediterranean," and a musician, a playwright, a novelist, a recital in a winter salon lend us an alien glow. We seem to belong to a generation before our own time. Lapwing and I come on as actors in a film. The opening shot of a lively morning street and a jaunty pastiche of circus tunes set the tone, and all the rest is expected to unfold to the same pulse, with the same nostalgia. In fact, there was nothing to unfold except men's humiliation, which is bleached and toneless.

The compliments and applause David received at the end of the recital were not only an expression of release and relief. We admired his stamina and courage. The varied program, and David's dogged and reliable style, made me think of an anthology of fragments from world literature translated so as to make it seem that everyone writes in the same way. Between fleeting naps, we had listened and had found no jarring mistakes, and Mr. Chadwick was close to tears of the humblest kind of happiness.

David looked drawn and distant, and very young—an exhausted sixteen. I felt sorry for him, because so much that was impossible was expected from him; although his habitual manner, at once sulky and superior, and his floppy English haircut got on my nerves. He resembled the English poets of about ten years before, already ensconced as archetypes of a class and a kind. Lily liked him; but, then, she had been nice to Hagen-Beck, even smiling at him kindly as he walked out. I decided that to try to guess what attracted women, or to devise some rule from temporary evidence, was a waste of time. On the whole, Hagen-Beck—oaf and clodhopper—was somehow easier to place. I could imagine him against a setting where he looked like everybody else, whereas David seemed to me everywhere and forever out of joint.

Late in the evening Mr. Chadwick's dinner guests, chosen by David, climbed the Mussolini staircase to the square, now cleared of stage and chairs, and half filled with a wash of restaurant tables. A few children wheeled round on bikes. Old people and lovers sat on the church steps and along the low wall. Over the dark of the sky, just above the church, was the faintest lingering trace of pink.

The party was not proceeding as it should: Mr. Chadwick had particularly asked to be given a round table, and the one reserved for us was definitely oblong. "A round table is better for conversation," he kept saying, "and there is less trouble about the seating."

"It doesn't matter, Mr. Chadwick," said Edie, in the appeasing tone she often used with her husband. "This one is fine." She stroked the pink-and-white tablecloth, as if to show that it was harmless.

"They promised the round table. I shall never come here again."

At the table Mr. Chadwick wanted, a well-dressed Italian in his fifties was entertaining his daughter and her four small children. The eldest child might have been seven; the youngest had a large table napkin tied around his neck, and was eating morsels of Parma ham and melon with his fingers. But presently I saw that the striking good looks of the children were drawn from both adults equally, and that the young mother was the wife of that much older man. The charm and intelligence of the children had somehow overshot that of the parents, as if they had arrived at a degree of bloom that was not likely to vary for a long time, leaving the adults at some intermediate stage. I kept this observation to myself. English-speaking people do not as a rule remark on the physical grace of children, although points are allowed for cooperative behavior. There is, or used to be, a belief that beauty is something that has to be paid for and that a lovely child may live to regret.

A whole generation between two parents was new to me. Mr. Chadwick, I supposed, could still marry a young wife. It seemed unlikely; and yet he was shot through with parental anguish. His desire to educate David, to raise his station, to show him off, had a paternal tone. At the recital he had been like a father hoping for the finest sort of accomplishment but not quite expecting it.

We continued to stand while he counted chairs and place settings. "Ten," he said. "I told them we'd be nine."

"Hagen-Beck may turn up," said Lapwing. "I think he went to the wrong place."

"He was not invited," said Mr. Chadwick. "At least, not by me."

"He wasn't anywhere around to be invited," said Mrs. Biesel. "He left before the Ravel."

"I told him where we were going," said Edie. "I'm sorry. I thought David had asked him."

"What are you sorry about?" said Lapwing. "He didn't hear what you said, that's all."

"Mr. Chadwick," said Lily. "Where do you want us to sit?"

The Italian had taken his youngest child on his lap. He

wore a look of alert and careful indulgence, from which all anxiety had been drained. Anxiety had once been there; you could see the imprint. Mr. Chadwick could not glance at David without filling up with mistrust. Perhaps, for an older man, it was easier to live with a young wife and several infants than to try to hold on to one restless boy.

"Sit wherever you like," said Mr. Chadwick. "Perhaps David would like to sit here," indicating the chair on his left. (Lapwing had already occupied the one on the right.) Protocol would have given him Mrs. Biesel and Edie. Lily and the Biesels moved to the far end of the table. Edie started to sit down next to David, but he put his hand on the chair, as if he were keeping it for someone else. She settled one place over, without fuss; she was endlessly good-tempered, taking rudeness to be a mishap, toughened by her husband's slights and snubs.

"It's going to be all English again," she said, looking around, smiling. I remember her round, cheerful face and slightly slanted blue eyes. "Doesn't anyone know any French people? Here I am in France, forgetting all my French."

"There was that French doctor this afternoon," said Mrs. Biesel. "You could have said something to him."

"No, she couldn't," said Lapwing. "She was sound asleep."

"You would be obliged to go a long way from here to hear proper French," said Mr. Chadwick. "Perhaps as far as Lyons. Every second person in Rivebelle is from Sicily."

Lapwing leaned into the conversation, as if drawn by the weight of his own head. "Edie doesn't have to hear proper French," he said. "She can read it. She's been reading a French classic all summer—'Forever Amber.'"

I glanced at Lily. It was the only time that evening I was able to catch her eye. Yes, I know, he's humiliating her, she signaled back.

"There are the Spann-Monticules," said Mr. Chadwick to Edie. "They have French blood, and they can chatter away in

French, when they want to. They never come down here except at Easter. The villa is shut the rest of the year. Sometimes they let the mayor use it for garden parties. Hugo Spann-Monticule's great-great-grandmother was the daughter of Arnaud Monticule, who was said to have sacked the Bologna library for Napoleon. Monticule kept a number of priceless treasures for himself, and decided he would be safer in England. He married a Miss Spann. The Spanns had important wool interests, and the family have continued to prosper. Some of the Bologna loot is still in their hands. Lately, because of Labour, they have started smuggling some things back into France."

"Museum pieces belong in museums, where people can see them," said Lapwing.

"They shouldn't be kept in an empty house," said the Admiral.

Lapwing was so unused to having anyone agree with him that he looked offended. "I wouldn't mind seeing some of the collection," he said. "They might let one person in. I don't mean a whole crowd."

"The day France goes Communist they'll be sorry they ever brought anything here," said Mrs. Biesel.

"France will never go Communist," said her husband. "Stalin doesn't want it. A Communist France would be too independent for the Kremlin. The last thing Stalin wants is another Tito on his hands."

I was surprised to hear four sentences from the Admiral. As a rule he drank quietly and said very little, like Fergus Bray. He gave me the impression that he did not care where he lived or what might happen next. He still drove a car, and seemed to have great strength in his remaining arm, but a number of things had to be done for him. He had sounded just now as if he knew what he was talking about. I remembered the rumor that he was here for an underground purpose, but it was hard to see what it might be, in this seedy border resort. According to Lily, his wife had wanted to live abroad for a while. So perhaps it really was as simple as that.

"You're right," Mrs. Biesel said. "Even French Communists must know what the Russians did in Berlin."

"Liberated the Berliners, you mean?" said Lapwing, getting pink in the face.

"Our neighbors are all French," said Edie, speaking to Mr. Chadwick across David and the empty chair. "They aren't Sicilians. I've never met a Sicilian. I'm not even sure where they come from. I was really thinking of a different kind of French person—someone Harry might want to talk to. He gets bored sometimes. There's nobody around here on his level. Those Spanns you mentioned—couldn't we meet them? I think Harry might enjoy them."

"They never meet anyone," said Mr. Chadwick. "Although if you stay until next Easter you might see them driving to church. They drive to St. George's on Easter Sunday."

"We don't go to church, except to look at the art," said Edie. "I just gradually gave it up. Harry started life as a Baptist. Can you believe it? He was fully immersed, with a new suit on."

"In France, it's best to mix either with peasants or the very top level," said Mrs. Biesel. "Nothing in between." Her expression suggested that she had been offered and had turned down a wide variety of native French.

I sat between Fergus Bray and the Admiral. Edie, across the table, was midway between Fergus and me, so that we formed a triangle, unlikely and ill-assorted. To mention Fergus Bray now sounds like a cheap form of name-dropping. His work has somehow been preserved from decay. There always seems to be something, somewhere, about to go into production. But in those days he was no one in particular, and he was there. He had been silent since the start of the concert and had taken his place at table without a word, and was now working through a bottle of white wine intended for at least three of us. He began to slide down in his chair, stretching his legs. I saw that he was trying to capture Edie's attention, perhaps her foot. She looked across sharply, first at me. When his eyes were level with hers, he said, "Do you want to spend the rest of your life with that shrimp?"

I think no one but me could hear. Lapwing, on the far side of Fergus, was calling some new argument to the Biesels; Mr. Chadwick was busy with a waiter; and David was lost in his private climate of drizzle and mist.

"What shrimp?" said Edie. "You mean Harry?"

"If I say 'the rest of your life,' I must mean your husband."

"We're not really married," Edie said. "I'm his common-law wife, but only in places where they recognize common law. Like, I can have 'Lapwing' in my passport, but I couldn't be a Lapwing in Quebec. That's because in Quebec they just have civil law. I'm still married to Morrie Ringer there. Legally, I mean. You've never heard of him? You're a Canadian, and you've never heard of Morrie Ringer? The radio personality? 'The Ringer Singalong'? That's his most famous program. They even pick it up in Cleveland. Well, he can't live with me, can't forget me, won't divorce me. Anyway, the three of us put together haven't got enough money for a real divorce. You can't get a divorce in Quebec. You have to do some complicated, expensive thing. When you break up one marriage and set up another, it takes money. It's expensive to live by the rules—I don't care what you say." So far, he had said scarcely anything, and not about that. "In a way, it's as if I was Morrie's girl and Harry's wife. Morrie could never stand having meals in the house. We ate out. I lived for about two years on smoked meat and pickles. With Harry, I've been more the wife type. It's all twisted around."

"That's not what you're like," said Fergus.

"Twisted around?"

"Wife type. I've been married. I never could stand them. Wife types." He made a scooping movement with his hand and spread his palm flat.

In the falsetto men assume when they try to imitate a woman's voice, he addressed a miniature captive husband:

"From now on, you've got to work for me, and no more girlfriends."

"Some women are like that," said Edie. "I'm not."

"Does the shrimp work for you?"

"We don't think that way. He works for himself. In a sense, for me. He wants me to have my own intellectual life. I've been studying. I've studied a few things." She looked past him, like a cat.

"What few things?"

"Well ... I learned a few things about the Cistercians. There was a book in a room Harry and I rented in London. Someone left it behind. So, I know a few things."

"Just keep those few things to yourself, whatever they may be. Was your father one?"

"A monk? You must be a Catholic, or you wouldn't make that sort of a joke. My father—I hardly know what to think about him. He won't have anything to do with me. Morrie was Jewish, and my father didn't like that. Then I left Morrie for a sort of Baptist Communist. That was even worse. He used to invite Morrie for Christmas dinner, but he won't have Harry in the house. I can't help what my father feels. You can't live on someone else's idea of what's right."

"You say all those things as though they were simple," he said. "Look, can you get away?"

She glanced once round the table; her eyes swept past me. She looked back at Fergus and said, "I'll try." She lifted her hair with both hands. "I'll tell Harry the truth. I'll say I want to show you the inside of the church. We were in it the other night. That's the truth."

"I didn't mean that. I meant, leave him and come to me."

"Leave Harry?"

"You aren't married to him," Fergus said. "I'm not talking about a few minutes or a week or a vacation. I mean, leave him and come to Spain and live with me."

"Whereabouts in Spain?" she said.

"Madrid. I've got a place. You'll be all right."

"As what? Wife or girlfriend?"

"Anything you want."

She let go her hair, and laughed, and said, "I was just kidding. I don't know you. I've already left somebody. You can't keep doing that, on and on. Besides, Harry loves me."

We were joined now by Michael Hagen-Beck. The stir caused by his arrival may have seemed welcoming, but it was merely surprise. On the way to the restaurant Mrs. Biesel had set forth considerable disapproval of the way he had left the concert before the Ravel. Lily had defended him (she believed he had gone to look for a bathroom and felt too shy to come back), but Lapwing had said gravely, "I'm afraid Hagen-Beck will have to be wiped off the board," and I had pictured him turning in a badge of some kind and slinking out of class.

He nodded in the curt way that is supposed to conceal diffidence but that usually means a sour nature, removed the empty chair next to David, dragged it to the far end of the table, and wedged it between Mrs. Biesel and Lily.

"Hey, there's Hagen-Beck," said Lapwing, as if he were astonished to find him this side of the Atlantic.

"I'm afraid he is too late for the soup," said Mr. Chadwick.

"He won't care," said Lapwing. "He'd sooner talk than eat. He's brilliant. He's going to show us all up, one day. Well, he may show some people up. Not everybody."

Lily sat listening to Hagen-Beck, her cheek on her hand. In the dying light her hair looked silvery. I could hear him telling her that he had been somewhere around the North Sea, to the home of his ancestors, a fishing village of superior poverty. He spoke of herrings—how many are caught and sold in a year, how many devoured by seagulls. Beauty is in the economics of Nature, he said. Nowhere else.

"But isn't what people build beautiful, too?" said Lily, pleading for the cracked and faded church.

A waiter brought candles, deepening the color of the night and altering the shade and tone of the women's skin and hair.

"This calls for champagne," Mr. Chadwick said, in a despairing voice.

David had not touched the fish soup or the fresh langouste especially ordered for him. He stared at his plate, and sometimes down the table to the wall of candlelight, behind which Lily and Hagen-Beck sat talking quietly. Mr. Chadwick looked where David was looking. I saw that he had just made a complex and understandable mistake; he thought that David was watching Hagen-Beck, that it was for Hagen-Beck he had tried to keep the empty chair.

"Great idea, champagne," said Lapwing, once he had made certain Mr. Chadwick was paying for it. "We haven't toasted David's wonderful performance this afternoon." From a man who detested the very idea of music, this was a remarkable sign of good will.

Hagen-Beck would not drink wine, probably because it had been unknown to his ancestors. Summoning a waiter, who had better things to do, he asked for water—not false, bottled water but the real kind, God's kind, out of a tap. It was brought to him, in a wine-stained carafe. Two buckets of ice containing champagne had meanwhile been placed on the table, one of them fatally close to Fergus. The wine was opened and poured. Hagen-Beck swallowed water. Mr. Chadwick struck his glass with a knife: he was about to estrange David still further by making a speech.

Fergus and Edie, deep in some exchange, failed to hear the call for silence. In the sudden hush at our table Edie said distinctly, "When I was a kid, we made our own Christmas garlands and decorations. We'd start in November, the whole family. We made birds out of colored paper, and tied them to branches, and hung the branches all over the house. We spent our evenings that way, making these things. Now my father won't even open my Christmas cards. My mother writes to me, and she sends me money. I wouldn't have anything to wear if she didn't. My father doesn't know. Harry doesn't know. I've never told it to anybody, until now."

She must have meant "to any man," because she had told it to Lily.

"It's boring," said Fergus. "That's why you don't tell it. Nobody cares. If you were playing an old woman, slopping on in a bathrobe and some old slippers, it might work. But here you are—golden hair, golden skin. You look carved in butter. The dress is too tight for you, though. I wouldn't let you wear it if I had any say. And those god-awful earrings—where do they come from?"

"London, Woolworth's."

"Well, get rid of them. And your hair should be longer. And nobody cares about your bloody garlands. Don't talk. Just be golden, be quiet."

I suppose the others thought he had insulted her. I was the only one who knew what had gone on before, and how easily she had said, "Wife or girlfriend?" Lapwing merely looked interested. Another man might have challenged Fergus, or, thinking he was drunk, drawn his attention away from Edie and let it die. But Lapwing squeaked, "That's what I keep telling her, Bray. Nobody cares! Nobody cares! Be quiet! Be quiet!"

I saw Lapwing's heavy head bowing and lifting, and Edie's slow expression of shock, and Fergus pouring himself, and nobody else, champagne. This time there surely must have been a flash of telepathy between two people with nothing in common. Fergus and I must have shared at least one thought: Lapwing had just opened his palm, revealing a miniature golden wife, and handed her over.

Then Edie looked at Fergus, and Fergus at Edie, and I watched her make up her mind. The spirit of William Morris surrounded the new lovers, evading his most hardworking academic snoop. Lapwing ought to have stood and quoted, "Fear shall not alter these lips and these eyes of the loved and the lover," but he seemed to see nothing, notice nothing; or like Mr. Chadwick he continued to see and notice the wrong things.

Three of the future delinquents at our table were ex-Catholics. They took it for granted that the universe was eternal and they could gamble their lives. Whatever thin faith they still had was in endless renewal—new luck, new love. Nothing worked out for them, but even now I can see what they were after. Remembering Edie at the split second when she came to a decision, I can find it in me to envy them. The rest of us were born knowing better, which means we were stuck. When I finally looked away from her it was at another pool of candlelight, and the glowing, blooming children. I wonder now if there was anything about us for the children to remember, if they ever later on reminded one another: There was that long table of English-speaking people, still in bud.

TITLES IN SERIES

J. R. ACKERLEY Hindoo Holiday
J. R. ACKERLEY My Dog Tulip
J. R. ACKERLEY My Father and Myself
J. R. ACKERLEY We Think the World of You
CÉLESTE ALBARET Monsieur Proust
DANTE ALIGHIERI The New Life
W. H. AUDEN (EDITOR) The Living Thoughts of Kierkegaard
HONORÉ DE BALZAC The Unknown Masterpiece *and* Gambara
MAX BEERBOHM Seven Men
ALEXANDER BERKMAN Prison Memoirs of an Anarchist
ADOLFO BIOY CASARES The Invention of Morel
CAROLINE BLACKWOOD Corrigan
CAROLINE BLACKWOOD Great Granny Webster
MALCOLM BRALY On the Yard
ROBERT BURTON The Anatomy of Melancholy
CAMARA LAYE The Radiance of the King
GIROLAMO CARDANO The Book of My Life
J. L. CARR A Month in the Country
JOYCE CARY Herself Surprised (First Trilogy, Vol. 1)
JOYCE CARY To Be a Pilgrim (First Trilogy, Vol. 2)
JOYCE CARY The Horse's Mouth (First Trilogy, Vol. 3)
NIRAD C. CHAUDHURI The Autobiography of an Unknown Indian
ANTON CHEKHOV Peasants and Other Stories
COLETTE The Pure and the Impure
JOHN COLLIER Fancies and Goodnights
IVY COMPTON-BURNETT A House and Its Head
IVY COMPTON-BURNETT Manservant and Maidservant
BARBARA COMYNS The Vet's Daughter
JULIO CORTÁZAR The Winners
ASTOLPHE DE CUSTINE Letters from Russia
LORENZO DA PONTE Memoirs
ELIZABETH DAVID A Book of Mediterranean Food
ELIZABETH DAVID Summer Cooking
MARIA DERMOÛT The Ten Thousand Things
ARTHUR CONAN DOYLE Exploits and Adventures of Brigadier Gerard
CHARLES DUFF A Handbook on Hanging
J. G. FARRELL Troubles
M. I. FINLEY The World of Odysseus
EDWIN FRANK (EDITOR) Unknown Masterpieces: Writers Rediscover Literature's Hidden Classics
MAVIS GALLANT Paris Stories
MAVIS GALLANT Varieties of Exile
JEAN GENET Prisoner of Love
EDWARD GOREY (EDITOR) The Haunted Looking Glass
PETER HANDKE A Sorrow Beyond Dreams
ELIZABETH HARDWICK Seduction and Betrayal
ELIZABETH HARDWICK Sleepless Nights